D0961238

THE DAY
THE SUN DIED

Also by Yan Lianke

The Years, Months, Days
The Explosion Chronicles
The Four Books
Lenin's Kisses
Dream of Ding Village
Serve the People!

YAN LIANKE

THE DAY
THE SUN DIED

A Novel

Translated from the Chinese by
Carlos Rojas

Grove Press
New York

The Day the Sun Died first published in Taiwan in 2015 as *Rixi* by Rye Field Publishing Company.

First published in Great Britain in August 2018 by Chatto & Windus.

Published simultaneously in Canada
Printed in the United States of America

This book is set in ITC Berkeley Oldstyle with Adobe Caslon Pro by Alpha Design and Composition of Pittsfield, NH.

First Grove Atlantic hardcover edition: December 2018

Library of Congress Cataloging-in-Publication data available for this title.

ISBN 978-0-8021-2853-9
eISBN 978-0-8021-4634-2

Grove Press
an imprint of Grove Atlantic
154 West 14th Street
New York, NY 10011

Distributed by Publishers Group West

groveatlantic.com

18 19 20 21   10 9 8 7 6 5 4 3 2 1

Translator's Note

History, Stephen said, is a nightmare from which I am trying to awake.

— James Joyce, *Ulysses*

Near the beginning of James Joyce's 1922 novel *Ulysses*, Stephen Dedalus famously compared history to a nightmare. It was also in 1922 that Lu Xun penned the preface to his first short-story collection, *Call to Arms* (published in 1923), in which he asks whether he should try to use his writing to wake up his fellow countrymen still trapped in the proverbial "iron house" of Chinese feudal values. In these almost simultaneous texts, two of the twentieth century's leading modernist authors both equated history with sleep and dreams. Whereas Joyce's Dedalus wants to *awaken from* the nightmare that is history, Lu Xun worries that his works might in fact succeed in rousing his blissfully oblivious readers, causing them to *wake into* a state of historical awareness for which they would then have no easy remedy.

Nearly a century later, Yan Lianke appeals to a similar set of oneiric metaphors in his novel *The Day the Sun Died*. Centered on a fourteen-year-old boy named Li Niannian, whose parents run a shop that sells items for funeral rituals and whose uncle runs a crematorium, the story describes a night during which most of the residents of the boy's village suddenly start sleepwalking—or, to translate the Chinese term for somnambulism more literally, "dreamwalking." The community degenerates into chaos, as many villagers act out the urges that they had kept suppressed during their normal waking state.

Like *Ulysses*, which famously unfolds over the course of a single day (June 16, 1904), the main narrative of *The Day the Sun Died* takes place over the course of a single night, beginning at 5:00 PM on the evening of the sixth day of the sixth lunar month, and concluding early the following morning. The novel is divided into a series of "books," each of which opens with a header that notes a temporal interval using the traditional Chinese *geng-dian* system, and each book is then divided into sections that similarly open with a header that notes the corresponding temporal interval using the Western twenty-four-hour system.

The Day the Sun Died also features a character named Yan Lianke, who is a well-known author of books whose titles are permutations of novels by the real Yan Lianke. For instance, *Dream of Ding Village* becomes *Ding of Dream Village*, *The Sunlit Years* becomes *The Years of Sun*, *Lenin's Kisses* becomes *Kissing Lenin,* and *The Four Books* becomes *The Dead Books* (in Chinese, the characters for *four* and *death* are homonyms). The novel also includes quotes from several of these fictitious texts, all of which are variations of passages from the real Yan Lianke's corresponding works. Although knowledge of Yan Lianke's earlier works is not required to appreciate *The Day the Sun Died*, it may be noted that many of these works similarly focus on the dark side of modern China's rapid development. For instance, *Dream of Ding Village* is named after a fictional AIDS village in Yan Lianke's home province of Henan, *The Sunlit Years* features a "cancer village" in which all of the residents die of throat tumors before they turn forty, and *Lenin's Kisses* is set in a remote village of disabled residents, who are exploited by a local official for financial gain. Through these fictitious communities of marginalized figures, Yan Lianke hopes to draw attention to actual communities and social phenomena that remain hidden in the shadows of contemporary China's rapid growth.

Even as Yan Lianke's dark vision has brought him considerable international recognition, it has also increasingly embroiled him with China's censorship regime. In 2016 the Chinese edition of *The Day the Sun Died* won Hong Kong's prestigious *Dream of the Red Chamber* Prize despite the fact that the novel was never published in Mainland China. Similarly, in 2014, when Yan Lianke was awarded the Franz Kafka Prize, it was in recognition of his entire oeuvre but specific recognition was given to two books translated into Czech—his novella *Serve the People!* and his novel *The Four Books*, both banned in Mainland China. Like many of Yan Lianke's works, all three of these books were published in Taiwan by Rye Field Publishing Company, which is increasingly serving as the primary Chinese-language outlet for his works.

Coincidentally, Yan Lianke was awarded the Kafka Prize the same month he began writing *The Day the Sun Died*. In his acceptance speech for the prize, he tacitly anticipates some of the central motifs of that novel. He opens his speech by recalling his experience growing up during the period of China's Great Famine of the early 1960s, which led him to develop "a very keen appreciation of darkness." He explains that even though today's China "has solved the basic problem of providing 1.3 billion people with food, clothing, and spending money, [and] therefore resembles a bright ray of light illuminating the global East," nevertheless "beneath this ray of light there lies a dark shadow. It is as if the brighter the light, the darker the shadow becomes; and the darker the shadow becomes, the thicker the corresponding sheet of darkness." He adds that he feels he is "one of those people who are fated to experience darkness," and views his recent literary work as an attempt to represent and explore this darkness.

Although in this speech Yan Lianke was ostensibly referring to the works he had published up to that point, his remarks about light and darkness anticipate this new novel, *The Day the Sun Died*, which he had only just begun to compose. As with his metaphorical description of contemporary China as a world shrouded in darkness, in *the novel* he describes a community from which the sun—and all hint of light—has disappeared altogether.

Yan Lianke caps his speech with an account of a blind man from his home village who, every morning when the sun came up, would say to himself, "it turns out that sunlight is actually black—but that is good!" Yan Lianke adds:

> *Even more remarkably, ever since he was young this blind man always had several flashlights, and whenever he went out at night he would always take one with him. The darker it got, the longer and brighter the beam from his flashlight would become. As a result, as he was walking through the village streets in the middle of the night, people would be able to see him coming and wouldn't run into him. Furthermore, when people encountered him, he would use his flashlight to illuminate the road in front of them.*

Yan Lianke offers this blind man as a model for his own literary projects, suggesting that he views his literature as a figurative flashlight to help others see a light that he himself is unable to perceive:

From this blind man, I came up with a new form of writing that is premised on a conviction that the darker it is, the brighter it becomes; and the colder it is, the warmer it becomes. The entire significance of this writing lies in permitting people to avoid its existence. My writing, in other words, is like the blind man with the flashlight who shines his light into the darkness to help others glimpse their goal and destination.

Yan Lianke not only hopes that his literature will offer readers a metaphorical "light," but further hopes that this light will help readers "perceive the existence of *darkness*," thereby allowing them to "more effectively ward off that same darkness and suffering."

In this parable of the blind man and the lamp, Yan Lianke borrows, and partially inverts, Lu Xun's famous metaphor of the iron house. Just as Yan Lianke compares his writing to a blind man with a lamp who helps guide others with a light that he himself is unable to see, Lu Xun describes how he ultimately resolved to compose stories that conclude with an optimistic twist, conveying to his readers a hope that he did not share. In this way, it may be said that Yan Lianke hopes to illuminate the darkness that underpins contemporary China, and in the process help readers wake up from what Yan, like Joyce before him, suggests is the nightmare of history.

—Carlos Rojas

Preface:
Let Me Ramble for a Bit

Hello . . . Are you there? . . . Is anyone going to come listen to me ramble?

Hello . . . spirits! . . . If you're not busy, then come and listen . . . I'm kneeling on the highest point of our Funiu Mountains, so you should definitely be able to hear me. Surely you won't be annoyed by the shouts of a child?

Hello . . . I've come on behalf of a village . . . a small village . . . on behalf of a mountain range, and the entire world. I'm kneeling here facing the sky, and simply want to tell you one thing. I hope you'll have the patience to listen to me, to listen to me ramble and shout. Don't be annoyed, and don't become anxious. This matter is as vast as the sky and the earth.

In our village, many people died as a result of this matter. In our town, many people also died. In our Funiu Mountains and the world outside, and in that night's dreamscape, as many people died as there were stalks of wheat being harvested. And the number of people who continued to live pathetically in the mountains was equivalent to the number of grains of wheat in the fields. Villages and infants, mountains and the world—what they share in common is that their internal organs are like paper bags of bloody water, and if you're not careful, the paper may rupture and the liquid inside will spill out. Fate would become like a drop of water that falls in the wilderness, or like a leaf that falls in a bitterly cold autumn forest.

Spirits . . . people's spirits! This village, this town, these mountains, and this world won't be able to endure another nightmare. Gods . . . bodhisattvas . . . arhats, and the Jade Emperor—I ask that you protect this village and this town. I ask that you protect these mountains and the world. It is on behalf of this village and town and people that I have come to kneel down on this mountaintop. It is to make sure that the living remain alive that I have come to kneel on the mountaintop. It is on behalf of the crops, soil, seeds, farm tools, streets, shopping districts, and the general hustle and bustle that I am kneeling here on this mountaintop. It is on behalf of the day and night that I am kneeling here on this mountaintop. It is on behalf of the chickens and the dogs that I am kneeling here on this mountaintop. It is with all honesty that I'm telling you the details of what happened on that day and night. If I make any mistakes, it's not because I'm dishonest, but rather because I'm simply too excited. My mind constantly feels muddy and confused, which is why I always ramble on and on. I like to talk to myself, regardless of whether or not there are people around. I like to mumble one sentence after another, with each one bearing no relation to the preceding one. The villagers and townspeople call me an idiot . . . an idiot. Because I'm an idiot, I don't have the patience to tease out the first strand of this jumbled mess. As a result, I have no choice but to recount everything in a halting, scattered way, thereby rendering me even more of an idiot. However, spirits . . . including bodhisattvas and arhats . . . you absolutely must not view me as a real idiot. Sometimes my mind is perfectly clear—as clear as a drop of water . . . as clear as the blue sky. For instance, it's as if a skylight just opened in my mind, allowing me to see the sky and the earth, and to see that night's developments. Each and every one of these developments is now clearly visible in my mind's eye, and I can even find the needles and sesame seeds that fell into the darkness.

The sky is so blue and the clouds are so near that, when I kneel here, I can hear my hair blowing in the wind, and can even hear the sound of the individual strands of hair bumping into one another. I can hear the clouds floating across the sky over my head, and can see the air passing in front of me, like yarn being pulled out of my eyes. The sun is bright and everything is still. The air and clouds smell like dew under the morning sun. I kneel—peacefully kneel here on this mountaintop. I am the only one here. In the entire world, there is only me—there is only me, together with the grass, rocks, and air. The world is so still. Everything under heaven is so still . . . Spirits, you should let me sit here and tell you about the events of that night. You have all hurried over to listen to me. I know you live in the sky over my head, and reside in the mountains behind me. I am also addressing these solitary mountains and trees, weeds and frogs, chaste trees and elm trees . . . Kneeling here facing the heavens, my heart like pure water, I will relate everything I have heard and experienced. I will relate that night's events, as though burning an incense stick in front of you, and under this sky . . . to prove that everything I'm telling you is true. This is like using weeds blowing in the wind to prove the existence of the earth and to confirm the destiny that the earth grants to the weeds themselves.

Now I will tell my story.

Where should I begin?

I'll begin here.

Let me begin by telling you about myself, my family, and our neighbor at the time. This neighbor was not any ordinary neighbor, to the point that you wouldn't even believe we lived in the same village and the same town. But he was, after all, our neighbor. He was our neighbor.

It wasn't that our family had wanted to be his neighbor, but rather it was our ancestors and God who had arranged it. This neighbor's name was Yan Lianke . . . This was that author, Yan Lianke, who could both write and paint. This author who had developed quite a name for himself. In our town, his reputation was even greater than that of the town mayor. Greater even than that of the county mayor. His reputation was so formidable, in fact, that comparing it with others would be like placing a watermelon on a bed of sesame seeds, or putting a camel out to graze with a flock of sheep.

As for me, my own reputation is as minuscule as a speck of dust lost in a pile of sesame seeds, or a flea nit hidden on the back of a camel, an ox, or a sheep . . . I am fourteen years old and my name is Li Niannian, though everyone calls me Sha Niannian, or literally "Stupid Niannian." Uncle Lianke is the only one who ever calls me Little Niannian . . . Little Nephew. Little Nephew . . . Little Niannian. Not only do our families belong to the same village, we are even neighbors. Our village is called Gaotian, and because it has streets and a market, and a town government, bank, post office, and police station, it should technically be considered a town. The village, however, is called Gaotian Village, and the corresponding town is called Gaotian Town. The county to which Gaotian belongs is Zhaonan County, and I don't have to tell you that *the reason China is called China is that from time immemorial the Chinese people have viewed China as the center of the world, which is why they call the country China, or literally the Central Kingdom. Similarly, the Central Plains are* called the Central Plains because the people there believe that they live in the center of China, which is to say, in the center of the Central Kingdom. These are not my words, but rather something Uncle Yan once wrote in one of his books. *Our county is located in the center of the Central Plains, and our village is located in the center of the county. In other words, our village is located in the center of China, and the center of the world.* I don't know whether or not Uncle Yan was right about this, but no one ever attempted to correct him. He even said, *My entire oeuvre was written to prove to the people of the world that that village and that piece of land are located at the center of the world.* But now he doesn't write anymore. In fact, he hasn't written anything for years. His inspiration has completely dried up, and his soul is exhausted. He also claims that it is as a result of his writing that he has become annoyed with this world. He wants to go somewhere to seek some peace and quiet. After having endured that night's events and being unable to write about them, he effectively died as an author—and as a living being, he didn't know where to go. Therefore, as I kneel here, I beg you—spirits . . . buddhas and bodhisattvas, Guan Yu and Kong Ming, the God of Literature and Li Bo and Du Fu, Sima Qian and Zhuangzi and Laozi, and also someone or other and someone or other—I beg all of you to grant Uncle Yan some inspiration. Let inspiration rain down on him, and let him continue to live as an author. Let Uncle Yan—over a span of three days and two nights— complete his novel *Night of the People*.

All of you spirits and human spirits . . . I beg you to protect our village. Protect our town. Protect that author, Yan Lianke. I've read many of his books. Because he is my family's neighbor, the books he writes when he is out traveling the world are mailed back to his house, and so I can go to his house to borrow them . . . *Years of Sun, Watery Hardness, Kissing Lenin, Ode, Hymn, Ballad.* There were also *Ding of Dream Village, The Dead Books,* and so forth. I read and devoured all of them. However, I have to tell you the truth—which is that when I read his books, it is as though I were asking my eyes to eat rotten fruit or to harvest dried-up winter crops. But, since there were no other books available, I was forced to find flavor even in these rotten fruits and dried-up crops. Who made me a bit stupid? Whose fault is it that my brain is a bit slow? Who was it that permitted me to finish elementary school, but then left me without anything to do? Good or bad, his books contain writing—and even though I may be stupid, I still like to read. Therefore, I read *Thousand Year History* many times over, to the point that I was able to memorize every stem-and-branch traditional date that appears in the work.

In early autumn, Uncle Yan, in order to write down the story of what happened to our town that night, once again moved out of his home and into a three-room house he had rented next to a reservoir to the south of town. It was a house with a courtyard, and he locked himself in there as though he were in jail. He remained in that courtyard for two full months, but in the end—despite covering the floor with discarded drafts and empty ink bottles—he didn't even manage to finish the opening of the story. When faced with the reality of what happened that year, that month, and that night, he found himself in a state of confusion—at a complete loss as to where to begin.

When it came to his writing, he felt an abject sense of hopelessness.

He felt a similar sense of hopelessness at the thought of living on this earth but being unable to tell stories. Once, I saw him gnawing on his pen until it was completely chewed up. His mouth was making loud grinding sounds, and he spat the plastic pieces all over the floor, the table, and the piles of wastepaper that surrounded him. Then he began banging his head against the wall, as though his head hurt so badly that he would be better off dead. Then he began pounding his chest with his fist, as though he wanted to beat the blood right out of his heart. Tears cascaded down his face, but his inspiration, like a dead sparrow, refused to take flight.

During that period, I would go every other day to walk around the ruins surrounding the crematorium, to look for Little Juanzi, who had disappeared. Along the way, I would often stop to see Uncle Yan Lianke, and give him some vegetables and noodles. And some fruit, and oil and salt. Then, I would borrow some books. On that particular day, I was taking him some spinach and soy sauce, when I saw him standing in the doorway. He was facing the side of the reservoir and the lake, and his face was as impassive as if it were a brick that had been removed from an old wall.

"Please leave the vegetables inside."

He didn't look at me, and his voice sounded like dust falling from a brick and flying everywhere. As I walked past him, I left that bag of spinach in his kitchen. Then, as I was proceeding into the room he used as his bedroom and study to grab the copy of *The Dead Books* that I wanted to borrow, I saw that the floor was covered in piles and piles of paper that he had written on and then ripped up—like someone who is ill and has vomited all over the ground. It was at that moment that I realized he had completely lost his inspiration. His imagination was dried up. He was unable to write the story he wanted to write, and consequently was so upset that he simply wanted to die. Astonished, I walked out of his room, and saw him heading toward the lake, like a ghost heading toward a grave. At that moment, I decided I would walk this fifty-*li*-long road by myself, and climb to the mountaintop—on behalf of our village. For our town, for our territory, for the people who live there, and for Uncle Yan Lianke, I want to tell you what happened that night. I ask that you . . . you spirits . . . protect our village and our people. I ask that you protect the dark night and the bright day. I ask that you protect the town's cats and dogs. That you protect that author, Yan Lianke,

7

whose ink has now run dry. Please give him some heavenly inspiration. Please give him an inexhaustible supply of heavenly ink and heavenly paper. Please permit him to keep writing and keep living. Please let him finish writing his *Night of the People* in three days and two nights, so that he may then include my family in his narrative and describe us in a complimentary fashion.

BOOK ONE

Geng 1: Pheasants Enter People's Minds

1. (17:00–18:00)

Where should I begin?

Let me simply begin here.

Those last few days had been the dog days of summer. It was the Dragon Festival, held on the sixth day of the sixth month of the lunar calendar, and it was so hot that the earth's bones were bending and breaking, and the earth's body hair had turned to dust. All the sticks and branches had dried up, and the fruits and flowers had fallen to the ground. Caterpillars were hanging in midair—desiccated and reduced to powder.

A car was rumbling down the street, but it hit a bump and its tire blew out. The car then swerved in the direction of the blown tire. The villagers rarely used horses and oxen anymore, and instead most of them used tractors, but when they were busy with the crops, families with more money would sometimes use cars.

When the car had a flat out in the fields, a family needed to use an old broken-down truck, or a tractor that smelled of red paint. Horses and oxen periodically appeared pulling carts, and there were even more people carrying bundle after bundle of wheat on their shoulders to the threshing grounds. They crowded greedily around the field and, as the road became blocked, they began arguing with one another.

Someone was even killed. In fact, several people were killed.

The night of the festival—the Dragon Festival was held on the sixth day of the sixth month—some people died because it was too hot, and my family's funerary shop sold its entire stock of burial shrouds.

Our funeral wreaths were also sold out.

Our golden foil was also sold out.

There had been boy and girl figurines made from yellow, white, and striped paper. There were gold and silver pots made from bamboo. Gold and silver mountains, and gold and silver horses. The entire room had been full of spirit money, like a bank that had just received a new shipment of coins. There was a white dragon-horse treading on the black hair of the child leading it, and several jade girls riding on the back of a green dragon. If you had walked into our family's funerary shop—which was called New World—several days earlier, you would have been startled by the opulent goods. But this was actually just as well, because on the eve of the Dragon Festival business suddenly exploded, and in the blink of an eye all of the store's goods were sold out. It was like when prices are about to soar, people go to the bank to withdraw their money in order to spend it. People empty their accounts, and even withdraw their old, overdue money. Then they buy the remaining goods from the stores along the main street.

2. (18:01–18:30)

Dusk arrived.

Dusk was embraced by the muggy air. There was no breeze blowing, and walls and pillars of all of the houses were covered in ash. The world was burned to the point that it was almost dead, and people's hearts were burned to the point that they were almost dead.

After working in the fields all day, everyone was exhausted . . . utterly exhausted. Some people fell asleep while harvesting their wheat, while others fell asleep while threshing it. The wheat crop was excellent that year, and the grains were as large as beans—so large that flour poured out of the gaps between the grains. It poured out. The golden ears of wheat covered the road, as people stumbled over the grains. The weather forecast predicted that there would be a thunderstorm in three days, after which the sky would remain overcast—meaning that those who didn't quickly harvest their wheat would find it rotting in the fields.

So, people quickly went to harvest their wheat.

They rushed out to harvest and thresh the wheat.

All of the village's scythes were busy, and people were hunched over whetstones sharpening them. Between heaven and earth, and between the fields and forest, there were people everywhere, and there was sound everywhere. Throughout the fields and throughout the entire world, there were people everywhere, and there was sound everywhere. One sound rubbed against another, as people with carrying poles brushed past each other and got into fights. Two families came to blows over a threshing machine, while, in the distance, my third and fifth uncles came to blows over a millstone.

I huddled in the doorway of the shop, reading Yan Lianke's novel *Kissing Lenin's Flowing Water Like Years*. My parents had dragged my cot out into the entranceway, and as the light swung back and forth I could see the words NEW WORLD on the sign above our family's funerary shop. The sign was written in gold characters on a black background, and in the twilight the gold characters appeared dull yellow. Not long after finishing dinner, my father brought out a glass of water, then sat on his bamboo cot on the side of the street. My mother hobbled over and handed him a paper fan, whereupon a man came and stood in front of him. The man was tall and had rolled up the sleeves of his white undershirt. A smell of sweat and wheat emanated from his head and body. He had a ruddy face and short hair, with a wheat leaf stuck in it like a tiny flag. He panted heavily, as though a rope were being pulled in and out of his throat. He said,

"Brother Tianbao, please prepare three wreaths and five paper ornaments for my father."

My own father stiffened, and asked, "What's wrong with your father?"

"He died. At midday today he went to sleep in his room . . . he had been harvesting wheat for two days straight, so I told him to take a nap. He went to sleep, but suddenly sat up in bed, grabbed a sickle, and said that if he didn't harvest more wheat, it would rot in the fields . . . if he didn't harvest it, it would rot on the ground. Then he got out of bed and headed to the fields. He wouldn't respond when anyone spoke to him, and didn't even acknowledge anyone's presence. He continued forward, focusing only on himself. When he encountered other people, they all remarked that it looked as though he was sleepwalking, and when others spoke to him, it appeared as though he couldn't hear them. It was as though he were sound asleep and no one could wake him. He kept talking to himself, seemingly walking in another world and speaking to another version of himself. When he reached the wheat fields, he said he was thirsty and wanted to drink some water, then he proceeded to the canal at the base of the West Hill, and drank from it. After drinking—and while still asleep—he fell into the canal and drowned."

This man who told us that his father had fallen into a canal and drowned was from the Xia family on the east side of town. I later learned that I should address him as Uncle Xia. Uncle Xia described how his father had drowned in his sleep, but also said that his father had been fortunate—Uncle Xia hadn't seen anyone dreamwalking for many years, but all of a sudden his father started dreamwalking, and since his father had died in his sleep, he must not have suffered in the slightest. With this, Uncle Xia stumbled away, his face ashen. He was wearing a pair of white cloth shoes, and his heels slipped into and out of the shoes.

I watched as Uncle Xia hurried away, like someone who remembers he has forgotten his key and runs home to fetch it. I sat under the light in the entranceway idly browsing a book. It was Yan Lianke's *Kissing Lenin's Years of Sun*. This novel was about revolution, which is like a year-round tornado, and revolutionaries run around in all directions like crazy people. *The four oceans are frothing and the clouds are seething; the five continents are trembling and lightning is flashing. When navigating the ocean, it is necessary to rely on a helmsman; and when living things grow, they must rely on the sun.* These sentences sputtered out like a string of firecrackers, like a thunderstorm in the heat of summer—dense and muddy, loud and raucous. The general plot of the novel involved a group of locals who wanted to go to Russia to purchase Lenin's preserved corpse. This was clearly a fabrication, but Yan Lianke wrote it as though it were true. I didn't like this story, nor did I like the tone in which he told it. At the same time, I couldn't figure out why this particular story was so seductive. As I was reading, Uncle Xia had come over, said something, then left again. I glanced up at my father, who was sitting on his cot in the entranceway. I saw that his expression was even darker than Uncle

Xia's—as dark as a cement wall. If Uncle Xia looked as though he had lost his key, my father looked as though he had just found an entire bundle of keys—including both useful and useless ones—and was unsure whether to throw them away or wait for the person who had lost them. Father hesitated, then stood up. Mother called to him from inside the shop, "Did someone else die?" Someone else had died. Father turned to her. "It was Old Xia from the eastern side of town, who fell into the West Canal while dreamwalking and drowned."

A question and an answer—the same way that when the wind blows, the tree leaves move. Father got up slowly and walked into the funerary shop . . . First I should say a few words about our shop. The shop was the sort of two-story redbrick building that you find along every northern town street. The second floor was used as a residence, while the first floor was used for business. In the front of the store there were two salesrooms, both of which were completely covered in papercuts and wreaths . . . including cutouts of oxen and horses, gold and silver mountains, and boys and girls. These are all traditional goods. As for modern goods, there were paper television sets, refrigerators, cars, and sewing machines. My mother was crippled and it was hard for her to get around, but she knew how to make papercuts, and she could make papercuts of window flowers, magpies, and mynas sniffing wheat and looking as if they were about to burst into song. She could make a papercut of a tractor, spurting plumes of smoke into the air. When villagers got married they would always ask her to make them festive papercuts, and even the village chief said that my mother was a master paper cutter.

But making papercuts for weddings wasn't profitable, because no one was willing to pay for them. Later, my parents opened our New World funerary shop. My father designed bamboo frames and my mother made papercuts. When the bamboo and papercuts were combined, they became funerary objects that people could purchase.

People were willing to buy things for funerals, but not for weddings. It was all very curious.

Everyone believed in dreams, but didn't believe in reality. It was all quite odd.

Speaking of my father, he was indeed very short—under one-point-five meters tall. As for my mother, she was very tall—much taller than my father. She was a head taller, though her right leg was shorter than her left. This was a result of having broken her leg in a car accident when she was young. After the accident, she was left crippled—permanently crippled. Therefore, my mother and father rarely went out walking together. My father was short, but when he walked, it was as though he were flying. He was short, but when he spoke his voice was as loud as thunder. When he became angry, the house would shake so hard that dust would fall from the rafters and petals would fall from the paper wreaths. My father, however, was a good man. He seldom got angry, and when he did, he usually didn't hit anyone. In the fourteen years I've been alive, I saw him beat my mother only once, and I saw him curse her only a dozen or so times.

The one time that he beat her, my mother simply sat there and let him. My father, however, was a good man, and after striking her a few times, he stopped.

Whenever my father cursed my mother, she also simply sat there and let him curse her. My mother was a good woman, and whenever she let my father curse her, after a while he would stop.

Both Mother and Father were good people, and they never beat me or cursed me.

Our family opened the New World funerary shop, which sold wreaths, burial shrouds, and paper ornaments. Our family made a decent living profiting off dead people. Whenever someone died, it was a happy day for our family. But my parents never actively hoped someone would die. In fact, sometimes they didn't hope for anything at all. When business at the funerary shop was good, my father would ask my mother, "What do you think is going on? What's going on?" My mother, in turn, would ask him, "What's going on? What's going on?"

I heard my father inside the funerary shop asking, "What's going on? What's going on?" I turned to look, and saw that the funerary ornaments, which had been piled up as high as a mountain, were all gone. My mother was sitting in the same spot where there had previously been a pile of wreaths, and in front of her there were mounds of red, yellow, blue, and green paper. She was holding a pair of scissors in her right hand, and had a stack of folded red paper in her left. The floor was covered with paper scraps. In that pile of colored paper, my mother . . . actually . . . actually my mother continued cutting until she fell asleep.

She fell asleep leaning against the wall.

She became so exhausted making funerary ornaments that she fell asleep.

My father stood in front of her and asked, "What's going on? What's going on? Someone placed an order for three wreaths and five paper ornaments, and tomorrow morning he will come to collect them."

I now looked back into the house, and when I saw my mother I was reminded of how Old Xia had died while dreamwalking. I was reminded how so-called dreamwalking is really a result of the way in which whatever you are thinking about during the day becomes engraved in your bones, so that after you go to sleep at night you continue your thoughts from when you were awake, and try to carry out those thoughts in your dreams. This is similar to what bureaucrats call *to implement,* but in popular discourse we simply say *to carry out.* In their dreams, people try to put their thoughts into practice. At that point, I began to wonder what I would do if my mother and father were to start dreamwalking. What thoughts might they have deeply engraved in their bones?

I began to wonder whether or not I myself would dreamwalk. And if I were to begin dreamwalking, what would I do? What, indeed, would I do while dreaming?

3. (18:31–19:30)

Unfortunately, I had always slept very little, and never became so exhausted that I fell into a deep slumber. Neither did I have any pressing concerns engraved in my bones. I was as incapable of dreamwalking as a man is incapable of getting pregnant, or a peach tree is incapable of producing apricot blossoms. But I saw people dreamwalking, and was surprised at how quickly it all started. I had never expected that they would begin in rapid succession, as though they were being summoned—much less that tens and even hundreds of residents of the village, the town, the Funiu Mountains, and even the entire world would begin dreamwalking overnight.

Family after family began dreamwalking.

Thousands and thousands of people began dreamwalking.

The entire world began dreamwalking.

I was still reading *Kissing Lenin's Years of Sun*. The novel was as odd as a peach tree full of apricot blossoms, or an apricot tree full of pears. Even if you don't like the story, it will still lead you by the hand and draw you in.

Gao Aijun picked up a cent in the street, and wanted to go to the store to buy some candy. One piece of candy costs two cents, but he didn't have enough money. He decided to sell his straw hat. He sold the hat for fifty cents, with which he wanted to buy half a jin of stewed pork. Although the pork was very fragrant, half a jin of stewed pork costs ten yuan, and he still didn't have enough money. He decided to sell his clothes, leaving himself only a pair of underpants to cover his private parts. He was able to sell his clothes for a lot of money: fifty yuan. With these fifty yuan, he decided he didn't want merely half a jin of stewed pork, but rather he wanted actual meat. Full of energy, he went to the hair salon on the other side of the village, and paced in front of it. The young women in the salon were also sex workers, and the salon was no different from a brothel. Everyone said that the salon's new girls from Suzhou and Hangzhou were very good, with tender skin and bodies like water. But to go to the brothel and fondle these girls with bodies like water was not something he could do with only fifty yuan. To get a room and a bed, he would need a hundred fifty yuan. And if he didn't want to leave promptly when he was done and instead wanted to stay for the night, then the price would increase to five hundred yuan. He thought and thought, and ultimately decided he had no choice but to make a significant sacrifice if he wanted to realize his plan. He gritted his teeth, took a step forward, and resolved to go home and sell his own wife, Xia Hongmei.

This story, this novel—why does it seem as though it were actually true? Why does it seem as though it were true? I thought about this, and wanted to laugh. Just as I was about to laugh out loud, something even more ludicrous appeared before me. There was the sound of footsteps in the street, like several hands beating a drum at the same time. I turned around and saw a crowd of children—some were seven or eight years old, while others were ten or more—who were all following a man in his thirties. The man was shirtless, and was holding a wooden shovel used to thresh wheat. He was mumbling to himself. "After a while it will start to drizzle. Yes, it will definitely start to drizzle. You're not like the others, in that you don't do business. You farm, and if you don't harvest the wheat, it will grow moldy, and an entire season's crop will go to waste. An entire season's work would have been for nothing!" The man's eyes were half-closed, as though he were falling asleep. He walked so fast that wind blew out from under his feet with every step. As he walked, it was as though someone were pushing him from behind. It was very stuffy outside, and there wasn't a trace of dampness or coolness in the air.

That man was coming from the west, and he crossed the street as though crossing a narrow ribbon. The streetlamps were the color of mud, as though there were ashes floating overhead. It was as if that man were walking through ashes. Of the children chasing him, there was one who was completely naked, his cock flapping between his legs like a wild bird. "He's dreamwalking . . . He's dreamwalking," the children whispered curiously—as if they were afraid that if they said this out loud, they might wake him up, but if they didn't, they would be unable to keep this miraculous occurrence to themselves.

The dreamwalker walked so fast, it was as if he were devouring the road in front of him.

The children jogged behind him. They stayed a few steps behind, so as not to wake him, so as not to bring an abrupt end to the spectacle.

The entourage appeared before me.

The man turned out to be Uncle Zhang, who used to live in the old house across from ours. In our town, Uncle Zhang was an infamous wastrel. He couldn't earn money, nor could he hold a job. Because of this, his wife would slap him, and would even go to the eastern side of the river with a man who *could* earn money, and would sleep with him in plain sight. She left home with that other man, and they went together into the city—to Luoyang or Zhengzhou. The other man eventually tired of sleeping with her, and no longer wanted her. After she was cast aside, she returned home, and as soon as she entered the courtyard, Uncle Zhang said to her, "You've returned. Quick, wash your face and go inside to eat something." He even cooked her some food and steamed her some buns. Uncle Zhang was truly a cuckold, but now he was dreamwalking. I stood up where I was sitting in the doorway of New World, and exclaimed, "Uncle Zhang . . ." My shouts sounded like popcorn popping, and the stuffy air was pushed forward by the sound. "Father . . . Uncle Zhang from across the street is dreamwalking . . . he's crossing in front of our house!" I shouted into the shop, then put down my book, hopped down from the doorstep, and headed toward Uncle Zhang and the children who were following him. When I caught up with them, I made my way through the crowd of children, as though cutting through a small forest. I made my way over until I was under another streetlamp, and there I tugged Uncle Zhang's arm and shouted, "Wake up, wake up! . . . Uncle Zhang, you're dreamwalking!

"Wake up, wake up! Uncle Zhang, you're dreamwalking!"

Uncle Zhang ignored me. He pushed my arm aside, and said, "After the rain, the grain will grow moldy out in the fields, but what can be done? What can be done?" I again rushed up and tugged at him, but once again he merely pushed my arm aside, and said, "The grain has gone bad, and when my wife and children return, they will be hungry. If my wife goes hungry, she'll run off again with another man." As Uncle Zhang said this, his voice softened, as though he were whispering to me and was afraid others might hear.

I stood behind him and stared in amazement, as my legs grew weak. After pausing for a moment, I quickly walked up to him, and I saw that his face resembled an old gray brick, and his body was as stiff as an old elm tree. His footsteps were as loud as a pair of hammers. His eyes were wide open, as though he were wide awake, but when he spoke, he didn't look anyone in the eye, and his brick-like expression demonstrated that he was sleeping.

Gazing out from Town Street, I saw that the sky was as hazy as though there were a cloud of fog floating overhead. When I looked more closely, I noticed a tiny light or two hovering in the haze, like summer fireflies. There was a hair salon and the grocery store—selling daily items, dishes, and cooking utensils. There was also a privately owned clothing store and a publicly owned electronics store. All of the stores along the eastern side of the town's main street had their windows open—regardless of whether or not there was anyone inside, or whether or not there were any lights on. Some of the store owners had closed shop and returned home to harvest their wheat, while others were sitting or lying down in their stores and cooling off with an electric fan. The street was very quiet, the night was impatient, and everyone was feeling lazy. When I passed in front of Uncle Zhang's store across the street, some people turned to look at me, while others didn't turn and merely continued what they were doing.

The children shouted, "He's dreamwalking! . . . He's dreamwalking! Quick, look at the dreamwalker!" The night was dark and murky. Perhaps someone heard them, or perhaps not. Perhaps several people heard them, but acted as though they hadn't. Those who did hear them would come out and take a look, stand by the side of the road and smile. After Uncle Zhang had walked away, those people would then go to the children and ask, "What are you doing? What are you doing?" Dreamwalking was a significant occurrence, but at the same time it wasn't really significant at all. For the past several hundreds or thousands of years, this sort of thing has occurred nearly every summer, and sometimes even several times in the same summer. When other people dreamwalk, it actually doesn't have an iota of significance. Who *wouldn't* end up dreamwalking once in their lives, or even several times—even just by rolling over and kicking the blanket off the bed? It's like how people talk in their sleep hundreds of times. Talking in one's sleep is a kind of light dreamwalking, and if one gets out of bed and starts doing things, that would be a kind of deep dreamwalking. Everyone who lives and works on this earth will inevitably have several instances of either light or deep dreamwalking.

The night was so hazy.

The sky was so stuffy.

People who were busy went to do what they had to do, and people who were idle remained idle. Meanwhile, people who were neither busy nor idle continued being neither busy nor idle.

Uncle Zhang, from across the street, headed out of town, to the edge of his family's field. He then went to a small threshing area in his family's field, in front of the ripe wheat. The landscape outside town was completely different from the landscape in town. In the fields, there was always at least some wind. There were small fields that were each shared by a pair of households, and medium-sized fields measuring half a *mu*, which were collectively threshed by several households. There were also some large fields measuring more than a *mu* each, which had been left behind by the production brigades. These fields lined both sides of the road, and at night the road resembled a sparkling river, and the wheat fields resembled lakes. In the distant large fields, there was the rumbling of threshing machines, while in the nearby small fields there was the creaking sound of horses and cattle pulling millstones. There was also the popping sound of people pounding the wheat as they lifted bale after bale onto the iron frame. Mixed together, all of these sounds resembled a boat—or several boats, or even several dozen boats— sailing across a lake.

The night sky was vast, the wheat fields were minute, and the sounds from the fields were swallowed by the night. In the end, there was a kind of stillness. The lamplights in the wheat fields were muddy yellow, and Uncle Zhang walked through this muddy yellow light as he left the town and headed north. After a while, the children stopped following him, and simply stood at the entrance to town. I, however, continued following him. I wanted to watch as he bumped into a tree or an electrical pole, because when he did, his nose would start bleeding and he would wake up with a shout. I wanted to see what his first response would be upon waking up from his dreamwalking. I wanted to see what he would say, and what he would do.

Fortunately, Uncle Zhang's family's field was not very far, and he reached it after proceeding north for about half a *li*. To get from the road to the edge of the field, he had to cross a rain-filled ditch. As he was doing so, he slipped and fell in. I thought for sure he would wake up, but he merely climbed right back out. "A man can't let his wife and children go hungry. A man can't let his wife and children go hungry." Without waking up, he kept repeating this phrase to himself over and over. In this way, he crossed the ditch and reached the edge of the field. Everything appeared very familiar, and he reached the field without any difficulty. He turned on an electric lamp hanging from a poplar tree next to the field. As soon as the light came on, he put down his wooden shovel and continued looking around. He pushed an iron threshing frame into the middle of the field, then carried over a bale of wheat. He untied the bale and, grasping a bundle of wheat stems with both hands, pressed the wheat flat and threshed it on the metal frame.

I stood next to him, and although he could see the entire field, he couldn't see me. As far as he was concerned, it was as if I didn't even exist. When people are dreamwalking, they see only the people and things they care about, and it is as if nothing else exists. The kernels flew off the iron frame as though from an explosion, and there was a faint whishing sound. The smell of ripe wheat was as fragrant as if it were coming from a hot wok. It seemed as if there were even more stars in the sky, and in the distance there was the sound of people arguing over the order in which they would use the threshing machine. Nearby, a nightingale could occasionally be heard singing in a tree. Apart from this, however, everything was silent. Everything was still and pure. Everything was murky grayish black. As sweat dripped down his face, he grabbed a handful of wheat kernels that had fallen to the ground. There was nothing else; everything was still and pure. After he finished threshing the wheat, he brought over another couple of bales. There was nothing else; everything was still and pure. I didn't want to keep watching—I didn't want to watch what he would do next.

I wanted to go back, but just as I was about to turn around, something happened. This something was like a glass bottle shattering, producing a loud sound. Uncle Zhang finished threshing another bale, then went to fetch a third. But as he was about to grab the new bale, for some reason he went to an area behind a pile of bales. As he was heading there, a night cat jumped out from behind the pile and stepped onto his shoulder as it ran across his back. Afraid that the cat's claws might scratch him, he instinctively covered his face with his hands. He stood there frozen in shock, appearing as dead as a post. After a moment, he began blaming himself. Sounding surprised and confused, he asked, "What am I doing here? What am I doing here?" He looked around, and added, "This is my family's field, but why am I here threshing grain? Why am I threshing grain?"

He woke up. At least it appeared as though he had woken up. "I was clearly asleep, so how did I end up here threshing grain? How could I be here threshing grain?" It appeared that he had woken up. He looked at the sky, with an expression of surprise and confusion that he himself was unable to see. He twisted his body as though looking for something, but when his gaze came to rest on the wooden shovel he had brought, he seemed to suddenly remember something. He squatted down and began slapping his face. "You are truly fucking debased! You are truly fucking debased! Your wife ran away with someone else while you were busy working, yet you still come out here to thresh grain for her. She is sleeping with someone else, yet you are still here threshing grain for her."

He slapped his face, as though he were repeatedly punching a wall. "You are truly fucking debased! You are truly fucking debased!"

After hitting himself repeatedly, he began making excuses for himself.

"I wasn't doing this for her. I was doing it for my baby.

"I certainly wasn't doing it for her. I was doing it for my baby."

Eventually, he stopped hitting himself, and he also stopped talking to himself. Instead, he collapsed like a sack of flour. After a while, he fell back asleep while leaning against a bale of hay. It was as if he had briefly woken up and then fallen back asleep. It seemed as though the period he had been awake had been but a musical intermission within a larger dream, and after the intermission concluded he returned to his original dream. I was surprised. Extraordinarily surprised. I stood in front of him, feeling as if he had been putting on a performance for my benefit. I couldn't tell whether to trust him when he said whether or not he was sleeping. When I stepped forward and pushed him, it was as though I were pushing a stone pillar, and when I shook him, it was as though I were shaking a water pouch. His body swayed, but then quickly returned to resembling a water pouch. I shouted, "Uncle Zhang, Uncle Zhang!" It was as if I were shouting at a corpse, even though he was still breathing and continued to snore softly. "Your wife has returned. Your wife has returned." I stopped shaking him, because I didn't think he would wake up. He was already sleeping soundly. Like a corpse. So I shouted at his corpse-like body, "Your wife has returned. She has returned with that man. While you were sleeping, she was with that man."

Then the situation was no longer like what came before.

It was completely different.

It was as though the sun had come out in the middle of the night.

It was as though there were a fire burning on Uncle Zhang's skin. His sleeping face, which resembled a dirty cheek or dusty brick, started moving in response to my shouts. He sat up, his cheeks trembled, and his entire face appeared ashen. He made an effort to open his eyes and stare at me, but it seemed he was merely peering at the road behind me. The road was like a river flowing over from afar—flowing in from far away, and then flowing away again. It flowed from north to south, and all sorts of sounds floated up onto the shore and mixed with the sound of flowing water. Uncle Zhang stared at the northern end of the street. His wife had taken this road on her way out of town. She had gone to Luoyang or Zhengzhou. Perhaps she had gone to Beijing or Guangzhou. In any event, she left with a man from some village, who was able to earn money.

She went out into the world.

He stared at this road leading toward the outside world. Under the light of the lamp, he chewed his lip. There was a grinding sound as his upper and lower teeth rubbed against one another, like two pieces of dark-green granite pressing against each other. The sound was dark green, like the night. It was also very humid, and there was an occasional breeze blowing in from the fields. The scent of wheat pounded people's nostrils, went down their throats, and became embedded in their lungs and stomachs. Some cars drove along the road from south to north, their lights slicing forward like a knife, then slicing away again. Uncle Zhang watched the lights recede. As the cars drove into the distance, the sound of his grinding teeth was replaced with a biting sound. A dark-green sound emerged from between the cracks in his teeth, like leaves that are covered in frost but have not fallen to the ground.

Those frost-covered leaves swayed back and forth. After a while, they separated themselves from the branches and drifted down to the ground. The air was as cold as his gaze. It was as if the sound was emerging from between his teeth.

He suddenly stood up, as though being pulled to his feet by the car that had just driven by. He stood up and gazed out in the direction that the car had gone. The muscles in his face collapsed, and there was again the sound of grinding teeth. He stood there as though a burst of energy were about to explode out of his joints. He didn't say a word. It was as if he had become a different person—as if he were no longer the same person who, a moment earlier, had been afraid that his grain would rot in the fields. It was as if he were no longer the same person who, a moment earlier, had been concerned that his wife wouldn't have anything to eat when she returned home. He had become a completely different person.

He didn't look at me, nor did he look at the world around him. His gaze was somewhat askew, as though he were looking at something I was unable to see. It was as if he were looking at another world and another scene. That other world and other scene must have existed in his dream, and in his hysteria. He seemed to be able to see that other scene very clearly, as it appeared drop by drop in front of him. He turned pale and a layer of sweat appeared on his forehead. It was impossible to know what he had seen after falling back asleep, what he had encountered, or what had taken place in front of him. He didn't say a word. He remained completely silent, and continued grinding his teeth. A thick vein was visible in his neck, as though a snake were crawling down his face.

Another vein began throbbing under the lamplight.

It was as though there were a couple of snakes crawling down his neck.

Three or four more veins appeared, like snakes crawling along his neck. He left the pile of hay and walked toward the threshing frame. He kicked the wooden shovel on the ground, as though kicking a branch or a bush on the side of the road. He was walking inside another dream—a dream that was completely different from his previous one. In this other dreamscape, he went over to the threshing frame, leaned over, picked up a steel rebar that was as thick as his thumb, and held it in his hand. He hefted it, then strode over toward the area beyond the fields.

The rebar was two feet long, and it seemed it had been sitting there for an eternity. It had been waiting for him to pick it up, and now, in his powerful hand, the rebar began striding toward the villages in town. He didn't follow the road he had taken on his way there, but rather proceeded within a new dream. From one alleyway, he walked toward a location in his dream. I followed him and called out to him several times. Seeing that he was still not responding, I stopped to watch as he entered the village. I watched as he, in the still night, strode past a wall and disappeared.

As for myself, I also headed south down the road, toward home.

BOOK TWO

Geng 2, Part One:
Birds Fly All Around

1. (21:00–21:20)

In New World, my family was also dreamwalking.

My mother was dreamwalking.

After I left, my mother cocked her head and entered the shop. In front of her was an array of multicolored pieces of paper. Different-sized scissors were scattered on the floor beneath her feet. Along the street, everything remained as it had been. The moon was bright white and the lamps were muddy yellow. The resulting combination of white and yellow resembled a basin of swill that had been dumped into a pool of fresh water—transforming the fresh water into foul, and then into swill.

Everything was very still—as still as death.

Like death, everything was extremely still.

Not long after dusk, the quiet night was broken by the muffled sound of fat pigs snoring. The sound was hot and dirty. Hot, dirty, and sticky. There was the smell of sweat, which seeped through the cracks in all the doors. The odors that gathered in the street were the odors of a summer night.

On this summer night, someone was sleeping on the side of the road. Someone else was sitting in front of a shop drinking tea and fanning himself. Someone else had brought out an electric fan and placed it in the doorway of his house, and the fan's blades sounded like whirling knives. Everyone was chatting while either sitting or lying in front of the fan. The town's streets were just as they had been, and the entire world was just as it had been.

But actually, the world would never be the same.

The great somnambulism had already begun. The footsteps of the dreamwalkers had gradually begun to enter my village, and my town. The somnambulism blotted out the sky and blanketed the earth, leaving everything in a state of chaos. No one knew that the somnambulism was already hanging over us like a dark cloud. Everyone assumed that what was overhead was simply a dark summer night's cloud. People assumed that this summer night was like any other. Feeling a bit lonely, I returned to town, and when I heard the sound of snoring and saw how peaceful the streets were, I assumed that the world remained as it had been. The only difference was that there were a few more ordinary dreamwalkers. I looked at the town's liveliest street—East Street. I gazed up at the immense night sky, and then returned to our New World funerary shop, where I saw that there was a small car parked across the street. My uncle had arrived. I saw that my uncle was standing in the doorway of our funerary shop, like a doctor standing in the central room of a patient's home.

"Please sit."

My uncle ignored my father, and instead continued standing in the doorway of the funerary shop, looking around in all directions.

Uncle was one-point-eight meters tall, and my father was one-point-five. Uncle was wearing the sort of silk shirt that wealthy men used to wear during the Republican period. Father, meanwhile, was in his underwear. Father wasn't particularly thin, but next to my uncle he appeared downright skinny. He stood there like a small tree beneath a larger one. My father stood in front of my uncle like a child in front of a tall, strong doctor. My mother was still sitting where she had been sleeping. Now, however, she was no longer sleeping, and instead was sitting on the stool where she always sat while making papercuts. On the stool, there was a filthy cotton pad. My mother's expression resembled not a stone in an old wall, but rather a dirty rag, or an old newspaper. She didn't look at anyone, and instead merely sat there talking to herself. "Whenever someone dies, you should always make sure there is a wreath over the grave. You should make sure there are several wreaths over the grave." As she said this, she continued cutting the pile of paper she was holding, as though she were kneeling down and carefully watering a flowerpot. She had already cut out many paper blossoms—piles and piles of them. She had also cut out countless green leaves—piles and piles of them. Father was now sitting next to her, and at his feet there were some bamboo strips, glue, string, and a knife. She continued cutting until she fell back asleep. Father said to Uncle, "I woke her up twice and then went to wash my face. But when I returned, I found that she had fallen asleep again." She continued cutting until she fell asleep, and even after she fell asleep her hands continued cutting. Her half-closed eyes continued staring straight ahead, and her mouth kept speaking as her hands kept cutting. This is how Father knew that she was dreamwalking. I also realized that she was dreamwalking. These past several days, we had entered a season of death. Our funerary goods sold out quickly, and Mother entered a somnambulistic state.

Uncle stood there looking at his sister, like a doctor examining a sick patient. When he turned away, his eyes resembled two chunks of ice bearing down on Father's face.

Father laughed.

"Hasn't business at your crematorium been very good these past few days?"

When Father turned to Uncle, he told him—as though telling a doctor—that Mother's symptoms were actually quite common, and therefore her condition was nothing out of the ordinary. But he forgot that Mother was actually Uncle's younger sister, and Uncle couldn't bear to watch his sister laboriously making papercuts. Even after she fell asleep, her hands would continue cutting out floral wreaths. "Bring over another basin of cold water, so that she can wash her face." Uncle glanced disapprovingly at Father. The room was filled with the scent of freshly made flour paste, mixed with the smell of sweat from Father's bare torso. After a brief hesitation, Father took the basin to fetch some cold water. "Given that everyone has relatives who have died, we have no choice but to work overtime to make wreaths for them." As he was saying this, Father turned to Uncle. He seemed a bit disdainful, but didn't dare do anything overt. Instead, he merely knocked the basin against the corner of the stairs leading to the kitchen, making a banging sound. He seemed to resent the fact that Uncle was meddling in his family's affairs. At this point, Mother suddenly looked in Uncle's direction. It appeared she had just woken up, but still seemed unable to see anything at all, and instead remained focused on her papercuts. The sound of her cutting resembled the calls of cicadas sitting on a jujube tree on a summer night. Uncle continued watching his sister. At this point, he noticed me—as though I were a child who had not remained standing by his parent's sickbed and instead was running around outside. Uncle appeared very displeased, and resentful. He raised his eyebrows, then kicked the stool in front of him, as his mouth drooped into a frown and his complexion came to resemble a piece of rusted iron.

"You need to haul away the corpse oil.

"Niannian, your father is busy, so you should help your parents out."

As Uncle was saying this, he shifted his gaze from my face to Yan Lianke's novel, which was resting on the corner of the stool in the doorway—as though the origins of the recent crises could be traced back to that work. He looked as though he wanted to kick that book out of the doorway, or light a fire and burn that copy of *Kissing Lenin's Years of Sun.*

But Father emerged from the kitchen over by the staircase. He brought over a basin of water with a cloth inside. Father summoned Uncle's gaze, placed the basin next to Mother's feet, then took out the cloth and squeezed out most of the water. Father took the cloth and wiped Mother's face as though he were a nurse wiping the face of a terminally ill patient. "The water is a little cold, and once you feel it you'll immediately wake up." Father said this to Mother, but it also seemed he was speaking to himself. I was surprised by the warmth with which Father was treating Mother. I knew that Father was saying this for Uncle's benefit, but was also saying it for himself. Uncle listened and watched as Father washed Mother's face. With a wet cloth, he washed Mother right out of her dreamscape. As the cold, wet cloth in Father's hand was rubbing Mother's face, Mother's hand suddenly paused in midair. As Father continued wiping Mother's face in a clockwise direction, the scissors dropped from Mother's hand and fell to the ground.

As Father continued wiping Mother's face in a clockwise direction, a papercut dropped from Mother's hand and fell to the ground.

Father wet the cloth again, then squeezed it out. As he was wiping Mother's face in a counterclockwise direction, Mother woke up. She recovered consciousness, as though someone had dumped a basin of cold water on her face. She woke up just like that, and angrily pushed Father's hand away. She blinked her eyes, then looked at the room as though seeing a new world for the first time. The room was warm. Very, very warm. The cold vapor from the water produced a faint scent that gradually dissipated through the room. It was as though the cold water in the basin was slowly being poured into a pot of boiling water. "Just now, I was making papercuts in my sleep, wasn't I?" Mother phrased this as a question, but it was also as if she were informing herself of this fact. "Brother, you've come." She turned to Uncle, and added, "Please sit down. I haven't seen you in over a month." Then she turned to me, and said,

"Niannian, hurry and bring your uncle a stool."

I brought over a stool, and placed it under Uncle's butt.

But Uncle didn't even glance at it.

"I came to ask your family to haul away the corpse oil from the crematorium. There is now another barrel." As Uncle was saying this, he looked around, and added, "However much money you've earned, it's enough. If you are tired, you should go to bed. There is no point in exhausting yourself like this only to earn a little more cash." My uncle was disdainful of the small change that my family was able to earn selling wreaths and funeral ornaments. As he was turning to leave, we heard the puttering sound of a motorcycle in the street.

The sound came to a stop in front of my family's funerary shop.

A very young, dark face appeared in the doorway, with an expression of surprise and congratulations. The visitor said, "Hey, Zhang Mutou, who lives across the street, has gone mad." It turned out that Zhang Mutou had found a two-foot-long iron pipe somewhere and taken it home, while repeatedly saying to himself, "Watch me beat him to death! Watch me beat him to death!" When he got home, he ran into his wife, who had returned with a man named

Wang, who worked at a brick kiln north of town. Zhang Mutou slammed down the pipe he was holding, and with a single blow he shattered Wang's skull. The young man added,

"You tell me, how did Zhang Mutou know that his wife and Boss Wang had returned home together? And, how is it that Zhang Mutou's timing was so good? His wife and the Wang fellow had just gotten home, and Zhang Mutou was right there waiting for them!

"I don't know who notified Zhang Mutou. Old Wang, the kiln worker, was very burly, but as soon as he entered the courtyard, an iron rod was smashed down on his head, and he collapsed in Zhang Mutou's courtyard like a sack of cotton.

"Bricklayer Wang is from one of our town's richest families, and Mutou's wife was not the first woman he had tried to seduce. After he died, the ground was covered in blood, as though he had scattered several dozen bundles of red hundred-yuan bills all over the ground.

"The blood startled Zhang Mutou awake. He stared in shock for a moment, and then woke up. It turns out that Mutou, that bastard, had been asleep. It turns out that he, that bastard, had been so brazen precisely because he was dreamwalking. After waking up from his dream, he lay on the ground, exclaiming and sobbing, 'I killed a man! I killed a man!' Then he became cowardly."

The person on the motorcycle laughed and gestured, and a pair of rat eyes flickered in front of my family's funerary shop like pearls.

"Everyone knows I am a distant relative of Old Wang from the brick kiln. But he was ruthless, while we were very principled. Now I've gone to notify Old Wang's wife that she needs to go to Mutou's house to collect the corpse. Being both affectionate and principled, I have also come to notify you here at New World, so that you can prepare some extra wreaths, paper ornaments, and funerary objects. His is the richest family in town, and whenever other families want to build a new house, they have to go to his family to purchase bricks and tiles. You should go there to prepare some extra funerary objects for him. If his family won't offer to pay for the funerary objects themselves, I'll do so on their behalf. Whose fault is it that I'm their relative? I'm willing to buy ten or twenty wreaths on their behalf, to place on his grave." The person on the motorcycle spoke quickly, as though someone had opened a sluice. He had a look of delight, as though his wife had finally become pregnant with a son. He was standing outside, with his head in the doorway. His eyes resembled those of a rabbit that has emerged from hibernation and is gazing out to where the spring flowers are blooming. As he was about to leave, his eyes again came to rest on my uncle's face. He laughed to himself, and his face appeared to burst into bloom.

"Director Shao, you're here! However much money Bricklayer Wang's family gave you for his cremation, I'll match it. Just be certain you instruct the crematorium workers well, because we need to make sure that Bricklayer Wang's bones are not completely burned and shattered. We need to make sure that, when they are removed from the furnace, there will still be some intact leg or hip bones. These need to be longer than the funerary urn, so that we'll have no choice but to smash them with a hammer in order to get them to fit into the urn . . . I'll give you some extra money, if you make sure you don't burn all of his bones to ashes. We need to leave some bones intact, so that we then have to smash them into pieces to get them into the urn."

That face in the doorway was talking and laughing—appearing as romantic as a peony blossom under the spring sun. After this person finished speaking and left, the echoes of his laughter continued to resonate in the entranceway. I felt a bit cold, as though someone had ridden by on a motorcycle and dumped a bucket of ice water over my head. Outside, there was the puttering sound of a motorcycle. "Damn it!" My uncle cursed as he looked away from the doorway. It was as if he had just seen a performance. It was as if, as he was walking along, he suddenly noticed he was stepping in a pile of vomit left by a drunk townsperson. The entire world once again became preternaturally quiet, and a cool breeze blew through the town, and through the entire world. But the entire world was once again condensed into our funerary shop. "Go haul away a barrel of corpse oil. If you leave it here tonight, then when we have another cremation tomorrow, we won't have anywhere to store the new oil. We definitely can't allow excess corpse oil to accumulate in the furnace room."

Upon saying this, Uncle departed.

He walked out of the room, like a doctor leaving a sickroom after having examined a patient. "Don't exhaust yourself to the point that you're making papercuts and wreaths in your sleep, only to earn a few extra dollars . . . If you need money, you can sell a few barrels of that oil." After leaving our house and going into the street, Uncle glanced back, but then looked away again. He got into a car waiting in the entranceway, and turned on the ignition. Two columns of light shone onto the street, and as Uncle was about to drive away, he rolled down the window and exchanged a glance with my father, who had come out to see him off.

My father stood there watching my uncle's car drive off. "When will I have a chance to make you a wreath." This seemed to be both a statement and a question. His voice was neither particularly loud nor particularly soft. When he turned and saw me standing behind him, he stared in shock. Then he patted my head and, with a smile, proceeded back inside.

He then went into the crematorium.

2. (21:21–21:40)

Bodhisattvas, Buddhas, Confucius, Zhuangzi, and Laozi . . . I've told this story in a highly fragmented and disjointed manner. Laozi,

Zhuangzi, Mencius, and Xunzi, together with Buddhists and Daoists. Local deities and kitchen gods. I have knelt here for a long time recounting my woes. Have you all heard my story of what happened on this night of this day of this month of this year? Ah, ah, I see your shadows as you stand there in midair. I hear your footsteps as you walk back and forth through the air. You sound like a breeze blowing. Oh, oh. So, there is, in fact, a breeze, and as it blows over my face it feels as though you are all reaching out to caress my cheeks. Mother Wang and the Buddha. Tripitaka and Monk Sha. Guan Yu and Zhuge Liang. The Star of Literature and the Star of Heaven. Can any of you tell me where the end of the thread of my jumbled story can be found? If you can't, I'll have no choice but to set aside this end of the thread and start looking for the other.

In that case, I'll start tugging at the other end of this story.

After Uncle left that night, I went to the crematorium to haul away the corpse oil my family had purchased from Uncle. That was truly a terrifying task, but I got accustomed to it and it no longer appeared so frightening—the same way that, over time, people can become companions with lions and tigers. It appeared there was no longer any boundary between day and night. The crematorium was devoted to cremating human corpses, and in this respect it marked a threshold through which people passed to another world. The crematorium had been in operation for more than a decade, and was older than I. Events from more than a decade earlier are like last winter's dried leaves and branches, and when a new spring rolls around they are rendered inconsequential. Everyone will forget about them. Truly forget. I don't know how my uncle became director of the crematorium. He had been running the crematorium since before I was born, and the only difference was that when he first became director no one in town was willing to speak to him, since he had switched from burial to cremation—reducing human corpses to ashes. He reduced complete and intact people to ashes, and furthermore asked the relatives to pay him several hundred yuan. Eight hundred yuan. It is as if after burning down my house and digging up my grave, you still expect me to pay for the kindling you used to light the fire. It is as though I have to pay you for your efforts in burning down my house and digging up my grave, and reimburse you for the money you spent on renting the tools you needed to accomplish these tasks. At one point, my uncle walked over to our funerary shop. Someone from behind threw a rock at him, and someone in front spat in his face. As he walked over, there was a warm and familiar voice behind him, saying, "Director Shao, Director Shao." My uncle turned around, whereupon the voice became cold and hard. "Director Shao, I'll fuck your grandma. Director Shao, your entire family is better off dead!" Those curses were coming from someone whose mother had been cremated a few days earlier or whose father had been reduced to ashes. The person stood behind my uncle and stared at him. In his hand, he was holding a brick that could be used to kill or a shovel that could be used to decapitate.

My uncle stood in the middle of the street, his face pale. He was one-point-eight meters tall, and resembled a sturdy yet powerless tree that could be blown over by the wind at any moment.

"Director Shao, let's fight!" As the person hollered and cursed, Uncle looked back and said, "Let's go! Let's go to the outskirts of town for this. I don't want to splatter your filthy blood all over the town's streets."

My uncle walked toward the man who was cursing him. He stood there silently, his face ashen. Everyone assumed that, after being cursed like this, Uncle would resign as director of the crematorium. Instead, he simply went up to the man, ground his teeth, and said, "We must change our customs to conform to the state's policies. I will definitely send all the corpses to the crematorium, and have them reduced to ashes."

Over the following day and a night, Uncle plastered notices and advertisements on the walls of the town's streets and alleys, as well as the walls of the villages surrounding the town. The advertisements said, *In order to leave some land for our children and grandchildren, we are switching from burial to cremation.* They said, *Only those people with no descendants of their own would dare to not leave any land for our children and grandchildren.* They said, *The state has specified that if it discovers that anyone has been secretly buried, then no matter how long that person has been buried, the corpse will be disinterred and cremated, and furthermore the family of the deceased will be fined a certain amount of money and a certain amount of land.* They said, *For the sake of the nation and the people, the government will award a certain amount of money and a certain amount of land to anyone who reports that a family has secretly buried a relative.*

As a result, none of the villagers dared to openly bury anyone.

No one dared to let a grave be visible.

The villagers had no choice but to take their dead to the crematorium to be cremated.

One night, however, a few people went to Uncle's villa, broke down his door, smashed his windows, and lit a fire in front of his house. From that night forward, Uncle stopped speaking to people and stopped doing things for them. He also stopped going out for solitary strolls. Instead, he stayed inside the crematorium day in and day out, as though he were so dedicated to his work that he barely even had a chance to return home.

I must confess. It was, in fact, my own father who informed on those villagers and townspeople who secretly buried their dead.

Whenever someone died and the family began to prepare for a burial while trying to keep it a secret, my father would go to the crematorium at night under the cover of darkness, and inform his brother-in-law. If he ratted out one person, he would earn four hundred yuan; and if he ratted out two people, he would earn eight hundred yuan. Villagers typically earned only a few hundred yuan a month, and even if they left the village to find work, they could never earn a thousand yuan a month. All my father had to do was to go a couple of times to the crematorium on the hill outside town, and he could earn nearly a thousand yuan.

At that point, our family and Yan Lianke's were neighbors. Yan's family had built a three-room, tile-roofed house, and every day the sulfuric odor from the brick wall behind his house would seep into our courtyard. My father and my grandmother would smell this odor every day. Once, my grandmother noticed the odor, then looked at the Yan family's wall and sighed, "When will my family be able to build itself this sort of tile-roofed house? When will we ever be able to build this sort of house?"

My father stood in front of his mother.

On another day, my grandmother asked, "Will our family ever be able to build a tile-roofed house in this lifetime? Because if we can, you will be able to find a wife and get married, and I will be able to die in peace."

Standing in front of my grandmother, my father blushed bright red.

On another day, after my grandmother fell ill, she carried over a jar of Chinese medicine and gazed at my father, saying, "I'm afraid I won't live to see you get married and find a job. I'm afraid you won't ever have an opportunity to live in a tile-roofed house." My father was twenty-two—an age at which many of the other village men had married, and even become fathers. They had all already either built tile-roofed houses or moved into apartment buildings. However, my father, apart from the fact that he resembled a twenty-two-year-old adolescent with his face covered in pimples, displayed no other hint of happiness. He stood forlornly in front of my grandmother, like a sheet of discarded wastepaper. He appeared ashamed and helpless. Autumn leaves fell from the sky, circling around Father's head as though beating his ears.

At this point, from a location not far away, there was the sound of footsteps. "Quick, quick, Grandma Zhang is not well. Take her to the hospital . . . Take her to the hospital." When my father heard those shouts, he rushed forward. He saw that the other villagers were also running over to the Zhang family's house. One person rushed over with a stretcher. Another rushed over with a rice bowl, then tossed the bowl to the side of the road. They were all so anxious, it was as if they were afraid the sky was going to collapse. My father stared at the front door of the Zhang family house. His twenty-two-year-old face was bathed in sweat. He didn't see anyone carry Grandma Zhang out of the house, so he waited a while, then a while longer. Some people entered with an empty stretcher, then reemerged with the same empty stretcher. When they entered, they looked surprised and alarmed, but when they reemerged, they appeared calm and mysterious. Beneath their mysterious expression, however, they had a look of excitement, like sunlight shining down into a deep well.

My father understood. He understood that Zhang Mutou's grandmother, from across the street, was already on her last legs. He knew that the Zhang family, in order to avoid having her cremated, had resolved not to publicly weep or hold a funeral procession after her death. They also resolved not to wear mourning clothes. Instead, they acted as though no one had died. They closed their front door, and the entire family knelt before the corpse for three days, but were careful not to let anyone see them, or know what they were doing. They all acted as though they hadn't seen or heard anything. As a result, the family managed to keep the death a secret. Three days later, in the middle of the night, they carried the body to a grave and buried it, then placed a pile of grass on top of the newly dug grave, together with cornstalks and tree leaves. In order to keep the burial a secret, no one breathed a word about the death, and instead everyone made only silent gestures. In those days, this was a common practice in the village after someone died.

However, my father disrupted this practice. As though he were piercing a boil, he put this secret on display for everyone to see, willingly serving as a spy and an informer. At the time, my father was only twenty-two, and the pimples on his face burned bright red. He hid in the courtyard and pinched his pimples until they were black and blue. He kept peeking out at the Zhang family's house across the street. He kept looking at the red bricks of the wall in back of the Yan family's new house, and kicking them. He suffered there until the sun had set, at which time he finally came out and proceeded toward the crematorium on a hill outside town.

He accepted four hundred yuan from my uncle at the crematorium.

By the time he returned, gripping four one-hundred-yuan bills, Grandma Zhang's corpse had been exhumed and hauled away, as though a prison van had hauled away an escaped prisoner. In the quietness of the village, even as the final traces of the setting sun were fading, you could hear voices exclaiming, "The Zhang family is cursed! The Zhang family is cursed!" This was the only expression of sympathy that the villagers uttered after Grandma Zhang's corpse was hauled away to be cremated. No one had any inkling that it had been my father who had exposed the family's secret. How could such a significant incident have been kept a secret? If they really didn't want people to know, they shouldn't have done it. After exposing the Zhang family's secret burial and returning to the village, my father was wandering the village streets in twilight, and when he saw other villagers eating their dinner, he acted as though nothing had happened. When he went to report the secret burial, he had taken an old hoe, explaining that he was going into town to repair it, and when he returned, he did, in fact, have a freshly welded hoe. He acted as though he were carrying it home after having had it repaired. It was truly as though nothing had happened. Under the setting sun, the birds returned to their nests, while the villagers ate their dinner and discussed their plans for the next day.

It was truly as if nothing had occurred.

The only change was that the Zhang family's door was now unlocked. Their house was as still as the dead of night.

When my father left, he was carrying a broken hoe, but when he returned he was holding a newly repaired one—meaning that now he had something to do with his hands. He could place his hand on the hoe handle, and in this way was able to calm himself down. He was like a bird returning to its nest at dusk. He acted as though nothing unusual had occurred. When he returned, he glanced over at the Zhang family's house. He paused and looked around, but the uncanny stillness made him return home. When my grandmother brought him a rice bowl, he looked up and stared at her for a long time. "Next year, our family should also build a tile-roofed house." As Father was saying this, he placed the hoe under the eaves of his house, then looked out at the Yan family's new brick house. "Next year, our family should also build a tile-roofed house. We definitely must build a tile-roofed house." He waited until Grandmother appeared pleasantly surprised, where-upon Father took the bowl and began gulping down his rice. He then squatted there without saying a word, his face pale. Crouched, his body resembled a cremation urn.

In this way, each time someone in the village died, my father was able to purchase several extra bricks for his house.

Each time someone in the village died, my father was able to buy another large tile for his house.

If anyone tried to secretly bury a relative, eventually the people in the crematorium would know. The enforcement brigade and the cart puller from the crematorium would invariably show up at the dead person's house shortly after the death. Amid the cries and wails, the cart puller would haul away the corpse. In this way, the law would be enforced. The corpse would be cremated. It would be reduced to ashes. At these moments, my father would never be in the village. Instead, he would always return to the village a day after the corpse had been cremated. It seemed as though every time someone in the village died, my father would just happen to be away visiting his relatives. It was as though he didn't know a thing. He would then return to the village and stay in his house without going outside. Sometimes it would be someone living in our own alley who would pass away, and although my father would be the one who informed the crematorium so that the carter could come seize the corpse, he would nevertheless ask my grandmother to go to the family's house to pay a condolence call and offer a funerary present. If everyone else was offering ten yuan as a condolence gift, he would tell my grandmother to give twenty yuan. If everyone else was offering twenty yuan, he would tell my grandmother to give thirty or forty.

Most of the time, however, there was no opportunity for him to offer condolences. This is because on the days when people were dying and being buried, Father was usually not in the village and presumably didn't know what was happening. This continued for half a year, during which time more than a dozen of our neighbors and fellow villagers died, and our family managed to save five thousand yuan to build a new house. But that winter, my father once again left the village for a couple of days, and on his way back he happened to run into the legal enforcement brigade and the family of a deceased person. That was a bitter cold day, and the earth and sky were both ashy gray. The wheat sprouts in the fields resembled the earth's body hair. My father walked back from our relative's house. He crossed over the mountain ridge and cut through a gully, and when he reached a hillside field he saw that the enforcement brigade was at the Yang family tomb. The men were like a flock of birds flying overhead and discovering pile after pile of cornstalks. With the sort of shovel typically used by prospectors, the enforcement brigade quickly dug a hole that was as thick as a man's arm in the middle of the grave. Then they placed several *jin* of gunpowder into the hole, resealed it, and lit a fuse protruding from the hole. Under the gray sky, the sparks produced by the fuse made loud popping sounds. They shouted, "Step back, step back!" as they retreated to a safe distance. Then they waited. And waited. And waited until an incredibly loud rumble exploded from the grave. The hillside trembled, the ground trembled, and everyone's heart trembled. Then everything calmed down again. The enforcement brigade returned to the grave and proceeded to kick into a pile the fragments of bone and flesh that had exploded out of the grave. Then they poured some gasoline and lit a fire. In this open-air grave, they cremated the remains of the deceased. Flames rose up into the air, as though someone's house had caught on fire. You could hear a popping sound as the flames leaped up. It sounded like a whip, as though the corpse were being repeatedly whipped. There was the smell of gas, and of burnt flesh. The air was full of a burning smell, and the people who lit the fire stood around it for a while. It was the middle of winter, and the mountain ridge was very cold. Some of the people standing around the fire held out their hands to warm them. My father observed from a distance. He couldn't believe his eyes, but it was real. He earned four hundred yuan from this. From the very beginning, he had been the protagonist of this story, and without him, there wouldn't even have been a story. In the area of the sky that was still illuminated, the predusk light of the setting sun was the color of fire, like gray ashes covering a still-burning fire. There was a faint smell of something burning. It reeked of burnt flesh and bone, as though someone had been cremated in the open air. There even seemed to be the sound of anguished cries as someone was being cremated. It was very faint, yet quite distinct. It was the sound of one agonized scream after another. Later, the voice grew hoarse. As the gasoline-lit fire died down, the screams also became quieter and quieter. Finally, they were replaced with sounds of moaning. My father stood next to another family's grave located about a hundred meters away. The trunks of the old willow and cypress trees on the family's grave were as thick as barrels, and were blocking his line of sight. There wasn't any trace of cold or shock on his face, and instead there was merely a look of astonishment. He continued staring at the Yang family's grave, which had been exploded and burned with gasoline. His face had a layer of pain, from where he had gotten burned by the fire. It was as if the blood in his face had been ignited by the gasoline. His face was baked dry by the gasoline, and the skin that was left behind was painfully cracked.

He stood there for a long time, staring straight ahead as he gingerly touched his face with his hands.

As the fire died down, the crowd dispersed.

The brigade headed toward the crematorium at the base of the mountain.

There were five or six men, all strong and burly. The eldest was around forty, while the youngest was younger than Father. They were all wearing the sort of standard dark-green uniforms that were worn by county and town employees. They were from a legal enforcement brigade that had been constituted at the county level, and were just like a real brigade. Every village and town had its own enforcement brigade, which would suddenly appear wherever there was a corpse that had not been cremated. This brigade would appear at the family's grave plot. They would explode and burn the tomb, and then leave.

After the enforcement brigade departed, my father went over to the Yang family's grave. The pit was two feet deep, and smelled of gas and scorched earth. After twenty minutes, the fire died out. The smell of gasoline and scorched earth, combined with the stench of burnt flesh and baked bones, resembled the stench that surges out of a furnace when you open it after having cremated a corpse. The handful of bones that had not yet been reduced to ash were like pieces of unburned kindling at the bottom of a dark hole. There was a round pit, next to which there were pieces of flesh and bone that the men had forgotten to kick into the fire. The bone had cracked open and turned grayish black, while the flesh resembled a piece of red clay sitting on the freshly scorched earth. Standing on the black and red soil, my father turned pale. Seeing that next to his feet there was a bone resembling a human vertebra, he turned pale. His face turned deathly white. He stared in shock. It was as though he already had centuries of experience, despite being only twenty-two.

In the distance, the Funiu Mountains fell silent. At the base of the mountains, Gaotian Village—or perhaps I should say Gaotian Town—also fell deathly silent. There wasn't a sound, and it was as if the entire world had died. As though everything was thoroughly dead. There were only the men of the enforcement brigade, who had already walked away, like a family returning home after having harvested their grain. The members of the brigade appeared calm and unhurried, and were laughing happily. Some of them were even singing, and the sound of their song soared into the solitary, deathly sky, like a flock of wild birds cutting through it. The predusk light of the setting sun resembled fiery embers in the gray sky, or white ashes being dumped on a still-burning fire.

It was extremely cold and a wind was blowing mercilessly through the graveyard.

My father stood next to the grave that had been exploded and burned. He stood there motionless, as though he were dead. At that instant, the red pimples on his face began to turn green. These pimples covered his forehead and nose, and he stroked the painful ones on his forehead. Then he leaned over to pick up that piece of flesh and bone that looked like a vertebra. He examined it, then quickly dropped it again, as though he had touched a piece of ice. Because the Yang family's grandmother was already ninety-two years old when she passed away, the family had decided not to cremate her. Therefore, they didn't weep when she died, and neither did they wear white mourning clothes or weep in the entranceway of their home to announce that someone in the family had died. But my father still knew. When he walked past the family's house, he noticed that their gate remained tightly closed, even though it was the middle of the day. Moreover, through the gate, he could smell the aroma of people gathered for a banquet.

He knew someone in the family had died.

He had already known that the family's ninety-two-year-old grandmother had been on her sickbed.

That night, Father had climbed the hill and had seen a light at the Yang family grave site. He saw that someone, under the cover of darkness, was digging a new grave there. Father then went to the crematorium to reveal the Yang family's secret. As Uncle was stuffing four hundred yuan into Father's hand, he patted Father on the shoulder and smiled. "Li Tianbao, don't worry that you are still young. In the future, you will definitely enjoy success. To survive, you must be willing to do things that others are unwilling to do." Father didn't respond. As he was leaving the crematorium, Mother was in a room in the crematorium sewing and selling funeral clothes. She opened her door and looked at Father, then dropped a piece of cloth in the doorway. "Someone else has died." It was hard to tell whether this was a question, or whether she was simply talking to herself. Father looked at her, and saw that her face was as sallow as a sheet of yellow paper. He nodded, as though in response, but also as though expressing respect and offering greetings to the younger sister of the crematorium owner who always gave him money.

Then he left.

Just as he always did.

He didn't return to the village. Instead, he went to see one of my aunts, just as he always did. He went to the house of his elder sister, who lived far away. He acted as though he didn't have a clue that someone in the village had died. But when he returned three days later, he found this scene at the grave site. The carter had not hauled away the corpse of the Yang family's grandmother for cremation. Instead, after waiting for the family to bury the corpse, the crematorium workers went to the grave site and blew it up, then doused the corpse in gasoline and burned it.

The weather was exceedingly cold, and the wind tore through the hills. He found a broken shovel that had been discarded by someone digging a grave, and used it to toss the soft earth back into the fiery pit. The rays of the setting sun resembled burning embers in the gray sky—like a lid of white ash covering a still-burning fire. Father scooped up one shovelful of soil after another. He wanted to re-cover the bones in the grave that had been blasted open. He filled the pit with soil, and then covered it once again with cornstalks and tree branches. This way, it looked as though nothing had happened. With this, all the problems were solved, and all that was left was a cold winter breeze blowing through the mountain ridge. However, someone was coming up from the base of the ridge. The Yang family had already been summoned out of the village and up the mountain ridge by the sound of explosions and burning. Leading the way were the young people, who could run quickly. Behind them was a large group of men and women from the Yang clan, appearing as though they were being blown over by the wind, along with the sound of mountains and seas. After seeing the crowd on its way to the Yang family grave, my father quickly left. He headed in the direction of the enforcement brigade. As he walked away, he kept glancing back to see whether or not that group of Yang family members was following him. He checked to see whether or not anyone had noticed his presence. He resembled a thief—a thief who, just before he manages to seize what he is attempting to steal, hears the owner at the door. My father felt cold, and his heart was shivering. Although he was wearing new padded boots and sweatpants, he was still extremely cold. As soon as he had money, he bought himself and my grandmother some padded clothes. At the time, he had been very warm, but now he was exceedingly cold. Heading east along the mountain path, the men of the enforcement brigade were already far away. In fact, there was no trace of them. In the predusk stillness, it seemed as if the entire world had died, and as though my father had also died. His face was deathly pale, and his forehead was covered in icelike beads of sweat. As he was about to reach the entrance to the crematorium, he sat down on the side of the road. Biting his lip, he sat down on the edge of someone's field. Without realizing what he was doing, he kicked the dirt under his feet into a pile. In front of the pile, there was a deep pit.

Finally, after the sky had turned completely dark, he headed into the crematorium.

I didn't learn about all of this until later.

But without knowing for certain, I assumed that this was what had happened.

This was the only explanation for how Mother and Father could have ended up this way while dreamwalking on that particular night of that month of that year. If this was not what happened, then my parents wouldn't have ended up this way. If things hadn't gone that way, my parents definitely would not have ended up this way on the night of the great somnambulism.

When my father reached the crematorium, he took out the four hundred yuan my uncle had given him. He took the four one-hundred-yuan bills and placed them on the edge of Uncle's table. "I'm not going to do this anymore. Even if my life depended on it, I still won't do it. Even if it means I won't be able to build myself a house and instead have to sleep out in the open, I still won't do it." After saying this, my father was about to leave. He was about to walk out of the crematorium office. My uncle didn't try to stop him, but neither did he accept the four hundred yuan. "If you won't do it, there are surely others in your village who will. All they need to do is say a few things and run around a bit, and in the amount of time it takes to eat a bowl of rice they can earn themselves four hundred yuan. Where else will you find this good a deal?" The office consisted of two rooms, and on the wall there was a slogan that had been copied from official documents: PROMOTE CREMATION TO SAVE FARMLAND. The lamplight was as bright as day. There were nightingales cooing in the crematorium courtyard. On the front wall of the two-story cremation hall there were the freshly painted words FAREWELL HALL, which appeared golden in the lamplight. One could see the water in the reservoir, appearing as though the moonlight had been gathered together and was floating on the water's surface.

As my father left the office, Uncle stood in the doorway like a giant, and declared, "I hope you don't regret this!" My father left the office. He walked away without saying a word. He was silent, and the entire world was silent. "I won't regret it." As my father said this, his footsteps sounded like water dripping onto tree leaves. The bricks for the new house had already been ordered, and cement had already been purchased. All Father needed was for five or six more villagers to die—and if out of five or six deaths there were three or four families who were not willing to accept cremation and instead tried to secretly bury their dead, that would be enough to allow him to buy the steel rebar he still needed. But his side job as an informer had become more difficult, since people increasingly would take their dead to the crematorium of their own accord—the same way that after the moon comes out there will inevitably be moonlight, and when the sun comes out there will inevitably be sunlight. Winter was the season of death. Every winter several villagers died, and inevitably there would be some families unwilling to accept cremation who instead would attempt to secretly bury their dead. Obviously, the crematorium could easily retrieve the corpses from the homes of the deceased. Uncle, however, would always wait until they had already been buried before blowing up their graves—insisting on going to the grave and using gasoline to light a fire. After my father left, my uncle came out and stood in the entranceway. "Li Tianbao, if you pass up this money, you'll come to regret it . . . You'll definitely regret it."

My father proceeded out of the crematorium. He departed without even a backward glance. He resembled a chick that was determined to fly away. The night sky opened up before him like a curtain, and the moonlight was stained with the smell of earth from the fields. He walked, and his footsteps continued to resonate as he went down the street. He also heard someone else's footsteps, and when he turned to listen more carefully he heard Uncle, behind him, cursing and telling him to go back inside.

It was all over. If people died and were buried permanently, there wouldn't be any more news about them. It was as if someone had been buried alive in the mud. It turns out that my mother had been standing in the entrance of the crematorium waiting for my father. She had watched as he emerged from the crematorium, as though flickering into view from the side of the road or from behind a shady tree.

"You mustn't ever do this again."

"I won't."

"But if you don't, how will you ever build your new house? I went to your street, and saw that while many of your neighbors have already built new houses, your family still lives in an old thatched-roof house.

"I can help you build a new three-room house. All you need to do is to marry me, and in lieu of a dowry, I will help your family build a new house. After we marry, we can open a funerary shop in the middle of Town Street. We can sell wreaths and burial shrouds, as well as paper ornaments and funerary objects to be buried with the deceased. After that, you'll never again need to do anything you don't want to do." As Mother was saying this, a cloud floated overhead and its shadow flickered over her body and her face. At that point, my mother was standing only three feet away from my father, and her breath was gently blowing onto his face.

She was waiting for Father to respond, but he barely glanced at her. Instead, he snorted and walked away.

She also walked away.

3. (21:41–21:50)

That night, during the second *geng* period—around nine o'clock—as I was heading toward the crematorium, I kept thinking about my family. I thought about affairs relating to my father, my mother, and my uncle. Uncle Yan wanted to know about these things, but I didn't reveal anything to him.

I don't know what happened between Mother and Father, but the following spring they got married.

I don't know what happened between Mother and Father, but after they got married I was born.

I don't know what happened, but after I was born my grandmother died.

Among all living things, every time one is born, another must die. And after one dies, another will be born. This way, the total number of living people, animals, and birds will always remain constant. There will never be one more or one less. The reason why the number of people in the world is constantly increasing is that the number of animals and birds is decreasing. One day, when the number of animals and birds finally increases again, the corresponding number of human lives will collapse like a demolished house. This passage is from one of Yan Lianke's books, but I can't remember which one. According to this logic, I was born because my grandmother was about to die, and my grandmother died because I was born.

When my mother was pregnant with me, my grandmother fell ill, and as my mother's belly grew larger and larger, my grandmother became sicker and sicker. It was like a race—a race between birth and death. Grandmother's belly hurt so much that she wasn't able to consume anything other than her medicine. As I grew increasingly fat inside my mother's belly, my grandmother grew increasingly thin lying on her sickbed. As my body grew larger, hers grew smaller. Each time my weight increased by one *jin,* hers would decrease by the same amount. As I was about to be born, she curled into a fetal position and prepared to die. I was born in the winter of the same year that my parents got married. There was a blizzard, and the entire world was white. At that time, I was inside my mother's belly struggling to get out, while my grandmother was lying on a bed in the southern room of our family's new house, about to die. As I was waiting to emerge from my mother's belly, Father went from the north room to the south room, where he stood in front of Grandmother's bed. "A baby boy! A baby boy!" When Father said this, Grandmother grinned. "My life has been worthwhile. We have a new house, and now I have a grandson to burn incense for me after I die." Then she smiled brightly and departed. It was as if she had been waiting for me to arrive before she left—like someone finishing a shift at work before someone else starts the next. After my grandmother completed her final shift, I started my first. I began living in Gaotian, and eventually began talking, crawling, and growing. Grandmother, meanwhile, died, after which she no longer spoke or did anything, and instead she entered a permanent state of rest.

Before she died, Grandmother didn't specify whether she wanted to be buried or cremated. Mother and Father were also not sure whether they should bury or cremate her. My arrival was a joyous occasion, while Grandmother's departure was a sorrowful one. When a joyous and a sorrowful occasion coincide, one doesn't worry about happiness or sadness. Father had a calm expression and Mother also appeared very calm as she lay in bed. My parents both acted as though I hadn't even been born, and as though Grandmother had not died. On that day, it was bitter cold, and had been snowing continuously for a whole month. The entire world was as white as the pristine snowy-whiteness of the inside of a grave. There were icicles hanging from the eaves of the house and from the tree branches. The snow in Gaotian Town came up to people's knees, and sometimes even their waists. The entire world was filled with snow, and everything under heaven was bitterly, bitterly cold. The village was so quiet that the basin of charcoal burning next to my mother's bed sounded like firecrackers. The snow visible through the window resembled blowing sand. The northern wind blew through the house and knocked down the icicles hanging from the eaves. In my mother's embrace, I could hear water boiling over the fire. Father was sitting next to the fire and mother was lying in bed holding me. Grandmother, meanwhile, lay in that bed waiting for her funeral arrangements.

Time was like an old saw being pulled between Father and Mother. I was born just as the sun was about to come up, the same way that Grandmother passed away just as the sun was about to come up. In this way, by noon I was crying and sleeping, sleeping and crying. When I was neither crying nor sleeping, I could hear my mother and father talking to each other, their voices very soft, as though they were about to fall asleep as well.

"Let me go out and take a look, and we'll talk more later." Mother said this as she rolled over in the bed. Father, who had been sitting next to the fire, stood up, and came over to the bed to caress my face. "Son, for generations, our family has had only one son per generation, and you should similarly also give me a son. That way there will be no karmic retribution, and I, Li Tianbao, will not have let anyone down."

Then he left. He went outside. In the blizzard, the world was so still that not even a single person's shadow could be seen, but on the wall in front of the entrance to our house, someone had posted a sheet of paper on which was written, in black characters, "Joyous news! Li Tianbao's mother has died. Let's see whether or not she will be cremated. Joyous news! Li Tianbao's mother has died. Let's see whether or not she will be cremated." This announcement was written in black characters on a sheet of white paper. The paper had straight edges, but the characters were twisted and slanted. The announcement was posted in the entrance to my family's home. It was posted on electrical poles. It was posted on the poplar and pagoda trees by the side of the road. After my father saw five or six of these announcements, he stood in front of an empty eatery, facing the silent snow. Then he turned and walked back.

On his way home, Father angrily kicked at the snow with every step. He was short and thin, and when the snow came up only to other people's knees, it came up to his thighs. And when the snow came up to other people's thighs, it came up to his waist. But he kicked the snow like a horse kicking up dust. In this way, he returned home, and on his way back, he began screaming,

"My wife has given birth to a son!"

"My wife has given birth to a son!"

He started out announcing the joyous news of the birth of his son, but by the time he reached my mother's bedside, he was talking about something else.

"Let's cremate her. Otherwise, everyone will either hate me, or hate your brother.

"Let's cremate her. That way, we can stuff people's mouths and eyes with her ashes."

They decided to have my grandmother cremated. On the third day, it stopped snowing in the morning, and when the sun came up and everyone in Gaotian was out sweeping the snow, my father didn't ask anyone to help him lift my grandmother's corpse, nor did he ask anyone to lend him a cart to transport it. He also didn't arrange for the crematorium's hearse to drive to our family's house. Instead, wearing a white filial cap and white shoes, he walked out of the house while carrying his mother—my grandmother—in her burial shroud. It was as if he were placing a wager with this world. It was as if he were fighting with the gaze of everyone in Gaotian. Father's white filial cap was made from calico, and was as white and delicate as snow. The burial shroud that my mother prepared for my grandmother was made from black silk that produced a black glow, and the golden lining around the collar and the sleeves glistened in the sunlight. The stitching was expertly done—indescribably so. No one had anticipated that my father would be so strong, or so bold. At that time, some people were sweeping snow from their entranceways, while others were out chatting in the streets that had just been swept clean. Breakfast and lunch were being served in the canteen. My father carried my grandmother's corpse past a crowded area, where many villagers and townspeople were watching.

Step-by-step, as if protesting.

Step-by-step, as though taking a vow.

Everyone stared in surprise. Everyone stared in shock.

The audience gasped in astonishment, then erupted into shouts as everyone's gaze was suddenly riveted on Grandma Mao Zhi, standing up onstage. After all, even at 109 years old, she was still a living person who had just been cracking walnuts, but now they found her wearing burial clothing like a dead person!

The burial garb was made of high-quality black satin with subtle sparkles that shimmered under the stage lights.

In this way, the blackness appeared to emit a white light, the redness emitted a purplish light, and the yellowness had a golden bronze luster. This resplendent burial outfit shocked the thousands of people in the audience into silence, and drew all of their eyes up to what was occurring onstage.

I was reminded of a passage from *Kissing Lenin*. I don't know whether it is because of *Kissing Lenin* that the events in our town subsequently came to pass, or whether it was instead on account of the events that happened in our town that *Kissing Lenin* came to be written. I don't know whether it was Yan Lianke's novel that foretold this night's events in our town, or whether it was this night's events that helped conceive a future Yan Lianke.

My father carried Grandmother, dressed in her burial shroud, from that area that was most crowded. The villagers stared in surprise. They all stared in shock. The brooms they were using to sweep the snow paused, as did their shovels. Their mouths, which were in the middle of exchanging gossip, paused. Their faces also paused in the bitter cold. Everyone watched quietly as my father walked over. They watched in deathly silence as this short man with a round face walked over carrying his mother's corpse on his back. He cut across the snow-covered ground. The snow had stopped falling and the sky had cleared, but between the sky and the earth there wasn't a single particle of dust. The snow-covered areas were white, and the areas that had been swept clean were the color of red earth. Meanwhile, my grandmother's body, which my father was carrying, was dressed from head to toe in shiny black fabric. The weather should have warmed once the sky cleared and the sun came out. However, because of my father and my grandmother, the town remained as bitterly cold as the middle of a winter night. It was as cold as a patch of uninhabited wilderness. The ground had frozen and cracked. People's hearts had frozen and cracked. Everyone's heart had cracked into deep fissures. Those announcements written on paper were posted on people's bodies and on tree trunks: "Joyous news! Li Tianbao's mother has died. Let's see whether or not she will be cremated." This was meant to be a very ordinary, playful remark. Father proceeded with Grandmother's corpse on his back and waded through that mortal realm. He cut across it, and jostled through it. Slowly. Bitter cold. Iron nails. It was as if he were shooting through a frozen forest. In the process, he knocked off all of the trees' frozen branches. He broke them off. He chopped down all of the frozen tree trunks. The entire world was filled with the sound of my father breaking off frozen branches. The world was filled with the sound of my father breaking off other people's gazes.

No one had any inkling that he possessed such strength.

No one had any inkling that he was strong enough to suppress the rotation of Gaotian's heaven and earth. Someone watching him from behind opened his mouth.

"Li Tianbao, what are you doing?

"Li Tianbao, what are you doing? Are you trying to put on a display of strength for the other villagers and townspeople? It's as if your mother's death was the villagers' and the townspeople's doing."

My father came to a halt.

His voice was as loud as thunder.

"I've never revealed anyone's secrets, because I've never revealed anyone's secrets!

"Whether or not the villagers and the townspeople are cremated or burned in the open isn't any of my business. It's simply not any of my business."

Then he proceeded forward again.

He showed everyone the shadow of my grandmother's corpse, as though he were holding a black cloth in front of people's eyes. As a result, no one was able to see what was really going on. The onlookers had no choice but to pursue him, shouting loudly. "What are you suffering from? What are you suffering from? Your mother died, but we are all from the same street in the same village. Therefore, if you had asked any of us to come help, we obviously would have been happy to do so."

Father once again came to a halt. He turned around, and in the process he reoriented the corpse he was carrying on his shoulders, such that my grandmother's face and eyes were now oriented toward the villagers.

"I haven't revealed anyone's secrets. In this village and this town, it is really of no concern to me who is cremated and who is torched by my brother-in-law.

"My mother has died, so I am taking her to be cremated. You must believe this.

"I'm taking my mother to be cremated. You must believe this."

Father spoke abjectly and magnanimously, as though retrieving from his pocket something that others had lost, and returning it to them. Or as if there were something he himself had lost and was now retrieving from someone else's pocket. He finished speaking and then, still carrying my grandmother's corpse, he walked away. He was a small, thin simian figure, carrying the corpse of a figure who had lived for sixty years, and had maintained close relations with the villagers and the townspeople for more than forty. This new development disquieted the villagers and the townspeople, making them feel that they had let him down. They also felt that they had let down my grandmother, and the entire Li family. Therefore, Zhang Mutou followed my father. Wang Dayou brought out a cart from his house, and followed him as well. The cart had bedding, sheets, and a thick pile of straw. Eventually, more than a dozen people, both noisily and quietly, lowered my grandmother from my father's shoulders. Then, following custom, they covered her face with a white cloth. They purchased some fireworks, wreaths, and spirit money from street-side shops, then lit the fireworks and scattered the spirit money along the street as though it were snow. In this bitterly cold frenzy, they transferred my grandmother's body to the crematorium.

A celebratory event unfolded against the backdrop of my grandmother's cremation.

The crematorium was located two *li* from town, and to reach it you had to follow the road directly south, and then climb a hundred-meter-tall hill. From the western side of the reservoir embankment, you could see a red courtyard wall. Inside the courtyard there were two rows of houses and a two-story building. There was also a tall exhaust pipe extending through the building's roof. This was why all of the villagers and townspeople—not to mention half of the residents of the county—hated the crematorium. At the time, the crematorium's farewell hall was simply a three-room house below the two-story building, with the words FAREWELL HALL written on the wall in black paint. That day, there were no trees or flowers, and instead there was only the crematorium's hearse parked in the snow. Several workers were gossiping while they swept the snow. My uncle was in his office sitting by a stove on which he was roasting peanuts, walnuts, and cloves of garlic. The smell of roasted garlic filled the crematorium as though several bottles of liquor had been spilled in the courtyard.

They brought my grandmother's body to the entrance of the crematorium. Then they lit some firecrackers, and the sound of the explosions alerted the people inside that someone had died and that they should begin preparing for the cremation. When my uncle emerged, he saw my father wearing a filial cap and standing next to the hearse. Then he looked around for the noisy crowd of villagers who normally form a funeral procession and accompany a corpse to the crematorium, but instead all he saw was my father with my grandmother's corpse. There were also a handful of villagers and a large wreath. Apart from this, all he saw was white snow, a northerly wind, and a solitary mountain ridge, together with the desolate and idle crematorium.

"What's going on?"

"Xiaomin gave birth, and my mother died."

My uncle fell silent. He summoned my father over to his office, then snorted and proceeded to say a multitude of things.

"Li Tianbao, you should have told me that my sister was going to give birth.

"Li Tianbao, look at how shabby and miserable you are. You should come work here. I'll offer you our highest salary in return for doing nothing, as long as you take good care of my sister.

"Li Tianbao, your mother died, but you didn't notify the crematorium. I would have sent a hearse to fetch your mother's body, its horn blaring to announce the death. I would have let everyone know that I, Shao Dacheng, was following the new customs and using cremation in order to help conserve land, without giving any preferential treatment to friends and relatives.

"Li Tianbao, remembering that we are relatives, you have voluntarily brought over your mother's corpse in the snow. After the cremation, I'll arrange for the hearse to return her remains. As for the cost of the funeral arrangements, I'll take care of them. But you must follow the relevant regulations. Even if you don't care about saving face, I—as your brother-in-law—certainly do, and I can't permit people to say that I, Shao Dacheng, knew about a death in my sister's family, and didn't handle the funeral arrangements."

After all these things were said, my father simply stared at his brother-in-law—my uncle—without saying a word. After my father left the room, my uncle called out to him and said something truly scathing.

"Li Tianbao, damn you, you can't even produce a fart on your own."

After this, my father should have said something in response, but instead he merely listened and silently came to a stop. When he saw that my uncle wasn't going to say anything else, my father continued walking out of the office, and closed the door behind him. He then proceeded outside and looked at the people standing in the entranceway. He looked at Zhang Mutou, Wang Dayou, Uncle Shu, and Uncle Wang, who were all waiting in the entranceway, and he laughed coldly, and said, "My brother-in-law has asked me to come serve as a foreman at this crematorium, and he promised to give me a very high monthly salary. But how can I possibly engage in cremating people? Even if I were so poor that I was starving to death, I still wouldn't do this."

No one said a word, and instead the villagers gazed at Father's face.

They all kept their eyes fixed on Father's face.

What followed was something that every villager had experienced, and something that had already occurred in many families. Without saying a word, Father transferred the corpse to the cart. Then, still without saying a word, he pushed the cart from the farewell hall into the furnace room. Without saying a word, he had everyone wait in the hall for the cremation—as though waiting for something that would come sooner or later. Because everyone was there to help my father, my uncle handed out cigarettes to all the visitors, and because they were cremating my grandmother, my uncle let the cremation go on for longer than usual, so that the body would be burned more thoroughly than usual. People stood in the hall smoking cigarettes while waiting for my grandmother's ashes, as though waiting for some late-ripening autumn crops. They brought over a wreath someone had left behind and lit it on fire, then huddled around for warmth while chatting with one another. Not having anything else to do, my father staggered over to the furnace.

When he reached the furnace, he stared in surprise.

The room with the furnace was located in a two-story-high building that was not divided into separate floors. The rust-covered furnace was sitting at an angle in the middle of the room, like an enormous metal pail suspended in midair, and appeared very rustic and awkward. It was said that this furnace had been used during the Great Leap Forward, in the forty-seventh year of the Republic, after which it had been sent to a factory. After that, it was sent to a recycling station in the city, and from there ended up in my uncle's possession. After having been repaired and adjusted, it became the furnace for the Gaotian crematorium. This furnace, moreover, had a special capability, which is that it could first excrete oil before cremating the corpse. Its high-temperature iron crucible was covered in an assortment of screws and bolts, like stones scattered across a loess plateau, but only the doors to the retort and to the slag hole could be opened. There was also a black exhaust pipe extending from the middle of the furnace and through the roof. There was a bare redbrick wall, and the ceiling was black with soot. Next to the brick wall, there was a three-legged table, on which were scattered some porcelain cups and several bottles of *baijiu*. On the floor, there was a trash can and piles of dust. Normally, this room was off-limits to visitors, but after my father married my mother he was allowed to enter. Normally, when people did enter they would merely stand there, but because my father was Shao Dacheng's brother-in-law, he was permitted to go in and look around.

He wandered until he was standing behind the furnace, where he stared intently at a thin metal pipe that extended out from the middle of the furnace. The pipe was connected to a meter-long leather tube, which led to a large metal barrel beside the wall. A stream of brown oil, as thin as a chopstick, was pouring out of the tube and into the barrel. The room was very warm, while outside the ground was covered in white snow and it was so bitterly cold that the trees and the earth had cracked. In this room, however, it was so hot that even if you were wearing just a shirt and unlined pants, the heat was still almost unbearable. There were two crematorium workers, both of whom were in their thirties. They had short hair and red faces, and their eyes were bloodshot from having stared into the fire for so many years. They also drank like fish. Each time they cremated a corpse, they would drink several shots of *baijiu*. As they were drinking and eating peanuts, my father stood next to that tube with warm liquid pouring out, and stared.

"What's this?"

"It's corpse oil."

"What is corpse oil?"

"When you cremate a corpse, you inevitably end up with corpse oil. When you cook meat at home, don't you find that the meat generates oil?"

They didn't say anything else.

My father realized that this was human oil.

First the furnace was heated to an optimal temperature for extracting oil, then it was raised to a high heat in order to cremate the corpse.

Realizing that the liquid dripping out of the tube in front of him was actually oil from my grandmother's corpse, he suddenly felt nauseated. He felt as though countless snakes were climbing up his legs and writhing around his chest and back, seeking an opening to enter his body. Then, he felt as though they were crawling up to his head and into his brain, where they proceeded to rest happily. He retched several times, to the point that he wanted to reach his hand down his throat and pull out several handfuls of his own intestines. Next to him, the furnace was so hot that soon he was covered in sweat, as the snakes continued to crawl happily over his head and body. Sometimes there would be only one snake, but at other times there were ten or more, and as they slithered around it also felt as though there were countless bugs crawling all over his body and biting him. The elder of the two crematorium workers brought over half a cup of *baijiu*. "I told you not to enter, but you simply had to come in and take a look . . . Quick, have a sip. Have a sip, and you'll feel better."

My father accepted the cup and took a sip.

Then he took another.

Finally, he turned to the large uncovered barrel and peered inside. He saw that the reddish-yellow corpse oil from his mother— my grandmother—was dripping out of the leather tube. The flame was very loud, and it completely muffled the sound of the oil dripping out. Or maybe the oil wasn't making any sound in the first place. Father looked again, took another sip of *baijiu,* then handed the cup back to the crematorium worker.

"Is corpse oil produced every time a body is cremated?"

"For that, you should go ask your brother-in-law."

"And where does the oil go?"

"For that, you should also go ask your brother-in-law."

Father didn't have anything else to say.

He didn't say anything else.

In the furnace room, apart from the sound of fire and—shortly after a body was inserted—the sound of bubbles bursting, there was also the sound of the crematorium workers sipping *baijiu*. My father stood in that furnace room, waiting for the spasms of nausea in his throat to subside, and then he walked out of the room. Outside, the entire world was covered in snow. From here, you could see the blue surface of the water in the reservoir. The parts of the reservoir that were not covered in snow appeared icy blue, while the snow on the water's edge was tinged in green. On the shore, there was a border of ice. He simply stood there and watched. My father squatted down and retched, then proceeded toward the office of his brother-in-law—which is to say, my uncle. He opened the door, walked in, and stopped in front of the director's yellow desk. He gazed at my one-point-eight-meter-tall uncle, the way an ant might gaze up at an elephant. He was like a blade of grass growing beneath a tall pagoda. After a moment of silence, my father told my uncle something so extraordinary that it was as if a moth had flown right into a mountain—as if it had flown right into the fire.

"Brother, I want to tell you something, but you mustn't get angry.

"You really mustn't get angry.

"Do you agree that it is because of karmic retribution that the heavens had me observe my brother-in-law cremating my own mother's body and producing corpse oil from it?

"Is it true that corpse oil cannot but be excreted, and that you cannot but profit from it?

"Tell me, what do you do with all of the corpse oil you produce?

"I am your brother-in-law, so you must tell me the truth—where does all the corpse oil go?

"In that barrel, there is my mother's flesh and blood, and her corpse oil. But where does the corpse oil go?"

Uncle's eyes grew large with amazement. The scent of the peanuts and walnuts being roasted over the stove's fire filled the room. The room was also filled with the scent of roasted garlic. The room was full of the warm scents of roasted nuts and garlic.

"Damn it, you went in there.

"You shouldn't have gone in, yet you did.

"Damn it, you are my brother-in-law, so I'll level with you. This oil is a financial resource, you know?

"Don't stare at me like that. If you do, I may get angry.

"If you want to eat, then go ahead. The roasted garlic and nuts are delicious.

"You can sell the oil anywhere you want. You can sell it to Luoyang. You can sell it to Zhengzhou. Factories in the cities all need this kind of oil. They need it to make fertilizer. They need it to make rubber. They need it to make lubricant. This is high-quality industrial oil. In fact, it would probably even be excellent for human consumption. During the Three Years of Natural Disaster, it was not unusual for people to consume one another."

My father stood there, and looked down at the garlic and nuts my uncle was roasting.

As my uncle ate, he looked back at my father. "Have some."

Father's entire throat began to spasm. "I don't want to eat. For how much can you sell this barrel of corpse oil?"

"For two hundred eighty or three hundred yuan. Normally a barrel would sell for three hundred yuan."

My father didn't say anything else. My uncle also didn't say anything else. My father reflected for a while. He seemed to be pondering for a long time, but, in fact, it was only the amount of time that it took my uncle to eat a peanut and a clove of garlic. Then, my father reached a decision. When he spoke, his voice was not particularly loud, but every syllable was clearly enunciated.

"Brother, given that corpse oil is produced every time there is a cremation, you should sell this oil to me. OK? I'll pay three hundred yuan per barrel. This way you won't need to pay to transport it to Luoyang or Zhengzhou. I'll come regularly to haul the oil away. As long as you sell the oil to me, I'll treat your sister well . . . As long as you don't sell it to anyone else, I'll be able to enjoy a good life with Xiaomin. We'll get along so well that you'll have no cause to worry at all. I'll treat Shao Xiaomin as though she were my own sister . . . You needn't concern yourself with what I'll be using this oil for. I promise, however, that I won't let anyone else know that when corpses are cremated they are not completely reduced to ash, and instead oil is secreted and taken elsewhere . . . You should sell it to me. I won't underpay you—I won't underpay you by a single cent. You don't need to concern yourself with the question of where my money is coming from. Xiaomin and I have already decided what kind of business we want to pursue. As long as you agree, then starting with this barrel of my mother's corpse oil, you can sell me all of your corpse oil. I will treat your sister as well as though she were my own, and you won't need to worry about our family . . . If our business makes a profit, then not only will I pay you every cent I owe you for the oil, I'll even repay you every cent I owe you for the three-room house you built us . . . You must trust me, Brother Dacheng. I'll keep my word. Although I'm only one-point-five meters tall, my promises are in no way shorter than those of others. You must trust me this time, Brother Dacheng. You must sell me all of these barrels of corpse oil.

"Sell them to me. As your brother-in-law, I'm begging you.

"OK? If you were to sell them to others, you wouldn't necessarily get three hundred yuan for every barrel."

At that point, as my father was going on and on, the shouts of
the Gaotian villagers could be heard outside.

"Li Tianbao, your mother has already been cremated, and yet
you are still in there with your brother-in-law warming by the fire!

"Li Tianbao, damn you, we came out here in the cold to help
you prepare your mother's funeral, while you are just sitting in there
with your brother-in-law warming by the fire!"

BOOK THREE

Geng 2, Part Two:
Birds Build a Nest There

1. (21:51–22:00)

Heavens! . . . Gods! This is how things were. This is how my parents ended up opening the New World funerary shop in Gaotian. The shop sold wreaths, paper ornaments, and burial clothes. In short, the shop sold everything dead people might need. Then, my parents used the money to go up to that embankment to buy corpse oil. It was like cutting down a tree and then planting another one, only to repeat the process all over again day after day, year after year. This is how I grew up, becoming who I am today. When I was three or four, I would remove some paper blossoms from a wreath and pin them to my chest, and when I was five or six I would take an entire wreath and walk down the street with it. When I was seven or eight, I would wear a burial shroud as though it were a raincoat or a windbreaker, and when I was eleven or twelve I began going with my father to retrieve corpse oil from the crematorium.

I was fourteen on that night, on the sixth day of the sixth month. I left the store and proceeded alone to the crematorium on top of the embankment, to retrieve some corpse oil—as though I were a fourteen-year-old going alone to harvest, collect, and transport the autumn wheat. The crematorium was to the south of town. I walked along that solitary, sweltering road. It seemed as though my father, for some reason, always walked along the side of the road, and never down the middle. Upon remembering how my father never walked down the middle of the road, I made a point of walking right down the middle. "The first time I went to inform on someone, I felt as though I was dreamwalking." This is what my father had told me. "The first time I went to the crematorium to fetch the barrel full of my mother's corpse oil, I felt as though I was dreamwalking." It seemed that my father had told me this as well, and this also made me think of dreamwalking. When I reached the wheat field at the front of a neighboring village, I stood there for a while. I looked to see whether or not there were any dreamwalkers like Zhang Mutou out in the fields threshing wheat. I expected that there probably weren't any, and, in fact, there weren't. Instead, the dreamwalkers appeared as impassive as bricks. While dreamwalking, a dreamwalker could see everything he could possibly imagine, but was unable to see anything from Gaotian and the world outside his dream. He was unable to see a tree or a shrub, unless that tree or that shrub had also appeared in his dream.

The wheat field was in the shape of an oval. There were two dreamwalkers at one end of the field, and a third in the middle. They were harvesting wheat under the light of a lamp, calling out to one another as they worked. The sound of their voices drifted over from the field, like birds flying overhead. "Aiya, do you know? I hear that an entire family was dreamwalking, whereupon the father raped his daughter-in-law out in a field." This remark was followed by hearty and obscene laughter—like an evil bird flying from one end of the field to the other, and then back with more lewd remarks. "If he raped his daughter-in-law, why didn't he also rape his daughter?" After listening for a while longer, I found I could no longer hear them clearly. I was more than a dozen paces from the field, and in the middle of the field there was a haystack that blocked my line of sight. In the distance, a field resembled a resplendent lake. The wheat had already been harvested and carted away. The familiar smell of the soil was like a steamer basket that had just been removed from the pot. It was radiating steam and fragrance. The smell of sweat and hot water noisily drifted over.

I had to quickly get to the crematorium to haul away the corpse oil. Uncle himself had come over in a cart to tell me. If we didn't haul it away overnight, Uncle would come over the next day and spit in Father's face. "You don't appreciate what I've done for all of you. Do you know for how much I can sell this oil in Luoyang? Five hundred yuan a barrel! Sometimes I can even sell it for six or seven hundred yuan a barrel. Now I'm selling it to you for only three hundred yuan a barrel, yet you don't haul it away quickly enough." This is how things were, but I didn't know why. When Father initially bought the oil, he bought several dozen—or even several hundred—barrels, but then he didn't want to buy any more. Uncle replied that if Father didn't want any more, that was fine, because the price of the oil had risen to eight hundred yuan a barrel. It was quite possible the oil could even be used to power a tractor. Father purchased oil generated over more than two years and hauled it away. Father didn't really want to buy any more, but Uncle said that it would be fine if he didn't, because Uncle could then take the oil to a rubber plant in Zhengzhou and have the plant convert the oil into rubber, for which he could then receive nine hundred yuan a barrel. Father considered this, then decided to continue buying and hauling away the oil. In this way, he continued buying and hauling away the oil right up to the present. Father secretly asked around for the price of the oil. In the suburbs of the provincial capital, some people called this lubricating oil, and if they were using it to lubricate their machinery, they would pay nine hundred or a thousand yuan a barrel. A decade earlier, three hundred yuan a barrel had seemed like an astronomical price, but now when Uncle sold the oil to our family for only three hundred yuan, it was as if he were virtually giving it away. He threatened that he was going to take the oil to a small factory in the countryside in the south, where he said he could sell it for eleven hundred yuan a barrel—and sometimes he could even get twelve or thirteen hundred yuan. Everything can increase in price—even a fart. However, Uncle never raised the price on the oil he sold to our family. Instead, we continued buying it for three hundred yuan a barrel, and could have resold it for a thousand yuan a barrel. In this way, for each barrel that Uncle sold us, our family could have made a profit of seven hundred yuan—or even as much as eight hundred or a thousand yuan—per barrel. But my parents didn't sell the oil. My parents were good people, which is why they wouldn't sell it. That oil was from people's bodies, and therefore couldn't be sold. Instead, Father took the oil to a cave below the reservoir and stored it there, as though storing a small trickle of water in a vast lake. Year after year, month after month, it was as if he were melting silver dollars back into ingots. Each time he hauled a barrel of oil over from the crematorium, it was as if he were taking a pile of money from the field, and every time he stored another barrel of oil in that cave, it was as if he were melting a barrel of silver dollars into ingots.

On that night, I again needed to go to the crematorium to fetch some silver dollars that I could then melt back into ingots. I left that neighboring village's field and followed the road toward the crematorium. It seemed as though once I left the town, I could reach the crematorium in less time than it takes to finish a bowl of rice. I saw the crematorium to the west of the embankment. It was surrounded by a brick wall, and inside there were two long buildings, and a two-story furnace building. This was the crematorium I was going to visit, and this visit would mark the beginning and the end of this night's events. It would mark the beginning and the end of this story.

I entered the crematorium through a small door inside the main iron gate. The crematorium was as peaceful as a cemetery. Originally, it *was* a cemetery—a cemetery where thousands or even tens of thousands of corpses were buried. Thousands, tens of thousands, an entire world of corpses—were all brought here in hearses, only to be reduced to ashes and taken away in urns. The building on the left was a new office complex that had been built by the crematorium, including the manager's office—this was my uncle's two-room office. The unfortunate thing was that after my uncle became the general manager, he no longer attended to the day-to-day operations. His office had fewer rooms than an office normally would, and his desk was covered in so much dust that you could write directly on it. My uncle would come by once every few days to collect his salary, and each time he would write several characters on his desk: "Life," "Death," "Corpse," "Money," and so forth and so on. Sometimes he would write the character for "Flower," or practice writing the phrases "Floral fragrance and hot days" or "The days are too hot." Because he was the general manager, after he finished writing the characters, an assistant would come in and help him wipe his desk.

The assistant would wipe Uncle's desk so that not a single speck of dust remained.

The office complex also included the accountant's office, the revenue collection office, and the reception room. The building across the way included the crematorium workers' dormitories and a utility room. There was also a canteen and a warehouse. The warehouse was used to store flour, rice, and funeral urns. When the crematorium was first built, living people would never enter this courtyard, but eventually they did begin to visit. When the crematorium was first constructed, everyone hated this site, but as time went on people gradually stopped hating it. When the crematorium was built, people wanted to smash my uncle's skull with a brick, but as time went on they began addressing him as "Manager" and "Boss." And if they wanted a relative's ashes to be left particularly white and the bone residue to be especially brittle—such that they wouldn't need to smash it with a hammer when transferring it into the urn—then they would address him as "Chief Director Shao." Sometimes they would even invite him out for drinks or for a meal, and slip him a couple of cigarettes. Sometimes, the relatives of the dead would need to wait in line, and priority would be given to those who had a note from my uncle. If family members wanted their relative to be cremated first, they would slip Uncle some money—the same way that someone wanting to buy a train ticket to return home often needs to have an acquaintance or relative pass someone some money.

I was as familiar with the crematorium as I was with my own home. Our family ran the only funerary shop in the entire town. In the past, I would often go alone to the crematorium in the middle of the night to take care of some things. I would often go alone to the New World flower garden, where I would write for a while and then nap. I would read from Yan Lianke's novels and then fall asleep, resting my head on a pack of gold foil. I would dream of a pile of treasure as tall as a mountain. While sleeping in the garden, I would dream that the village and even the entire town had been transformed into a garden, a public park. Flowers bloomed, there were birds flying, and a willow branch was floating on the water's surface. Fish were leaping out of the water, as butterflies and dragonflies flitted around on both banks.

It was very poetic.

It was very amusing.

The birdsong mixed with the flower fragrance.

The flower fragrance mixed with the birdsong.

Countless shades of red and purple mixed together. Not even Yan Lianke's novels contained a scene like this.

The sky was heavy with clouds, but their footsteps were as light as cotton blossoms. I gazed up at the sky, then at the two-story furnace room and funeral parlor. There were several stone steps, and when I climbed them I found the farewell hall. Actually, there were two farewell halls, and I stood in front of the second one for a while. The cries of the crickets were soft and bright. Behind the farewell hall, there was an area that no one—other than the crematorium workers and the relatives of the deceased—was permitted to enter, because it was from there that the deceased entered the furnace room. In that room, the crematorium workers had to perform many tasks that outsiders shouldn't be permitted to observe. Before placing each corpse in the furnace, the crematorium workers would always drink several cups of *baijiu* and smoke several cigarettes. Sometimes they would have strange ideas, and would go to the incense burner next to the wall and light a stick of incense. If they were going to cremate one of their relatives or someone they knew, they would light three sticks of incense. They would also kowtow once, or three times. If they were cremating one of their enemies, or a rich owner or manager, however, they might kick the corpse several times. They would close all of the doors to the furnace room from the inside and would drink some beer or *baijiu,* as everyone outside waited impatiently, banging on the door and shouting:

"Are you done or not? Just get it done!"

The workers would reply, "These people did so many things while they were alive, we should send them on their way in a respectable fashion. We certainly can't send them off as though they were merely ordinary people."

In reality, the crematorium workers weren't doing anything out of the ordinary, but rather they were simply sitting in the crematorium room and drinking.

While drinking, they would sometimes even spit on a corpse's face.

Or they would shatter a beer bottle over a corpse's head.

By afternoon or evening, whenever there were no more corpses to cremate, those two crematorium rooms would be filled with ashes, and the floor would be covered in bottles. Against the wall next to the furnace, there would be a barrel full of corpse oil. Hanging from the wall and at the base of the wall, there would be the funeral objects that had not been sent into the furnace with the corpse. Everywhere, there were bone fragments from one corpse or another, together with shards of stone or plastic that had fallen off a funeral urn. But as long as it wasn't the busy season for deaths, it was fine. People were always cremated either at dawn or later in the morning, and in the afternoon the crematorium workers would straighten up the rooms. But during the busy season for deaths, they wouldn't have time to clean, and instead they would drink and stagger around, and sometimes they would collapse onto a pile of funeral objects and clothing, and fall asleep.

Alcohol can give people courage, which is why the crematorium workers always needed to drink.

Alcohol can eliminate foul odors, which is why they always needed to drink.

Whenever the two crematorium workers got drunk, they would ask someone to come help them clean up. Eventually, they simply hired an assistant specifically tasked with cleaning the furnace room and the cremation hall. This was a young girl—the Little Juanzi I mentioned earlier. She was a year or two younger than I, and her family was from one of the villages to the east of the embankment. Her parents had both died, as had her grandparents. Consequently, she had come to know the crematorium like the palm of her hand, and was hired to clean it every evening. At that moment, she was straightening up the furnace room. She swept the ashes, and the lamplight. She emerged from the room and then went back inside, like a butterfly fluttering around. She left behind a sweet fragrance wherever she went, as though a stream of water were flowing toward me on a humid summer night.

I waded through the light encircling the cremation hall, toward the furnace room.

Meanwhile, Little Juanzi reemerged to grab something, and then went back inside. There was a shimmering shadow, like the rustling of a sheet of black silk. I heard her say something. She wasn't speaking to me, but there wasn't anyone else who could hear her, other than a pile of flowers and plants next to the entranceway—and each time she went out and back in, she would bring in some of those flowers and plants.

When I arrived at the entrance to the furnace room, Little Juanzi was in the process of placing some plants and wildflowers next to the iron door of the furnace. She had already decorated the entire room with flowers and plants. The ones on the wall resembled a vertical garden, and on the furnace itself flowers had been placed everywhere they could potentially be mounted. There were red, yellow, and green ones. There were wild camellias and wild chrysanthemums, producing strings of purple and clumps of red. There were also coxcomb flowers and small orchids. These flowers could be found everywhere outside the crematorium. There were carriage-wheel blossoms and another kind of little yellow flower of which I didn't know the name. There were also Chinese roses and peonies planted in the crematorium courtyard, as well as roses in full bloom. The building resembled a greenhouse. The semi-inclined furnace resembled an enormous flower pistil.

In this way, the furnace building became a greenhouse.

When I showed up, Little Juanzi was in the process of inserting tiny yellow and red flowers into the cracks in the barrels of corpse oil, making it appear as though the flowers were growing right out of the barrels. I had assumed that when she realized I was observing all of this, she would stop. However, when I appeared, she turned and looked in my direction, appearing completely unsurprised, as though she hadn't even seen me. It was as if she were looking at a tree. She blinked without saying a word, then continued inserting the flowers into the barrels. I was baffled by this reaction. I knew why she was decorating this furnace room as though it were a heavenly greenhouse.

"You are dreamwalking."

She was in the process of fastening a wildflower onto the metal pipe leading into the oil barrel. Her expression was as calm and impassive as a flower secretly blooming in the moonlight.

She again turned to look at me. Her mouth moved, as though she were speaking to someone. She mumbled to herself, but it was impossible to tell what she was saying. I watched her face move as she spoke, then watched as she took a step back to see whether or not the flowers were attractive. It was as if I were looking at a painting or a scene that she had designed. I went over and tugged on her shoulder. "You should go into the courtyard and wash your face." She stubbornly pulled her shoulder away. "When people die, we have to bring their corpses into this room. After their friends and family have bidden the deceased goodbye in the farewell hall, the body is brought into this room between the farewell hall and the furnace room. The body is brought in adorned in flowers, and remains adorned in flowers when it is taken to the furnace room. It would be ideal if we could have dragonflies and butterflies flying around this room. That would be a true heavenly world."

As she said this, she stood there regretfully.

"Can you help me catch some butterflies to put in this room?" She looked at me, then smiled. "Oh, it's you. I thought you were my cousin.

"My cousin has become a drunkard. Every time he cremates a corpse, he drinks half a bottle of *baijiu,* so you can imagine how much he ends up drinking on a day like today." She shifted her gaze back to the flower she had just inserted. "Tomorrow, I'll catch some butterflies and dragonflies, and will release them in this room. That way, the room will look like a garden. When people die and are brought here, it will be as though they were returning home. That way, no one who enters this room will ever want to leave, the same way that no one ever wants spring to be displaced by summer, or summer to be displaced by fall." At first she mumbled to herself, as though reading an article, but gradually her speech became clearer. As she was speaking, she turned toward me, though her gaze remained fixed on a bucket of water in the entranceway.

Then, she went to bring over the bucket, and sprinkled water on the flowers and plants. I clearly saw her gaunt and sallow face. Her eyes were half-open, and her expression looked like a flower blooming in a foggy night. She was wearing a black skirt and a floral shirt. Her hair was arranged into two messy braids, and her face was filthy. Her front teeth protruded slightly over her bottom lip. She did not smile easily, but she nevertheless made a point of always smiling. Her father was dead, as was her mother. Her grandmother and grandfather were also dead. She lived in the crematorium, and every day after the cremations concluded, she would clean the crematorium's two main halls. She would straighten up the farewell hall, and would also clean up the furnace room. She truly lived in a dead, corpse world. She had lost her father, and had lost her mother. She had also lost her grandfather and grandmother. But she would always smile whenever she saw anyone. She would smile while sweeping the ground, and would smile while cleaning the farewell hall. Sometimes she would even smile while rushing to apply makeup to a corpse. She resembled a flower that would never accept defeat.

As I was preparing to haul away a barrel of corpse oil, I knocked down the coxcomb flower and the green sprig that she had placed on the barrel. She then picked them up and placed them back on the barrel, with an expression that still resembled a reddish-yellow blossom.

"If you don't take this barrel, there won't be anywhere to store tomorrow's corpse oil. After you take it away, I'll put a flowerpot here. I notice that there are wildflowers as large as my fist growing on the embankment outside the crematorium. They are red with traces of yellow, and they produce a sweet fragrance even stronger than that of osmanthus blossoms.

"I want to plant some of those osmanthus-scented flowers here in the furnace room.

"I want to fill this room with the scent of osmanthus. That way, when people walk over from that other world, they will enter a world filled with osmanthus fragrance. They will feel no pain as their bodies are being cremated. They will feel no pain as their corpses are being burned and their bones are reduced to ash. They will feel no pain as oil flows from their remains. This osmanthus fragrance comes from plants called intoxicants, and after one whiff, people will pass out and forget everything. They will forget their pain and the world, as though they had been anesthetized. That way, they will move from that world into this one without feeling the slightest trace of pain.

"Tomorrow, I will dig up some intoxicants, and plant them here in the furnace room.

"Now, I am going to go dig one up and plant it in a flowerpot. I will place the pot next to the furnace. When you replace the oil barrel, be careful not to knock over my pot."

She walked out of the room, like a butterfly fluttering away. Even though she was speaking to me, she wasn't looking at me. Instead, her gaze remained focused on her own affairs. Her gaze remained focused on her somnambulistic world. Even when I brought over a cart to haul away that barrel of corpse oil and asked her to help me push it, she didn't seem to hear me. She went outside, as though flying away. I saw her in the entranceway, walking under the lamplight with a shovel. The door in the courtyard wall behind the crematorium was open. Perhaps it had always been open. After all, not even thieves were willing to come here. She walked out through that back door, appearing to float away into the empty, empty mountain ridge. She walked along the ridge, casting her shadow on the mountains.

She resembled a flower blooming on the mountain ridge in a nighttime dream.

2. (22:01–22:22)

One barrel of corpse oil weighed about six hundred *jin*, but I don't know how many corpses had to be cremated in order to generate so much oil. In the off-season for deaths, one month might yield less than a barrel, but in the peak season you could generate a full barrel in just ten days or two weeks. The oil was initially light yellow, but when it congealed it darkened—turning so dark that it appeared as though there was a light-black layer beneath the yellow.

Because the oil came from humans, I won't say any more about it. Whenever I speak about it, my body begins to throb with pain, my heart tenses up, and I become extremely anxious—as though I accidentally got my fingers caught in a door hinge. The crematorium was built on a road leading to the mountain ridge, with the reservoir on one side and the road on the other. At that point, the night was still very shallow, and all sorts of sounds were walking over from the villages below the ridge. The weather was warm and muggy, but the breeze on the mountain ridge was as cool as a mountain spring. In the reservoir, a clear white light leaped from the surface of the water, as the water vapor drifted out over the mountain ridge. The wheat in the fields on both sides of the road had already been harvested, and the sweet smell of wheat stubble mixed with the water vapor, like milk flying everywhere. It was as if a woman had given birth to a baby, then secreted her excess milk all over the mountain, splattering it all over the fields.

I hauled a large barrel of corpse oil up from the mountain-ridge road to a cold cave on the side of the reservoir. Tendrils of scent hung from the tip of my nose. Because the barrel was full, some of the oil had spilled out and splattered over the metal exterior, just as there is always a layer of salt and water on the outside of a salt canister. As a result, the barrel's white metallic exterior turned oily red, then oily black. The oily red and oily black tint produced an icy stench—smelling mostly of ice, with a slight stench. If you didn't know this was human oil, you might not have noticed this icy stench. Most of this coldness was produced from people's hearts, and without it the barrel would simply have been an ordinary barrel of oil—either mechanical or vegetable oil. Although the odor emanating from the barrel was not that of sesame or peanut oil, it was nevertheless a greasy, oily smell. It was human oil, and upon remembering this I felt a chill. It had the stench of bone, flesh, and fat. Fortunately, I didn't fear this smell of human oil, since I was a bit stupid. Stupid people are always fearless. I never feared death or corpses. Our family lived in the funerary shop, and ever since I was little I had grown up surrounded by wreaths, paper ornaments, and piles of funerary objects. Before I was even three, my parents would take me to the crematorium to see my uncle, and by the time I was five, I had entered the furnace room. When I was five and a half, I sat on the front handle of the cart used to transport human oil, going with my father once or twice a month to store the barrel in the cold cave.

I made several trips a month.

Now it was my turn to go alone to carry the corpse oil to the cave. At the age of fourteen, I felt like a tree that had grown up at the entrance to the underworld. I had to stand in that entrance, braving wind and rain. Alone, in the night of the great somnambulism, I would move a barrel of corpse oil from the furnace onto a cart, and then proceed one *li* down the mountain-ridge road. I passed the courtyard of the house Yan Lianke had rented, proceeded another half a *li* down the gently sloping road, then another half a *li* down the hill. I took this barrel of corpse oil, which was the product of the cremation of seventy to eighty corpses, and stored it in an overflow cave that stayed cool in the summer and warm in the winter. Then I left. I walked alone along the mountain ridge, and up the gently sloping path. In order not to think about all of those corpses and the corpse oil, I told myself that I wanted to reflect on some things relating to men and women. But what? I ended up thinking about Xiaojuan, or "Little Juan," who cleans the furnace every day and applies makeup to the corpses. Her full name was Xu Xiaojuan, but everyone calls her Juan . . . Juanzi . . . and Xu Juanzi.

I should have gone with her to dig up some intoxicants. I should have leaned close to her ear and shouted, to wake her up from her somnambulism. I should have taken her a basin of water, to wash her face. I should have rubbed her face with a wet cloth. If only she were a bit prettier—just a bit—I would definitely have woken her up from her somnambulism. I would definitely have accompanied her as she dreamwalked to dig up some intoxicants, and then let her accompany me as I went to store the corpse oil. We would have walked together along this one-*li* mountain-ridge road, and up this half-*li* hill, and nearly another *li* down another hill. But I already covered that ground myself. The squeaking of the cart's wheels sounded as if the moon and the stars were all following their respective paths through the sky. As I proceeded forward, the cart's wheels bumped against each other, and as the wheels turned they produced a grinding sound that consumed the night road inch by inch. In this way, the cart had led me to the cave next to the reservoir. In front of the cave there were two trees, and a field of grass. There was also a pair of rusty iron gates that were large enough to drive a cart through. Inside the gates, my father himself had erected a wooden door. I opened both the outer gates and the inner door, then felt around on the right-hand side of the inner door. I quickly found the lamp string that was hanging there, and pulled it.

The lamp came on.

The lamplight shone forlornly on this area in the entranceway to the cave. In order to save electricity, Father had not arranged for lamps to illuminate the entire five-hundred-meter-long cave. However, this lamp still energetically shone down on those barrels of oil in the cave's dark depths. The lamp made a panting sound, as though it were about to expire. There was the sound of water dripping down the cave walls, and the sound of a bitter cold breeze blowing from the depths of the cave. There was wave after wave of a cold, oily stench emanating from the barrels of corpse oil. This stench was sometimes heavy and sometimes light, but it was always very pungent. I had opened the door, gone inside, and stood under the lamp. The light from the forty-watt bulb gradually dimmed, as though it were so tired that it wanted to die. I looked into the cave, and immediately my entire body felt chilled and began to tremble. The cave was as wide as a street and as tall as a house. It extended from one end of the embankment to the other. The walls were made of stone and cement, and the cement-filled fissures between the stones were two fingers wide. Whether deep or shallow, these fissures lined the cave's walls and ceiling. The ceiling was in the shape of an irregular dome, and over the years it had developed damp areas that were stained by water, like a stream that would never dry up but also would never flow abundantly. When the reservoir was first built several decades ago, it was designed so that when the water rose above its target level, the excess would flow into this cave abutting the embankment. But later, the amount of rain in the region decreased, as did the amount of water flowing into the cave, and even after the reservoir had accumulated water for years, it still didn't reach the lower lip of this cave. The cave was therefore abandoned, until my family began using it to store their corpse oil. In exchange for a meal and several cigarettes, the person in charge of overseeing the cave handed my father the keys. It was as if this cave had been constructed specifically for my father's use—so that after the crematorium was built nearby, my father could then use the cave to store corpse oil.

Everything proceeded smoothly.

Everything was formed naturally.

If heaven decides that people must die, it also decides whether they will have an earth burial, an ocean burial, a river burial, or a mountaintop burial. After these various forms of burial had been practiced for years, people were eventually forced to abandon their burial customs and begin practicing cremation. After switching to cremation, my uncle, as though embezzling gold, let the human oil flow, whereupon my parents began to buy it and store it here—barrel after barrel, year after year. From the beginning, my parents wanted to store the oil underground in order to keep it safe. It was only after my father went up to the ridge in the middle of the night to look for a pond, a hole, or a gully that he realized that the population of the Funiu Mountains was as dense as a field of grass, and there wasn't any remote spot where he could store the oil for a long time without others—including spirits and demons—potentially finding it. Accordingly, he had no choice but to store the barrels one after another in this cave, and wait for the day when the oil could achieve its maximum potential. What potential? This would be a truly astonishing use, because otherwise Father would not have continued storing this oil for so many years. He would not have filled this five-hundred-meter-deep cave with oil. The lamp's electrical cord extended from one end of the cave to the other, and if you stood at one end, the cave appeared as deep as the night sky. Barrel upon barrel of corpse oil was stored there, as though it were a village about to hold a ten-thousand-person meeting, or as though it were a ten-thousand-*li*-long road full of people wearing black clothes. There was barrel after barrel, and if all of the oil had been poured out, it would be enough to form a river, a lake, or even a vast ocean.

However, I had never seen the ocean.

Yan Lianke's novels rarely mention the ocean, but he often writes about fields and wilderness, mountains and plateaus. His settings are typically cold and desolate, stretching endlessly in all directions. Even after walking for three days and three nights, you still would not be able to reach the end of his wilderness. His novels are each very long, and when placed together they resemble a vast wilderness. They could also be said to resemble a simple yet messy grave. Pines, cypresses, and wild pagoda trees would grow out of the body buried in this grave. Beneath the trees there would be a plot of dry grass and wildflowers, and locusts and crickets living between the grass and the flowers. Grasshoppers and crickets would sing there every day. This person—this Uncle Yan—I don't know why all of his novels are like messy graves, or an expanse of wilderness. More concretely, if you want to say something good about his novels, then the best thing you could say is that his novels are about a village. The people, soil, and houses all sing a song of everlasting sorrow. Or, if you want to be more precise, you could say that it is a funeral song involving a tree, a plant, and a person. Or someone blowing a suona horn to sell goods from our New World funerary shop. You could say that the funerary shop our family opened was simply waiting for Uncle Yan's works to be completed. All of our family's business—including that of my father, my mother, and myself—everything we say and do should be recounted in those books. Unfortunately, my father cannot read, and neither can my mother, while I myself can't write or tell stories. At the end of the day, even if I felt that Uncle Yan did not write well, I would have no choice but to accept him, and would have no alternative but to read his books—the same way that even if you don't like sweet potatoes, you still have no choice but to eat them if that is all you have. Or you might want to live in Luoyang, Zhengzhou, Guangzhou, Beijing, or Shanghai, but all you can do is go from Gaotian up to this cave, and then from the cave back down to Gaotian. Gaotian is simply Gaotian, and this cave is simply this cold cave. The barrels of corpse oil stored in this cave are as endless as Uncle Yan's novels. Desolate and lonely. Even if you were to spend three days and three nights—or a hundred days and a hundred nights—hauling the barrels out of the cave, you would still never finish. I stacked one barrel next to a row of others. With the back of the cart facing a row of barrels, I would hoist the barrel up, whereupon it would slide down off the back of the cart and land with a thud next to the others. It was as though someone had jumped into the ranks of his army regiment. It was as if when a new story was added to one of Uncle Yan's books, that regiment suddenly gained an extra member. In this way, the troops became more numerous, and the regiment gradually became larger, stronger, and more imposing.

The sound of barrels knocking against others was low and resonant. The cave swallowed that sound like a famished wolf devouring its food, and the sound abruptly disappeared. In this way, the cave once again became perfectly still, and the barrels of oil once again became countless columns of death. As I was about to leave, a dragonfly landed next to my foot. There were bats flying in the light of the cave's lamp. There were spiders climbing in the spaces between the walls and the oil barrels. They all seemed to be hoping I wouldn't leave, or at least that I wouldn't turn off the light when I did. They seemed to be hoping I wouldn't leave them in the darkness, in the dampness, in the oily stench. I had no choice but to turn off the light and leave. Outside, everyone had begun to dreamwalk, and if I didn't turn off the light and leave, then what would I do if my parents started dreamwalking?

I turned off the light and closed the door. The pitch-black sound resonated through the cave. It resonated through the world of the embankment. The moonlight was as soft as water, and the night was as still as a cave. After I walked outside, I stood there facing in the direction of Yan Lianke's house, then used the light from his window to follow the path down the hill and into town.

BOOK FOUR

Geng 3: Birds Lay an Egg

1. (23:00–23:41)

It was a hot, stuffy night.

Heat emanated out through every door and window crack, from every house in every village.

I left the embankment and returned to the road below. Entering the town streets, I felt as though I were stepping into a steamer basket. There was the sound of restless movement everywhere. The night birds cried plaintively, as though they had just woken from a dream. In their cries, there was the stench of sweat and the smell of fear and confusion. The crickets were still singing and dancing outside town, but when they reached the main street they suddenly fell quiet. There were beams from lanterns and flashlights, which blew in front of me. There was the sound of footsteps running, and it seemed as though something were happening in town. After the light and the sound of footsteps receded, the deep silence appeared as distant as winter is from summer, and as the Qing dynasty was from the Ming dynasty.

It was only upon reaching the street that I once again saw the light of the lamp and the shadowy figures of people rushing around. The figures were emerging from my family's store, having come to report recent deaths and order funerary wreaths. Father looked up when he saw me enter, and muttered to himself, "How could someone jump into the well and drown while dreamwalking? Someone else also jumped into a well while dreamwalking. It's the strangest thing—how can people kill themselves while dreamwalking?" With the knife, he cut a bamboo stem in half, then into quarters, and finally into eighths. In this way the stem, which was originally as thick as a person's wrist, was reduced to a bundle of sticks as thin as chopsticks or noodles. Father tied an old shoe sole against his leg, then placed the bamboo and the knife against the sole. Mother was silent. She was quietly making papercuts, and carefully folding paper blossoms. Using glue to stick them together, she worked until a blossom appeared in her palm. The room was filled with the familiar odor of flower paste, the crisp smell of bamboo, and the sweaty smell of my parents' bodies as they worked. There was also the odor of newly made wreaths and funerary objects. The entire room was full of these odors. The entire world was full of these odors.

"Today, five people died." I stood in the entranceway watching my father.

"Six people," my mother said to my father.

"We're insanely busy. Insanely busy." My father's voice grew louder. "It is the peak dying season, combined with the somnambulism. I'm concerned that tomorrow there may be ten or twenty families coming here to buy wreaths."

My mother reacted with surprise. Her hand resting on her knee, she turned to look at the clock on the wall. She saw that the clock had stopped, with the hour and minute hands frozen at two o'clock in the afternoon, which is the hottest time of day. I closed the door to the shop. "The empty barrels in the cave have almost been used up, so we'll have to purchase more." As I was saying this, I went to gulp down a glass of cold water, like a cow. "Juanzi, from the furnace room, has started dreamwalking. A three-person family out harvesting wheat have all started dreamwalking." As I was saying this, I sat down next to my father, and in the process pushed aside a pile of bamboo sticks. Father turned to look at me. "Aren't you sleepy? If not, you should go fold some more gold foil. Two more families have had a relative die, and will want to buy some funerary objects. Before, people wouldn't buy wreaths and paper ornaments until two days after a relative's death, but these days they come the very next night. They want things immediately. It is as though people want to be buried the day after they die." As Father was saying this, he went to open the door. He wanted to let in a breeze, but outside the air was still.

"Father, what would it be like if I were to start dreamwalking?"

"Whatever you are thinking about, that is what you'll do when you dreamwalk."

"I'm thinking about reading books."

"Then, while dreamwalking you'll open a book."

"I think that some day I definitely want to leave this village and this town."

"Where do you want to go?"

"I don't know. I just want to leave."

"Then you certainly mustn't dreamwalk. If you were to start, you might leave home and head out in an unknown direction."

"I want to be like Yan Lianke, and earn fortune and fame from writing and telling stories."

Father stared at me. "Fold some more gold foil. If the Yan family can produce an author, that is a product of their family's fate. It is because several generations ago a literary root was buried in their ancestral grave. In our ancestral grave, however, there is no such literary root, and instead our family has no choice but to devote ourselves to the funerary shop. Even though we aren't able to do very much for the living, we do decently for the dead."

Father's voice sounded as remote as though it were floating in midair. Mother had finished folding a colorful paper ornament. She had cut out a basketful of birds and butterflies, which would fly around the paper blossoms and wreaths. When she placed the basket next to her leg, it resembled a pile of auspicious clouds and cranes. Without saying a word, she continued cutting and pasting, pinching and folding. When she finished, she extended her legs, stretched her back, and lifted her arms into the air. Then she lowered them and let out a long sigh.

I noticed that her expression resembled an old newspaper.

Surprised, I turned to look at Father's face.

"Let her sleep. If she wakes up, there's no telling what she'll do. People keep dying and dying, and there's no telling how many people will have died by tomorrow."

As he was speaking, Father's face appeared warm and gentle. He rarely looked at Mother with that sort of expression, but he began looking at her like this after I was born and turned out to be a boy. Later, when I was two and still hadn't learned to speak, some villagers speculated that I might be an idiot, whereupon Father stopped having this expression. One day, Father ripped up all of the shop's wreaths and paper ornaments and stamped them underfoot, then hurled all of the bowls, plates, and spoons against the wall. Mother shouted at him, "Retribution! This is retribution." My father furiously slapped her, and then my mother hugged me and sat there weeping. My father bashed his own head against the wall. He wailed and bashed his head; then bashed his head again and wailed some more. Eventually, he once again looked at Mother with this same expression, as he was looking now. His expression was as gentle as a wildflower blooming in a clump of dried trees in autumn. He even went over and gathered the hair that had fallen over Mother's face, and carefully put it back in place. "When your mother dreamwalks, it is not ugly." He said this and smiled. "There is still time for me and your mother to give you a younger brother or younger sister. No matter how evil God might be, he wouldn't be so evil as to condemn all of our family's children to be idiots." Father said this to me, and also to all of the funerary objects in the room. At that moment, Father and I heard someone shouting in the square. The shouts sounded as anxious as though a sluice had suddenly been opened, or as though a pot were boiling over.

"Wang Ergou, where the fuck did you go? Our father has started dreamwalking, you know? After you discussed the situation with those somnambulant old men, they all went to the West Canal and jumped in. Did you know?

"Wang Ergou, our father has died, yet you are still at someone's house gambling. Why didn't God arrange for you to gamble yourself to death, while letting our father live?"

The person shouting was a woman, and although her voice was hoarse, her exclamations nevertheless erupted as if a bamboo pole as thick as a man's arm was being split in half in the middle of the street. As she shouted, she also seemed to be stomping her feet. It was as if the street were burning hot, to the point that she didn't dare keep her feet on the ground. "Wang Ergou, I'm going to call you one last time, and if you still don't appear, that will mean you must have died in someone's house. You will have died at a card table, using your life as an exchange for that of our father. If you are able to bring him back, you will have fulfilled your filial obligations.

"Wang Ergou, go quick to the West Canal! Go rescue our father!

"Wang Ergou, our father and several other old men jumped into the canal and drowned. Did you know?

"Wang Ergou, our father has already died, but you can't die as well."

After she finished shouting, the woman turned and walked away, leaving the other onlookers standing in the street. At least she had stood there and hollered, and had reported this death to the world. She had no idea whether or not the men heard her, and couldn't care less whether or not they returned home. She herself anxiously hurried home, heading south. She needed to take care of her father-in-law's funeral. She left behind a crowd of people in the square, all staring in shock and discussing what they had seen. They were commenting on how hot it was, and how several more dream-walkers had headed over to the West Canal and drowned themselves. They discussed how they shouldn't go home and sleep—because if they did, they might very well start dreamwalking, and then they, too, might try to commit suicide. When I emerged from the store with my father, I stood in the street and watched the woman who walked away, as though watching a dream. Just as I was about to make my way over to the square to talk to the people standing there, a middle-aged man emerged from that group and headed toward us. He came to a stop right in front of my father. "Heavens, you're here! Has your family succeeded in selling all of your wreaths? Our neighbor, Old Hao, is not yet seventy, but he went with those old men who liked to gather at the West Hill and gossip. He, too, jumped into the canal, but was rescued. After being rescued, he woke up, but then went back to sleep. And after falling back asleep, he started dreamwalking again, and while sleeping he confessed that he had a terminal disease such that, if he lived, he would only become a burden to his children, and therefore decided he might as well kill himself. In fact, he proceeded to drink dichlorvos while asleep. This was insecticide he had been hiding for several years. For years, he hadn't dared to drink it, but he ended up ingesting it while dreamwalking, for the sake of his children. He drank it as though it were water, and afterward he began to have convulsions, collapsed, and fell unconscious. In no time, he was dead. On behalf of my neighbors, I have come to order three large wreaths, two small ones, and a set of paper ornaments and funerary objects." Under the lamplight, the middle-aged person's face resembled an old tabletop. His eyes were mere slits, like rotten melon seeds. He looked as though he had been woken up just after falling asleep. He looked as though he had not yet fully woken, but was nevertheless impelled by an urgent matter. He looked as though he had come to visit my father while dreamwalking, to report the death and to relate those various matters. "As for my neighbors, I must help them take care of their funeral arrangements. I also need to notify the crematorium. I need to ask your son's uncle whether, when he is performing cremations tomorrow or the next day, he could also cremate my neighbor. Old Hao was a good man, and we should treat him well. We should prepare a particularly hot fire for him, and pulverize his bones." As the man was saying this, he stepped forward. Upon seeing my father standing in the light in front of the store, he stared in shock, then slowly turned back. "You must remember the funerary objects I mentioned to you. We mustn't let our neighbor be buried in a coffin that is completely bare. If we do, we'll truly be letting him down." As the man was exhorting us, he suddenly seemed to remember something. He took a couple of steps back. His voice was so low that it was barely audible. "Tianbao, I hear that when your brother-in-law is cremating corpses, the bodies secrete human oil. That's incredible, but what does he need human oil for? Currently, a *jin* of soy oil costs only ten yuan. One *jin* of sesame oil costs less than twenty yuan. Does he dare take this human oil to the marketplace and sell it as cooking oil? Given that he is obviously not lacking

in money, how could he be so lacking in morality? This is not the
Three Years of Natural Disaster, when it was not unusual for people
to consume others. In the current world, it would be extraordinary
for people to consume human oil. If the villagers and townspeople
were to learn about this, I'd be surprised if they didn't beat him to
death. And if they didn't do so openly, someone would surely do so
in secret. I heard others discussing this possibility, but I definitely
don't believe your brother-in-law would dare to do it. If he did have
the guts to do this, he would have died long ago. Isn't that right? No
one would go so far as to sell corpse oil for money. Although others
are gossiping about this, I still don't believe it. When I was young, I
was in the same class as your brother-in-law, and when I later went
to see him to give him some funerary gifts on behalf of my neighbor,
I asked him about it directly. Brother Tianbao, you mustn't look at
me that way. I'm not dreamwalking or sleeptalking. I simply spent
all day harvesting wheat, and am now so exhausted I feel I could
die. After I fell asleep, I was woken up by my neighbor to help him
take care of the funeral arrangements.

"Don't forget to prepare three large wreaths, two small ones,
and a set of funerary objects.

"When I come to pick everything up tomorrow or the next day,
I'll bring you the money.

"I'm leaving now, but don't forget what I told you."

He did, in fact, leave. As he retreated into the distance, he
resembled a shadow disappearing into a dream. My father continued
staring at that man's face, which resembled an old tabletop. That pair
of half-closed eyes looked like those of an idiot. Father knew that the
man was dreamwalking. He was taking care of his neighbor's funeral
arrangements while dreamwalking. A live dreamwalker was taking
care of the funeral arrangements of an old man who had died while
dreamwalking. I watched as he took one high step followed by a low

one, appearing as though he were floating along. As he was speaking, he didn't let Father get a word in edgewise. He remained completely absorbed by his own speech. Most dreamwalkers are like this. Either they keep their heads down and do their thing without saying a word, or else they babble continuously to themselves, not caring whether or not anyone else is listening. I was reminded of that woman who had been yelling at her husband, Wang Ergou, in the square. She had been running around, cursing, and shouting to herself. The woman had gone to sleep, had been woken up, and after becoming active had promptly fallen asleep again—but even after falling asleep, she continued doing the things that urgently needed to be done.

She was dreamwalking.

She, too, was dreamwalking.

By this point, there were many villagers and townspeople who were dreamwalking.

Among the townspeople standing in the square, weren't there also some who were dreamwalking? Why is it that the woman who had been cursing the men had left, yet the men remained standing in the square? My father headed over there. "Keep an eye on your mother. Don't let her go outside while dreamwalking." As he turned around and shouted to me, I saw that in the lamplight he resembled a dream shadow heading forward.

When he reached the square, Father looked at everyone's face, as though he were searching for something. Then, he stood in surprise in front of those men and women. He saw that half of the people had faces the color of bricks in an old city wall. They were dusty and wooden. Or light yellow and dark gray, or dark yellow and light gray. They were all dreamwalking. Their eyes were half-closed, but they believed they were actually awake. They were asleep, but their spirits were awake. Meanwhile, the faces of the people who were not dreamwalking were also light gray and light yellow. Their eyelids were heavy and it looked as if they were about to doze off. They wanted to sleep, but made an effort to remain conscious. Perhaps if they toppled over they would fall into a deathlike slumber, and it was simply by virtue of the fact that they remained standing that they were able to stay awake. They remained awake, but didn't notice that everyone around them had entered a dreamscape. They had no idea that everyone else had already entered a dreamscape, and instead they simply continued standing in the square, appearing disheveled and whispering to themselves. The lamplight shining down on their heads resembled muddy water, and was the same color as their faces. A dog was barking, and there was the sound of footsteps walking back and forth. A night cat ran out of the square, and as it passed us it began to slow down. It leaped up onto a wall, then lay there and watched the people in the streets, the events in the town, together with the consequences that this night's developments would have for the entire world.

My father stood for a while longer in the square. He stood in front of that crowd, and said to one of the people, "It looks as though you are dreamwalking. Quick, return home and go to bed." Then he said to another, "It looks as though you are dreamwalking. Quick, return home and go to bed." No one paid him any heed. It was as if people couldn't even see him standing in front of them. He shook the shoulder of a young man from the pharmacy across the street. "Look, your eyelids are as heavy as iron plates. Quick, return to the store and go to sleep." The young man from the pharmacy removed my father's hand from his shoulder and flung it aside. "In telling me to go to sleep, you are telling me to dreamwalk. But if I were to start dreamwalking, all of you would then be able to rob my store." He said this as quickly and clearly as someone who was awake. My father also shook the shoulder of the owner of a tea shop. "Are you really not asleep? I see that your eyes are struggling to focus." The man also removed my father's hand from his shoulder. "Why are you shaking me? Did you think I was dreamwalking?" He said this angrily, but avoided meeting my father's gaze, and instead continued looking in another direction. He gazed out into the hot, grayish-black night, and into the murky grayness at the other end of the street. After a moment, the man turned around and said to the group of people assembled in front of him, "I'm advanced in age, so you should listen to me. Tonight, the entire town of Gaotian has collectively begun to dreamwalk. So, none of us should go to sleep, because as soon as we do, we'll become infected with somnambulism. And as soon as you become infected, you won't know what to do.

"Tonight, none of us should sleep. Instead, we should all stand guard and make sure no one robs my shop. We should also make sure we don't die while dreamwalking without realizing it."

Everyone crowded around the owner of the tea shop, and said, "We'll do as you say, and tonight we'll all stay here in this square. If someone tries to rob the store, we'll be here. We'll help guard the store, and the people inside. We'll stay here all night, if need be." The other man replied, "You can't stand here all night . . . Go have a drink . . . Go have a drink . . . If we have a drink, we'll be able to stay here all night. We'll be able to outlast the dreamwalking. We'll guard the store, and we'll guard you. And if anyone tries to take advantage of the general somnambulism to rob you, we'll pounce on him like a swarm of bees."

Then everyone left.

They dispersed.

In the end, the only person left in the square was Father. He watched everyone depart as though watching a herd of sheep walking through a field. He was now alone, as though there wasn't anyone else living in the Funiu Mountains—only him, standing all alone in front of the village on top of the mountain. It was as though he were the only one left in the world—standing alone in this square.

It was late at night. Extremely late. At the very least, it was already the third *geng* period, which is to say, between eleven-thirty and midnight. In the past, it would have been peaceful at this time of night. Everyone in Gaotian would have been asleep, and from the streets you could have heard everyone snoring. But on this particular night, the stillness was broken by a faint roar—a roar that contained a deadly terror. After standing in the square for a while, my father finally returned home. His footsteps started out slow, then gradually picked up speed, but after a while they slowed down again. When he finally returned to the funerary shop, he saw that my mother was no longer cutting paper blossoms and wreaths in her sleep, but rather had collapsed against the wall and was now sleeping soundly. No longer dreamwalking, she had returned to the peacefulness of deep sleep. Father stood in the entranceway, thought for a moment, then dragged my mother away as though dragging a sack of grain. "If you want to sleep, then sleep. Just make sure that you don't die in your sleep." As Father was saying this, he hauled Mother to the top of the stairs so that she could sleep in her room on the second floor.

Our house had four rooms in all, two upstairs and two down-stairs. The upstairs rooms were used as bedrooms, and one downstairs room in the front was used as a business space for New World and the one in back was used as a kitchen and storage area. The stair-way was located against the back wall. The stairs were made from elm wood. The wood was originally painted red, but now the paint had worn away and all that remained was the original grayish-black wood. In the center of each step, there was a pair of depressions left by people's feet. My mother stepped in those depressions as she went upstairs to go to sleep. After watching my mother go upstairs, my father returned to the front room and stood there looking in both directions. "Niannian, you're not sleepy? If not, then it would be best if tonight you simply didn't sleep." He went into the kitchen and washed his face in the sink, and when he emerged he handed me a wet cloth. "Wipe your face and come with me to take a look at our old home. I don't want anyone to take advantage of the somnambulism to pry open our front door!"

As he said this, he walked away. He led me out into the street, and into the dreamscape night.

2. (23:42–24:00)

Father and I walked along, one in front of the other. I told Father countless things, but now I can't remember what exactly I said. I think I asked him, "Are you afraid of dreamwalking?" I myself wanted to dreamwalk, but was not at all sleepy. There was a strange energy surging through my body, like what I felt years ago when I entered the Luoyang Zoo for the first time. At that moment, I glimpsed an extraordinary new world. Father said, "Tonight, something extraordinary may happen in our town. We may face a mass death." I replied, "Hopefully, we'll at least be able to make it through the night." Father then said, "As soon as the eastern mountains light up, and the sun rises in the east, everyone will wake up. People who need to go and harvest wheat will go and harvest wheat; and those who need to thresh grain will thresh grain. The stores in town that need to open for business will open for business."

I think he said a lot more, but I can't remember what.

After a while, he walked away.

The moonlight was truly the color of water. But in that water-colored moonlight, there was no longer the coolness that there used to be at night. Instead, that water-colored moonlight resembled boiled swill that had not yet cooled. The moonlight was steaming, and as the steam that was rising from the ground blew away, sweat poured down my father's face and his back. We walked away from the liveliest part of the street toward the village street on the west side of town, which was less than two *li* away. Or perhaps it was a little more than two *li* away. I originally thought we would be able to get there in no time, but on this particular night I felt as though it were ten or even twenty *li* away. Or even a hundred or a thousand *li*. On the road, I saw someone who had been sleeping but needed to take a piss. So, like a child, he opened his door and peed into the street. The street had been repaved with cement several years earlier, and the combination of his urine and the steam rising from the cement produced a boiling sound. As the man urinated, he continued muttering to himself. "That feels good. That feels really good!" Heaven permitted men and women to enjoy that sort of pleasure, and it sounded as though he and his wife had just done it. It was as if just as they were doing it, he suddenly needed to stop and go outside and take a piss, planning to then return to bed and finish what he had started. But it turns out that when he finished peeing, he forgot that his wife was still in bed waiting for him. Instead, he remembered something else he wanted to do. He wanted to walk to the fork in the road. He simply stood there, staring at the sky. "Has the sun begun to come up? Because if it has, I have to go and buy my mother some mutton soup. If I do so now, my wife won't know. If I go early, I can purchase the first serving from the first pot. That way, there will be a lot of meat and oil. Mother said she hasn't had any mutton soup for several days, so she immediately tied up her pants and headed toward the town's train station, where people selling beef and mutton were gathered." Upon seeing me and my father, the man said, "Hey, has the sun begun to come up? It looks like both midnight and early dawn." My father peered at that person's face. "Zhang Cai, are you dreamwalking?" "Hey," the man replied, "I'm asking you whether the sun has come up or not." Father suddenly struck Zhang Cai's shoulder, and Zhang Cai recoiled as he opened his eyes and shook his head. "How did I end up here in the middle of the street? Didn't I go to the bathroom to pee? How did I end up out here in the street?"

Zhang Cai turned and returned to his home, as though he had suddenly woken up. "How did I end up in the street? How did I end up running out into the street?"

Farther ahead, there was a woman in her thirties who was coming out of her home holding a cleaver. "I'm exhausted, I'm so exhausted." Mumbling to herself, she suddenly threw down the cleaver. "I'm about to give birth! I'm about to give birth!" She bent over, then squatted down. She looked as though her belly hurt so much that she was about to roll on the ground in agony. We hurried over, thinking that she was about to give birth right there in the middle of the street. We helped her up, whereupon I saw that her expression resembled a cloth that was glowing bright red in the lamplight. But even as she was talking and shouting, her eyes remained tightly closed, as though transfixed. "Are you dreamwalking?" my father shouted, then shook her. My father and I both stared at her belly.

She really was pregnant. Her belly swelled, becoming more and more rotund. She was wearing a large, thin shirt, and the pictures of flowers and plants printed on the shirt were soaked with sweat. "Quick, wake up and return to your home. Make sure that nothing happens to your belly while you are dreamwalking," Father shouted while standing in front of her. She was, in fact, startled awake, then began to laugh. "Tianbao, this time I'm pregnant with a boy. My first three children were all girls." She laughed as she said this, and continued laughing as she returned home.

After this, there was a noise from the house next to that of the pregnant woman. The door was made of willow wood, and the creak it gave as it opened resounded through the emptiness. Following that sound, a man in his sixties emerged. He was thin with white hair, was wearing slippers, and had a bag strapped to his shoulder. The bag was so heavy that he was doubled over at the waist, and every time he took a few steps he would need to stop and rest, and stretch his shoulder. As he walked, he muttered to himself, and his mutterings seemed to flow out of his bag like water—flowing onto the ground and onto the street. But after he walked past several houses, we all realized what he was carrying, and we knew what he was going to do with it. He headed toward Liu Datang's house. Then, *thump thump,* he knocked on Liu Datang's door.

"Brother Datang, please open the door.

"Brother Datang, I want to return a sack of wheat I borrowed from your family more than a decade ago. After we fought several years ago, I thought that I had returned it, but in my dreams tonight I suddenly realized that I hadn't.

"It wasn't that I wanted to keep your grain. I really did forget. If I had wanted to keep your grain, I wouldn't be considered human. I'd be a pig, a dog. Instead, I'm even worse than a dog or pig, because I really did forget. I wasn't trying to keep your family's grain."

The door opened.

The two old men stood there staring at each other, with one of them standing inside the door and the other standing outside. The one outside stood there for a while, then placed the sack of grain inside the doorway. A brusque, embarrassed sound came from inside. "It was just a sack of grain. If you forgot it, it's OK." But then the sound of embarrassment changed to one of surprise, as though someone suddenly noticed that what he had just picked up was not a ball of warm cotton but rather a lump of ice.

"Are you dreamwalking? You have a confused look, and your eyes are shut. Brother Qingshan, come here and wash your face.

"Quick, come over. I'll bring some water for you to wash your face."

Along the road, we kept running into dreamwalkers. Some of them woke up when Father tapped them on the shoulder, but others ignored him, staggering away as he shouted to them. There were men and women, ranging from young people in their twenties to old people in their seventies and eighties.

This is how the great somnambulism began.

The quiet night sent the sound of the great somnambulism outside the village, outside the town, and throughout the entire mountain range. It transmitted the sound to villages and households in the nearby mountains. The entire village was sleeping, but it sounded as though it were awake. The entire town was sleeping, but it sounded as though it were awake. The entire world was sleeping, but the dreamwalkers made it sound as though it were already morning and everyone was waking up. I saw a man dreamwalk out of his home, completely naked. Both his torso, which was generally left bare in the summer, and his thighs, which he always covered with underwear, were as black as the night. His skin resembled the sunrise. Naked, he walked outside, but we didn't know where he was heading. He hurried along without saying a word. His member was dangling between his legs like a dead bird. I was startled by that ugly thing, and my gaze was so pained that I couldn't look away. "Father . . . Father," I shouted, as I grabbed my father, who was walking in front of me. I pointed at the naked man, who was in the process of turning into an alley. Father abruptly came to a halt, as though the town street was sucking at his feet and holding them in place. "Hey, do you realize you're not wearing any clothes? Do you realize you're not wearing any clothes?" Then he went up to the man and tugged at his left arm. The man immediately shook off Father's hand. Without saying a word, he continued toward one of the houses in that alley.

"Do you realize you're not wearing any clothes?

"You are Zhang Jie, from the street in front of ours, aren't you? Do you realize you aren't wearing any clothes?"

3. (24:01–24:15)

Our old house was still quietly ensconced there. The door handle resembled a bird sleeping in a summer night. The house was still a house, and the door was still a door. There were several containers of grain propped against the wall, and apart from some rat droppings, nothing appeared to be out of the ordinary. Grandmother's portrait was still sitting on a table in the main hall, and the spiderweb was still hanging from the wall. The stools were covered in ashes, as were the chairs. When the door opened, the ashes and dust blew around. The stale air also blew around. There was the sound of a straw hat falling off a nail in the wall. Our footsteps were echoed by the sound of night sparrows singing. In the courtyard, there were trees—tung trees and poplars—that were growing crazily with no one to stop them. One tree trunk had a fork resembling a pair of legs that had taken a wrong turn. There were old chests, old clothes, and rusted hoes and scythes. There was an unused well in the courtyard, and dried-up flowers in a pot. There was also the musty stench of death that had accompanied us home. The house had a lonely and desolate smell, as though no one had entered for a long time. We looked around, and eventually came out and stood in front of the rear wall of Yan Lianke's house, which abutted our courtyard. The bricks in the wall were no longer new, and had long since lost that fresh sulfur smell of new bricks. Yan Lianke's house was not as good as ours. Originally, it had been a new three-room mansion, but now it was an old three-room tile-roofed house. Residents of the west side of town had all headed to the east side to buy luxuries, purchase apartments, and do business, and only Yan Lianke's house was left in this empty, empty alley. Every year, that famous Yan Lianke would say he wanted to go to the developed region to buy a house, but in the end he never did. Perhaps he wasn't earning enough from his book royalties. In any event, he never bought a new house, and he stopped being one of the wealthiest people in town. In fact, even my family ended up with more money than he. When Yan Lianke wrote novels, he wanted people to live in his stories. My family's business, meanwhile, helped people live in another world after they died. We used different methods to achieve a similar goal. We both had the same basic objective. Our family opened a funerary shop and sold funerary objects, and anytime anyone died in the village or the town, the relatives would come to us to purchase funerary objects and burial shrouds. Currently, our family is one of the town's richer households, like a great tree in a prosperous forest. This way, every time my father returned to the old compound and saw the Yan family's house and wall, he would stand there and reflect for a while. He would reflect, then go to the Yan family's rear brick wall and knock several times. He would knock several times, reflect for a while, then kick the door. But on that particular night, Father didn't knock on the Yan family's rear wall and then kick the door. Instead, he knocked on the wall, then gazed up at the sky. "His family doesn't have anyone out working in the fields, so there won't be anyone dreamwalking . . . His family doesn't have anyone out working in the fields, so there won't be anyone dreamwalking." Father had a skeptical expression, and his eyes had an impatient look. It wasn't clear whether he hoped someone from the Yan family would start dreamwalking, or whether he was afraid someone might do so. In the end, I simply stood beneath the family's rear wall and waited. I listened carefully, and heard an urgent shout coming from the alley outside our house.

"Has anyone seen my mother? Has anyone seen my mother?"

"Your mother is on the riverbank at the base of West Hill. There are several elderly people there. They appeared to be discussing whether or not to jump into the river, but they were stopped by a passerby."

Both people were shouting at the top of their lungs. Upon hearing the sound of shouting and footsteps, Father rushed out to stand in the doorway. "It appears that Guangzhu from North Street is looking for his mother," Father muttered to himself as he watched Yang Guangzhu's shadow go around the wall, as though a log had fallen into a gully.

After a brief hesitation, Father locked our house's front gate behind him, then together we followed Yang Guangzhu's footsteps.

I remembered how others had said that the year before my parents married, a grave that had been exploded, so that the corpse inside could be cremated, actually belonged to none other than Yang Guangzhu's grandmother. His father had led him to the ancestral grave, and when his father saw that his mother's corpse had been exploded, her flesh scorched, and her hair burned, he began to curse—but before he finished, his breath caught in his throat and he fell into the grave. He had suffered an aneurysm, and never recovered consciousness. Therefore, Yang Guangzhu simply buried him in the grave that had just been blown open. He was not cremated, and instead was buried. After the burial, Yang Guangzhu knelt down on the grave holding a cleaver and a shovel, waiting for someone to come spy on him so as to reveal this secret burial. He waited for someone to come from the crematorium to blow up the grave and burn the corpse. He even made a grenade from gunpowder, which he hooked to his waist—so that when anyone arrived he could simply detonate the grenade and die as the grave was blown up.

However, the enforcement brigade never arrived.

He waited day after day, but they never arrived.

He waited week after week, but they never arrived.

He waited month after month, but they never arrived.

Finally, he placed a dagger in his belt and walked down the street shouting, "I buried my father's uncremated corpse in our ancestral grave. The informer can go to the crematorium and inform on me. I buried my father's uncremated corpse in our ancestral grave. The informer can go to the crematorium and inform on me."

His shouts landed in the street's quiet and deathly solitude. The village's quiet and deathly solitude. The town's and the entire world's quiet and deathly solitude. No one went to inform on him. No one went back to blow up his family's ancestral grave and burn the corpse. For a day, for a week, and for month after month, he kept watch over that grave like a wild hare sitting in a field. In the end, he returned home. In the end, he stopped in the village's empty streets and shouted, "Informer, come out! Don't make me wait for months. If you come out, we won't fight or curse. All I want is for you to tell me why you are serving as an informer. I just want to know who you are. I want to know why you are acting as an informer. I want to know why, despite the fact that your family has been living in the area for generations and has close ties with the other residents, you nevertheless are still not able to turn down the few hundred yuan you might earn from serving as an informer."

He shouted, "You informer, come out! Let me see you!"

He cried, "Come out! Let me see you, so that I can know who you are! How did our Yang family ever wrong you? It was your fault that my ninety-year-old grandmother's grave was exploded and her corpse burned up. It was your fault that my father died on her grave because of this. When he died, he had just turned sixty, and he didn't have a trace of illness."

He cried and shouted as he knelt down on the side of the village road. "Come out, come out! You owe me two lives, but if I beat you when you come out, I won't even be considered a person. I'll be a beast, a pig, a dog. So, I won't curse you or beat you, and won't even say a word. If I want to say something or do something, I'll be a beast, a pig, a dog—and as soon as I go outside, I'll be run over by a car. I can be tossed onto the hearse, like a pig. I can be cremated in the furnace, like a pig. My ashes can then be scattered over the grass and muddy ground of the crematorium, as though they were pig or cow manure. They can be poured into the reservoir next to the crematorium, to feed the fish and the shrimp.

"You must come out. You must come out!

"You must come out, so that I can see who you are. You must come out!"

As he shouted, the sun set.

As he shouted, the sun came up again.

He shouted and cried day after day, as the sun repeatedly rose and set.

The daytime heat was left on the streets of the village, and when night fell the heat and dryness would be scattered everywhere. At midnight, when ordinarily the temperature should be cooling off, the daytime heat would still blanket the streets and the entire world. There was the sound of footsteps, and people's shadows were also flickering all around us. In the square up ahead, it appeared as though there was someone heading west. He seemed to be in a hurry, and his footsteps alternated between being light and being heavy. He lifted his feet and lowered them again, as though he had noticed a depression—or a series of depressions—in the street. With every step, he would lift his foot and then lower it again. Someone was following him, hurriedly following him, as though running after him. The person following him was shouting, and the sound of his voice was like water that had just been released from a sluice gate.

"Father, don't you dare go down to the riverbank!

"Father, don't you dare go down to the riverbank!"

Father and I were stopped in our tracks by these shouts. We rushed over to the square, and saw a middle-aged man following an old man, as they both headed toward the riverbank to the west of the village. The old man was in his seventies, and his son was in his fifties. When the son caught up with his father, he hugged him tight. "Have you gone mad? Have you gone insane? Have you gone mad? Have you gone insane?" Then, the son half-hugged and half-carried his father home. When they reached us, both of them stopped and stared as though they had suddenly run into a doctor.

"Tianbao, you've returned home! Tell me, do you think my father has gone insane? He was sleeping, then suddenly got up and ran outside.

"I'm going to find my mother. You know, more than ten years ago my mother was still alive when she was taken to the crematorium to be cremated. She was in the hospital and her catheter had not yet been removed, whereupon the doctor announced that there was nothing else he could do. He said that if she didn't want to be cremated, then she should be taken away while still alive. I don't know who called to notify the people at the crematorium, but the crematorium's hearse was waiting in front of the hospital. We hadn't yet decided whether to bury her or have her cremated, but they proceeded to haul her away to the crematorium. As she was being hauled away, her heart was still beating, and she was cremated while still alive. It is because of this that my father, whenever he falls asleep, keeps repeating over and over again that he has to go and find my mother, he has to go and find my mother."

As the son was saying this, he dragged his father in front of me. My own father stood there, remaining perfectly still. It was as though someone had slapped him in the face. He was as pale as the moon, and his forty-year-old round face appeared as contorted as though he were in his fifties or sixties. He looked cold, though the night was actually very hot and humid. Father stood there without saying a word, as though he were cold. The look of comprehension with which he had been watching the dreamwalkers was replaced with an expression of utter confusion. Bewildered, he said to me, "Go home and see your mother. I'm going to the West Canal, to take a look." Then he headed toward the West Canal.

He headed out of town.

BOOK FIVE

Geng 4, Part One:
Birds Lay Eggs There

1. (24:50–1:10)

When I returned to Town Street, I was astounded by the dream-walking chaos I found there. Initially, everything was very calm, and as I walked along I could hear people grinding their teeth in their sleep. They were talking in their sleep, and I also heard rapid footsteps in front and in back of me, as though people were running around. All of the dreamwalkers appeared to be anxious and confused. I saw a young man jump out of the window of a hair salon, hugging bottles of shampoo and conditioner to his chest. He was also holding a pair of electric hair clippers and scented soap. Someone else was standing in the street and shouting, "Thief! Thief!" As that person was shouting, I saw someone else break down the door of a meat shop and, without stealing anything, he placed a large pot used for boiling mutton over his head. He then went up to the person who had been shouting, removed the pot, peered at the other person's face, and slapped it.

The person stopped shouting.

The world became quiet.

Then, like a pair of brothers, the two men picked up the pot and walked away.

It was all extremely odd. The world had become an exceedingly strange place. Originally, it had been just old people who were committing suicide while dreamwalking, while strong and healthy dreamwalkers either went to harvest grain or else went to steal things. For instance, the young man who was robbing the hair salon had also opened a hair salon of his own on the other side of town, but because business wasn't as good at his own salon as at this one, he came and stole from it while dreamwalking. In his mind, it was the owner's fault for not arranging for someone to keep watch, and simply leaving the salon open at night. I would come to this salon every month to have my hair cut, and after the young man ran off, I went up to the window to peek inside. I saw that not only had it been robbed, but furthermore everything inside had been smashed. The mirrors on the wall had been shattered, and either the pictures of models with beautiful hair had been crunched up into a ball and thrown to the ground, or they had been torn up into pieces and tossed in the air. A lamp was rolling around under a table, and a salon chair was lying on its side next to the table. There was also an electric fan that had been crushed and left on the floor behind the door. The fluorescent ceiling light tirelessly illuminated all of this, like the sun coming out from behind some clouds to shine on the desolate earth. On this night of this month of this year, the world was suddenly turned upside down, as though a strong wind had toppled an entire forest. Trees had been uprooted, and the leaves and branches were left broken and bare. On the side of the road and in the fields, and in the entranceways and on the walls in front of every home, there were piles of leaves and branches and plastic bags that had been deposited there by the wind. The world was no longer as it had been, and the mountain ridge was no longer as it had been. Gaotian Town was also no longer as it had been. I stepped back from the window of the hair salon and stood astonished in the middle of the street, where I saw people running back and forth. One person was dragging a sewing machine, and as he ran past, some yarn fell to the ground, as though he had spit out a spiderweb.

Someone else walked past me carrying a television set, and the sound of people grinding their teeth while they slept was like a television.

I was completely discombobulated. The world had become a world of thieves. Worried about my mother, I hurried home, and when I arrived I discovered that on East Street every house and every store had its lights on. Some people were standing in their doorways watching the excitement, even as they stood guard by their own houses. Someone brought out a large glass of water, and placed a chair in the entranceway to his store. He waved a fan as he drank his water. Next to the legs of his chair, he had either a knife or an iron rod. When I walked over, we glanced at each other, as we always did, and I held up my knife. After waiting for him to recognize me, I put it down.

"Oh, it's you. Li Niannian. You're running up and down the street like a ghost.

"If you're not going to go to sleep, where are you heading?

"With all these people dreamwalking, why are you not home watching your parents and your store? Why are you running around like a ghost?"

I returned home, and when I pushed open the door to our family's store, the first thing I saw was that there were now six or seven more wreaths than before. The front room was completely full of wreaths, with some placed on top of others. The entire room had twenty or thirty wreaths, which would be enough for ten families to buy wreaths at the same time. In the past, it had been exceedingly rare for two townspeople to die on the same day. But tonight was different. I didn't know what might happen tonight. I didn't know how many people might die. Perhaps our shop wouldn't have enough wreaths to meet the demand. Perhaps even two or three stores wouldn't be enough. When I thought of the dead people, I didn't feel at all frightened, and instead merely had a faint sense of unease. Walking through the wreaths in that room, I felt as though my heart were a pot of boiling sweat, and as though my body were dry, cold, and pure. My body was dry and cold and pure, but my heart had a layer of warm sweat, like a ripe peach that had been rinsed in water.

"Mother, Mother!" I shouted as I entered the room. As I passed through the world of funeral objects, the sound of my shouts remained stuck in the first-floor entranceway.

My mother was not sleeping in the upstairs room. After passing back through the room filled with wreaths, I found that she had boiled herself some water in the kitchen behind the stairs. She boiled it in a large aluminum pot used for steaming buns, then poured the water into the teapot and added some tea leaves. She wasn't sure how many tea leaves she should add, so she kept adding one pinch after another. She blew away the steam from the teapot, as though she were serving freshly cooked rice.

"Mother!"

I stood in the light, facing the kitchen.

"Where's your father?"

Mother looked back at me. Steam had condensed on her face, producing droplets of water and leaving her face covered in a layer of red blush. The light on her cheekbones was a sort of yellow, while her hair, which was disheveled from sleep, looked like scattered straw. Her expression had gone from resembling paper from an old book or an old newspaper to resembling a wet rag. Her body was like a toppled tree. She had clearly turned to speak to me, but then turned away again before I could answer. She seemed to have forgotten what she had just asked me, and fallen back into her dreams. She focused only on her boiling water, and the tea leaves she was adding to the teapot. This was Xinyang tea from Henan, which the fat owner of the farm tools shop next door had brought from home. The shop owner had given this to my mother, saying that the tea was heavenly good, and if you add a few leaves to a cup of tea, you can boil them until they are standing upright. It looked as though a small sprout had appeared in the water. It was said that if you drank a cup of this tea, your exhaustion would evaporate and you would become reinvigorated, and if you had a cold and were running a fever, you could drink several cups to get better. People from China's Central Plains very rarely drink tea, and the people from the Funiu Mountains almost never do so. Only at the height of summer do they boil some green bamboo leaves and drink bamboo tea, which is cooling and helps defeat the heat. But the fat shop owner claimed that her tea not only had the same effect as bamboo tea but also had a number of additional side benefits. She said that her tea was unusually effective in dispelling drowsiness. If people drank a cup they would immediately perk up, and if they drank two cups, they wouldn't be sleepy at all.

In fact, we each drank one cup, and lost all desire to sleep.

After drinking two cups, we felt as though we could stay up all night.

Our entire family drank that tea. Once, after drinking it, our entire family stayed up all night, chatting until dawn. Mother said, "If people feel sleepy, they should simply drink a cup and they'll immediately wake up. If they drink the tea, they won't sleep, and neither will they dreamwalk." While sleeping, Mother said she wouldn't dreamwalk, and would help prevent others from dreamwalking. The smile on her face resembled a peach, elm, or tung blossom. She removed the aluminum pot from the stove, then found two teacups and three bowls and said, "Let's go. Let's go to the entranceway. We can give a bowl of tea to whoever is dreamwalking." I stood under the kitchen light without moving. "Father told you not to leave. He said you were dreamwalking, and that I absolutely shouldn't let you leave home." I went up to Mother and handed her a bowl of tea. "You should first drink a bowl, and after you do so, you'll wake up from your somnambulism." Mother lunged backward, and her left elbow struck the wall, sending the bowl she had been holding to the floor. "You said that I was dreamwalking. Actually, I wasn't dreamwalking. I was tired from making wreaths, but my mind remained as clear as a pool of water." As Mother was saying this, she picked up her bowl, and proceeded toward the door of the store. She laughed as she walked. "Tonight, God has been good to our Li family. The entire town is dreamwalking, and our family is the only one still awake. The dreamwalkers are like confused demons, and those who are not dreamwalking are like awake gods. Awake gods are best positioned to help the confused demons, and if we help them, we'll be able to wipe clean our debts. If they wake up, they will be grateful to your father and me, and to our entire family." She said this as she walked— taking light footsteps as though she were dancing.

As I listened to Mother, for some reason I began staring at her legs. As a result of the car accident, she had always walked with a limp, but she no longer appeared crippled. I was so surprised that I took two steps forward, and clearly saw that as Mother passed through the gap in the wreaths, her lame leg seemed to have grown a bit longer, and appeared a bit stronger than it had been. It was now full of energy, and could easily support her weight. Astonished, I stood there in the middle of the room and watched as Mother moved some tables back and forth. She took some bowls and cups, and placed them on the table in the entranceway. Under the lamplight, she pulled over a chair and sat down in the entranceway. She scanned the street, and saw that someone carrying a bundle of wheat was coming toward her—making a sound like someone's dying scream. The bundle of wheat rose and fell, like a boat sailing down a river.

"Now that you've gone out to harvest wheat in the middle of the night, you should come over here and drink a bowl of tea."

The person carrying the wheat ignored her, and instead passed right by. As he was passing in front of her, he switched the wheat from one shoulder to the other. Then, someone else appeared carrying what looked like a sack of grain. He walked urgently, staring straight ahead and breathing heavily. "Come here and drink a bowl of tea. You are very busy in the middle of the night." The man glanced in our direction, then began walking even faster, as though he were fleeing someone or something. A bottle fell out of his bag and rolled from the middle of the road to the side of the road. "You just dropped something. You just dropped something." Not only did the other person not stop to pick it up, he remained perfectly upright as he continued to run away.

Bewildered, my mother watched the man rush off, then went to pick up the object he had dropped. It was a baby's milk bottle and a packet of condensed milk. The packet was printed with an image of an infant so chubby that its cheeks drooped down. The bottle and the milk packet both still had the colorful brand name and the price, and upon seeing this, I realized that the man must have just robbed someone's store, and had a baby at home that needed milk. I watched as the thief ran away.

I noticed that my mother really was no longer lame.

She no longer walked with a limp, and was now not very different from ordinary people. I'm not sure what time it was by this point.

It may have been late at night, or perhaps it was not late at all. The scene on the street was different from that on the riverbank, in that it was still hot and humid. There were some people who were heading toward us, their footsteps as loud as explosions. There were several of them, a large group. They were all in their thirties and forties, and were all strong, energetic, and wild. As they walked, they muttered mysteriously. They were discussing whether to rob the department store next to the town's train station or the electronics store next door. The latter was called Electronics City, though in reality it was merely an electric goods shop with a grandiose name. The thieves concluded that the items in the department store were simply too random, and even if they grabbed a sackful of goods, they wouldn't necessarily be able to sell it for very much. But if they instead went to Electronics City and each of them grabbed one item, they'd be able to sell it for several hundred or even several thousand yuan. "I want you to stay in the street and keep watch. Also, pry open a window and stand outside it. The three of us will go inside and hand you the goods." The person giving these directions was the head of the town's moving company. He was tall and burly, and normally directed men who were responsible for performing the town's moving jobs. When the thieves came up to our house, they saw that we had placed some tea on the table in the entranceway, and so—without waiting for my mother to summon them—they each proceeded to drink a bowl. One of the men didn't drink, and instead appeared as though he were about to fall asleep.

"You should also drink a bowl. If you do, your drowsiness will disappear."

"Drowsiness my ass," the burly one retorted, looked at his companions. At the mention of the possibility of getting rich, he became more enthusiastic than the others. Then he turned to my mother. "We are awake while everyone else is dreamwalking. This is a remarkable opportunity." He was drowsy, but unable to fall sleep. He threw the empty bowl at the stool in the entranceway, where it made a clattering sound as it spun around. Then he told his companions to follow him. Usually, they would move things to other people's houses, but this time they were moving things back to their own homes. The men's faces trembled with excitement. They were carrying bundles they had made from bedsheets or sackcloth, and either had hooked them at the waist or were carrying them in their hands.

In front of the shop, everyone was nervous as though the air were too thin.

Out in the streets, everyone was nervous as though the air were too thin.

My palms were so sweaty, they resembled pools of water. "Relax," the burly one said. "No one is going to rob your family's funerary shop." After they finished drinking, they left. And as they were leaving, they turned and said, "You can go to sleep. Stealing from your family's funerary shop would be as bad as stealing from a grave. No one in the entire town, or even the entire world, would want to come and steal a wreath from your shop and put it up at home."

After they said this, there was a laugh. A hearty laugh. A crazy laugh. It sounded like a firecracker exploding in the quiet night. They walked away. The entire world fell quiet. In this momentary stillness, however, there was an anxiety that could not be dispelled. My mother's face was pale with fear. Her eyes no longer appeared blank as though she were sleeping, and instead it appeared she had woken up. In fact, she *had* just woken up. Those five or six men had woken my mother from her dreams. Mother pushed the hair out of her face, and looked in the direction of the men. "They are thieves. They have gone to rob someone." I couldn't tell whether she was asking me this, or simply talking to herself. "My God, we have to take some of this tea to all the families in town. If they drink it, they will no longer be drowsy, and they can guard their property. They can guard against all of that deadly activity." As she said this, she went back into the house. It looked as though she wanted to get something. She took rapid steps—both light and powerful.

That night, it really did appear as though my mother was no longer crippled. She appeared even and balanced, as though she were wearing perfectly fitting clothes. She walked briskly back and forth, as though she were flying.

2. (1:11–1:20)

During the night of the great somnambulism, stealing things was as easy as simply leaning over and picking them up.

Electronics City was located about a hundred paces east of our house. If you turned west, however, just before you arrived at the town's train station, there was more tumult. As the thieves approached Electronics City, they saw it was located between a convenience store and a wineshop. It was a three-room house, with two windows and a door. The thieves agreed that they should break the door and windows, and go inside. They weren't carrying any hammers or drills, but claimed they didn't need them. The lamp inside was as bright as the sun, and light streamed out the windows as though the sun were rising in the east. In the lamplight, they could see a drop of saliva dangling from the corner of the owner's mouth, as he appeared to sleep. The owner was in his fifties, with a round face and a slightly hunched back. When he spoke, delight was visible in the corners of his mouth, and when he didn't speak, happiness was still visible in the corners of his mouth. When people came to buy appliances, he would smile, and if they merely looked around without purchasing anything, he still smiled. The display shelves were arranged against the wall, and there was a large as well as a small one. The large shelf had television sets, while the small one had a variety of small appliances. There were also some refrigerators, but the owner rarely sold any of those. In town, people had begun using electric rice cookers, irons, and fans. There were also light bulb plugs and sockets. These items were all carefully placed on display. The owner had nothing else to do, and he would always be dusting those display cases with a feather duster. In this way, he swept out the thieves, who stood in astonishment in the entrance to his store. It turned out that this owner was not asleep, and instead was now dusting his goods with the lights on. The thieves stood in the darkness in front of the store, then decided not to take the risk of trying to steal from there. Instead, they decided to continue on and steal from whichever houses didn't have any lights turned on. But as they were about to depart, the owner came out and stood in his doorway. "Don't leave! Even if you don't want to purchase anything, you should still come inside and take a look." He sounded as friendly as though he were speaking to a neighbor or his own brother. In the end, they were all from the same town, and they all knew one another as if they were brothers or neighbors. "We have no choice but to leave." The big burly one gestured to his companions. But the owner took two steps outside and waved his feather duster in the air. "It's time for the wheat harvest, and the weather is very warm. I therefore haven't had any business for days. Please come in, so that I can have some business. Come in so that I can have some business."

They all stood motionless.

One of the bolder ones walked over toward the entrance to the store, and waved his hand in front of the owner's face. He then went back out and stood in front of the burly one. "Damn it, it seems he is dreamwalking. He was originally my neighbor, but now he views me as merely a customer." The man's burly companion stared in surprise, then laughed. He waved, and led the others to the lighted area in front of the store, where they saw that the owner was, indeed, smiling. He was staring straight ahead, and although he was smiling, his eyes didn't light up. The whites of his eyes exceeded the black portions, and he would periodically lift his hand and rub his eyes. "Come inside and look. Regardless of whether or not you plan to buy anything, you can still come inside and take a look." Then, smiling, he rubbed his face with both hands. "Whenever fieldwork is at its peak, business at my store becomes as cold as the dead of winter, and sometimes I may go for several days without selling anything. At the end of the month, however, I still need to pay rent on the land." This building was one that the owner, Wan Ming, had built himself. At the time he built the house, the thieves were not yet thieves, and they had all come over to lend him a hand. But now, in telling them that at the end of the month he would need to pay his rent, he was treating them as though they were total strangers. When people started dreamwalking, they entered a different world.

The tall one waved his hand in front of the owner's face. His eyes looked as though he were asleep, and he wasn't even blinking.

"Do you want to buy anything? If you do, I can give you a discount."

"How much of a discount?"

"That depends on how much you want to buy."

"I'll buy a television set."

"What size?"

"This one. It has a twenty-nine-inch screen."

When they first saw each other, the thief had addressed the owner as Boss Wan. But now the owner treated these men as though they were total strangers. He was in a dreamworld while they were in the waking world. In his mind, he was a businessman eager to sell his goods, while they were customers who had come to buy his goods. "I noticed this television set . . . I noticed this refrigerator . . . If you can sell them to us cheaper, each of us would buy one." Originally, in bartering with him the men were simply trying to waste some time while waiting for their opportunity to rob the store. But Wan Ming asked if they were each willing to purchase something, and added that, if so, he would be happy to give them a discount. "I can sell them to you for a thirty percent discount. Thirty percent off is my lowest possible offer, and even in your dreams you won't find anything so cheap. As long as each of you purchases at least two thousand yuan worth of goods, I'll make sure that you get everything for thirty percent off . . . This is cheap . . . Dirt cheap . . . So, will you buy anything? If so, you can go select your goods, and while you are doing so, I'll have a drink of water." As he said this, he turned and proceeded toward the counter, but walked right into it. "Damn it. I'm falling asleep. It's too hot, and I can't see anything. If you want, you can come in and I'll shut the door and go to sleep."

He did, in fact, sit down on a stool and, leaning against a cabinet, proceeded to fall asleep, his hand still resting on the glass.

The sound of early morning snoring resonated through the store like a swarm of mosquitoes. The thieves were startled and delighted, and it was as if each of them had a bird's nest full of eggs sitting on his head. They all felt warm and happy. The one who had been standing in front of the televisions pretending to select one, initially reached for a television set but then paused and smiled. The man who had been pretending to examine an electric rice cooker turned around and placed the rice cooker under his arm, but when he noticed that everyone else was standing in front of the refrigerators and television sets, he dropped his rice cooker and went to stand in front of the television sets as well.

In this way, they all stole what they needed, and in the blink of an eye they had emptied out the entire store.

3. (1:21–1:50)

In addition to the aluminum pot Mother had just prepared, she boiled another pot of water for tea.

In the first pot, she had placed seven or eight pinches of tea leaves, and in the second she placed two large handfuls. This freshly brewed tea was as thick as Chinese medicine. It was dark red, and was steaming. The tea leaves were floating on the surface, like sticks drifting down a river. "Take this bowl to the house of the man you call Fifth Grandpa, on the next street over. Take it, so that whoever in his family is drifting off can drink some. Tell his relatives that they absolutely must not let those in their family fall back asleep, because if they do, they will start dreamwalking—and if they start dreamwalking, there's no telling what might happen." I didn't respond, nor did I move a muscle. I simply stood there and looked into Mother's eyes. At this point, Mother's eyes did not appear in the least bit sleepy. Instead, they resembled a couple of dried-up ponds that had been refilled with water. I don't know whether that pair of grayish-white dreamwalking eyes had been startled awake by someone, or had been woken by the steam from the tea. The wrinkles around Mother's eyes were so numerous and so deep that they resembled trenches. "Take this over to them." My mother took a step forward, and waved that bowl of tea in front of me. "Your father has let them down, and your uncle has also let them down. If we send them a bowl of tea, our debts to them will be met, and we will no longer owe them anything."

This plan sounded simple and easily implementable: it appeared she was proposing that we use bowls of tea in order to repay our debts. I took the bowl and hurried down the street in a state of confusion. It was as if I knew that a bowl of tea could cancel our debt, but I also felt that a single bowl couldn't possibly be enough. When I reached the house of Fifth Grandpa, I shouted, "Fifth Grandpa, outside everyone is stealing things. If you drink this tea you won't fall back asleep, and that way you'll be able to guard your house and prevent people from robbing you." After the door opened, Fifth Grandpa looked suspiciously at that bowl of tea, as though it were a bowl of soup into which someone was planning to add poison. "If you don't trust me, you can try it. If you take a few sips, you'll find you aren't sleepy at all. You really won't be sleepy at all." Clearly skeptical, he brought over a bowl and asked me to pour him a little of the black-red tea. Under the streetlamps the ground was the color of yellow mud, while elsewhere it resembled a pool of sewage. Some people ran by in front of me, while others ran behind me. They ran frantically, to the point that if they dropped something—like a pair of plastic sandals or a red silk dress—they wouldn't even stop to pick it up. Meanwhile, I accepted the bowls of thick tea that Mother handed me, and delivered them as she directed. At each house, I would first knock and then hand over the bowl of tea. I would always say the same thing, and as I was leaving I would keep an eye on the ground and pick up whatever I found.

As I was delivering tea to the sixth household, I encountered a family of three in the intersection. The man was in his forties. He was shirtless and wearing shorts, and was carrying a pair of bamboo baskets. In one of the baskets there was a sewing machine, and in the other there was its stand. There were also some neatly folded piles of cloth, and some newly sewn clothes. The family had just robbed a tailor's shop. They must have robbed a tailor's shop. The man's wife was carrying a bundle of cloth. When some of the cloth fell to the ground, I immediately knew which shop it had come from. When they saw me, they all scurried into the street, as if they had just seen the owner of the tailor shop returning home, or they had just seen the owner's family come out. I stood there watching the family of three. Under the lamplight, their faces appeared sallow and were covered in sweat. "Have some tea. If you drink this tea, you won't fall asleep, and neither will you dreamwalk." When the child—who was several years younger than I—saw me, he quickly went over and held his mother's hand. His hand went from yellow to white, becoming the same color as hospital walls. The man immediately stood in front of his wife. "Go away! You're the ones who are dreamwalking. If you take another step forward, I'll kill you." He shifted his bag from one shoulder to the other, so that the sewing machine was now in front. I stood there, staring blankly. I tried again to explain, "This is a bowl of tea that has been specially designed to dispel drowsiness and give you a lift." I extended the bowl to him, and took a small step forward. "This is thick tea, and upon drinking it people who are drowsy will no longer feel drowsy, and people who are dreamwalking will suddenly wake up." I extended the bowl to him, and when it was close enough that he could reach out and grab it, he put down the baskets he was holding. From the side of the sewing machine, he took out a knife—a cleaver. The back of the blade was black with rust, but the edge still gleamed brightly.

"Do you want to live or not? If you take another step, I'll chop you down."

I stood there frozen, and pulled back my hand.

"Get out of here. If you don't, then regardless of how young you may be, I'll still chop you down."

"It really is just a bowl of tea. If you drink it, you'll wake up and will no longer be drowsy."

As I was stepping back, the tea splattered my hand. It was neither hot nor cold, but rather lukewarm. I looked at this man and his family, and proceeded into the middle of the street—but wasn't sure whether I should drop the bowl of tea and run home, or continue to the house of the sixth family. This sixth family was surnamed Gao, and when a member of the Gao family died, my father had secretly earned four hundred yuan. When my uncle cremated the family's relative, he let all of the corpse oil flow out, and then took some ashes and bone fragments from the furnace, and gave them to somebody. The Gao family didn't know about any of this—the same way that, during the day, people may well forget about what they dreamed the previous night, or the way that people, while dreaming, don't remember what occurred when they were awake.

In the meantime, I continued standing in the middle of the street until I saw someone walking over. The man who had just robbed the tailor's shop also saw this person approaching, and he quickly put his knife away and placed his bag back on his shoulder. "When the sun comes up tomorrow, if you dare tell others that you ran into us tonight, I'll send your entire family to the crematorium." He made a point of telling me this before leaving, to frighten me. He also gave me a fierce glare. It was as if he either hated me or feared me. Because I feared his gaze, it was as if it were a blade of light slicing my face in half. As the family walked away, the pace of their footsteps suddenly increased, such that it sounded as though they were fleeing. It was not until they were already far away that it finally occurred to me that I should have checked to see what the man looked like, what his family looked like, and whether or not they were from Gaotian. However, I was so frightened I completely forgot. My mind was a complete blank, like a bald mountain in the middle of winter, or like Yan Lianke's novels that resemble deserted graves. It was as though everything was a dream, and everyone was dreamwalking. Was I also dreamwalking? If so, that would certainly be a very odd occurrence—an extraordinary occurrence. I tried to take a sip of the tea I was holding, then vigorously pinched my thigh. It hurt, but my throat felt moist and comfortable. In this way, I confirmed that I was awake and wasn't dreaming. I felt somewhat disappointed. The light on the street was unevenly distributed, and I moved a step from an illuminated area to a darker one, where I saw that family of three walking away.

However, someone else was approaching.

The person came closer, with footsteps that sounded as familiar as a sentence in a book I had read.

The footsteps sounded as familiar as the titles of Yan Lianke's novels and the names of the characters in them.

It was my father.

It really was my father. He was returning from the banks of the river outside town.

But the closer he got, the less he sounded like my father. His body was so hunched over that he looked like a rat running down the street, and he was breathing coarsely and heavily, like an elephant that had hiked a long distance. His clothing was wet and there was a gaping hole in his left breast, where the fabric was still hanging from his chest. His pants had a long rip, through which you could see a bloody wound. His round face was yellowish-white, or pale yellow.

He had been beaten. At least it looked as though he had been beaten, and no mild beating at that. The left side of his mouth was bruised and swollen, and it looked as if the blood were about to start flowing but was still bottled up inside.

Outside town, my father had done something very saintlike. On the West Canal, he had washed the faces of many dreamwalkers, as though performing baptisms, and in this way he had succeeded in waking them from their slumber. He had used a bamboo pole to reach into the canal and fish out the bodies of several old people who had jumped in while dreamwalking, and then woken up realizing that they didn't want to die. Someone said that after Father awakened all of the old and young dreamwalkers, he carried back to the village the corpse of someone surnamed Yang, whom he hadn't managed to wake in time. He returned to the east side of town, but as he was making his way back to the center of town from an alley on the east side, he ended up like this. Like a mouse. Like a lamb. Like a chicken that had been killed by a cat or dog. Like a dog that had been beaten by someone passing on the road. He was sick. He was disabled. But he was also extraordinarily sleepy. He was exhausted. It was as though, in a single breath, he had sown several decades worth of crops, or had walked for several decades. But as soon as he stopped, he would fall asleep, and as soon as he fell asleep, he would topple over. Therefore, so as not to fall asleep and topple over, he stood in front of me—as though a short, rotten post that had been buried underground for many years suddenly rose up before my eyes.

"Father . . . Father . . ."

I repeatedly called out to him. I called out to him twice, but he didn't answer. He didn't answer, and instead stood planted in the middle of the street as though he were in the middle of a deserted field. He looked at me as though he were looking at something else.

"I deserved to be beaten. Who told us to let everyone down?

"I really did deserve to be beaten. Who told us to let everyone down?"

It was hard to tell whether he was saying this to me, or simply speaking into the void. He seemed to be talking to himself, mumbling to himself. As he spoke, a sallow smile hung on the corners of his mouth—an ambiguous, forced smile. As he smiled, he cast a glance toward South Street behind me. "Niannian, you are my son. Given that you are my son, you should go with me to kneel down in front of the others. We must let them beat us and curse us. Who told us to let them down? Who told your uncle, that beast, to let them down?"

I saw the whites of Father's half-closed eyes, which resembled two pieces of dirty white cloth, while his pupils resembled drops of ink that had fallen onto the cloth. The ink was no longer black, and the white cloth was no longer white. Instead, they were now mixed together, so that the boundary between the black and the white was no longer discernible. If you looked carefully, you could see that the white portions of his eyes were dirty, that the pupils were a mixture of black, yellow, gray, and white, with some parts being slightly darker—enough to show that these were his pupils.

I knew Father was dreamwalking.

I knew that now Father was also dreamwalking.

His expression was like a brick or a block of wood. Perhaps no one had beaten him. Perhaps he had fallen while dreamwalking, and had ripped his clothing and hit his mouth. His mouth wasn't terrifyingly swollen, it was just the sort of swelling that's the color of blood, and his expression was not entirely like a brick or a block of wood. "Father, what's wrong? Take a few sips of this tea Mother brewed." I handed him half a bowl of the tea, which had already cooled down. But he was still in a somnambulistic state, and his entire attention was directed toward whatever it was he was thinking about. He knocked over the tea bowl I was holding and the tea splattered to the ground—the same way that he had deliberately knocked over the face-washing basin I had handed him earlier. "Are you or are you not my son? If the other townspeople look down on your father, you must do so as well.

"Even if I were shorter than I am now, I would still be your father.

"Even if I had sinned more than I have, I would still be your father.

"Let's go. Go with me to those families' homes, to kneel before them."

Father led me to those households on the south side of town. It turned out that those were the same households I had visited to deliver tea. They included the homes of Fifth Grandpa, Uncle Liu, Auntie Wu, and Sister-in-Law Niu. When we reached the first house, Father pounded on the door, and when it opened, he pulled me down to kneel in front of the person opening the door. He looked up at the person's face and, without waiting for the person to realize what was happening, he began to sob and plead. "Fifth Grandpa, you must beat me. You must beat me. I, Li Tianbao, am not a person, but rather a beast. You must beat me!"

Fifth Grandpa was terrified by this.

In front of the entrance to Fifth Grandpa's home, there was a small ten-watt bulb, which produced a dim and muddy light. Fifth Grandpa's complexion was oddly sallow. "What's going on? What's going on?" Staring in shock, Fifth Grandpa came over to lift me and Father from the ground. But as he was standing in front of Father, Fifth Grandpa seemed to remember something. He turned pale, and stared as Father's eyes turned icy cold and his voice turned frigid.

"Tianbao, what are you talking about?"

Father looked up. He appeared to be still half-asleep, and when he spoke his voice was somewhat hoarse. "More than ten years ago, it was I who went to the crematorium to inform on people. It was I who reported that Auntie had been buried, as a result of which her body was pulled from the grave and burned."

Fifth Grandpa froze.

Fifth Grandpa stared at my father as though staring at a dog eating human flesh. As I knelt next to Father, I looked up at this old man in his eighties. His gray hair moved in the lamplight, as did his goatee. The sagging and wrinkled skin of his face tensed, trembled, and then tensed again. It seemed as though he wanted to say something, or as though he were about to slap Father's face. At the same time, he was still an old man in his eighties, who was unable to hit or curse anyone. The corners of his mouth trembled, as he turned to look at the courtyard behind him. Then, as he turned back, his face appeared red and frightened.

"Tianbao. You and your son must go quickly.

"You mustn't let the rest of my family know about this."

My father peered into Fifth Grandpa's courtyard, then stood up, whereupon I stood up as well. When Fifth Grandpa pulled us forward, we peeked into the courtyard behind him. "Father, who is it?" This was the sound of his son shouting to him from some room. Then, the sound of Fifth Grandpa answering his son drifted back into the courtyard. "It's nobody. It's the village notifying every household to guard against theft." Then everything was quiet again. In the ensuing silence, Fifth Grandpa pushed me and my father out of his house. Father frantically knelt down and began kowtowing, then he and I frantically backed out of Fifth Grandpa's house. We stood on the side of the street, as Fifth Grandpa waved and repeatedly warned us not to mention this to anyone. "You can say that Niannian brought us some invigorating tea, but you mustn't mention what else happened."

Fifth Grandpa quickly shut the door and, in the process, he shut the events of the past into the back of Father's mind.

Father and I stood on the side of the street. I saw Father let out a long sigh—a sigh as long as a rope tied around a bundle of wheat stalks, and when the rope is undone the wheat stalks will fall apart. Father was also relaxed, and under his somnambulistic pallor his face was blushed slightly.

"Let's go. Let's go to the next house. The more I think about it, the more I think this is not a big deal. If we go to a few more households, I'll be able to put everything I've done in this life behind me. Then, you'll be able to live happily with your mother."

The hand with which Father was holding mine was covered in sweat.

My own hand also had a small pool of sweat. When Father released my hand in order to wipe his own on an electrical pole, I felt a chill on the back of mine. I hadn't realized that I had clenched my hands into fists, but after I released them, I discovered that in each of my palms there was a pool of coolness.

With this coolness, I suddenly felt very relaxed. It was as though there were no somnambulism. It was almost as if there were no longer any somnambulism. Father could now think and speak clearly. Apart from the fact that when I looked down at his face I saw that it was the color of wood or brick, even Fifth Grandpa, who was awake, did not think my father was sleeping. Father, however, was half-asleep when he knelt down in front of others to atone for his acute sense of guilt and shame. This is really how he was. It's the way someone talks and acts after getting drunk, but then forgets everything the next day after sobering up. He swayed slightly when he walked, but otherwise no one would have been able to guess that my father was asleep—or even half-asleep.

We proceeded forward. We went to the next house, which belonged to Uncle Liu. Out in the street, it seemed as though terrifying sounds were hidden everywhere, but when you listened carefully, you couldn't hear anything. The moon remained as it had been, murky grayish-white. The air seemed to be both moving and congealed. The clouds remained as they had been, accumulating in some areas and dispersing in others, and leaving the town's streets and alleys muggy and murky. What time was it? I didn't know what hour and what minute of this day and night it was. I followed my father. I left the empty bowl on a stone in front of Fifth Grandpa's home, planning to take it back when I returned.

We reached the next house, and knocked on the door.

We knocked, and also called out.

A man opened the door, and Father—upon seeing that it was the head of the household or someone important in the family—immediately knelt down in front of him. As he did, Father cried, "Beat me . . . You must beat me . . . Spit in my face . . . You must spit in my face . . ." Then he described how, when someone in this family had died, he had informed on the family for money. When he said this, the man who opened the door appeared startled, speechless, and at a loss. After all, the events in question had occurred more than a decade earlier, and the regulations on burials and cremations were determined by the state. My father and I had not only confessed, but even knelt down in front of the man. What else could be done? The other man simply stared for a while, and reflected. "So, Tianbao, this was really something you did." Still kneeling, Father nodded. The other man was angry for a while, but then expressed forgiveness. He said something that was a mixture of hot and cold. "I never imagined you could have done something like this. You are such a small person, I never imagined you were capable of accomplishing such an extraordinary deed. Everyone says you and your wife at the New World funerary shop are completely different from the director of the crematorium. The wreaths you sell are large and cheap, and you never try to profit from the families of the deceased. I would never have imagined that you were capable of something like this . . . Get up! It's certainly true that you can't judge a book by its cover . . . Get up! I'll never strike someone who is offering an apology . . . Get up, it's the middle of the night, and the two of you should return home and go to sleep. Just now, your wife told Niannian to bring us a bowl of tea to prevent us from falling asleep and dreamwalking."

We stood up.

We proceeded to another house.

Then we proceeded to yet another.

This home belonged to a man called Gu Hongbao, who was a bit older than my father, and a bit taller. I needed to get the tea bowl we had left in front of Fifth Grandpa's house, and take it over to Gu's house. I just needed to take it to Gu's house. But first I needed to get the tea my mother had prepared. My pace was a bit slower now. I placed the refilled bowl in the entrance of Fifth Grandpa's house on the southern side of the intersection. By this point, things were different from before. They had gotten blown out of control, and had exceeded Father's plans. They had exceeded even my own wildest imagination. We knocked on that door, then went inside. When we saw Gu Hongbao standing in his courtyard, we immediately knelt before him.

"What are you doing? What are you doing? Li Tianbao, what are you and your son doing here?"

The light in his courtyard was very bright, and it was not entirely clear why his family had so much money. The piles and piles of money seemed to come from nowhere. They had money to go drinking, and money to gamble. They had built a three-story house lined with white porcelain, and were able to lead a very prosperous life. Under that fiery red light, we could see that the doors to the house were made of iron and were painted red with touches of silver and gold. The windows had green steel bars that had been soldered into the shape of flower blossoms. The courtyard was full of flowers and plants, and there was also a flower pond. A black sedan was parked in the courtyard under a new tile-roofed garage. Father and I knelt down on the concrete in front of the door to the garage, and could smell the alcohol coming through Gu Hongbao's pores. Father told Gu about how he had previously served as an informer. He described his feelings of shame and guilt, and how he had always wanted to find an opportunity to confess, but had been hesitating for more than ten years. He explained that on that night, while all of the townspeople were dreamwalking, he himself felt simultaneously clearheaded and confused, as though he were dreaming as well.

He therefore had come to confess.

He therefore had come to acknowledge his crimes.

"If you want to hit me, go ahead.

"If you want to curse me, go ahead.

"Brother Hongbao, if you want to hit or curse me, you are perfectly entitled to do so."

We thought nothing would happen. We thought that, at worst, Gu Hongbao would simply utter a few cold words, like the previous families, particularly since his mother's cremation was not actually the result of my father's actions. Before my father went to inform on him, the crematorium somehow already knew that the Gu family was planning to conduct a secret burial. The hearse was already parked in front of the family's entranceway, but my father still went to the crematorium, and my uncle still gave him two hundred yuan as a reward. This is why my father had now come to the Gu family—to confess his sins. What he didn't expect, however, was that after hearing what Father had to say, Gu Hongbao would immediately turn green with fury. He stared straight ahead, then suddenly grabbed a pole from in front of the garage and held it up.

"Damn your mother, so it was you after all!

"Damn your grandmother, so it was you, Li Tianbao!

"Damn your great-grandmother. All these years, I've never forgotten about that. I never expected that on this night of the somnambulism, you, Li Tianbao, would come over in such a confused state and confess."

It turns out that when Gu spoke, his voice was high-pitched like a woman's. When men with high-pitched voices get angry, it is as though their bodies are suffering an electric shock. Jumping and hopping around, he had grabbed a wooden pole and continued hopping around under the lamplight while mumbling to himself. Afterward, he looked off in another direction, like a frightened horse that lowers its head and runs away. When Gu uttered his first curse, my father, who believed he was sleeping in his bed, reacted as though someone had just punched him in the gut. He appeared as though he wanted to wake up, but was sleeping too soundly and simply couldn't rouse himself. But when Gu screamed at him a second time and reached for his pole, my father finally woke and opened his sleepy eyes. "Aiya, what's going on?" he shouted, then pulled me away from Gu Hongbao's raised pole. He pulled me and I quickly took a couple of steps back, then he positioned me in front of him, to block him from the pole.

"Brother Hongbao, were you really going to hit me?

"I'm not scared that you'll hit me, but were you really going to hit your nephew Niannian?

"Go ahead, hit me. Hit me. If you can, go ahead and beat Niannian to death."

My father pushed me toward Gu's wooden pole, even as he simultaneously gripped my shoulders and prepared to pull me away.

Ultimately, it was I who blocked Gu's pole. It was I who, on account of my age, was able to defeat him. At the time, I was frightened and confused, and my mind was in turmoil. My head and body were covered in sweat, and sweat also dripped down my face. But when Gu Hongbao saw my father push me under his pole, his hand suddenly froze. In fact, his entire body froze. My father had won—he used wakefulness to defeat sleep.

"Brother Hongbao, just now I was speaking to you in my sleep. Did you take what I said as the truth? You often get drunk, but after you sober up, do you take what you said while you were drunk as the truth? In court, they don't accept what people say when they are drunk or asleep to be reliable evidence, and instead they treat it as equivalent to the ravings of a madman. So, how could you accept what I just said while asleep as true? How could you accept what I said or did while dreamwalking to be true?"

Gu Hongbao stared in shock. He stared at the spot where my father had been kneeling, as the pole remained frozen in midair. Perhaps he was remembering how he liked to get drunk, or was thinking about the oddness of that somnambulism. He stared at Father's face, and into his eyes, as if he wanted to determine whether or not my father was, in fact, dreamwalking. At any rate, after staring blankly for a while, he ultimately put down the pole he was holding. My father seemed to be afraid they would continue to argue over something, so as soon as Gu Hongbao put down his pole, Father pulled me toward the front entrance of the house and walked away. He walked very quickly, as though he were fleeing. He ran as though he were fleeing. "How could I have been sleeping, woken up, and then fallen back asleep? And then start dreamwalking again? How can I endure a beating, and then fall back asleep and start dreamwalking again?" He was talking to himself. He was muttering to himself. He strode over to the entrance, then turned around and looked back at Gu, who had followed him out, and shouted:

"Gu Hongbao, what people say while they are dreamwalking doesn't count as true, and you mustn't take what I said as true. Just now, the mother of Yang Guangzhu, who lives at the eastern end of the street, went to look for her husband, who died more than ten years ago, then proceeded to drown herself in the river. It was I who carried his mother home from the river, but after doing so, I told his family that it was I who killed his mother, his father, and his grandmother.

"If you say that I harmed the three members of his family, then how could I tell his family?

"Such an insignificant person as myself, could I have harmed the three members of his family?

"Gu Hongbao, did you hear? Don't forget that several times when you fell down drunk on the side of the street, I was the one who carried you home.

"Gu Hongbao, go to sleep. I'm telling you that the fact that your mother's body was taken away and cremated has nothing to do with me. Like you, for the past ten years or more, I had no idea who in town could be so amoral, and therefore, while asleep, I confusedly attributed this act to myself.

"Go back to sleep. Don't forget that my own mother wanted to be buried, but in the end was afraid someone would inform on her, and so it was I who took her to the crematorium."

Standing in the middle of the street, my father told Gu Hongbao many things. Standing in the doorway, Gu listened intently as my father told him everything that had happened. It was as if he were sobering up, and was slowly remembering everything he had said and done while drunk. Initially, when Gu and my father first encountered each other, one of them had been asleep and the other had been awake, but now that they were both awake, the more they spoke and listened, the more confused and murky the situation became, and the harder it was to distinguish between truth and falsity.

After everything became confused, we really did leave.

Father kept saying, "I don't dare sleep, I don't dare sleep. If I fall asleep, I'll start dreamwalking, and something awful may happen. Something deadly." Ignoring Gu Hongbao, who was still standing in the entranceway, Father pulled me away and said we had to return home.

Then we hurried home.

BOOK SIX

Geng 4, Part Two: An Entire Clutch of Chicks Hatch

1. (1:51–2:20)

Something awful occurred.

Something deadly.

After Father pulled me away, we hadn't gone very far before we arrived at the tailor's shop, which was positioned kitty-corner from the Gu family home. When we initially arrived on that street, we had focused only on getting to the Gu family home, and didn't see the tailor's shop. On our way back, however, I noticed the tailor's shop. Out in the street, there were the sounds of countless footsteps going back and forth. The dreamwalkers were stealing things, while those who were not dreamwalking also took the opportunity to steal. "Thief! . . . Thief!" It was unclear where this cry was coming from. It was as though a piercing wind were blowing over. In the street and alleys, the yellow lamplight seemed as though it were there to let the thieves find their way, while remaining dim enough to obscure their faces. Another crowd of people came forward, carrying an assortment of bags. When they passed us, I turned to look at them, but Father pulled me back. "You're all busy. Very busy. We didn't see anything." Father hugged me close, then led me over to the entrance of the tailor's shop.

The door was open. The shop was located on the side of the street, and there was a wooden sign in the entranceway. On the sign, there was the word TAILOR in large red characters, though in the darkness the red characters appeared black and indistinct, yet at the same time very clear. In this clarity, a pungent smell of blood wafted over. When I turned in the direction of the smell, I saw that in the entrance to the shop someone was lying in a pool of blood. He was dead. His arms were extended awkwardly in front of him like a couple of tree branches, and he was still grasping a sewing machine belt. When my father and I saw this, we both gasped and stood there frozen. Before I had a chance to look more closely, Father used his body to block my sight. He didn't want me to see that bloody corpse, but I still saw it. The blood looked like mud, and the corpse's skull had been shattered like a melon. The body and the blood were mixed together, as though someone were trying to wash himself by crawling through the mire. My father stared silently at the body, and continued to stare until finally he shouted, "Hey . . . Tailor Liu . . . Something horrible has happened at your home . . . Something deadly . . . You are all still sound asleep . . . Heavens, you are all still sound asleep!" At this point, I remembered how, a little earlier, that family of three had passed me while carrying a sewing machine, some cloth, and a large knife. It was only then that I noticed once again that, although my father was not very tall, his voice was nevertheless as tall as a tree. It was so loud that if you were to place the sound upright, it would be like a ladder reaching the sky and leaning against the clouds, such that people could use it to grasp the moon and stars.

Then, a light appeared in a window in back of the tailor's office, and Father quickly led me home. We ran like crazy.

Someone had died.

Someone really had died.

Because they were dreamwalking, people had died one after another. Not all of them committed suicide by jumping into a river or hanging themselves. Others had been cut down while robbing and stealing. Out in the streets, it seemed as though the footsteps of thieves and bandits could be heard everywhere, but it also seemed as though there wasn't anyone there at all. There were shouts of "Stop, thief! Stop, thief!" followed by a deathly stillness. It would become so still that you could hear the fear circulating through the town streets. From one street, you could hear the sound of stealing and killing coming from a different street, but when you went to another street, you would hear sounds coming from an alley off the first street.

Everyone appeared to be very busy. Very, very busy. People were muttering to themselves, and when they brushed by one another in the street, they acted as though they didn't even know one another. They acted as though there wasn't anyone near them. They acted as though the entire world were asleep, and as though they were the only ones who were awake and busy doing things. One person who didn't know what he wanted was simply running around aimlessly. He wandered back and forth, and if he bumped into a wall he would simply turn away, but if he bumped into a tree, he would slap his own forehead, followed by his thigh or butt. It was as if he had just woken up, or had realized that this was not what he should be doing. He simply stood there staring blankly, then went to either do something or not do something. He wandered aimlessly along that street, like someone swimming through a muddy pool—and he was making an awkward snoring sound, as though it was not easy for him to breathe while underwater.

The street resembled a market—not the sort of bustling market where everyone was constantly bumping into everyone else, but rather the sort of idle market that comes at the end of the busy harvest season. It was as if everyone had finished work and was now simply relaxing, and had come out to the street to take a stroll and look around. People didn't have any fixed plans to buy or sell anything in particular. But in the process of strolling about, someone began anxiously running, his feet moving so fast that it seemed as though he were flying. It was as if he were trying to catch a car or a train. In the ensuing tumult, no one knew what was happening.

Or what might happen.

In fact, someone died.

Someone really did die. And it wasn't just one person, but rather several.

Many people walked past the body of a dead person, acting as though they hadn't seen anything. They looked at a dead body on the side of the road as though it were someone sleeping on the riverbank or on the roadside. But my father woke up and saw all of this with me. He even climbed up onto several corpses to take a closer look. He had woken up when he came out of Gu's house, and as soon as he saw the corpse in front of the tailor's shop, he lost all traces of drowsiness. It turned out that a corpse could dispel drowsiness. The stench of blood could drive away a person's drowsiness, just as insect repellent can drive away mosquitoes. "We have to tell the village chief about this. We have to tell the town government about this. We have to go immediately to the town's police department and report this, and ask that the township police take care of it." My father originally wanted to take me home, but when we reached the intersection, he changed his mind. Instead, he led me to the house of the village chief. We strode past one dreamwalker after another—one group of dreamwalkers after another—as though we were striding through a forest. As the dreamwalkers proceeded, they lifted their feet and then lowered them again, over and over. They were all stumbling along, but only very rarely did any of them fall down because they couldn't see the road clearly.

I'm not certain what time it was at this point. It must have been around *chou* period, from one to three o'clock in the morning, and more accurately perhaps around the fourth *geng,* which is to say, two o'clock. On our way to the village chief's house, we ran into our neighbor Yan Lianke, who was returning from his writing studio on the embankment. He appeared to be dreamwalking as well, and quickly crossed over from the other side of the street. Like the others, he alternated between high and low steps. But unlike the other's, his clothing was neatly arranged and his shirt was tucked in. He was wearing a pair of slippers, as though he had woken up to go to the bathroom, and then had simply continued walking until he reached the town. He didn't say a word, and his face was like a book full of miswritten characters that no one could read. When he walked past me, I shouted out to him, "Uncle Yan, what's wrong? . . . You've come back to town." He ignored me, and continued onward. In a dream, he continued walking in the direction of his house.

So, it turned out that even this author could dreamwalk. Even he could be infected with this secret disease. I tugged at my father's hand, and pointed to Yan as he walked away. My father looked at him as though looking at a tree that could walk. He watched as that tree crossed from one side of the street to the other. "The fact that even he can dreamwalk is incredible, simply incredible!" As my father was saying this, he took my hand and quickly led me to the house of the village chief. It was as if he thought that in finding the village chief, he would be able to make everyone stop dreamwalking. As if in that way, he could make daytime be daytime, and nighttime be nighttime. As if in that way, he could make it so that people would do things when they were supposed to do them. Dreamwalking is like being summoned or infected, and it turned out that even this author was capable of being summoned or infected. Even people located in remote and isolated locations were capable of being infected. It was quite possible that this somnambulism affected not only Gaotian Village, Gaotian Town, and the Funiu Mountain Range, but also the entire county, the entire province, and even the entire nation. It was quite possible that the entire world was dreamwalking in the middle of the night, with only my father and myself still awake, together with the thieves and the bandits. As we proceeded forward, my father and I mumbled to each other as though talking to ourselves. I gazed up at Father's face, and he patted me on the head, saying, "Father won't go back to sleep." His head was as clear as a mountain stream, and he didn't have the slightest trace of drowsiness. The fact that he wasn't sleepy was actually a torment, because it meant that he had no choice but to attend to the dreamwalkers, the same way that those who were able to stand erect and walk had no choice but to help those who had fallen by the side of the road. Father had no choice but to assist them to their feet, and to help them pick up what they dropped. Of course, many items simply fell and rolled away, and someone helping to retrieve them might be tempted to slip something into his own pocket. This was to be expected. I myself picked up many items lying in the street and took them home—including a pot, a pouch of milk, a milk bottle, as well as some clothing and shoes that thieves had stolen and then dropped by the side of the road. There was also a scythe used to harvest wheat, and a cloth sack used to collect it.

The village chief's house was located in the entrance to the second alleyway off the main street. It was a new three-story house, built with red bricks and red tiles, which resembled a large fire burning day and night. There was a seven-foot-tall courtyard wall and a two-yard-tall gatehouse made from old bricks with a roof that had the inscription GONG MANSION in large gold characters. The light bulbs below the door resembled the eyes of the village chief's wife, as if she stood in the street cursing people. Father and I arrived at the village chief's house, and as we were about to knock on the door, we saw that it was already ajar. The courtyard was as illuminated as though it were the middle of the day. The house was also as illuminated as though it were the middle of the day. Although it was already well past midnight, and was even entering the latter half of the night, the village chief and his wife had not yet gone to sleep. Instead, they were preparing hot and cold dishes, and drinking wine. The smell of the wine filled the house, and drifted out into the courtyard and into the street. There were pear and apple trees in the courtyard, and in the lamplight the fruit was dangling there like miniature hammers. Mosquitoes and moths flew around tirelessly, and the village chief, who was in his fifties, was shooing them away while drinking wine. He was neither fat nor thin, and was a bit hunchbacked. His thick, mournful mien was wooden and gray. Hanging on the wall, there was an image of a deity and a landscape painting. There were portraits of Deng Xiaoping and Mao Zedong. The village chief's shadow fell on the latter portrait. There was also an enormous painting of the eight celestials crossing the ocean, which was hanging on the wall between the two main rooms, making it appear as though the entire wall were a deep blue sea. The village chief was sitting on the seaside drinking wine. When he raised the cup to his lips, it made a whistling sound like ocean waves; and when his chopsticks knocked against the side of his bowl, they sounded like oars striking the shore. "Damn it, you're not opening the door. How dare you not open the door?" He continued cursing as he drank, running through a litany of complaints. "I never did anything to offend you. I've treated you well, but now, regardless of how loudly I knock and shout, you still won't open the door for me." He wife emerged from the kitchen with a plate of eggs and chives. Her shirt was half-unbuttoned, revealing breasts that resembled fallen eggplants. She walked past me and Father as though walking past a pair of stone columns. She was under fifty years old; her smiling face, which, was reddish-brown, was like a pile of dried paint. "Gong Tianming, I've prepared another dish of eggs and chives for you. Now you can say who treats you better—me, or that widow!" She sat down in front of her husband, served herself a cup of wine, then toasted him. "Apart from her youth, I don't see any way in which that widow is better than me! Now you can determine whether her treatment of you is real or fake. Not only did she throw you out, she even slapped you in the face." The chief's wife pushed the plate of eggs and chives up to her husband. "Here, have some. These green chives are the shreds of that widow's skinny flesh, while this yellow egg is her fatty meat. The dish is called fat with fried widow." She then placed a bowl of soup in front of him. "This is a soup made from her ribs . . . This is a cold dish prepared from the widow's tongue . . . These are the widow's breasts prepared with garlic sauce . . . Eat her. Drink her. In this way, you can help resolve my anger, and can also help resolve your own anger." The chief gazed at his wife, looking resentful and befuddled. But, in the end, he did accept her toast. Looking at her face, which resembled a pile of dried paint, he didn't say a word. Instead, he put his chopsticks in that dish of skinny-fat widow eggs and chives.

Father and I knew that the village chief was dreamwalking, and we knew that his wife was also dreamwalking. While sleeping, they would eat, drink, and complain about each other. In the entranceway to one of the halls, there were two pots of Chinese roses that were as red as blood. That night the village chief and his wife were drowned in the smell of food, flowers, and wine, like a pond full of mud and blood. Standing in the entranceway to the village chief's house, I gazed at the faces of that couple who had lived together for nearly thirty years, like a board that had been split in two.

"The two of you are both dreamwalking.

"The two of you are dreamwalking, so you should wash your faces or drink some tea. If you do that, you'll wake up."

My father walked into the hallway of the village chief's house and stood next to the small table where they were drinking wine. "Chief, you have to wake up. I have to find a way to ensure that no one else in this village falls asleep tonight, because if people do, they'll start dreamwalking, and if they dreamwalk, there will be major problems. Some people have already died. In fact, quite a few people have already died. Some of them drowned themselves in the river, while others were beaten to death while being robbed. If you don't attend to these issues of life and death, the village and town may well fall into utter chaos— becoming as chaotic as a bowl of porridge." Upon saying this, Father went to look for the village chief's face basin, then brought it over, half-filled with water. "Wash your face. Wash your face and wake up, so that you can quickly attend to the village's affairs. You can't simply stand by and watch as one villager dies after another."

The chief looked at my father and at the basin, then poured himself another cup of wine. He said, "I had thought you were Wang Erxiang, but it turns out you aren't. Given that you are not Erxiang, why are you asking me to wash myself? And drink wine? And eat vegetables?" My father turned to the chief's wife. "I want you to wash the village chief's face." He glanced at the wife, then quickly looked away again. Her breasts were visible through her shirt, like sagging eggplants.

"Go wash the village chief's face, and also wash your own.

"Given that there has been a momentous incident in the village and in town, as village chief he has no choice but to look into it. If he doesn't attend to people's lives, then one by one they will all be lost.

"After you wash your own face and wake yourself up, you should wash the village chief's face. Hey, don't start eating now. You should first wash your face to wake yourself up, and then wash the village chief's face."

Father stood there while saying this. Meanwhile, the village chief and his wife ate and drank as though no one were around. In the end, when Father and I attempted to wash the chief's face ourselves, he grew angry. He immediately stood up and threw down his chopsticks. "You fuckers, who do you think you are? How dare you touch my face? Do you think you're my wife? Do you think you're Wang Erxiang? If you make another move, I'll have my wife fry you as though she were frying Wang Erxiang, and then I'll consume you with some wine." He said this in a powerful voice, such that his entire face appeared to be possessed by an angry and heroic spirit, and as though he wanted to grab a stool and smash it over my father's head and body.

My father froze. "I am Tianbao. Don't you recognize me?"

My father took a step backward. "I am Li Tianbao, who sells wreaths. I am awake, and you are asleep."

"Get out!" The village chief sat down again, and poured himself a cup of wine. He picked up a pair of chopsticks and, without wiping off the dirt, stuck them into a dish of cold vegetables. His wife laughed as she watched her husband and my father. "You say we are dreamwalking. Look at your own face, with sleepiness as thick as a wall. What are you doing coming over to our house in the middle of the night, rather than going back to sleep in your own? It's the middle of the night. Why can't you let my husband rest in peace? He's the village chief, and not your family's hired hand, whom you can summon at will. And you, you are eating and drinking, and saying that this is meat from that widow's thigh, that it's meat from that widow's breast. You claim you are eating her and drinking her—but if you eat her and drink her, it is as if you were sleeping with her. There is no need for you to long for her so fervently." She thought that, in saying this, she would be flattering her husband, but the village chief raised his wine cup while staring coldly at his wife, whom he hated. She immediately looked away, and her voice dropped to a whisper.

"If someone doesn't open the door for you, is that my fault?

"If someone pushes you and slaps your face, is that my fault?"

Father and I emerged from the village chief's house, and from his family's dream. The night was as it had been, and there were still footsteps and mumblings everywhere. The night was seeped in mystery and disquiet, which circulated everywhere like air. It was as if there were someone hiding behind every tree and every wall. For some reason, all of the streetlamps along the main street were suddenly extinguished, as were all of the streetlamps in the entire town. It was unclear whether they had been extinguished on schedule—during the *chou* period from one to three o'clock in the morning—or whether they had been shattered by dreamwalking thieves. At any rate, the road now consisted of sheet after sheet of darkness, and in isolated alleys there were streams of thick blackness. Through this black night, the sound of invisible footsteps was simultaneously murky and indistinct but unusually clear and resonant.

The night became a good night for thieves and bandits.

The town became a good town for thieves and bandits.

The entire world became an optimal world for thieves and bandits.

My father tugged at my hand. "The electricity has gone out. Don't be afraid." In the darkness, I nodded in my father's direction, and gripped his left hand even more tightly than before. Every day, he would split bamboo to make wreaths, leaving his fingers as rough as the bottoms of a pair of sandstone shoes. We headed back, and after taking a few steps through the darkness, we could make out some stars in the sky. I noticed that the road under our feet seemed to be emitting a muddy glow. As we proceeded forward, we heard footsteps following us. We stopped and spun around. Without waiting for the footsteps to get closer, Father offered a pleasant greeting. "Hi, whoever you are. You can do whatever you want. My son and I didn't see anything, and we won't say anything to anyone." However, the shadow continued to approach, with the footsteps becoming faster and faster.

"You two, whoever you are, was it you who just came to my home?

"It must have been you who came to my home."

It turned out that this was the village chief.

The village chief had been chased out of his home, and out of his dream. He was holding a flashlight, which he shone on me and my father. Then he turned off the flashlight and stood there in the murky darkness. In the darkness, he appeared to be pondering something. "Chief Gong, if you have any tea leaves at home, you should have your wife brew you some tea to drink. Otherwise, you should go back and I'll have Niannian bring you a bowl of tea." The village chief initially didn't say anything, but after a while he remarked:

"A moment ago I was very sleepy and confused, but now I am less so, and feel as though a seam has opened in my brain. Just now, when you were in my home, were you saying that in the village there had not been just one death, but many?"

"Ah, yes, there really have been many. They are all people who either died while dreamwalking or were beaten to death. This is why you must wakefully attend to these things."

The night was eerily quiet, but in the stillness there were some people who were feeling irritable because it was hot and stuffy. When Father spoke, I could sense his anxiety, and could feel his sweaty hand. The village chief, however, remained calm. In the murky darkness, the chief's face dissolved into the depths. In the dark depths, it appeared as though he had no face, but only a body standing before us like a column. This body stood there silently for what seemed like an eternity.

"Li Tianbao, given that you can sell wreaths and burial shrouds every time someone dies, you will surely make some money. But, it won't be very much. I'll give you more, if tonight you can help me with something. OK?

"I want you to go fetch some poison. Then, I want you to take advantage of the fact that my son's family is not home and the entire town is out dreamwalking, and go slip some poison into my wife's wine cup or soup bowl, so that Erxiang and I can marry each other. OK?"

Upon saying this, the village chief stood there motionless, staring at me and my father. It was as though he were staring intently at something he couldn't see. The sweat that had accumulated in my father's palm began to drip. His warm palm became a pool of cold liquid, and then became a mass of frigid air. "What are you talking about, Chief? How could I, Tianbao, possibly do what you are asking? I came to find you simply because I was worried that the town's dreamwalkers might run into trouble . . . You can continue doing whatever you were doing, and I'll return home and fetch you a bowl of thick tea." As Father was saying this, he pulled me away and we quickly left the village chief and headed home. Initially we took small footsteps, but then we shifted to large strides. As we broke into a run, Father glanced at the dark shadow following behind, and immediately slowed down.

"Go back, Chief, go back! It's not easy to be alive. I'm going to go home and fetch you a bowl of tea."

The village chief didn't immediately respond. After a while, however, his voice emerged from the darkness. "I really do like Erxiang, so what do you suggest I do? What should I do?" His voice sounded hot, anxious, and helpless, but it also seemed to have hints of warmth. It was unclear whether he had really woken up, or was still asleep. Father focused only on dragging me home, and when he spoke again, it was to look back and gesture symbolically. "Chief Gong, go home. In the entire town, there is no one as tight-lipped as I. I'll go fetch you some awakening tea."

We heard the village chief's footsteps as he turned around and headed home. He proceeded very slowly, as though he remained bewildered over whether or not he should murder his wife and marry Erxiang.

2. (2:21–2:35)

In town, there was a police station.

The police station was located in a courtyard across from the town government compound. In the courtyard there were trees, lamps, and electric fans. The station's police were all in the courtyard taking advantage of the coolness to sleep. The yellow lamplight was like a bright pond. The courtyard gate was made of iron and steel bars, and if you climbed up, you would see that inside there were five bamboo cots nestled together like corpse pallets. The five township policemen—who were asleep on the cots like soldiers in the barracks—each sat up, one after another. Like soldiers, they put on their shoes, then turned and proceeded to the wall in the rear of the courtyard, where they urinated against the wall, each of them holding his member with his hand. After they finished, someone—perhaps it was the station chief—said something, and the five policemen shook off the remaining drops of urine, then turned and marched back.

In a neat and uniform fashion, they removed their shoes and lay down to sleep. The sound of their breathing and snoring flowed out into the courtyard like water through a canal.

"A deadly event has occurred in town. Aren't you going to do anything? . . . A deadly event has occurred, aren't you going to do anything?" Father and I both shouted through the gate's iron bars. Three policemen sat up, and together they hurled a curse at the gate as though throwing a brick. "Get out! . . . What are you doing, making such a commotion in the middle of the night? Do you want us to arrest you? . . . Do you want us to arrest you?" After they finished shouting, the policemen lay back down in an orderly fashion, and there was the sound of their bodies striking the wooden cots—as though a wreath's several dozen bamboo strands simultaneously snapped in the middle of the dark night.

Then, all was silent again, except for the rhythmic sound of teeth grinding.

3. (2:36–3:00)

The town government cadres also began dreamwalking.

They began dreamwalking, going off in all directions. Only the light bulbs and fluorescent tubes were awake and shining. The cracks in the old bricks used to pave the town government courtyard were clearly visible. If a needle were to fall into one of those cracks, it could be located immediately. Mosquitoes and moths were flying around in the light. Standing in the interstices between light and darkness, the grape trellises resembled a mysterious matrix of light and shadow. This building was more than a hundred years old, and the bricks and tiles looked as though they had been taken from an old temple, or from Beijing's Imperial Palace. It had originally been a home belonging to a member of the landed gentry from the Republican era, and later it had been adopted as the site of the town government. One town government regime after another used this as its office complex; and one town mayor after another worked and relaxed in this brick and tile structure. Here, officials would read newspapers, study official documents, and hold meetings. They would oversee the various villages under the town's jurisdiction, together with everything in the Funiu Mountain region. On that particular night, however, all of the town government cadres began dreamwalking. The town mayor and the deputy mayor also began dreamwalking. As the mayor and the deputy mayor began dreamwalking, the other people in that tile and brick building—including both important and unimportant ones—began dreamwalking in accordance with the mayor's decree.

While dreamwalking, they enacted a historical scene of the emperor attending to governmental affairs. Half a month earlier, a theatrical troupe had come to the town to perform the palace operas *Saving General Yang* and *The Cases of Judge Bao,* and now the costumes from those operas were put to a very important use. In particular, the town mayor wore the emperor's robes, while the deputy mayor wore the prime minister's robes. The emperor's robes were embroidered with a dragon and phoenix, with gold borders and sleeves as wide as pants legs. Both the emperor's and the prime minister's robes had gold borders and a red waistband. Meanwhile, the clothing of the empress dowager and the various imperial concubines was studded with jade ornaments that sparkled in the light. Periodically, there would be the sound of jade striking gold. That night, the town government's entire entrance hall and meeting room were transformed into an old-style imperial court. In addition to the mayor and deputy mayor, all of the other county cadres followed convention and wore either military or civil robes. The county's former messengers and cooks were effectively promoted and dressed as officials and eunuchs. Their clothing was magnificent and resplendent with jewels. The lamps were burning brightly, and a row of red lanterns was visible in the doorway. The workers who had previously been responsible for cleaning the town government building had now become officials who stood in the entrance hall next to the ministers and held up signs reading SILENCE! The former announcers from the town government's broadcasting station were now empresses, princesses, and palace ladies responsible for fanning the emperor. The atmosphere was one of solemn silence, and apart from the look of exhaustion in everyone's eyes, all the faces had an expression of curiosity and enchantment as people struggled to stay awake. They were like people who, every night before going to sleep, made an effort to listen to something, watch something, or do something. The court officials and military officers knelt down in front of the mayor-cum-emperor, who was sitting on his throne, in front of a gold-edged, engraved table that would be used in the palace drama. On the table, there was a large imperial jade seal wrapped in yellow silk. The seal was placed in the center of the table, and on either side of the seal were a pen holder, a writing brush, and a small teacup with a lid. The palace ladies brought the mayor some bird's nest and white fungus tonic soup. Somewhat annoyed, the mayor looked at his bowl of soup, then raised his arm slightly, motioning for the palace ladies to retreat. "You should speak. It is not possible to resolve all of the world's problems simply by bowing." The mayor's intonation sounded exactly like that of an emperor. He spoke slowly, and sounded slightly annoyed. The prime minister and court officials glanced up at him, and saw that he was lifting his bowl of soup to take a sip. Knowing that the emperor was in a peaceful state of mind, they set aside their worries. The emperor said, "Everyone sit down, and after you have done so, you can each report to us, one after the other." With this, the prime minister, cabinet ministers, and military officers all stood up, bowed deeply to the emperor, ceremonially flapped their sleeves, and loudly expressed their gratitude. Then, they all stood or sat in front and on either side of the emperor.

"Who will speak first? Perhaps the prime minister could speak first? Please tell us what you investigated during your trip to Jiangnan this past month."

The deputy mayor quickly came forward, bowed deeply, and ceremonially flapped his sleeves. "Zha! . . . Thanks to his majesty who, in his infinite royal graciousness, sent your humble servant south for over a month. Your servant passed through Shandong and Xuzhou, and then took a boat down a canal through a band of cities, from Nanjing to Wuxi, Yangzhou, and Suzhou, all the way down to Hangzhou. Wherever I went, it was always undercover, and I never inconvenienced anybody. Everywhere I went, I found peace and prosperity, and there was no one who did not express the utmost gratitude to the emperor, shouting, 'Long live the emperor! Long live, long live the emperor!'"

When the emperor heard this, he waved. "This is the same old thing. These are the same things as always." However, as he said this, he had a smile on his face, and there was a gleam of delight in his eyes. "But these words still need to be spoken. Transportation from Beijing to Jiangnan is not very convenient. It is a long and arduous journey if made on foot, and even on horseback it takes over a month, and is difficult and exhausting. I grant you a vacation for you and your family, to go to the Chengde Summer Palace for a holiday retreat." He waved again, and gestured for the prime minister to step back. The mayor then gestured to the officers standing on either side of him. "Governor Li, it has been several days since you returned from the frontier. Please report on the conditions there. Please tell us about the condition of the people living there, together with the miserable life on the border." Deputy Director Li Chuang, from the town's department of armed forces, stepped forward and ceremonially flapped his sleeves. Then he knelt down, and looked up. His voice was as sonorous as a drum.

"Thanks to his majesty who, in his infinite royal graciousness, sent your humble servant to the northwest, to survey the frontier. Three years ago, the frontier was undergoing the ravages of war. There was one military engagement after another, and people could barely make a living. Everywhere I went, I saw countless people who were starving or victims of natural calamity. Often people would block our way to beg for food and water. The Xiongnu living along the frontier would repeatedly attack. At night, they would steal and pillage, and during the day they would loot and capture. During harvest season, they became particularly unruly, and riding their horses and armed with bows and arrows, they would burn, pillage, rape, and kill. As a result, those living along the frontier found that they could no longer rely on cultivating the land, and experienced severe food shortages—to the point that many of them ultimately had to abandon their fields and their homes, and relocate to the interior. But after your majesty sent me out there, I followed your directives, and attempted to bring peace to the outer regions before turning to the interior ones. We defended the frontier and waged a series of furious battles. There was not a single battle that did not result in casualties and injuries, but our soldiers did not flee a single time. Instead, the entire army fought as one, as everyone preferred to die on the frontier rather than retreat. I led the charge, trying to ensure that when the enemy soldiers arrived, they would be blocked, just as when the floods arrive we build embankments to contain them. During the battle of Qilian Mountain, I was wounded three times by arrows, but even with my injuries, I still charged ahead. For three days and three nights, I did not dismount from my horse, and my knife never left my hand. I ate on horseback and slept in the saddle. In the end, we managed to defeat the enemy, and forced the Xiongnu to retreat more than a hundred twenty *li*. Following this battle of Qilian Mountain, the war of the northwest was broken wide open, and afterward we were able to win every battle. Conversely, the enemy lost every engagement, and continually had to retreat. As a result, the northwestern territories were finally restored to the interior, and the region was again at peace. The residents of the frontier could move back and resume cultivating the land, and enjoy the pleasures of home and hearth. Currently, the entire band of territory covering Shanxi, Gansu, Ningxia, and Mongolia is at peace. There was a bumper harvest, the nation and the people are at peace, and industry is prospering. Throughout the northwest, whenever members of any other nationality see a Han general or soldier, they immediately kneel down to you and your army, and shout, 'Long Live' three times. Whenever I return to the court, I must ask to pay obeisance to your majesty from all the different peoples, and offer wishes of 'Long Live, Long Live, Long Live!'"

This long directive from the deputy director of the department of armed forces was extremely eloquent and forceful, and when the other officers heard it they were speechless. They were astonished that the deputy director of this tiny office, who was a twelfth-generation descendent of Li Zicheng, could be such a talented orator. Even the town mayor was delighted, and the deputy mayor stared in admiration. The other town cadres in charge of the economy, administration, and education were all leading ministers in their own right, but when they observed the eloquence of that official from the department of armed forces, they felt ashamed of their own inferiority. They knew that the mayor would definitely favor this cadre, and were concerned that he would be promoted to a position of section chief, or deputy mayor charged with overseeing the public order, or even of military governor in charge of guarding the frontier. As all eyes remained fixed on this frontier governor dressed in his boots and military attire, the cadres heard the town mayor-cum-emperor begin to laugh. He stood up and walked toward the table, then turned, walked back, stood next to the throne, and moved the imperial seal that was sitting on the table.

"Governor Li, your civic achievements and martial strategies are excellent, you are virtuous and talented, and you have achieved your objectives in defending the border. These past three years the Xiongnu also admired you from their hearts, and sent tributes every year. To ensure that the imperial government will remain in order, and that the rewards and punishments will be strict and impartial, I hereby decree that you be promoted to the position of general governor, with authority over military affairs and border skirmishes in the northwest and the northeast, as well as Yunnan and Taiwan, Guangdong and Guangxi, and other border regions." With a smile, the emperor looked over the civil and military officials assembled in front of him, then he let out a deep sigh. It was as though he finally felt safe now that all matters under heaven were in harmony and at peace. "Do the ministers of education and civil administration have anything further to report?"

The ministers of education and civil administration looked at each other, whereupon the minister of civil administration stepped forward, flapped his sleeves, and bowed on one knee. "Your humble minister has one item to report, but doesn't know whether it is appropriate or not?"

"Speak." The emperor gazed down at the minister, just as a scout on patrol might gaze at a commoner complaining about injustice he had encountered. "Today I am in an excellent mood as I hold my morning conference, so you are welcome to say whatever you wish."

The minister of civil administration stood up and gazed at the emperor, then he turned and looked at the two rows of officials standing on either side.

"This summer the citizens blessed by the heavenly grace of the emperor have enjoyed ten thousand *li* of bountiful harvest. The ears of wheat are as large as ears of millet. But recently the royal astronomer sent an urgent message, reporting that in three days there would be a torrential downpour, and that it would continue to be overcast for at least half a month or a month, and the rain will completely flood most of the land under our jurisdiction. If we don't quickly harvest the remaining wheat, I'm afraid that most of it will end up rotting in the fields, leading to a catastrophic winter without grain and starving people throughout the region. Based on the royal astronomer's projection, our realm may currently be stable and at peace, and the people may be celebrating, but beneath this surface peace there lies a great calamity. I know that the emperor is prepared for danger in times of peace, that you see the future as an immortal, and preemptively that everyone should work through the night harvesting grain and storing it in a warehouse, after which all should help combat the floods by building embankments and securing the villagers' houses, so that when the flood does arrive, the people won't be caught unprepared and taken by surprise. That way, the people won't be left destitute, the region's hidden instabilities will not be triggered, and catastrophe can be avoided. I hope that the emperor will consider my humble advice."

After the minister of civil administration finished, he again ceremoniously flapped his sleeves and bowed, while peeking up at the town emperor. The emperor seemed displeased but didn't say anything. Instead, he merely yawned and appeared annoyed. As a result of this, the minister of civil administration looked uneasy, and was about to launch into a searing self-critique when suddenly, at that moment—at precisely that moment, the same way that during an opera performance, just as the performance reaches a climactic point, the performance shifts to another story—one of the sentries stationed outside the palace came rushing in and stood in front of the ministers assembled before the emperor. He quickly performed the ceremonial flapping of his sleeves, then announced:

"Reporting to the emperor, outside the palace there are a couple of troublemakers who have forced their way in, and your humble servant was not able to prevent them from entering. They insisted on seeing you in person, and claim that even though outside the city there is abundant grain, the peasants continue to harvest the grain through the night, as though they were dreamwalking. Meanwhile, in the city, some people have taken advantage of the fact that everyone else is either sleeping soundly or dreamwalking, and have begun stealing, pillaging, and killing people. In short, everything is in chaos, and the dynasty is on the verge of collapse. Please indicate whether or not you are willing to see these troublemakers."

The mayor glanced over at the sentry. "Can you confirm that they are both troublemakers?"

The sentry rubbed his sleepy eyes. "They definitely are. They are the father and son who run the town's funerary shop, and sell spirit money to burn at funerals. They sell money for the dead, in order to make money for the living."

The emperor looked away from the sentry, and cast a cold glance at the minister of civil administration, who was reporting on hidden disasters. He gazed coldly, then snorted. Finally, he looked over at Li Chuang, the military governor of the frontier region as well as the deputy director of the department of armed forces. "Governor, you are needed to help resist external aggression and maintain internal peace. Go outside to take a look . . . To all of those who do not respect our court, who bring false charges against our nation, claiming that we are not prosperous or at peace, I have just one word: Execute!" When General Li heard this, he was left speechless. He looked away from the ministers, and left the palace with the soldiers serving as sentries.

In his position, the deputy director of the town's department of armed forces, who was already in his thirties, was charged with maintaining the peace and handling petitions. He had been doing this for more than ten years. During that time, he had groveled while privately nursing a grudge, but continued to hold only a deputy position. Now, his opportunity had finally arrived, and he strode toward the outer gate of the town government courtyard.

The town government building was not located in the liveliest part of town, but rather was in the far northeast corner. In front of the main entrance, there was a pair of solitary Republican-era stone lions, and the gun turrets located at the four corners of the compound were also still there. The six-story stone staircase was also still there. Clouds floated by overhead, casting shadows onto the earth. All of the town's streetlamps were extinguished, but the lamp in front of the main entrance to the town government courtyard was illuminated. As a result, in the middle of the night, the town government compound was different from the village streets, and the government buildings were different from ordinary people's houses. Father and I both waited at the outer gate of the town government's Forbidden City. As we were waiting at the entrance of the town government compound for the sentry to return, someone approached us from behind. It was an old man who was dreamwalking. He had dry hair and missing teeth, and when he closed his mouth it left a depression in his face. He was one of the town's lowly officials, who relied entirely on petitioning the government for food and money. He was seventy-two years old, and had already been petitioning the government for eighteen years. Whenever he didn't have any money, he would go to petition for redress, and after the government gave him a bit of money, he would turn around and head home. Whenever he didn't have enough to eat, he would go to petition, and after the government gave him a bit of rice and flour, he would eat and drink in town and then return home. When the old man wasn't petitioning, the town would be peaceful, but he continued to petition month after month, and year after year. In another instance, his son died in one of the county's factories, but the factory claimed that his son actually died from some illness. When the factory didn't offer the father any compensation, he went to petition. Later, when no one offered him any support for the elderly, he went to petition. On this night of the great somnambulism, Father and I assumed this old man had come to bring charges of injustice and to petition for redress while dreamwalking, but as he walked by me, his eyes appeared yellow under the lamplight and he was muttering something that was only half-intelligible. He nevertheless had a bright, muddy smile.

"In the future, I will no longer petition for redress. I will no longer petition.

"In the future, I will really no longer petition for redress. I will really no longer petition."

As he mumbled, layer upon layer of smiles appeared on his face. After Father asked him why he would no longer petition for redress, Li Chuang—who had been charged with suppressing external aggression while also internally keeping the peace—emerged at the entrance. Li Chuang was wearing the type of uniform a military officer would typically wear in a traditional opera. He was marching in a military fashion, and was speaking as though he were asleep and dreaming. He appeared at the entrance to the town government compound and stood on the stone steps, gazing down at Father and myself standing below him. Before Li Chuang could speak, however, the old man stepped up to him.

"Deputy Director Li, in the future, I will no longer petition for redress.

"Deputy Director Li, I have come to tell you and the town mayor that each time I come to petition for redress, the two of you ask me how is it that I've already managed to spend the money you gave me the previous time I came to petition, but the truth is that I myself don't know how I managed to spend it so quickly. I clearly

remember putting the money under my pillow, but after a few days
the money would be gone and I would have no choice but to come
petition for more. But tonight, as soon as I went to sleep, I had a
dream. I dreamed that, because I was afraid of losing the money you
had given me, I hid it in a hole in an old persimmon tree in back of
my house. I therefore went out and looked in the hole, and found
more than thirty thousand yuan. Then I looked in the hole of another
tree, and found more than two thousand yuan. I looked in a crack in
the wall behind my bed, and in the ridges between the bricks in the
floor under my bed. In all, I estimate I found one hundred twenty-
three thousand and eight hundred yuan.

"With one hundred twenty-three thousand and eight hundred
yuan, I no longer need to petition. This is enough for me to live comfortably for the rest of my life. This is enough to support me in my
old age, and to cover my funeral after I die. Deputy Director Li, I have
come to tell you and the town mayor that I really won't petition anymore. Even if someone were to try to kill me, I still wouldn't petition."

Talking and laughing, the old man proceeded up the steps. He
walked up to Li Chuang and repeated three more times the phrase
"one hundred twenty-three thousand and eight hundred yuan." But
as he tried to proceed further, Li Chuang blocked his way, and as
Li Chuang was blocking his way, Father and I heard Li Chuang say:

"You really won't petition anymore.

"You guarantee that you won't petition anymore."

Li Chuang pulled the old man toward him, and spoke to him
softly and with a trace of coldness.

"If you stop petitioning, then what will I do, as the person in
charge of handling petitioners? If you stop petitioning, the town will
no longer receive its monthly allotment of several hundred yuan for
resolving petition claims. If you stop petitioning, how will I become
a great general responsible for resisting external aggression and

maintaining internal peace? Listen to me—you must continue to petition every month. Every month and every year, you must go to the county and the city center to express your grievances. You know?"

As he said this, Li Chuang shook the old man's shoulders, and the shaking appeared to wake him up. The old man stared in shock for a moment, and gasped. It appeared that he had really woken up. He stared at Li Chuang, as his voice grew louder and more urgent.

"Deputy Director Li, you are wearing a military-style opera costume and squinting. Are you dreamwalking? Earlier, I was half-awake and half-asleep, but I really did find the money that I hadn't known was there. There was one hundred twenty-three thousand and eight hundred yuan. Now that I have all this money, I no longer want to petition. I really don't want to petition anymore."

Deputy Director Li didn't say anything else, nor did General Li. Instead, he simply stared at the old man for a while. He then pushed the old man backward, rolled up the sleeves of his opera uniform, and pulled up the war robe, which was dragging on the ground.

"You still expect me to resist external aggression and maintain internal peace? In doing this, you are making it such that the town employee responsible for overseeing petitions will be left unemployed and have nothing to do. If you stop petitioning, this not only affects my and the mayor's future prospects, it will also have an impact on the finances of the present dynasty. You know?" As he was speaking, he deftly removed his war robe and let it fall to the ground, then he stood in front of the old man. "I am no longer that nitwit deputy director of the department of armed forces, but rather the general of the present dynasty, in charge of the nation's foreign engagements and internal affairs. I'll kill anyone who doesn't listen to me, and if you dare not listen to me, I'll kill you, too."

As he was saying this, he punched the old man in the chest, striking so hard that he staggered backward. As Li Chuang did so, the old man—who had been petitioning for eighteen years and now no longer wanted to petition anymore, but who still didn't understand how the government worked, and simply didn't understand questions of national stability—stood there frozen. "You must be dreamwalking. If you are, I won't speak to you. Instead, I'll go speak directly to the mayor. I really don't want to continue petitioning. I really don't want to continue petitioning." As the old man said this, he edged toward the town government compound. Li Chuang jostled his way among the passersby who had assembled. He kept shoving and shoving, until finally he succeeded in pulling out a pole from somewhere. The pole was a foot long and as wide as a man's wrist. He abruptly brought it down onto the old man's head, and blood immediately gushed out. "Aiya . . . Aiya . . ." With these shouts, this lowly official who had been petitioning for eighteen years collapsed onto the town government steps.

The old man died on the town government steps.

Before dying, however, he gazed up at the sky and uttered one final cry: "I really won't petition anymore! I really won't!"

Blood followed the sound of his shout and flowed down the stairs. Father and I remained still at the bottom of the stairs. A sentry wearing a military uniform was a young man from the town government who was in his twenties and had secured his job because he and the town mayor shared relatives. He had been standing behind Deputy Director Li the entire time, and watched the commotion in front of him. When he saw the old man fall down the stairs, he ran back to the town government courtyard, shouting,

"Someone has died! Someone has really died!

"Someone has died. Someone has really died."

His shouts sounded like a house collapsing—like the heavens falling and the earth cracking open.

Deputy Director Li didn't move a muscle. He stood there motionless and stoic, like a high official. "I've been stationed on the frontier for three years now. The Xiongnu have already killed thousands upon thousands of people, and I'm afraid that one or more of you will create a disturbance." He dropped his pole and picked up his opera costume from the floor. Then he cast his gaze onto me and Father, who were both standing below the stage. "The two of you must be the father and son who run the New World funerary shop on Town Street, selling wreaths. I've just given you some additional business." He brushed the dirt from his costume. Actually, he wasn't sure whether or not there was any dirt on it, but he still went through the motions.

"I'm telling you—this is not the town government, but rather the Forbidden City's Throne Room. I am also not Deputy Director Li, but rather this dynasty's general commander. If any of you dare trespass on the imperial palace, create a disturbance, or disobey instructions, you will all fucking have to leave.

"You will have to leave, just like that troublemaker, Deputy Director Li."

While carefully patting his uniform, he turned around and headed into the town government's palace. Taking one step at a time, he proceeded slowly and deliberately. Under the lamplight, his shadow entered that old-style courtyard. This was the town government's courtyard. It was the majestic palace of that night of the great somnambulism.

Father and I watched this scene in shock. We felt chilled and our hands were trembling. The hand with which Father led me away was covered in cold sweat, and my own hand was covered in my father's sweat, which was so cold it felt like ice water. My entire body was covered in an icy cold sweat.

BOOK SEVEN

Geng 5, Part One: The Chicks and Birds Fly Away

1. (3:01–3:10)

We couldn't permit everyone to continue dreamwalking.

People died as easily as someone grinding his teeth while dreamwalking. They stole and looted as easily as someone mumbling something while dreamwalking. We walked back from the town government compound, but Father didn't have any idea how to stop everyone from dreamwalking. He asked Mother to take a gas stove and an aluminum pot out to the square, where he lit the stove, brought the water in the pot to a boil, and added several handfuls of tea leaves.

Then he went to the pharmacy and bought all of its realgar ice-crystal for dispelling sleepiness and refreshing oneself, and added that to the pot.

In the middle of the night, the town was pitch-black, but the fire in the square was burning bright. There were no dreamwalkers in the square, or else they had all escaped from their dreams. Instead, there were groups of awake people: three and five, or four and six, standing in the square drinking realgar brew and tea.

That night, my father became an extraordinary saint. He arranged for my mother and for the awake passersby to prepare more tea and realgar medicinal brew. He found a gong somewhere and began beating it while they walked up and down the town's streets and alleys, each of them shouting:

"Hey . . . On this night of the somnambulism, everyone needs to guard against theft and looting."

"Hey . . . The village chief and the members of the town government are all dreamwalking. My own family needs to guard against theft and looting."

"Hey . . . Everyone who is unable to conquer sleepiness should go to the square and drink some tea. Go drink some realgar brew. Your drowsiness will immediately be dispelled and you'll feel as though you just woke up."

Following the sound of his gong, many front doors and windows opened. It seemed as though all of the dreamwalkers really *were* going to gather in the square, where it was loud and noisy. They drank the tea and the realgar ice-crystal brew. As they were drinking, they discussed the events of that somnambulistic night. "How could they . . . ? How could they . . . ? How could they have let our Gaotian Town experience this once-in-a-century or once-in-a-millennium somnambulistic hysteria? Even if you are skeptical, you'll have no choice but to believe it." Footsteps resonated up and down the streets and alleys, and it seemed as though the entire world was filled with footsteps. Everyone was headed toward the square, to drink tea and hear extraordinary stories about the night of the great somnambulism.

A large crowd gathered in the square—so many people that it appeared as though they were holding a convention. The area was filled with the smell of tea and realgar ice-crystal brew. People were drinking while standing and squatting, and my mother was as busy as if she were at the market. She ladled several bowls of tea and the realgar ice-crystal brew from the pot, and distributed them to the people gathered in the square. As for my father, as he was banging his gong and heading south, he encountered two things—two things that I have no choice but to tell you about, Spirits.

The first is that as Father was hollering and striking the gong, he encountered someone. This person was anxiously emerging from a narrow alley, and seemed to be carrying a heavy sack on his shoulder. He put down his sack and rested for a while, and it was at that point that my father happened to walk by, shouting and striking his gong. The two men were standing about three to five paces apart, separated by the night's murky darkness. In struggling to discern who the other one was, each stared as though encountering a mortal enemy. "Who . . . ?" . . . "I . . . I'm Li Tian-bao." As Father said this, he walked toward the dark shadow in front of him. "Stop right there! If you take another step closer, I'll stab you!" My father came to a stop about two steps from the other man. "Li Tianbao, things are now even between our two families. When my father died, you must have been the one who informed the higher-ups that he had been buried, and for more than ten years I've been looking for an opportunity to beat you and break your legs, leaving you crippled like your wife. Now you've caught me trying to steal things, but if you don't report me, then we can call it even. In the future, neither of us will have any need to bear a grudge against the other." As he said this, the man began to lift the sack back onto his shoulder, but kept running into difficulty. My father walked closer and gave the man a hand, at which point the man turned and expressed his gratitude.

"Li Tianbao, thank you. From now on, you and I will be brothers."

My father finally recognized the man. His name was Zhao Huanhuan, and he lived on East Street. Father thought that it looked as though the man's bag were full of something like stone heads. In town, there was a stonemason who specialized in carving statues of Buddhas and Buddha heads. A Buddha head could sell for a lot of money, and whoever purchased it would have to burn several sticks of incense in front of it. The home of that stonemason who specialized in Buddhas was located in the alley from which the man had just emerged. Father watched as Zhao Huanhuan proceeded down the road. He expressed his thanks to my father, and his heart appeared to be full of gratitude. Father, however, didn't feel a trace of gratitude in his veins. "You've even stolen some Buddhas? How dare you steal spirits?" He watched as Zhao Huanhuan disappeared into the distance, and then he began heading back to the square. He wanted to beat his gong, but in the end he didn't. He wanted to continue shouting, but he was too lazy.

At this point, the second thing occurred. In the main street, the doors of some stores were open, while those of others were closed. The doors that were closed were locked from the inside, and were blocked with tables and bars. As my father left the southern part of town, he again saw a shadowy figure emerge from the stonemason's alley. This figure was carrying a leather bag and was pulling a suitcase. "Ershun, what do you have there? How is it that your hands are empty? Didn't you manage to grab anything?" The man obviously mistook my father for someone called Ershun. "Who are you? I'm not Ershun, I'm Li Tianbao." My father walked over and, as before, the two men stood facing each other in the dark. When they were a few paces apart, they finally recognized each other.

"Li Tianbao, I thought you were my brother, Ershun. Why are you carrying a gong? How much is a gong worth? It's not even worth as much as you would get from selling half a wreath."

"You are dreamwalking." My father gazed at the man, whose name was Dashun. "You, too, should go to the square to drink a bowl of the tea my family has brewed. The police and members of the town government are also dreamwalking, and several of them have gone there to drink tea."

"The fuck I'm sleeping!" Dashun laughed, then quickly became serious again. "So, it's you and your wife who are boiling tea in the square?" Dashun approached to look at Father's face. "Tianbao, you must want some tea leaves? This store specializes in selling suitcases and purses, but there is one counter full of tea leaves and other things. I don't drink tea and there is no one else in my family who does, so I didn't take a single box."

My father looked at the door out of which Dashun had just emerged.

"Go on in. You would be doing this on behalf of everyone, so it wouldn't count as stealing."

My father went inside.

He quickly grabbed several boxes of red oolong and green tea. He didn't know which kind of tea was best, nor which would be most effective in dispelling drowsiness. Instead, he simply picked the largest boxes. As he was emerging from the store with five or six boxes of tea, he discovered that Dashun had not left and was still standing outside the store waiting for him.

"You haven't left yet."

"I was standing guard for you." Dashun lifted the purse he was holding and pulled the suitcase in front of him. "This way, Li Tianbao, you have stolen things and so have I, so now both of us are thieves. When the sun rises tomorrow and people wake up from their dreams, I won't expose you, nor should you expose me. You and I are both thieves to equal extents, and neither of us is more innocent than the other."

As he said this, he smiled proudly. He looked again at Father, and walked away.

He walked away.

My father stood there staring in astonishment. In the end, he returned to that Luggage World store and placed the five or six boxes of tea back where he had found them.

He left them where he found them.

2. (3:11–3:31)

Spirits . . . People's spirits! I just told you about a minor matter, and now must tell you about a major one.

This was a very significant matter. Even the employees in the town government had begun dreamwalking. The townspeople had no choice but to look after themselves. A second gas stove appeared in the square, and the number of pots also increased. The two stoves produced a fire that pushed against the bottoms of the pots. However, these fires could heat up only a small pot, so someone had set up a large, clay stove. This brick and stone stove spat out flames from all sides. Pieces of dismantled doors and stools had been thrown into the stove, and the resulting fire lit up the entire street. There were small pots and large ones, aluminum ones and iron ones. The realgar ice-crystal brew was black and bitter, and no one was willing to drink it. Instead, everyone came to drink the tea, and take it away. There were three or four pots, or four or five, all being heated by a raging fire. The water came to a boil. In the light of the fire, they brewed the tea. The scent of bitter tea streamed freely through the night, extending to the mountains outside town. Soon, the entire world was pervaded by the fragrance of tea.

At this point, at this moment, some people brought over some coffee, which hardly anyone in the town had ever drunk before. It was dark brown and silky red, and when they opened the canister a red scent flowed out. They poured some boiling water, and added a spoonful of coffee grounds. In the water, the coffee looked like a piece of silk fabric in a fire. The townspeople with some worldly experience, who had drunk coffee before, began shouting.

"You need to add sugar and milk powder!

"You need to add sugar and milk powder!"

Someone brought out some white and brown sugar from home, and some infant's milk formula. With this, the coffee did, in fact, taste better—it had a bitter and sweet taste that resembled the licorice flavor of Chinese medicine. Drinking the coffee was like chewing on licorice when you are thirsty. They passed the coffee around, with everyone drinking a cup or half a cup. The coffee helped dispel everyone's drowsiness, making people increasingly excited and spirited, to the point that they no longer had any desire to sleep.

In the dark night, everyone's spirits were exactly as they had been during the day. It was as if it were a holiday. It was really as if it were a holiday, and they were having a performance.

I decided to take a bowl of coffee to the Yan household.

I wasn't sure whether or not anyone else in Yan's household was dreamwalking. It seemed, however, as though every household in town had dreamwalkers, so why would his be any different? When my father asked me to take a bowl of coffee to every household that he had previously betrayed, I also took one to the Yan household. Needless to say, this was the most famous household in our town, since Yan had written so many books, and earned so much money. On New Year's, both the town and the county mayor would go to his home to pay their respects. After Yan became an author, he would frequently leave town on business, and every time he returned home he would bring back the best and most expensive cigarettes. While out of town, he definitely would have had a chance to eat all sorts of delicacies and drink all sorts of expensive tea. He definitely would have also drunk a lot of foreign coffee. But tonight, he didn't necessarily have any tea or coffee to drink.

I saw that Yan had returned from the embankment. It appeared as though he was still in a somnambulistic state. He walked unevenly, and when he proceeded down the street he resembled a spirit walking over from the country path. This Yan Lianke, this person who became an author after leaving town, would return to town to spend a few nights when he didn't have a story to write. After spending a few nights in town, he would again come up with an idea for a story that would once again bring him fame and fortune. For Yan, this town and this village functioned the way that a bank did for a thief—offering him an inexhaustible warehouse full of goods. His novels *Time Like Water* and *Both Stiff and Hard* and *Kissing Lenin*— all of these works described events in our town and in the nearby Balou Mountains. Every detail in every story—even something as seemingly insignificant as a leaf on a tree—was as familiar to me as my hands and feet, my fingernails and toenails. But now, he was in his fifties and couldn't write anymore. Our town was still the same as before, and our days still passed just as before. The town's stories and random events continued to unfold as before, but he found that he could no longer write any new stories. He didn't even know *how* to tell a new story. Even after he returned and went to the picturesque reservoir near town, he still found himself unable to write. It seemed as though this inability to write had caused him to age precipitately. His hair turned gray, just like our town's Old Cao's. He no longer retained the pure and clean quality he had while traveling in the outside world, nor did he have the neat clothes or the look of delight that he once had.

He had aged. As a result of being unable to write, he had aged precipitately.

When he first left town he was not yet twenty years old, but in the intervening thirty years he had become overweight and somewhat hunchbacked. From his appearance, it was not at all obvious that he was an author, much less a celebrity. Apart from the fact that he had a trace of an outsider's accent, in all other respects he was just like one of the locals. He was just like the village's accountant. He had thin, graying hair, and the skin around his eyes resembled red grapes. But when he spoke in the local dialect he would occasionally add some unfamiliar words. None of the villagers realized that he had aged precipitately because he found himself unable to write. For the villagers, there was no obvious connection between the aging process and an inability to write. They could understand, for instance, why as Carpenter Zhao aged he would become less able to perform carpentry, or why as a large black dog aged it would no longer be able to run about as it used to, but as for Yan Lianke, everyone speculated that he must have developed some sort of illness after spending his entire life sitting at a desk and writing. To have back problems was a very aristocratic condition; and to the rest of us here, who frequently suffer from paralysis or terminal disease, his illness seemed as insignificant as a pebble beside a mountain. Particularly if you are someone whose medical expenses are covered. It was, therefore, to be expected that he would develop an illness from writing, and they couldn't understand why this needed to become a matter of life and death. This Yan fellow made everyone envious and jealous, and made everyone feel heartache and pity. This author had returned to town. I wanted to go see him. I wanted to take him a bowl of ice-crystal coffee to wake him up, as though I were taking an invalid a bowl of Chinese medicine capable of curing any illness.

I took a sleep-dispelling concoction consisting of ice crystals and coffee that had been brewed together, and headed to Yan's home.

When I arrived, what I found was as different from my expectations as though grains of sand were growing in a field of wheat, or rice plants were producing millet. No one knew how those ears of wheat had suddenly become ears of sand, nor could anyone transform the ears of millet back into ears of rice. That is how things were.

There was an old courtyard, and an old house. The courtyard was full of old willow trees that were so tall they could touch the sky. Yan's eighty-one-year-old mother lived in that courtyard, charged with guarding her ancestral roots. Perhaps she was very lonely. But what guard of ancestral roots isn't lonely? As I carried the ice-crystal coffee to Yan's home, the sound of my footsteps echoed to every lonely and isolated corner of the town. I had assumed that only Yan and his mother were living in that courtyard, but when I reached his alley—which was also our own family's alley—I heard the sound of crying coming from the courtyard. As I rushed up to the entrance of the Yan family home, I heard footsteps in the courtyard. As I was standing in the entrance to the courtyard, that scene became like an ear of wheat producing an ear of sand.

There was a light in the courtyard. There was a lantern hanging from a tree, an oil lamp sitting on the window ledge, and a candle sitting on the branch of a tree. The light from the courtyard flowed out the main entrance. Yan's elder sister had returned from her mother-in-law's home, and her husband had also returned. The neighbors from the alley had also come over, and the courtyard was crowded and noisy. Everyone was gathered around Yan as though around a deity suffering from hysteria. Yan was sitting in the center of his courtyard, and in front of him was a face-washing basin half-filled with water. There was a wet cloth in his mother's hand, as though she had just washed his face. His face was pale and anemic, as though it had been soaked in water. His head was covered in sweat. The sweat had also soaked his cotton shirt, and his pants legs. His face was pale, and tears were streaming down his cheeks. His face, that nondescript face, was common-looking with drooping jowls. He appeared dull and blank. He was staring off into space, as though he had glimpsed something from another world—a ghostly world that he could scarcely believe. At the same time, he also looked as though he hadn't seen anything at all. Or as though he had seen something, but was unable to talk about it. Therefore, his garlic-bulb-like nose in the middle of his face began to display a glimmer of life. He shuddered, then began to weep, as a bright, ugly sound emerged from his nose.

Arranged in front of him were more than a dozen copies of his books and books by others. There were also several manuscripts and a bottle of paste. It had been in order to retrieve these items that he had dreamwalked back to his house in the first place, and while dreamwalking he had maintained a wide smile and kept repeating the same phrase over and over again: "I have a story to write . . . I have a story to write." It was as if inspiration had suddenly struck, like flower petals raining down on him. The story's plot twists rushed toward him like a cloud of wheat fragrance, or as if a ripe, fragrant fruit had fallen to the ground. He kept speaking and mumbling to himself, and after he returned home he didn't look at anything, nor did he say anything to his mother, and instead he began rummaging through all of his cabinets and counters—looking for books, pens, and paper. "Inspiration has struck, so I have to jot this down . . . Inspiration has struck, so I have to jot this down . . ." At this point, his mother got out of her warm bed and saw that her son's sleepy face resembled a miswritten character. She saw that—apart from his mouth, which was still moving—the rest of his face was frozen, as though he were dead. His eyes remained open and were staring straight ahead, though they were as dull as a corpse's.

"You are dreamwalking . . . You are dreamwalking. . . ."

As she said this, his mother walked toward him. "Lianke, if you're dreamwalking, you should go wash your face."

"Mother, where is my pen and paper? I have a story I need to write. Inspiration has struck me like fruit that has fallen from a tree and landed on my head."

"You really are dreamwalking. Lianke, you really are dreamwalking."

"Where are those books that I left in the chest? When I begin to write, I need for the table and the room to be full of books. Only when I'm surrounded by piles of books do I feel as though I've returned home."

Yan's mother went to ladle out half a basinful of water, and as Yan was leaning over to look for his pen and paper, she tossed a wet towel onto his face. His face was hot and the water was cold, and he immediately gave a start and stared in surprise. He straightened his body and looked around, then covered his face with his hands, squatted down, and began to sob. "I can't write anything . . . I can't write anything at all . . ." He wept like a baby, as though suffering from hysteria. "If I can't write, I might as well die . . . If I can't write, I might as well die . . ." As he wailed, he squatted in front of his mother and covered his face with his hands. Tears streamed out from between his fingers, like a mountain spring pouring out of a crevice in the ground.

His mother didn't know what to do. She didn't know how to encourage this very accomplished son of hers.

He, meanwhile, continued to wail.

"What does it matter if you can't write? Won't you still be able to live comfortably, as before? Won't you still be able to live comfortably, as before?" His mother stood next to him, and patted her son gently on the head. Tears were also streaming down her own face. "If

I can't write, it's as if I were dead. It's as if I were dead!" he shouted to his mother, but between talking and shouting, he stopped crying. It was as if he remembered that he was a man in his fifties, and that his mother was in her eighties. He stood up, looked at his mother, then looked again at his old house. "So, this is what dreamwalking is like." He smiled humorlessly. "It never occurred to me that I might also dreamwalk. The reason I was dreamwalking was that these past several days I haven't been able to sleep, on account of not being able to write, and my fatigue accumulated until I began to dreamwalk." He returned with his mother from the outer room to the inner room, and even supported her as they stepped over the threshold. It was exactly as though he were returning from the sleeping world to the waking world. It was as if he were stepping back into his home, as if he were rolling down the window shades and returning from his dream to the real world. He sat down on his mother's bed and told her many things. He told her how he had seen people dreamwalking in a village on the embankment. It was as if while dreamwalking, he found the streets full of dreamwalkers. They were all dreamwalking. He also asked his mother—his mother, who had been alive for more than eighty years, from the Republican era to the present—whether, in this long, dark alley of time, she had ever witnessed a situation in which the entire world started dreamwalking. He asked whether she had ever witnessed a situation in which everyone, while dreamwalking, suddenly returned to a childlike state, where everything was either simply bad or simply good.

But in asking this, and without realizing it, he once again climbed into his mother's bed and fell asleep.

It was as though a soporific breeze had blown over his body, and the room was filled with the sound of his snoring and mumbling. "Go to sleep. Go sleep in that bed. Lianke, you need to get up and go to sleep in that bed." He made an effort to open his eyes, but after he went to the other room, it was as if he were entering another world. Standing on the border of this other world, he turned and looked at his mother, with a smile on his face. "Mother, I have a story to write. I reached out and grabbed a handful of inspiration, which gave me the idea for the beginning of a story." Then, with a broad smile, he began searching around furiously for a pen and paper, and for his books. He moved so quickly, it seemed as though he were from another world. He had an undecipherable expression, as his face instantly became an unreadable text. His eyes were open, but the only thing he could see was that space of his imagination. There wasn't any light in the distance, nor were there any things or people outside his imagination. "I have a story. I have a story that is different from everyone else's." As he was loudly muttering, he continued to laugh happily.

His mother stood in front of him. "Lianke . . . Lianke!" she shouted at him, as though attempting to wake him from his dream.

"Have you seen that book with the black cover? The book that you said had a cover that was as black as night?"

His mother came over and patted his shoulder. "Do you think you'll die if you stop wanting to write?"

"Now I won't." He smiled at his mother. "Now I have a story to write."

His mother slapped his face.

"If you don't wake up, you'll die inside your story."

He stared at his mother in astonishment.

"Quick, come out of your story," his mother roared like thunder. "If you don't, then you'll be written to death inside your own story."

Another slap landed heavily on his cheek, as a teardrop hung suspended on his mother's face.

The world calmed down. The town calmed down. The tumultuous house calmed down. Yan's body swayed back and forth.

His head also swayed back and forth. He no longer had a trace of excitement on his face, and instead his cheeks were blushing with embarrassment—like someone who had encountered some sort of abject humiliation. He woke up, he woke up from his dream. Looking at his mother, he rubbed his face, as though trying to rub away some sort of pain.

"I'm not going to write anymore. I'm not going to write another word as long as I live." He stated this quietly, yet firmly. "Actually, if I don't write, I'll be able to live much better. I'll be able to live better than anyone else." He lowered his hand and led his mother back into her room. In doing so, he wiped the tear from her face. But as he was leading his mother to her room, she instead dragged him toward the courtyard. "Sit down out here. The bedroom is hot and stuffy, and if you go inside you will surely fall back asleep." Mother and son proceeded to the courtyard, where a cool breeze was blowing. In the distance, clouds were floating over. There were old trees. It was an old courtyard, with old walls and columns. Everything was as peaceful as a thousand-year-old river, or an endless mountain ridge. Or like a night cloud that had continued floating uninterrupted for thousands upon thousands of years. Mother and son sat opposite each other in the courtyard. They could hear the sporadic sound of footsteps out in the alley and in the street. There was also the sound of my father's gong, as he was shouting for everyone not to sleep, so that every household would have someone to stand guard against thieves and looters.

"These are the shouts of Li Tianbao, who lives in the house behind us."

"Yes, it's him. But he's a good person."

"The funerary shop is good work, and the money simply pours in. Every month and every day, there will always be people needing to purchase funerary objects."

At this point, Yan's elder sister returned, as did her husband. Afraid that the dreamwalkers would enter the old courtyard, they had rushed back. They were both sitting in the courtyard, and because the light was on, the neighbors also hurried over. The neighbors gathered around Yan, and also gathered around the half-filled basin. They were all discussing recent chaotic events in town, including the great somnambulism. Whenever any of them felt drowsy, they would dip a towel into the water and wipe their face with it, to wash away their drowsiness. Yan's mother brought over a bowl of peanuts and a bowl of walnuts. Some neighbors also brought over some sunflower seeds. They brought over a table, put an assortment of items on it, then stood around the table and chatted. As though it were New Year's Eve, they resisted their drowsiness and somnambulism. While listening to the tumult out in the street, they talked about the crops, and the harvest. They discussed families who got into fights while competing over the wheat harvest, and how the families fought until they were bloody. They observed that dreamwalking was not entirely a bad thing, and recalled how, during a fight, someone's skull got bashed in and blood started gushing out. The aggressor was someone who was quite fierce during the day, and would say to his opponent, "If you fight me, that means you're my mortal enemy, and I'll knock your head right off your shoulders!" Although he was proud and arrogant during the day, at night he began sleepwalking and lost that heroic valor, and instead got some eggs and milk and went from house to house to apologize, saying, "I'm sorry. I'm sorry." He added, "It's my family that was at fault. It's my family that was wrong." He added, "Look at these dreamwalkers—it is not that they're all bad!" Dreamwalking, it turns out, could transform someone who is heroically bad into someone who is quietly good.

They proceeded to say millions of good things about dreamwalkers.

They asked what was so strange about dreamwalking, and added that there was an even stranger incident involving Ma Huzi's family from East Town. One of Yan's neighbors came to the front of the crowd and waved his hands frantically to underscore what he was saying.

"You remember that Ma Huzi died three years ago? Everyone in the village, and everyone in town, knows that he died from a terminal illness. But during this past half night, as soon as people began to doze off and dreamwalk, guess what happened! Ma Huzi's wife dreamwalked over to the town police station. She went to the police station to turn herself in. She said that her husband had not, in fact, died from a terminal illness, but rather she, after caring for her paralyzed husband for twelve years, couldn't bear it anymore, and put poison in his bowl.

"She claimed that for three years after her husband died, she had not had a good night's sleep. Her remorse over having poisoned him was so strong that it was as if she had injured her own parents. Tonight, after finally managing to enjoy a good night's sleep, she decided to turn herself in. She said, 'I know I'm dreamwalking, but it is only while asleep that I could have dared turn myself in. Because if I turned myself in, what would happen to my three children? My youngest is not yet three years old, and was born half a year after his father died. Now that I've come to turn myself in, however, none of you should wake me up. If you do, I'll deny that I poisoned my husband. Furthermore, you don't know what my husband said before he died. While foaming at the mouth, he said to me, "Thank you for sending me to the other side. This way I don't need to continue enduring this punishment. It is you who have completed me. But you mustn't tell anyone, because if you mention this to anyone, then our family will suffer a disaster and our children will end up not only without a father but also without a mother." '

"This is what happened.

"This is also what happened.

"If it hadn't been for the somnambulism, who would have ever known that Ma Huzi was killed by his own wife, or that she was even capable of something like this? Normally, she appeared to be so good and weak, so docile and obedient, so diligent and tolerant. The second year after they got married, Ma Huzi became paralyzed, so she began caring for him, and did so for the next twelve years. But, in the end, he died at her hands. Fortunately, there had been this night of somnambulism—a once-in-a-century occurrence. While dreamwalking, she had turned herself in and confessed the truth. Had it not been for this somnambulism, who would have ever learned the truth of what happened? She herself said that it is actually better when people are dreaming, because that way they are able to do everything they wanted to do during the day, when they are awake. 'If it had not been for this night of somnambulism, even if you killed me a hundred or a thousand times, I would never have admitted that I murdered my own husband.'

"It was very odd that she said this while dreamwalking. She added, 'I have turned myself in, but you mustn't wake me—because if you do, I'll simply deny everything. Instead, you must consider who will look after my children now that I have confessed.'

"She did indeed say this. It was all very odd.

"It was exceedingly odd that even while asleep she was nevertheless aware that she was asleep and that she was dreamwalking. So, was it indeed possible for people who are asleep to know that they are sleeping? And to instruct people, while they are sleeping, not to wake them up?"

Upon relating this bizarre story, the neighbor began to laugh, then he bent over and noisily washed his face. "I'm also feeling sleepy. You must make sure that I don't become infected with this somnambulism disease. Because if I am, there's no telling what I might say." He laughed as he said this, but no one else did. The others were all still absorbing the information that Ma Huzi had been murdered by his own wife. They were digesting the fact that a murderer could turn herself in while dreamwalking. Yan's eyes were as large as dates, or as a couple of rotten grapes, as he stared at the neighbor as though seeing someone he had never met. He stared at the neighbor as though staring at a key plot twist in a story.

"It's true.

"It's all true.

"Why can I not write a story about someone who knows she is sleeping while sleeping? About how she is able to interact with and speak to the waking world while still in her dreams?" Yan stood up and walked around the courtyard. As he passed the crowd of people, he spoke and continued walking. His face was flushed with excitement—so red that it looked as though there were a wet piece of silk stuck to his face. "I have another story—I have another story to write. I don't want people to claim that my inspiration has dried up, or that I'm in my sunset years." He laughed, producing a stupid cackling sound.

"Now inspiration is raining down onto my head like raindrops. It is blowing against my breast like a breeze . . . Mother . . . Sister . . . Apparently, you've both left. I want to return to my studio on the embankment. If I don't write this down, then after I wake up all of these stories will blow away like the wind.

"All of you should leave. I want to go to my studio on the embankment.

"You should leave. I want to go and write.

"All of you should walk and talk more slowly. I don't want you to wake me up, because if you do, my stories will disappear. My inspiration will also disappear, and even if I were to bang my head

The Day the Sun Died

against the wall, I still wouldn't be able to produce another novel. It is good to be asleep. While sleeping, people are indeed really good. Sleep is like the sun and rain—in that when sleep comes the crops start to grow, and when sleep is deep the crops become ripe, and are ready to be harvested and stored in the warehouse. I should take advantage of being asleep in order to write. All of you should leave. No one should bump into me, and no one should say a single word to me. Don't wake me from my dreams."

He continued walking as he said all this, his voice growing increasingly softer as he progressed from light into deep sleep. He walked around the courtyard, then began looking around his room for his books. He took his pen, pencil, and paper, together with the glue, paste, and tiny scissors that he couldn't do without when he was revising and editing. Finally, his crystal-clear voice degenerated into an indistinct mumble. His words and sentences became murky. His nostrils, which would always flare when he spoke, became still. His wide eyes were half-closed, as though he were so exhausted that he couldn't keep his eyelids open. The determination to write that had been visible on his face was now visible only in his eyes. It accumulated there. It was as if he had already sat down and was staring at the composition paper's individual boxes for writing Chinese characters.

Everyone quieted down. Everyone stared at Yan, who was standing there waiting for everyone else to leave, although in reality he had been planning to leave first. "Let him wash his face." Yan's mother pulled aside the person who said this; she also pulled aside Yan's sister and her husband. Then Yan's mother went over and stood in front of her son for a while. She stared at him, as though she had suddenly learned how to read and could finally understand the text written on her son's face.

"Do you really want to write?"

He nodded.

193

"When you aren't able to write, do you feel as though you were physically sick?"

He nodded.

"Do you really feel that living is no different from dying, and that if you are unable to write you would prefer to die?" His mother's voice suddenly became louder.

He was silent, looking as though he were pondering the question. Then he nodded very slowly and solemnly—like someone in court nodding to indicate whether he wishes to be executed by decapitation or by hanging. He didn't say a word, and instead sat in the light as though he had just drowned in a deep lake. The sky was very murky. The night was very murky. Yan's face had the murky look of a middle-aged man. A book he was holding fell to the ground, and he bent down to pick it up. The ice-crystal coffee I had brought had already cooled off. The coffee odor had disappeared, to the point that it seemed as though what I was holding was a bowl of ordinary flour-paste soup. Initially, I had been standing in the entrance to the courtyard, watching. Initially, I had been in the Yan family courtyard watching and listening, but I don't know when I put down the bowl I had been holding and instead squatted there watching and listening. In just the same way, I don't know who later told me about town matters from before I was born. And about world matters. And about matters relating to the Yan family. Because I was stupid, I forgot many things, and I even forgot myself. In particular, I forgot I had brought some drowsiness-dispelling ice-crystal coffee. Upon hearing someone discussing Ma Huzi's family situation, I felt as though I had fallen into one of Yan's novels. As I watched Yan walk back into his dream, back into his somnambulism, I felt as though someone had locked me in a dark room. Yan's mother stared at her son for a while, as though she had been staring at him for millennia. She said to the others, "Don't wake him up. Let him sleep." They stood there staring, like wooden puppets watching a puppet show. "He says that if he can't write, he'll go crazy and die, so just let him write. Even if he writes himself to death, he'll still feel as though he's alive." As Yan's mother said this, tears streamed down her face, like rain in the wilderness. "Given the fact that he has already become like this, let him stay that way. Let him live as though he were already dead, because being dead is just like being alive." When she finished, she looked at her son, and then gazed out into the night. She looked into the courtyard, and at the people standing there. Then she said something very simple but very solemn.

"No one wake him up. Let him sleep."

After this, she shifted her gaze from her son's face to his body, and then back to his face again. "You should go. Let your sister and her husband escort you back to your home on the embankment."

While asleep, Yan was calmly pondering, as though he had woken up. "There is no need for them to escort me. If they do, they may wake me up, and if I wake up, my story will dissipate. It will fly away, and I will be left without any inspiration. If I'm unable to write, then life will be even worse than death." He was sleeping as though still awake, and he faced the night as though it were daytime. He looked at his mother. He looked at his elder sister, her husband, and their neighbors. Then he picked up his things and left. "All of you go back." Saying this, he, like a shadow, climbed the stairs, went down the hallway, then out into the night streets and alleys. His footsteps sounded like wooden mallets striking a soft and hollow surface. He swayed back and forth, then gradually fell into a rhythm. It was a rhythm, but was also like a breeze. In this way, swaying back and forth while still asleep, he walked away. His mother and sister both came out of the courtyard to watch him, as though watching a dream, and in the dream they were watching a willow tree on the shore swaying back and forth in the wind.

He walked away.

The night fell even further.

The people prayed that the sun would come soon, and that everything would return to normal.

3. (3:32–4:05)

It was I who escorted Yan back to his house up on the embankment. It was I who wanted to escort him.

His family said, "You are small and your footsteps are light. You won't wake him, so you should escort him to his house on the embankment." They also urged me not to speak to him on the way there, so as not to wake him. However, I spoke to him anyway. I couldn't help speaking to him. He walked in front of me with one heavy step followed by a light one. Unable to see the road clearly, he would occasionally step into a hole. Each time he did so, he would suddenly lunge to one side, and I would think that this would surely wake him up. But instead, he would merely mutter, "There's a hole here," and continue forward. As he proceeded, he would periodically kick a brick or a stone, and would then lift his aching foot and cry, "Aiya, Aiya," and walk away. I followed him, like a lamb following its mother. Whenever he stepped into a hole or kicked a stone, I would step forward and support him, and as soon as he walked away, I would follow him. We passed through the town's alleys as though through a tunnel beneath a dam. When we finally reached a broad, flat road, it was as though we had reached a large square. By this point there was no one in the square—only bricks and stones, for the stove used to brew tea and coffee, and the lingering scent of tea and coffee.

Everyone had dispersed.

Everyone drank realgar tea and ice-crystal coffee. This dispelled drowsiness, and therefore everyone stopped dreamwalking. Out in the streets, meanwhile, there were still the shadows and footsteps of the last people taking home their pots for brewing tea. It was like the nighttime movement that one would originally have expected. Apart from Yan, who was walking in front, I very much wanted to find one or two more dreamwalkers. But in the town streets there was only lamplight and stillness, and there were no more dreamwalkers to be found. Occasionally I could hear screams—but these were not the sort that one would hear from someone being chopped down and killed, but rather the kind one might hear from someone who glimpses a shadow but then realizes that it is just a cat or a dog.

Surely, the night of the great somnambulism couldn't possibly have concluded so easily? How could it have ended so simply? But the town streets were, in fact, now as still as a grave. I was rather startled, and also a bit afraid. I instinctively stepped forward and grabbed Yan's hand, like a frightened child grabbing his father's hand. Yan's hand was warm and soft. His palm was soft and supple, and completely lacking in strength. This hand was completely different from my father's. Because of this hand, I began speaking to him, asking him a series of questions.

"How many years has it been since you left Gaotian?

"Was this return trip worth it? You arrived just in time to find the entire village, and the entire town, in the middle of a great somnambulism.

"What did you see while asleep? How can someone know he's sleeping while he's sleeping?"

He turned to me, then patted me on the head and laughed.

"In my next novel, I'll write about dreamwalking. This is a gift heaven has sent me in my moment of despair."

It turned out that dreamwalking was a gift—a gift from the spirits in heaven. I myself suddenly wanted to dreamwalk. Moreover, like Yan, I wanted to be able to know I was dreamwalking while dreamwalking. It would be like being able to observe the events of this world while in another world, or knowing that you are still alive even after you've died. I held Yan's hand, and carried his books for him. We walked past the square, and past East Street and West Street. I saw that the door of my family's funerary shop was open and there was a light on inside. I wanted to go in and tell my parents that I was escorting the dreamwalking Uncle Yan back to the house he had rented on top of the embankment. In the end, I only thought about doing this, and didn't actually return home or to our family's shop. I saw that there were people in a clothing shop stealing things and carrying them away, and I wanted to exclaim, "Stop! People are no longer sleepy, and the store owner will return and grab you!" But in the end, I only thought about doing this, and didn't actually walk over there. I saw that in the fields outside the town people had hung a lantern from a tree branch and were harvesting wheat. After every few swipes of the scythe, they would pull the tree branch out of the ground and move it forward. I wanted to go up and say, "You should return home and drink some tea, and also brew a bowl of realgar ice crystals and drink it as well. When others drink this, they immediately stop feeling sleepy and stop dreamwalking." At the same time, it also occurred to me that dreamwalking might well be a good and beautiful thing for some people, so why was I trying to wake them up?

I didn't end up doing any of the things I had thought of doing, so I was the complete opposite of people who are dreamwalking, who generally end up doing everything that comes to their minds. If people are able to do whatever they are thinking, isn't that a dream come true? I wanted to ask Uncle Yan about his novels. I wanted to know how much money he earned from writing a book. I wanted to ask him to bring me some more books when he returned. Therefore, I asked again—as though beginning to sharpen my scythe.

"Uncle Yan, do you think it is better for people to spend their lives listening to stories, or to focus on telling stories to others?

"Uncle Yan, can you tell your stories more warmly? Whenever I read your books, I always feel chilled to the core. The *yin* in your books is simply too strong. When I read a book in winter, I want for that book to contain a warm stove, and when I read a book in summer, I want for that book to have an electric fan.

"Uncle Yan . . . Uncle Yan, ah, Uncle Yan!"

We proceeded to the end of the town's South Street, and stopped under the square's pagoda tree. This was an old tree—like the one under which people from Shanxi's Hongdong County gathered to begin their migration. The trunk was so wide that two grown men couldn't reach around it. The tree was over two hundred years old, but its branches were still as strong and dense as an umbrella's spokes, and its canopy blocked the wind and rain as effectively as an umbrella's canvas surface. The base of the tree was protected by a wall of bricks and stones, like a younger generation looking after its elders. I stood beside that pile of dirt and said, "Uncle Yan, you know, all of your books are about occurrences in our village and our town. But other than myself, no one in the village or the town actually likes your books. Apart from myself, no one is even able to read one of your books from beginning to end. People all ask what your books are about. Actually, you could take any classic novel—whether it be *The Romance of the Three Kingdoms* or *The Water Margin* or *The Investiture of the Gods* or *The Three Heroes and Five Gallants*—and literally open it to any random page, and what you would find would definitely be better than any of your books. What this means is that your books aren't worth a cent. They are like the spirit money we sell in our shop, which, although it nominally is money, you could throw to the ground and no one would give it a second glance."

Uncle Yan stared in alarm.

As Uncle Yan stared, he released my hand. He looked down at my face, the way a fortune-teller might stare at a divination book. The night was murky, but the moon was bright. I saw Uncle Yan's face, which was like an undecipherable divination book. I looked at him, and he looked back at me. Then, he pulled me over to sit down on that wall under the pagoda tree and proceeded to ask me some very peculiar questions—some very mysterious and abstruse questions, like a woman unable to bear children who goes to a bodhisattva to ask when she will be able to get pregnant.

"Niannian, tell Uncle Yan the truth, which of his books do you like the best?

"Tell Uncle Yan the truth, which of his books describes the events of our village and our town most accurately?

"Niannian, Uncle Yan is begging you to tell him about your family's and your uncle's affairs. Your father, your mother, and your uncle—the things they've done in their lives all concern momentous matters of life and death for us. I want to write a book about life and death in our village. Once I have finished, hopefully not only will you enjoy it, but furthermore the other people in the village and the town who can read will also enjoy it. Tell me, tell me—tell me about your father, your mother, and your uncle. If you do, then the next time I come, I'll bring you more books. Your Uncle Yan may not have written any good books himself, but he can bring you many good ones."

"What books?"

"I'll bring you a copy of *The Plum in the Golden Vase*. It's so good, it's out of this world."

In the end, I didn't tell Uncle Yan about my family. Instead, I kept my lips sealed and refused to say a single word. I didn't realize that what he said and asked while dreamwalking was completely without rhyme or reason, but I looked up at his face and saw that it really truly resembled a pile of books full of miswritten characters, or a divination book that no one can understand. However, I was not dreamwalking, nor was I stupid, as everyone thought I was. I certainly wouldn't tell him my family's matters simply for a copy of a "Golden" something or a "Plum" something. I didn't tell him about my uncle and the crematorium, nor did I tell him that my father was a local informer who encouraged the higher-ups to cremate corpses that had been illegally buried, and who had also hidden barrel upon barrel of corpse oil in a cave under the embankment—right next to the courtyard Yan had rented for his studio. "What is there to tell about our family? We eat food, we put on our clothes, and when someone dies, we may sell a wreath and earn a bit of money. We then use this money to buy colored paper to make more wreaths, and gold foil with which to make funerary ornaments. With whatever remains, we buy some food to eat."

I didn't say anything else.

I didn't know what to say. The moon and clouds were slowly passing overhead. We walked away—we left the pagoda tree and headed toward the embankment. We left without saying anything else. We were no longer as close as we had been. I didn't tell him I felt a bit ashamed and conflicted when it came to what my family had done, as though I had stolen something from him, owed him something, or had somehow done him wrong. In order to regain the intimacy we had enjoyed beneath that pagoda tree, I took his hand and asked him piles of intimate questions.

"Uncle Yan, do you think people spend their lives telling other people stories, or do they spend their lives listening to the stories that others tell them?

"Uncle Yan, when I grow up, do you think I should leave Gaotian, as you did, or should I stay here with my parents?

"Uncle Yan, when a man gets married, do you think he should look for only one woman, or for two or more?"

In this way, we soon arrived at the embankment. Up on the embankment, I felt that we were closer to the sky. Closer to the moon and the clouds. I felt we were farther from the world of Gaotian, from the bustling life of the villagers who were fighting and dreamwalking, and from their eating, dressing, sowing, weeding, chatting, drinking, and sleeping. When we reached the entrance to the courtyard that Uncle Yan had rented on the embankment, I saw that the reservoir below was perfectly blue, as though all of the light from the moon had been stored there. It was as bright as a mirror, as ice, or as a dream. There was a breeze blowing, and some lonely voices drifted over. I saw an owl, which was standing in a nearby field with eyes like a pair of red lanterns. I saw the funeral parlor, and on the distant hill its lights resembled a couple of clouds that had descended from the sky. The two of us stood in his entranceway, and the prospect of parting hung like a frosted leaf over his face and over my heart. In the end, we had no choice but to part, since he had to go to sleep. If he had fallen down while dreamwalking, he probably would have fallen asleep, but instead he continued talking and writing as usual. Everything he thought and did was just like what he wrote about in his novels. Perhaps as soon as he went inside, he would sit down and begin writing a novel that would function as a warm stove in winter and a cool electric fan in summer. For the sake of this book, we had to separate—but as we were parting, he told me something my own parents had never told me.

"Niannian, you should continue to learn from your parents how to make funerary paper ornaments, so that when you grow up you can make a good living.

"Niannian, if a girl likes you, you should marry her. Heaven and God have decreed that each man should have only one woman.

"Niannian, you should leave. Uncle Yan wants to take advantage of his somnambulism to write a story. Uncle Yan wants to follow your suggestion, and write about a warm stove in winter and a cool fan in summer. A book that the villagers and townspeople will all want to read."

He patted my head, and proceeded into his courtyard. After telling me to go home, he shut the courtyard gate.

I continued standing in the entranceway, as though I were slowly falling into a dream or into a well. I again thought about the somnambulism. I thought about the town and the village. I thought about my parents, but then felt a sudden chill. I shuddered, and wondered whether or not anyone would take advantage of the somnambulism to steal from my family. I wondered whether, in order to steal from us, someone would tie up my parents and beat them. With my mind feeling like a bolt of lightning just before a downpour, I left Uncle Yan, and left his house up on the embankment.

I rushed home.

BOOK EIGHT

Geng 5, Part Two: Some Are Living and Some Are Dead

1. (4:06–4:26)

When I reached the entrance to the funerary shop, I froze in my tracks.

I felt as though a brick had smashed into my head.

It was just as I had feared, and I felt as though I had already glimpsed what was happening in our funerary shop from the embankment two *li* away. I frantically pushed open the door and stood in the entranceway. My sudden arrival startled my parents and the two thieves. The light glowed, as lights do. Wreaths, spirit money, and paper ornaments were scattered around the room as though a strong gust of wind had just blown the flower blossoms and the green leaves to the ground. There were also broken stems and branches from the fruit trees, trampled twigs from the wreaths and bamboo baskets, and the wire and sticks used to make funerary figurines, together with painted busts of boys and girls—all scattered on the ground and piled against the garden wall. Inside the room, red and yellow items were fluttering around and hanging down, against a blue-green and violet-crimson background, like a flower pond shattered by hail. It was extremely cold, but also extremely hot. Mother and Father were tied to chairs positioned on opposite ends of the room, and the faces of the two men were obscured by their masks. The taller man was standing with his arms crossed, while the shorter one was holding a wooden pole that was as thick as his arm. Sweat was running down the thieves' necks, chests, and backs, but they seemed to have no desire to remove their masks. Instead, they stood there, staring at my parents while waiting for something. Their eyes were visible through the holes in their masks, appearing both dark and bright, and not at all sleepy. They were wide awake, as a result of either having been woken by my father or having drunk my mother's tea. After waking up, they may have taken advantage of the general somnambulism to try to steal things. As for my parents, who were tied up and sitting on opposite sides of the room, their faces were a mixture of white, yellow, and yellowish-white, and were covered in sweat, as though they had gotten caught in a rainstorm. The thieves periodically stared ahead, then glanced at the stairs leading to the second floor, and into the inner room. They seemed to be waiting for something, but I didn't know what. It also seemed that they were waiting for me to push open the door and walk in.

I stopped in the entranceway, and stood there staring straight ahead. It was precisely as I had imagined, like a screw fitting perfectly into a screw hole. I had assumed that if someone were going to rob our family's store, he would be wearing a full-face mask or else would have a handkerchief over his face, and these men were, in fact, wearing masks. I had thought that if someone were going to rob us, it definitely wouldn't be just one person, and, in fact, it turned out to be two people. And perhaps it wasn't just two people, but rather three—because otherwise why would the thieves keep glancing upstairs? Also, I had assumed that if people came to rob us, they would definitely rip up those wreaths and paper ornaments and scatter them everywhere, and, in fact, the room looked as though a hurricane had swept through it.

Everything was exactly as I had imagined it.

It was like a screw fitting perfectly into a screw hole.

I entered the room and stood there staring in shock, astonished by the fact that everything was exactly as I had imagined it. I looked at Father, and at Mother. Then, when I looked again at the two thieves, the taller one lunged forward and brought his hand down on my shoulder. Grabbing my shoulder as though it were a gold brick, he pulled me inside, and I was standing directly in front of him. Just as I was thinking that my parents were going to say something, my father exclaimed, "He is still a child. Daming, why don't you let him go?" My father struggled to come toward me, ripping the paper blossoms under his chair. "Don't call me Daming! I already told you, I'm not Daming! Didn't you hear me?" The tall thief went over and kicked Father's chair. When Father didn't respond, the thief kicked the chair again until his foot hurt, then he hopped around the room gasping in pain.

The shorter one, who was carrying the wooden pole, suddenly burst out laughing.

The taller one glared in annoyance, whereupon the shorter one immediately fell silent.

"Don't grab him. Don't frighten the boy!" Mother also leaned forward. Her voice was urgent and pleading, but also somewhat calm. "We are all fellow townspeople, and after tonight—after everyone wakes up—won't we still see one another?" As she said this, Mother gazed at the two thieves, but they placed no stock whatsoever in what she said. "We aren't from your Gaotian Town." The shorter one waved his wooden pole at Mother. "If we were from the same town, do you think we'd come and steal from you, or from your funerary shop? If someone were going to steal from anywhere, who would steal from a fucking funerary shop? Given that your fellow townspeople have already robbed the town's valuable stores, outsiders like us need to rob a shop like yours so that we won't have to leave empty-handed." He said this as though offering an explanation. At least it sounded like an explanation, but his voice was so loud and coarse it seemed as though it could shake the blossoms that blanketed the ground. At this point, the sound of footsteps could be heard coming from the inner room. The sound was somewhat familiar to me—like the way that, while eating, I would knock my chopsticks against the side of my bowl. When I turned to see who it was, I saw two fat men come down the steps. One of them was carrying a backpack, and the other was holding a bag. As they came forward, they put their masks back on while shaking their heads at the original two thieves, who were watching them.

They shook their heads with a look of disappointment.

It was also with great disappointment that the tall thief grabbed my shoulder and pulled me toward him. "Niannian, you returned at precisely the right time. Tell me where your family's money is hidden! This is the season of death and everywhere—both in town and out of town—people are dropping like wheat being harvested. Therefore, business at your family's funerary shop must be as good as this year's wheat crop, but we've searched your house upstairs and downstairs, and have found only a few hundred yuan. Who do you think you're fooling?" As he said this, he gently turned my body, such that I was facing Father, with my back against his belly and his thighs. He gripped my throat with his arm, as though trying to choke me, as though he were trying to squeeze money right out of my throat, and I felt as if I was being strangled. Sweat poured down my forehead like water streaming down a mirror that had just been pulled out of a pool, or like rain pouring from a house's awning during a thunderstorm. I felt as though he were lifting both my feet off the ground. A button from his sleeve got jammed into my mouth and caught in my throat, and I wanted to cough, but the button was wedged in my throat such that I couldn't cough it out, nor could I talk or even breathe.

"How do you expect him to say anything if you're choking him? How do you expect him to say anything?" As Father struggled to speak, the shorter of the two thieves pushed him back, and he was once again sitting where he had been. But even as Father's body returned to its original location, his voice continued to resonate throughout the room. "Let him speak . . . let him speak. . . . Wherever he says there is money, you can go look there.

"You can also have him go look on your behalf. But how is he going to be able to help you if you choke him? How is he going to be able to help you if you choke him?" As my father shouted, he stomped his feet. He was struggling to stand, but despite his best efforts, he couldn't get out of his seat.

The taller thief loosened his grip on my neck, and air rushed in like wind through an open door. I coughed repeatedly, and the hot sweat on my forehead and face quickly cooled. I knew that I would no longer feel sleepy, and therefore wouldn't dreamwalk. I felt wide awake as though my brain were a block of ice or covered in icicles. "Don't you just want some money?" I turned to look at the thief who had been choking me. His nose was poking through his mask, while the area in front of his mouth had a damp patch from his breath.

"If you want money, you shouldn't choke me like this, because if you do, how am I supposed to get you money?

"I know where the money is.

"Listen to me, and I promise you'll end up with a lot of money.

"Why steal from a funerary shop when you could rob the crematorium? How much do you think our family possibly earns from selling each wreath? And furthermore, we still need to buy food and clothing, and pay the rent. The crematorium, however, needs only a bit of oil and electricity to cremate each body. When people go to a hospital for treatment, they may try to bargain for a cheaper price, but after someone dies and is sent to be cremated, no family would dream of trying to bargain for a cheaper price, and instead the relatives simply pay however much the crematorium asks. So, rather than coming to steal from our funerary shop, you should go steal from the crematorium."

No one spoke or even moved. Instead, everyone stayed frozen like a statue. It was very hot and stuffy in the room. The short, fat thief wanted to remove his mask to get some air, but when the tall, fat thief turned to stare at him, the man quickly pulled his mask back over his face. Some people were walking down the street, and looked in our direction. One was carrying something, and shouted, "Even the funerary shop is being robbed." Then he walked away, laughing. Father looked at me, as did Mother. The thieves looked at me, then exchanged glances with one another through the eyeholes in their face masks. Their eyes appeared bright and happy, as though I had just helped them think of something—as though I had reminded them where the key to the front door of a bank or a safe-deposit vault was located. The tall, fat man suddenly tossed aside the bag he was carrying and laughed. "Fuck, why didn't we think of that?"

The taller one stared at the bundle on the ground, a skeptical look hovering over his eyes like mist over a pond.

"It's just a bedsheet, and not worth anything." As the fat one said this, he glanced at the tall one. The two of them had a quick conversation with their eyes, during which the short and fat thief on the stairs tossed down the items they had with them. Then, the tall thief looked again at the short one, whereupon the short one threw his pole to the ground. Then, all four men removed their ski masks and proceeded to use them to wipe their sweaty faces. My parents and I saw that the tall thief was Sun Daming from Third Street. The fat one was Daming's cousin—his mother's nephew—from a neighboring village, but I didn't know his name. The other two were also from neighboring villages—they were the children of Daming's uncle. The four of them were all relatives who had come out to steal together. Although they were neither sleeping nor dreamwalking, they were taking advantage of this night of the great somnambulism to steal things. After removing their ski masks, they stood in the middle of the room, and Daming told the short thief to go untie my mother, and told the tall one to go untie my father. Then he stepped forward and stood in front of my father.

"Li Tianbao, tell me the truth. After my father died, was it you who informed the crematorium that he had been buried?"

My father shook his head, and rubbed the marks the rope had left on his wrist. "If it were up to me, I would have preferred to die tonight while dreamwalking, without realizing it." Father looked around the room, then turned to Mother. "There's still tea in the pot in the kitchen. If you drink some, you will no longer be sleepy, and will no longer do nonsensical things." When the fat thief heard this, he laughed, then stepped up to my father. "It was precisely because we were confused that we didn't come out sooner to take advantage of the somnambulism to steal things. That's why we didn't come out until now, after all of the town's stores had already been robbed bare." Then he looked at his cousin Sun Daming, and declared to my parents, "We'll return all of your things to you. If you didn't inform on my cousin, then we don't have a score to settle with you. Now you just need to let Niannian accompany us for a while."

Father stood up, as though he wanted to retrieve me from Daming's grasp. But Sun Daming pulled me to his chest. He laughed coldly.

"Don't you despise the boy's uncle? The entire town knows that you and your wife bear a grudge against her elder brother, but that neither you nor your wife can take any action against him. Tonight, my cousins and I will help you get your revenge." He let his gaze come to rest on my mother's face, and seeing that she appeared pale and scared, he softened his tone and said, "Sister, don't worry. We won't do anything to your brother. For the past ten or more years, he has been profiting off other people's deaths. You know that this is true. Don't you often say, 'He is my elder brother, so what can I do? What can I do?' If there's nothing you can do, we can do it for you. We'll take advantage of tonight's somnambulism to go to his house and claim his dirty money. If we're lucky, we'll be able to steal a lot of it, and use it to build a public bridge over the river above the town; and if we aren't, at the very least we'll be able to reclaim the cremation fees that our relatives have unjustly had to pay over the years."

Then, they pushed me out the door.

My parents stood there, astonished, and watched us leave.

I followed them out.

Out in the street, everything was as dark and murky as before. It was as if the nighttime had remained stuck there and hadn't moved. Compared with inside the room, it was much cooler outside, so everyone took a deep breath. We didn't know what time of night it was. Everyone stood in the doorway of the funerary shop and looked around. At this point, my parents finally came to their senses and rushed outside. "Daming . . . Niannian is still a child. Regardless of what I, Li Tianbao, may have done wrong in this life, I've never done anything to your family. I'm begging you not to let anything happen to Niannian. I'm begging you to let him return soon, since he is our only child."

Daming turned and looked back at the funerary shop, and at my parents. "Why don't you clean up your house? As long as we don't start dreamwalking, we won't let anything happen to Niannian." Then they walked away. Their voices resonated down the street like water rushing down a river.

2. (4:30–4:50)

It turned out that they were riding a motorized three-wheeled cart.

It turned out that the cart had been hidden in a dark corner of the street.

It turned out that the cart was empty except for some cloth sacks, iron rods, and scythes.

It turned out that they had no intention of robbing the crematorium, and instead they planned to rob the home of my uncle, the crematorium director. They pushed me into the cart, making me sit in front. They told me to hold on tight to the railing, so that I wouldn't fall off. Looking after me as though I were their own brother, they made me feel as though my heart were being warmed in an oven on a cold winter day, or as though it were being cooled by a breeze on a hot summer day. The motorized cart backed out of the shadows, and then with a puttering sound it rumbled out of town. On the road, we saw others driving the same sort of cart, as people stood on the other side of the street and shouted, "You've struck it rich!"

"The fuck we have! Other townspeople have already robbed the stores bare."

"Then rob their houses."

"But they've fucking drunk tea and shit-piss coffee ice crystals and are no longer sleepy, and are no longer dreamwalking. So, how do you expect us to steal from them?"

A motorized cart heading into town suddenly stopped by the side of the road.

Daming and his cousins, meanwhile, continued heading out of town, into the dark night.

"Where are you going?"

"We're going home to rest. We're no longer interested in trying to strike it rich."

As Daming and his cousins shouted this response, they saw the other cart pause on the side of the road, hesitating about whether to continue into town or proceed to another village, but in the end it turned around and left.

Then they saw another cart heading toward them.

"How are things in town? It is possible to strike it rich there?"

"Go quickly. The entire town is dreamwalking, and the doors to every house and store are wide open."

"Then why is your cart empty?"

"Our cart? We didn't want those large items, but rather only what we could fit in our pockets."

As Daming said this, he stood up in his cart and heroically patted his pockets. The other cart rushed even more quickly toward town, with its occupants shouting and hollering as though they were enjoying a New Year's Eve party.

It turned out that there were countless people from the countryside riding tractors and motorized carts, and driving cars and trucks. Tonight, they were all either rushing into town or heading toward the county seat. They were heading anywhere they could find valuables. They were all trying to strike it rich. I saw someone sleeping, and his head periodically slipped down, appearing as though it would have fallen off had it not been held up by his neck. Some people were dreamwalking, but they looked as though they were still awake. They were staring straight ahead with faces that resembled the boards of a coffin. But there were even more people whose faces didn't seem to have a trace of drowsiness. They were wide awake, but were taking advantage of the great somnambulism to steal things. I didn't know what time it was. Perhaps it was already four or five in the morning— either the *yin* period or the *mao* period—when most people are asleep. The fat man riding on our cart had fallen asleep, and in his dreams he was saying, "I want to go home and sleep, I want to go home and sleep. What is there to steal?" The man's brother patted him on the shoulder, whereupon the other man woke up and began saying something different. "My entire life I've never had a chance like tonight. After one succeeds in making a fortune, it will always be possible to earn additional money." However, it was at this point that Daming told his short cousin, who was driving the cart, to pull over to the side of a road outside town. Daming then led me to the center of the cart bed, which was as large as a tatami mat, and told me to sit or squat there. The dark night surrounded me and the cart was like a cool lake, making it a perfect time to go to sleep. There were no dreamwalkers harvesting or threshing wheat in the fields by the roadside. Instead, the world was quiet and asleep, but it was also in tumult. Everyone was dreamwalking, and everywhere there were faint sounds and movement. Daming gazed up at the sky and down the road. When he finally looked back at me, his eyes were as bright as tiny black specks of light. "Niannian." He rested his hand with the mask on my shoulder.

"Your uncle is not a good man, is he?

"Your uncle got rich on our death money, isn't that right?

"Even today, if the relatives of the deceased don't offer your uncle gifts, he won't completely reduce the corpse to ashes, and instead will smash its bones with a hammer right in front of them. Isn't that right?

"Your uncle always makes customers pay for a marble cinerary urn, but then gives them only an ordinary stone one. Isn't that right? He always makes them fork over money for the price of a casket made of real mahogany, but then gives them only one made of ordinary wood. You know this to be true, right?

"Your father hates your uncle, and your father is kind and gentle, but given that Shao Dacheng is your uncle, your father has no choice but to have your mother add several paper blossoms to the wreaths she sells to the families of the deceased, and to use high-quality cloth and tight stitching for their burial shrouds, and to make sure that the embroidery is strong and beautiful, and all the villagers and townspeople know this and have seen it with their own eyes, and they all say that your parents are good people but that your uncle would be better off dead, and they say that your mother married your father precisely in order to be able to escape your uncle, and that your parents have spent their entire lives attempting to absolve your uncle's sins and repay his moral debts, and everyone from the town and the village knows, and you yourself know, that your parents and your uncle are positioned at opposite ends of the heavenly scale of justice, and even as your uncle is at one end earning soiled money, your parents are at the other end trying to do good deeds and repay your uncle's moral debts, and the more money your uncle earns, the more he sins, and the more your parents have to do good deeds on this side of the scale to compensate for his actions, such as by making their wreaths and paper ornaments better than usual, and selling them cheaper than usual, and although your family's store may appear to be doing good business, in reality it is not making very much money at all, which is why we weren't able to find anything at your house tonight, nor did we take any of your things, and this is all because your parents are good people, which made it impossible for us to take action, and it was on behalf of your father, your mother, and your entire family that we decided to leave your home empty-handed and accept your recommendation that we rob not your house but rather the crematorium, though now, looking back, we have decided that on behalf of your father, your mother, your entire family, and everyone in and outside the town, we have decided not to rob the crematorium, but rather to go directly to your uncle's home and rob it, and in this way we can help resolve the enmity that your father, your mother, and you yourself bear toward your uncle, as well as everyone who bears enmity toward the crematorium, so now you won't need to accompany us to the crematorium or to your uncle's villa, given that it would be awkward for you to see your uncle, which is why at this point we just need for you to tell us the specific address of your uncle's residence in that scenic residential compound up on the embankment, and tell us where your uncle normally hides his money and his valuables, and where he hides the jewelry belonging to his wife, which is to say, your aunt, and given that I know that your father doesn't often go to visit your uncle, and neither does your mother, since she has a hard time walking, that means that in your family, you are the only one who often goes, and if you tell us what we need to know, you are welcome to get off the cart and return home, where your parents are waiting for you, and furthermore we can't bear to drag you with us as we continue robbing until dawn, because in the event you were to have an accident, we would be letting you down, and also letting down your parents, so you should just tell us the specific address of your uncle's villa and where he hides his valuables, and you will then be free to return home, where you and your parents can close the door to your funerary shop and go to sleep, and at daybreak tomorrow, regardless of what happens, I won't blame you or call you out, but rather we will feel extremely grateful to you and your parents, and tomorrow we will purchase many things and go visit you at your home, and will even give your family a portion of the valuables that we take from your uncle's villa, so that you won't have told us this information for nothing, and so that your parents won't have paid and suffered for your uncle's sins over the past decade for nothing.

"Niannian, tell us! We just need you to say a few things.

"That's right. If you tell us these things, you will accumulate considerable virtue on your family's behalf.

"Niannian, you should get off the cart and go home to sleep. If you run into people who are awake or dreamwalking on the way, you mustn't speak to them, and you definitely mustn't tell them what we are doing."

After he finished, I got down from the cart.

I watched as Daming and his cousins turned at the three-way intersection and disappeared into the night. In the distance, there was a light where my uncle lived, as though the sun were about to rise. In the villages closer by, there were also lights and sounds, as though everyone had already woken up and was preparing to get out of bed.

Standing at the three-way intersection, I remained in the pit I had dug, where I felt cold and chilly. I didn't feel at all sleepy, and I felt as awake as though someone had thrown open doors and windows after the sun came up.

3. (4:51–5:10)

I walked toward my uncle's house.

I ran toward my uncle's house.

I sprinted toward my uncle's house.

My uncle was a pig, but he was still my uncle. My uncle was a dog, but he was still my uncle. I wanted to warn him that bandits were going to rob his house, and therefore he absolutely mustn't go to sleep, mustn't dreamwalk, and mustn't open his door. To reach my uncle's scenic villa, the motorized cart would have to circle around the crematorium on the embankment. It would have to circle around the road to the west of the embankment. It would have to cross over the top of the embankment. It would have to proceed to the eastern end of the embankment before coming down and circling around a forest and a pond at its base. I, however, proceeded from the opening of the path directly to my uncle's house, and in this way was able to shorten the distance by two or three *li*. I knew that if I ran, I'd be able to make it to my uncle's house before the others, and I did. On the way, I encountered wind and trees. I ran into a couple who were completely naked under a tree doing couple things. It was unclear whether they were awake or dreamwalking, but their cries of pleasure were loud enough to shake the trees along the side of the road. As I observed them from a distance, I felt the blood rush to my head, and the thing between my legs became as stiff as an iron bar. I very much wanted to approach them to see more clearly, but for the sake of my uncle I had no choice but to continue forward. A lantern the couple had placed under a tree produced a faint, yellow light, like a star that was about to fade from the sky.

I moved farther and farther from that light.

Of the couple's cries of pleasure, I couldn't understand a single word.

I proceeded through the wilderness, along the river down the embankment. The Yi River was like a broad and tangled silk ribbon dangling down from the sky. The water sounded like a song, a ghost's wail, or the couple's cries of pleasure. Later, it occurred to me that the couple must have been taking advantage of the great somnambulism to enjoy themselves. But at the time, I asked myself why the couple couldn't do their thing in the privacy of their own home? Why weren't they in their own bed? As I walked along, I saw a dark shadow and felt very frightened, but when I remembered that couple, my fear dissipated. When I heard the night bird's calls of alarm, I felt a chill run down my spine and, like the man lying on the woman, I cried out, "Ah . . . Ah . . ." and frightened away the night bird. As a result, I was no longer afraid, and felt like a young hero.

I could see my uncle's villa. He lived in what was known not as a village, but rather as a small compound. His neighbors were all very rich, including one who had opened a mine and was selling and shipping coal long distances, another who had opened several chain stores in town and in the county seat, and several bureau directors and department heads from the county seat. I heard that there was even a county mayor living there. That was our town's wealthy compound, our aristocratic compound. It was a compound that ordinary people were not allowed to enter, and furthermore ordinary people wouldn't even have any business going in there. It was a sunny area surrounded by water flowing out through the dam. The trunks of the pine trees were as wide as cypresses, and the cypresses were as wide as pines. The trunks of the cypresses, pines, and pagoda trees were as wide as buckets. Each tree was surrounded by a small pool lined with stones, and in front of every house there was a pair of flower ponds. In front of every house there were four stone steps, at the top of which there was a pair of ceramic dogs, one lying down and the other standing up. The dogs always had their tongues hanging out, as though they didn't have anything to drink. The compound's doors were always closed and locked, as though someone might come by at any time and try to rob the houses.

But in more than ten years, no houses in that compound had ever been robbed.

No one had ever tried to steal from them.

Tonight, however, someone was going to rob and steal from this compound. Daming's cart was loaded with cleavers and iron bars, and he and his cousins were prepared for a fight. If there was a slaughter, someone would die, and if someone died, someone else would need to be killed to exact vengeance—and not just one or two people, but rather three or five, or even seven or eight. I ran over from the old bridge, and headed up the hill. Light was radiating out from a grove of trees, as though the tree leaves had shattered the moonlight into tiny shards. As I followed a path to a concrete walkway leading to one of the compound's back entrances, I found my body and clothing completely covered in sweat. Each of my hair follicles seemed to be wide open, and inside each of my canvas shoes there was a small pool of liquid. My breathing was as loud and urgent as if someone had opened a sluice and released the water in the reservoir, but when I finally reached the residential compound and witnessed the situation there, I felt it wasn't worth it.

I shouldn't have done it.

It appeared to have been a huge mistake for me to come to notify Uncle and the other residents of this compound. When I reached the compound, I found that the back gate had been left open. Normally, Uncle would lock it every night, but on this particular night the gate had been left wide open. Light was streaming out through the entrance, as though an enormous pane of glass had fallen to the ground, like a golden stream flowing along the ground. Inside, no one was sleeping, and instead the people were all gathered in the center of the compound. The streetlights were on, and the lights in every house were burning bright. On that night, this residential villa was as brightly illuminated as though it were midday. It was as if the villa had never entered that year's or that month's or that night's darkness. The pine trees that pierced the sky were adorned with lights as though their branches were full of diamonds, and the cypresses were standing as though covered in glowing mercury. The flower ponds were illuminated as though they were under the midday sun, and the flowers were emitting a fragrant scent. People were rushing back and forth along the cement, asphalt, and brick roads and paths, and were carrying either cooked vegetables or cups or bottles of wine. They were drinking, walking, and eating as though it were New Year's Day or a wedding banquet being attended by dozens or hundreds of families. However, the residents wandered around the courtyard with stupid smiles and faces looking like shiny bricks that had just been painted red, white, and yellow.

They were all dreamwalking.

While dreamwalking, everyone was eating, drinking, and chatting.

Several plazas were surrounded by fountains, with their lights glittering brightly. As the columns of water from the fountains rose and fell, they emitted a jade-white and crystal-yellow light. In a flower pond that was half a *mu* in size, there was an array of yellow, green, and white lights, and consequently all of the goldfish were hiding in the shadows of the pond's rockeries. At the twenty or so round dining tables and square mah-jongg tables that surrounded the pond, people were eating and drinking, while others were playing mah-jongg. The sound of them clinking cups as they toasted one another resembled the chaotic music of an opera. The mah-jongg tables were covered with dozens of wads of cash, with each wad containing ten thousand yuan—meaning that there must have been several tens or even hundreds of thousands of yuan on the tables. The drinkers were enjoying the world's best *baijiu*, including Maotai and Wuliangye, and the bottles and liquor cups were scattered everywhere. It was unclear whether they were dreamwalking or simply drunk, but after toasting one another they proceeded to lie down on the tables and fall asleep, and as they slept they kept mumbling, "Damn it, I drank too much! I really drank too much!" The wives and other women were wearing pajamas that revealed their jade-white skin. They stood next to the men, watching them play cards and bringing them more money. When the men won, their faces shone like flower blossoms, and when they lost they resembled dishrags. There were also large, fat children running around with faces like wooden boards—yet, unlike their parents', the children's faces resembled recently split wood or freshly baked bricks. Some of the children were sleeping on their front steps, against their mother's chest, or on their father's lap. Their pink faces were covered in sweat, as though they had been sitting in hot water.

They were all asleep.

They were all dreaming.

It also seemed as though they were dreamwalking, like my parents.

Because it was so hot, all of the rich residents of this residential compound had emerged from their houses and were chatting happily, at which point they all began to feel drowsy and started to dreamwalk. In order to enjoy themselves, they had taken their wine and cigarettes outside, and each family asked their maid to cook some food and take it out to the courtyard. It turned out that even when dreamwalking, they were different from the villagers and townspeople. When villagers dreamwalked, they went to harvest and thresh their wheat, while also stealing, robbing, and killing. For the residents of this compound, however, dreamwalking consisted of eating, drinking, and playing mah-jongg. Some of them had their eyes open, while others had them half-closed. Some of them played mah-jongg in their sleep exactly as they would have had they been awake. They had their shirts off, and were wearing only an undershirt. There was also a charcoal seller I knew, who had removed both his shirt and his pants, and was wearing only a pair of underpants. He looked as if he had just rolled out of bed after having been doing it with his wife, and in front of him there was an array of three wine cups and three empty wine bottles. One woman, after drinking with a man, had removed her shirt and was wearing a pink-and-white bra embroidered with flowers and with a gold lining. Under her bra, her breasts were as plump as freshly baked buns coated in a layer of flour. There was the smell of alcohol and women's fragrance everywhere, as well as the smell of flowing water and the sound of snoring in the middle of the night. Some of the men were sleeping on the side of the road, and next to them were the foreign suits and ties that only they wore. One man was wandering inside the compound like a specter, and with each step he would lower his foot very carefully, as though afraid he might step on a needle, a nail, or a rock. "They are dreamwalking, dreamwalking. Everyone is dreamwalking," he said as he walked around, as though he were the only person still awake. "I definitely can't allow myself to fall asleep and dreamwalk, because then what would I do if someone were to try to rob me?" Then he proceeded to wander around the outside of the compound until he reached the main entrance. "Where's the guard? . . . Where's the guard? . . . I should go warn the guard that, no matter how drowsy he might become, he absolutely mustn't fall asleep. He mustn't permit anyone from outside to enter, nor permit any of the compound's nannies or other outsiders to leave."

As he said this, he wandered back and forth between the compound's front and back rows of houses. As he followed the path, he discovered he was unable to find the main entrance, or the guard stationed there.

I went over, wanting to tell him where the main entrance was and where the guard was, but when I reached him I discovered I didn't want to say anything. I saw that he was a man, but for some reason he was holding a woman's floral bra in his hand, like a pig holding a flower blossom in its mouth. When he looked in my direction, it was as though he couldn't even see me, and I distanced myself from him as though from an inanimate log. As I headed toward Uncle's house, which was the sixth house in the third row, I turned and saw that the man had bumped into something and fallen asleep on the ground.

My inability to find Uncle among that group of people who were eating, drinking, and playing mah-jongg was like being unable to find a certain pig in a passel. I followed a path lined with cypresses to the third row of houses, and when I reached one with a courtyard, I saw a middle-aged nanny open an iron gate and walk out. She was carrying a sack and was pulling a large suitcase. When she saw me she took a step back, but then—realizing that I had already seen her—she simply stood in front of me.

"It's obvious you're not from here.

"Just take something and leave. If the guard catches you, you'll be punished in place of the actual thieves."

As she said this, she hurried along, avoiding the lights and heading toward the compound's northern entrance. She walked so quickly, it seemed as though the soles of her feet were made of nails and the road was covered in fire.

I saw a guard hide a suitcase in a grove of trees, and when he emerged he was clapping his hands and looking as though he were making his rounds.

I saw someone's dog standing at the edge of a lawn and barking urgently. Meanwhile, the dog's owner was sleeping on the lawn, snoring like thunder.

I quickened my pace until I was nearly flying. I knew that the compound was about to be ransacked. Those people from the town and neighboring villages wanted to steal and plunder, and they knew the residents were likely to be asleep or dreamwalking, and they also knew where their heavenly bank accounts could be found.

Without saying a word or stopping to look around, I ran to Uncle's villa. I ran so fast that the several-hundred-meter-long forest path seemed as short as a chopstick. In some of the houses the lights were on, while in others they were off. The front doors of some houses were locked, while in others the key had been left in the keyhole, as though waiting for thieves, robbers, and relatives from other families to come and use it.

I finally reached my uncle's villa.

I paused in front of the sixth house in the third row, and wiped the sweat from my face. I hopped up those four steps, and leaped over the stainless steel railing beside the steps. I stood in front of Uncle's front gate and called out to him, then pushed the gate upon and went inside as though stepping into a dream. Uncle wasn't upstairs in the room they called a bedroom. My aunt wasn't upstairs in the room they called a bedroom either. Only their child was upstairs asleep in the room they called a bedroom. The area they called a living room was as large as three normal-sized rooms. The light was so bright that you could see ants crawling across the floor as clearly as though they were cars driving up and down the road. The television was on and the walls were snowy white. The sofa was empty, and the sound from the television was reverberating through the room. The tea table was so cluttered that it resembled a market. In the living room, the bamboo plant and two flowerpots were watching the people who were busily squatting there—my uncle and my aunt, who were both topless and were wearing only slippers and underwear. They didn't look at all like people from a rich household, and instead resembled the town's poor. My aunt had prepared four dishes herself, as well as two bowls of soup—one of three-flavored egg drop soup and the other of shrimp, shredded meat, and pickled vegetable soup. The dishes and the soups were all placed and piled and arrayed on the market-like tea table. Uncle was big and tall, and when he squatted down he resembled a collapsed wall. Aunt was thin and small, and when she squatted beside the wall she resembled a freshly planted flower or shrub. When I entered, they were in the process of pouring a bottle of something or other onto the vegetable dishes and the soups, as though they were adding salt or MSG. Uncle was pouring it and Auntie was using chopsticks to mix it in. When they heard the door open, they both turned and stared at me in surprise, their faces a mixture of white, yellow, and yellowish-white. But that yellowish-white hue quickly faded, and their faces returned to their previous murky-sleepy state. They became shiny and stupefied like porcelain under the lamplight. "Didn't you lock the door?" Uncle asked Auntie in a recriminatory tone, but he continued pouring the bottle over the dishes and soups as though scattering sesame seeds over a field. "I did, but the wind must have blown it open." As Auntie said this, she continued mixing the dishes with her chopsticks. They were both so busy with what they were doing that it appeared they didn't even see me—it was as though I were but a gust of wind, a tree, or a dreamscape that disappears in the blink of an eye.

"Uncle . . . Auntie . . . What are you doing? Something has happened in this compound, don't you know?

"The world is falling apart, don't you know?"

The room was so quiet, it seemed as though there wasn't anyone there. It was as though I hadn't even entered. Uncle continued carefully pouring whatever that was over the dishes and the soups, and Auntie continued stirring it up. As the sugar-like crystals fell onto the dish of scrambled eggs and dissolved, the eggs developed a trace of gray, appearing as though the eggs were slightly burned. "Don't add too much, because then it won't taste right." . . . "Don't worry that we'll add too much. If we do, then as soon as they take a bite that will be the end of them, and it knocks off the possibility that they might wake up again after a long night of many dreams." Then

Uncle proceeded to add some more to one of the bowls of soup. As Uncle was adding the substance to the soup, he switched to a different bottle, which contained what looked like muddy water. From this bottle he added one splash, and another. And another, and another. "Don't add any more, don't add any more. If you do, it won't taste right . . . If we add too much, then these sons and grandsons will immediately collapse as soon as they take a bite." After he added the final splash, Uncle lifted the bottle up to the light. He saw that the bottle, which had previously been full, was now half empty. Under the lamplight, the bottle appeared dark yellow, and the portion that still contained liquid was dark brown. The edges of the bottle's label were slightly curled, and a black skull and crossbones appeared in the upper center of the label, as though a bloody fingernail were stuck to it. I immediately recognized the skull and crossbones, and the word "dichlorvos" beneath it. It was at this point that I realized that the most significant development was actually unfolding right here inside my uncle's villa, and not out in the compound's main courtyard. "What are you doing? Uncle, Auntie, it is the middle of the night. Why aren't the two of you asleep?" A cold breeze blew toward me from the tea table, and from where Uncle and Auntie were squatting. Initially, it appeared to be merely a breeze, but then it developed into a major burst of wind, and was so cold that I began shivering. As soon as I started shivering, I broke into a sweat. My shirt stuck to my back, and my forehead and eyes became filled with the hot, salty scent of sweat. There was also a sweet scent in the air, like saccharine water. I knew that the more it smelled of sweat, the stronger the poison was—and that this was the smell of the insecticide dichlorvos. I realized that the room's increasingly sweet odor was the smell of poison crystals in the food.

"Uncle, Auntie, it's the middle of the night and you still haven't gone to bed. What are you doing?"

"Don't say anything. If you've come, you can just sit over there."

"Outside, there are people looting and stealing, and soon they will come here."

"Huh?" Uncle finally looked at me. "If they come to steal from me, I'll simply invite them to have some scrambled eggs and drink a bowl of three-flavored soup." He laughed, and then, with Auntie, focused on adding the dichlorvos crystals to the remaining dishes. "This once-in-a-millennium somnambulism is truly a gift from heaven. Tonight, everyone who usually looks down on me will die." I saw that the chopsticks with which Auntie was stirring the food were turning black from the poison, and the smile that floated over Uncle's face as he was speaking resembled a yellow cloud. He added the poison to the food as though he were sowing seeds.

"Niannian, it's good that you came. You came at just the right time. In a little while you can help your uncle take these dishes out to the courtyard. Put them wherever I tell you, and take the soup to whichever table I specify. The county's Mayor Miao lives in this compound, but he has never spoken with either me or your aunt. The director of the department of civil affairs also lives in this compound, and has visited everyone's house except ours. They all resent the fact that I work at the crematorium, and are afraid of being contaminated with the air of mourning and death. Even the damned director of the coal mine, who is himself dark and dirty, tries to avoid me whenever we run into each other in the street. All of them fucking look down on the crematorium—but if they can manage it, they are welcome to simply not die, and not need to be cremated in the first place. One of our neighbors struck it rich while gambling in the county seat, and another did so while stealing in Luoyang. I don't look down on them for gambling and stealing, yet they resent me as a neighbor for being inauspicious, and consequently they sold their houses and moved to the front of the compound. But that's fine. If they resent me, then tonight I'll simply cook them some vegetables and soup.

"I'll send all of them to the western heaven!

"After they have wept to the point that heaven itself has no more tears, their relatives will have to beg me to cremate them, and reduce them to ashes.

"After I cremate them, their relatives will still need to come bring me gifts, and say that we all live in the same compound and affirm that we are neighbors. When someone dies, they'll ask that I burn the body completely, and not leave behind any intact arm or leg bones.

"It's not that I won't report them for what they've done, but rather that it's simply not time yet. When the time comes, I, Shao Dacheng, will certainly have no choice but to report them!

"Niannian, come here. Take this dish of three-flavored soup to the table next to the fountain, where Mayor Miao is sitting. You've seen Mayor Miao before—he's the thin, bald man. You don't need to say anything, just place the serving bowl on the table and then serve a bowl of soup to each of the people sitting there. If anyone asks, you can say that you are from the second house in the first row. Actually, it doesn't matter which house you say you are from, since they will all die after they drink the soup. At that point, they won't know anything, and their troubles will be over. And then there are those who are playing mah-jongg. No one knows what business they are in, but they have even more money than I. After you deliver the soup, you can take them these vegetable dishes, with some bowls and chopsticks. I don't need to curry favor with those who have money. And after they get tired of playing cards, you can take them this soup. You don't need to say a word. They will start eating and drinking, and once they start eating and drinking, it won't matter how much money they have.

"There is also this dish of greens. The high school principal is vegetarian, so you should serve him this.

"This dish . . . Niannian . . . Niannian . . .

"Niannian . . . Niannian . . ."

The night became deeper. Uncle's voice swept the night's darkness out of the room. It tumbled down the stairs, like water flowing downward. It followed my footsteps, as though trying to drown me.

4. (5:11–5:15)

As Uncle was mumbling to himself, I took the opportunity to leave his house. I ran toward the compound's main entrance, and as I proceeded I heard footsteps pounding behind me like war drums. As I ran, I didn't think about anything. In my mind, there was only one thought, which was planted there like a tree: "Daming and the others have to arrive soon. Daming, come quick and bring the others to rob my uncle's place. Steal his money and his things. You can take whatever you want. All of Auntie's jewelry is in the cabinet at the head of her bed, and Uncle's money is hidden inside the wall on the other side of his bedroom. Daming, come quick. Come quick and rob Uncle's villa." As I ran, I shouted to myself, and the sound of my feet crawled up my throat like a snake. The sky was bluish-gray and the ground was murky-gray. The world would be dreamlike, if dreams themselves were so poisoned. The light across the street was burning brightly, as though the sun were still suspended there. The surrounding brick wall was three meters high, and the top of the wall was covered in barbed wire and shards of glass. Between the two marble gateposts there was a large iron gate, which was locked, and inside it there was a smaller door, which was also locked. Of the two night guards, one was asleep in the doorway, and I didn't know where the other one was. When I reached the doorway, I saw Daming and the others arriving. It was unclear where they had left their motorized cart. Each of the four men was carrying a sack, and they were also carrying an assortment of iron and wooden poles. They stood in the entranceway, unsure of how to enter the compound. When they saw me standing in the entranceway to the compound, it was as though they had seen a monkey escaped from its cage. They stared at me with a suspicious expression.

We stared at one another through the iron gate for several seconds.

Then, I went and pressed a button in one of the columns, whereupon the gate swung open. The two worlds became one.

"Brother Daming, my uncle doesn't live in the second row; he lives in the sixth house in the third row.

"My uncle's money isn't kept in a chest or a cabinet; it's kept in an iron safe that is hidden in the wall of his bedroom on the second floor.

"My aunt's jewelry is in a red silk pouch that she keeps in the third drawer of the cabinet at the head of her bed.

"Brother Daming, hurry up and come in, then go to my uncle's villa, which is the sixth house in the third row. You can take advantage of the fact that my aunt and uncle are both dreamwalking, and tie them to chairs the same way you did my parents. Then, you can steal whatever you want.

"Come in, come in! What are you staring at? It was precisely because I was afraid you wouldn't be able to enter that I took a shortcut and hurried here so that I could open the gate for you."

A look of surprise and delight fluttered like a piece of silk fabric over the faces of Daming and his cousins, who were still standing outside the gate. It was only after I finished what I had to say and stepped out through the gate that they finally attempted to come inside. As they brushed past me, I looked again at Daming's face. He pressed a flashlight into my hand, and I turned and shouted to them,

"It's the sixth house in the third row. You must go only to my uncle's villa, and not anyone else's!

"Brother Daming, remember you absolutely mustn't taste any of the food or soup that my uncle and aunt prepared, because if you do, you will die!"

My shouts hovered like a song in the night air over my head. The footsteps of Daming and his cousins accompanied my shouts like rhythmic music. I returned to town, while the others headed into the compound. "Regardless of what we end up finding, we'll make sure to set aside a portion for you and your family. I, Sun Daming, can personally guarantee this, so Niannian, you can rest easy." This was the last thing Daming said as he entered the compound, and even today, when I remember this, I feel delighted and thrilled—as though Brother Daming's shouts were a bucket of ice water dumped over my head in the middle of summer.

BOOK NINE

Post-*Geng*: The Birds All Die
in the Heart of the Night

1. (5:16–5:30)

The night became deeper and deeper.

The birds all died in the heart of the night.

It seemed as though I had spent the entire night running around. I suddenly became a bit drowsy and felt my legs swell up. The night road was murky, and its stern face unfolded at my feet. The heat in the fields was replaced by coolness, as the earth's final traces of warmth gradually dissipated. It was like the aftermath of a tantrum: a kind of dissipation unfolded across the villages and throughout the vast silence.

I could see the streetlamps in distant villages.

I could hear the rumbling of cars in distant streets.

That night, a smell of unease continued to pervade the entire land. But that smell seemed both weaker and stronger than before. I knew that people always feel sleepiest just before the sun is about to come up, and it is precisely when people feel sleepiest that they are most likely to dreamwalk. I walked away from the western wall of this scenic compound. The original road was still waiting for me, and the dark was also still waiting for me. I went to the riverside to wash my face and drink some water. As I was passing over the bridge, I gazed out at the river, and saw the water's bright light and heard its clear sound. I remembered how, earlier, a couple were doing couple things under a tree on the river's opposite bank, and I was oddly reminded of Juanzi, the young woman responsible for cleaning the crematorium. If only she were pretty. If only she didn't have buckteeth. If only she could read . . . I began walking faster. As I thought about her, I no longer felt sleepy. So, it turned out that Juanzi was capable of dispelling sleepiness and providing energy. I thought about Juanzi in a deep, remote area. I imagined the two of us doing that sort of couple thing, and doing it in this night's vast wilderness. I imagined this until my hands, forehead, and entire body were covered in sweat, as though I were really embracing her. The couple were no longer where I had seen them. They weren't on the side of the road, nor were they under the tree. When I reached that location, I looked under the tree and listened, and the stillness rushed toward me, such that it seemed as though I could see and hear the bare footsteps of the silent night. I shone my flashlight on the matted grass where the couple had been lying. There was a box of matches, as well as a woman's hair clip.

I was once again reminded of one of Yan Lianke's novels. This work was as rough as one of Gaotian's early adobe houses, but this was precisely the sort of novel I liked to read. In fact, I had already read this particular work countless times, and could even recite many passages from memory.

At this point, he again removed his clothes and quickly put them away in her cabinet, as though putting them aside forever. Completely naked, they locked the front gate as well as the house's front and back doors. It was as if they had entered a different world. There was an unprecedented sense of relaxation, which made them feel an unprecedented sense of happiness and freedom. They embraced each other. She wanted to stroke him down there, so she continually reached down, like a mother tenderly caressing her baby. He wanted to kiss here down there, and she permitted him to do so, as though he were kissing a statue. They pursued their hearts' desires, without any inhibitions or restraint. Whenever they began to get tired, they would sit down to rest, and she would either sit down on him or else he would rest his legs on her thighs. They would either sit or lie on the ground, or else he would rest his head on her waist or her belly. He had just gotten his hair cut short, and when the stubble brushed against the tender parts of her inner thighs where the sun never shone, it gave her a pleasurable tingling sensation that she couldn't put into words, and whenever he slightly moved his head, that tingling sensation would increase. Because of this, she would produce a mature woman's crisp laugh. Her laughter grew louder, then faded, and finally it would arouse his hidden male instinct, and he would once again begin caressing her body. Acting as if she were a child again, she ran around the room, and when she began to tire and he caught her, she would be taken by him, as he would endlessly do that sort of couple thing on her body. She permitted him to plow clouds and sow rain on her body, fornicating crazily like a goatherd running crazily through the fields.

As I remembered this passage, my steps grew lighter. I felt the sun was about to come up, and the great somnambulism was about to end. As soon as the sun came up, temporal order would again be restored.

But the sun didn't come up.

It really didn't. The night was as deep as a dark well, and we remained as far from daybreak as the Qing dynasty was from the Tang dynasty.

That night's catastrophe seemed to have just started. It seemed as though the world had only just fallen into a state of somnambulism.

For all of the earth's villages and towns, the chaos had only just arrived. When I turned from the path onto the main road, I saw many cars and tractors taking people from the mountains to the town. The headlights of both the cars and the tractors resembled columns extending into space, and their rumblings resembled a hammer shattering stones. In the lamplight, I could see that the people inside those cars were holding hoes, shovels, pitchforks, and axes, and hanging from the hoes and shovels were an assortment of burlap sacks, cloth bags, and sheets and bedcovers that could be used to carry bundles—as if they were going somewhere to fight a battle and, in the process, clean up the battlefield.

The people were having an uprising.

The people were dreamwalking.

While still asleep, the people were driving cars and heroically heading into town. Their faces were bright red, and they didn't look at all drowsy. As for the passengers in the cars, they were mostly strong, young men, but there were also some young women in the group. The young women were carrying baskets and crates, as though they were going to divide up the grain harvest. I knew that the world was in tumult, and had been turned upside down on this night of the great somnambulism. Those who were not dreamwalking took advantage of the general somnambulism to make trouble, and there were more people pretending to dreamwalk than there were actual dreamwalkers. Everyone was using the general somnambulism as a pretext to rob and steal—the same way that people might take advantage of a popular uprising to wage war, or take advantage of a war in order to make a profit.

I thought I must be only a few steps away from town, and from home, but after having carried me back and forth along this road all night, my calves felt as heavy as lead and my legs felt as if they were dead. I trudged toward home, and when I reached the intersection at the edge of town, I saw that the cars, tractors, and motorized carts were stopped there. People had gotten out of their vehicles, and they were holding flashlights and lanterns. They were grouped based on their village or clan, and each group was in animated conversation while waiting for instructions. Some people were stomping their feet and cursing the others, saying, "Hurry up, Hurry up! Let's go into town. If we don't go into town, the others will wake up and we'll lose our chance to steal anything."

The sound of voices flowed, like water through a newly opened sluice.

The sound of the crowds walking back and forth was like water flowing through a newly opened sluice.

I walked through those vehicles and crowds like a mouse running under people's feet. I saw that the weapons everyone was carrying were not ordinary farming tools, but rather real knives, large hammers, and even hunting rifles. One large group came running over, followed by another. When I reached the entrance to the town, I saw that the townspeople had stopped dreamwalking and were now sound asleep. The streets were quiet, the houses were quiet, and even the shops that had been robbed and left with their windows and doors wide open were quiet. Some people walked over from the main street, but it was unclear whether they were awake or dreamwalking. They walked very slowly, appearing to have no inkling that the town was on the verge of a great calamity. All of the visitors had gathered at the town entrance. They exclaimed:

"A battle of thievery has surrounded the town, and is about to overtake the town itself."

"A murderous war is anxiously waiting just outside town."

I was no longer sleepy, and my eyelids no longer felt unbearably heavy. I had already returned from the dreamworld to a state where I could see the world very clearly. My calves, which had fallen asleep, regained sensation. I walked briskly through the town entrance, and began to run as soon as I was through it. By the time I reached the main road, I was sprinting so fast it was as though I were flying through the air.

"Outsiders have come to rob our town!

"Outsiders have come to rob our town!"

I shouted as I ran, with my shouts echoing like the cries of an ox about to be slaughtered—as though the blade were being held to the ox's throat. But not a single person in the town's houses and streets woke up in response to my screams. The people had already died—they had died in their sleep. After awakening from their dreamwalking, they were pushed back into sleep and died. Or else they heard my shouts and assumed they were the crazed shouts of a dreamwalker. Continuing to shout as I ran, I dashed through the deep night until I reached my home. Upon seeing the light in the doorway of the New World funerary shop, I came to a stop and, facing the street, shouted frantically:

"Outsiders are coming to rob the town!

"Outsiders are coming to rob the town!"

After shouting this twice, I decided there was no need to continue. I simply couldn't continue. A voice emerged from my family's store: "Fuck your grandmother, what is all this shouting about?" Then someone kicked me in the rear, almost lifting me into the air. As I was still reeling from the kick, someone pulled me into my house, where I saw a group of men in a configuration similar to the one in which I had found Sun Daming and his cousins. There were several half-filled bags and sacks, and the men were standing unhappily in the center of the room. My parents were kneeling in the center of the room, and behind them were two burly young men. The floor was covered in shredded wreaths and floral ornaments. My parents were kneeling in the middle of all of those blossoms and pieces of paper as though kneeling in a funeral hall. The men standing behind them were as expressionless as funeral directors, their faces betraying neither joy nor sadness. They appeared to be awake, and their eyes were open. One young man—who had a fierce look and a mole on his shoulder, and whose face became dark when he was upset—came into the room screaming and shouting. It was his foot that had kicked me in the rear, and it was he who had pulled me inside. He pushed me toward my parents. "This is your son, isn't it?" My parents stared in alarm, then nodded and said the same thing they had said to Sun Daming: "He's still a boy, you mustn't hurt him." My parents were about to plead, but were cut short by the men standing behind them.

"Where are your family's valuables?"

It was this question again.

"Where do your parents hide their money?"

It was this question again.

Like Sun Daming, the man with the mole on his shoulder used his left arm to put me in a choke hold, while grabbing my shoulder with his other hand. "If you tell me where they are, I'll let you go. If you tell us where they are, we'll simply grab some things and leave." Unlike Daming, however, these men weren't wearing masks, nor did they choke me while waiting for me to speak, nor had they tied my parents to chairs. They were outsiders, and weren't worried that other townspeople might recognize them. While waiting for me to speak, they even patted my shoulder, like brothers, to express a friendly warning.

So, I spoke.

I had no choice but to speak.

What I said pleased them, but alarmed my parents.

"My uncle's villa has many things.

"My uncle's villa has money and jewelry, but someone has already gone there to rob it.

"All of the residents of my uncle's compound are very rich. Every family has lots of money. Given that their compound is so close to this town, if you don't go there after having come here, you will have wasted a trip."

The men stared in surprise, as if I had woken them from their dream. My mother and father also stared at me, as though I had been talking in my sleep. The atmosphere in the room became tense. They were all so surprised that the delight on their faces was replaced with a look of shock. "Where the hell is this place you are talking about?" . . . "I'm talking about the scenic compound. If you don't go steal from there, you will have wasted your trip. My uncle lives in that compound. His is the sixth house in the third row, and anything you take from his house is guaranteed to be worth a lot more than anything you could possibly find here. His television is as large as a table, and his tables and chairs are all solid mahogany. You know how valuable mahogany is, don't you?"

There was no response.

Not even a peep.

The house was so quiet that you could even hear the breathing of the funerary flowers. Father's face was as pale as the paper in the wreaths. Mother's face was also as pale as the paper in the wreaths. My parents stared at me as though I wasn't their true son, but rather an unfilial son or grandson. The man with a mole on his shoulder gestured toward the others, and they all gazed at him, waiting for him to speak.

"Why didn't we think of this?"

As the man with the mole mumbled to himself, he released his grip on my throat and shoulder, then gently pushed me forward. In doing so, he indicated that everything was OK—that it was all over, and they were going to leave. Then he nodded, and the others picked up their sacks and headed for the door. It was over. It was indeed all over. The robbery had concluded. But at this moment, the man with the mole suddenly remembered something. He stopped, turned around, and looked at me.

"What is your uncle's name?"

"Shao Dacheng."

A look of alarm flickered over the man's face. He stood in front of my parents. "You must be Li Tianbao, Shao Dacheng's brother-in-law? And you are Shao Dacheng's crippled sister?"

My father nodded.

My mother also nodded.

And that was that. The situation no longer continued along the path it had been following. The situation suddenly started all over again. The man threw down the sack he had been carrying, and viciously kicked my father in the chest. "Motherfucker, I've finally found you!" He stomped on my father's legs. "So, it was you who harmed my father and my entire family! It's your fault that for the past several years my family has experienced nothing but misfortune." Roaring and stomping his feet, the man slapped my father's face. Then, without waiting for my father to process what was happening, he slapped my mother's as well. "Your brother is a pig, a dog. He isn't even human. And since you are his sister, you'll have to be slapped several times as well."

He slapped her like crazy.

He cursed her like crazy.

I stared in astonishment, and just as I was about to beg him to stop hitting her, the others grabbed me, as though they, too, realized what was happening. My sense of filial duty became frozen with fear, and I simply stared in alarm. Without resisting, I permitted the other young men to pin me to the ground. Everything happened as quickly as a car running over someone's head and splitting the skull open, such that the person dies without even making a sound. The man with a mole on his shoulder continued slapping my mother and kicking my father in the chest and stomach. My father sat on the ground like a sack of sugar, and as the man hit and kicked him, my father's butt slowly slid across the floor. The paper wreaths that covered the floor were pushed backward by my father's body until they formed a pile against the wall. Once my father was pressed against the wall, the man began to hit and kick him even more viciously, but my father sat there like a pile of clothing or a sack of sugar.

"Fuck your grandmother! After my father was buried three years ago, you must have been the one who informed on him. Do you admit it?"

Several punches rained down on Father's face like tiles being smashed on the ground.

"Fuck your grandmother! Three years ago, when you informed your brother-in-law, that bastard sent someone to our home in the mountains and dug up the corpse, saying that the Reform and Opening Up Campaign had reached our remote village, and that we needed to change our customs. Then he ignited my father's corpse and cremated his body in the open, you know?"

He repeatedly stomped on my father's head and chest, making him gasp for breath as his face came to resemble one of the white flowers with red petals that were lying on the ground.

"Your brother-in-law cremated my father in the open, and in the process made me a model antireformist. In the village, I was put on display and made to parade around. They even wrote me up in the county paper. Did you see the report?

"If you saw it, then how did your conscience permit you to live with this? Are you even human?

"After my wife read the article and heard the broadcast, she left me. Your Li and Shao families have been profiting off other people's deaths, and have condemned others to a lifetime of misfortune. How can you live with yourselves?

"Shortly after my father was cremated, my mother died of anger, and it was three months after her death that my wife left me. Half a year later, my sister developed a mental illness as a result of our parents' deaths, and leaped to her death from a cliff. In this way, what had been a stable family was torn apart and destroyed, even as your Li and Shao families didn't know anything about it. As I have gotten older, I've become increasingly dissolute, and if I wasn't drinking, I'd be gambling or stealing. It is all your fault that I became bad. When I was released from prison six months ago, I vowed to become good, but tonight while I was sleeping, God came to me in a dream and said, 'Ma Guazi, your time has come. You should gather some friends and go into town and steal some things.' After I woke up, I insisted that I didn't want to rob or steal, and instead I wanted to be good. But God was still in my heart, saying, 'You should go, you should go! Quick, get out of bed and go!' If God demands that I do something, I have no choice but to do it. So I brought the others to town, and to your shop. I originally assumed that entering your funerary shop had been a very unlucky thing, but I never expected that this was actually God's way of letting me get retribution for what your Li and Shao families have done to mine. God wants you, Li Tianbao, to repay me in full, and he wants your crippled wife to repay me on behalf of her brother. I have already come to terms with the collapse of my family and the deaths of my relatives. Other than in my dreams, I never imagined I would find you, and make you pay. But this night of the somnambulism has allowed me to think of all of this, and to encounter all of this."

He once again slapped my mother and kicked my father in the face and chest. He then stomped on my father's legs and feet and ankles. He stomped on him for a while, said a few things, then slapped him several times. He beat him, said something, then stomped on him some more. He grabbed one of the room's bamboo stalks and struck my parents over the head. After he grew tired from beating them—and after he had run out of curses and left the store a mess with paper blossoms, shreds of paper, sticks, and bamboo stalks all over the floor—he noticed that, throughout his beating and cursing, my parents hadn't moved a muscle or uttered a word, and only raised a hand to protect themselves when he brought his foot or the bamboo stalk down on their faces. After a while, my father stopped doing even that, and simply sat there and allowed himself to be beaten. It was as if the person being beaten was not him, and as if the punches and kicks that were raining down on his head and face did not hurt him in the least.

Blood poured out of his head.

Blood poured out of his nose and mouth.

The blood flowed onto his body, his shirt, and splattered all over his thighs. Everyone was astonished by my parents' lack of response. I knelt down and—assuming that my father must have died—I stared in shock and called out to him, and also called out to my mother. I could see that they were both looking at me, as though they were trying to use their eyes to communicate. I knelt there without moving or saying another word. The room was very hot, and Ma Guazi's clothes were soaked in sweat. The room was very cold, and everyone's face was covered in frost.

"Damn it!" Ma Guazi once again stomped on my father's legs. I saw my father's legs tense up, as though he were going into convulsions. Then he extended his legs and waited for them to be stomped on again. Sure enough, he was stomped on again, and his legs tensed up again. Then he extended his legs once again, and waited.

"You sure can take a beating. If you just beg me once, I'll stop.

"All you need to do is beg me, and everything that happened tonight will be forgotten."

Ma Guazi continued stomping and speaking, speaking and stomping. "Could it be that you really weren't the person who informed on me, which is why you refuse to speak or struggle? Damn it, if you don't struggle, then it must be your own fault. If you don't struggle, that means it must have been you who informed on me." He slapped and kicked, kicked and slapped. Ma Guazi hoped that my father would either beg him to stop or else would try to defend himself, but instead it appeared as though he were the one who was begging my father. At this point, Mother crawled from Father's side and begged Ma Guazi while hugging his leg. But as she was looking up to plead with him, Father reached over and pulled her back.

My father spoke.

My father finally spoke.

"Thank you for coming to beat me. Actually, your father's cremation was not a result of my having informed on him. However, for more than ten years I did do that sort of thing to others. So, in coming to beat me tonight, you are letting us repay those debts. This way, we will no longer owe anyone anything."

My father had a smile on his face as he said this—a miserable smile. As he grinned, his voice resembled a fly buzzing around. As he was speaking, he looked at Ma Guazi, and the smile on the corners of his lips spread to the rest of his face, as though his face were covered in white blossoms and red leaves. But as Father was expressing his gratitude, Ma Guazi slapped him. "Does that feel good? Then I'll let you feel even better." He knocked Father's smile from his face, leaving it red with blood. He turned and glared at his companions, who were standing there staring. "Why aren't you beating them? Could it be that these past several years, no one ever informed on you when your elders or relatives were buried?" Then, after using all his strength to kick my father and mother one final time, he announced that he was done.

This was truly the end.

As Ma Guazi was leading his companions away, he picked up a large, white paper blossom from the ground and placed it on Mother's head. Then he picked up half a wreath and hung it around Father's neck. Then he left. He did, in fact, leave. In the room, there were only my parents, myself, and a mess of wreaths and flowers. We looked at one another. The lamplight and the dusk were the same color as the paper and blossoms that littered the floor. Mother sighed, removed the white blossom from her head, and placed it on the ground; then she wiped her face. From somewhere she had managed to find a rag-like piece of cloth and handed it to Father. By this point, Father's shirt was completely unbuttoned, and both his shirt and his chest were dark with blood. He carefully turned to accept the rag, as though afraid his neck might be broken. Upon discovering that he could still turn his neck and move his body, Father wiped his face. It was as if he were checking to see whether or not his face was still there. Fortunately, it was. The left side of his face was as swollen as a freshly steamed bun. Then, as though he were afraid that the flesh on his face might suddenly fall off, Father slowly raised his hand to his left cheek. He ripped a strip from the rag Mother had handed him, and stuffed it into his bleeding nostril. The result was rather farcical. "Now our Li family doesn't owe anyone anything. I am grateful to Ma Guazi, because it was he who permitted our family to repay our debt." Father said this softly to himself. After removing the dead man's wreath from his neck, he attempted to stand up. His joints creaked loudly, as though his bones had been displaced and were now returning to their correct positions.

It turned out that Father was OK.

I had assumed that Father's bones would surely be shattered, but it turned out that he was OK. I had never thought that Father, as small as he was, would be so resilient. I went to help Mother, but saw that as soon as she stood up, she almost fell down again. She nevertheless made an effort and managed to stay upright. Seeing this, Father was relieved. He kicked the blossoms and paper ornaments lying on the ground, together with the spirit money and the paper ingots. And then, leaning against a chair and the wall, he headed toward the entranceway. "The sun is about to come up. As soon as it does, everything should be OK." His mumbling became a sigh. "Be sure to straighten up the room. God, if they are willing to rob a funerary shop, there's no telling how they must have left other people's houses."

As he said this, he made his way out of the store, as though wanting to check on the condition of the other houses that had been robbed.

Father stood outside the store and gazed at the street. The pre-dawn coolness rose up from the street, as though water were flowing into the room. Mother didn't clean up the mess, and instead hobbled into the kitchen to wash her face—to wash the blood off her face, and to wash the bloody wounds on her arms. "Your uncle's family is going to come to a bad end. Tonight, your uncle's family is going to come to a bad end." She muttered this to herself as she walked, but before she passed the stairs and went into the kitchen, Father returned. He was walking much faster than when he left, and while it looked as if he still needed to lean against the doorframes and the walls for support, he was nevertheless moving at a fast clip. I knew he had seen that the outsiders were taking advantage of the somnambulism to arrive in cars with their shovels, hoes, and weapons. He had turned pale—as pale as white funeral paper. Sweat was flowing down his face as though he had been drenched in a downpour of bloody rain.

"The town will experience a crisis.

"The town will experience a major crisis.

"This town will really find itself unable to escape its doom."

Father spoke so quickly, it was hard to believe he had just been beaten. In a single step, he leaped across the room and strode past the stairs to Mother's side. "Go quickly, and leave this town! Don't lock up the store on your way out, because the messier you can leave everything, the better. Niannian, you should scatter those shredded wreaths in the entranceway, and leave the front door wide open. Make it appear as though others have already robbed this store countless times."

2. (5:31–5:50)

I went to do as Father instructed.

I took the shredded wreaths that were scattered around the shop, and placed them in the entranceway. I took the ornamental boys and girls that had gotten stepped on, and placed them on either side of the door. I also took the funeral ornaments that were covered in my parents' blood, and placed them in a visible location. I left the door to the store wide open, then fled with my parents. I don't know where Father had managed to find a motorized three-wheeled cart, which could either be pedaled or could run on a motor. "Here . . . here." Father was calling out from the darkness, and I ran over to him. I hopped onto the motorized cart, and Father headed toward a street in town.

Behind me, there was a loud and chaotic sound of footsteps, and there was also the loud and chaotic sound of voices. The voices were like floodwaters rushing toward the town. The town was smothered by the sound of the voices, and was lifted up by this tide of sound. My family rode that three-wheeled cart from East Street toward West Street, and from the town entrance to the center of town. The cart sounded as though it were about to fall apart, and as though the chain were about to snap at any moment. In the cart's tin trunk, there were sacks, hoes, and also a heavy-duty battery-powered radio. Around here, whenever middle-aged or old people ride a motorized cart, they like to carry a radio with them. The radio would play as it was being knocked around, but whenever you wanted to listen to it, it would go silent. I wasn't sure which family had driven this cart and abandoned it while they went to steal things, but now the cart was carrying my family.

The door to the farm tools store was closed.

The door to the nearby grain and oil store was also closed.

The door to the hair salon that was kitty-corner across the street, however, was open.

The door to the store selling glass for windows and doors was half-open.

The entire town was still half-asleep. Some people had woken up from their dreamwalking, and then fallen asleep again. Others had been sleeping soundly all night, and not only had they not dreamwalked, they hadn't even gotten up to use the bathroom. But now, there were some people—I couldn't tell whether they were awake or dreamwalking—who staggered along the street and had no idea what had happened or what was happening on this night in this town, in this world.

"People from other villages have come into town to rob and steal!

"People from other villages have come into town to rob and steal!"

As several shouts came from the intersection, Father turned the cart around, and proceeded north. He began screaming at the top of his lungs, and told Mother and me to do the same. So, we all stood in the cart, cupped our hands around our mouths, and shouted.

"Everyone, get up! Outsiders with hoes and shovels have come to steal and loot.

"Everyone, quickly get up! Outsiders who have come to rob us have already reached the entrance to town."

Father's shouts were as rough and urgent as shattered stone and cracked bamboo, while Mother's were as thin and delicate as a ripped silk sheet fluttering in the wind. My shouts, meanwhile, resembled a partially grown branch swaying back and forth—and although they were short, they nevertheless flew the farthest. Some people emerged from their houses and stood on the side of the street, and after watching for a while, they went back inside and shut their doors, and we could hear them using wooden bars to barricade them. Father once again drove his cart forward, and our family's shouts once again sounded out, one after the other. It was as if on this night, the town hadn't succeeded in silencing my parents, and it was as if they had lived their entire lives so that tonight they would be able to travel the town's streets shouting and hollering. In this way, the town's streets and alleys were all woken up again, only to die down again.

The square. The town's northern entrance. South Street and West Street. All of the town's streets and alleys were filled with the sound of our calls and shouts. Wherever we ran, the sound of our shouts would pour out like the wind. When we reached the entrance to the village chief's house, Father had wanted to shout as we knocked on the door, but in the end he didn't have a chance, and our family had no choice but to run away. The entrance to the village chief's alley was suddenly filled with lights and the sound of footsteps. In the dark night, we couldn't hear anyone talking or shouting, and all we could see was that light flickering. The sound of footsteps surged toward us like an earthquake, or like a flood that had inundated the houses and inundated the entire world.

The outsiders gathered around so that, when the time came, they would be ready to surge into town.

It was like water accumulating in a reservoir until it is ready to overflow the embankment.

Or like troops gathering until they are ready to go to war.

I stared in the direction of those lights and sounds. Mother looked at those lights and screamed, "They've arrived! Quick, run away! . . . Quick, run away!" Father's foot, which was about to kick the door to the village chief's house, froze in midair. By this point, the street was already full of the sound of people running, and it seemed as if everywhere we looked there were people fleeing town with their bundles of possessions. They were carrying lanterns and flashlights, even though the road leading out of town was well lit. The main road was as brightly illuminated as it had been before dusk, and everything could be seen perfectly clearly. When my father ran forward, he could see, in the lamplight, a key hanging from the handle of another cart, and tied to the key there was a dirty embroidered monkey. Father, without appearing to give the matter much thought, grabbed the key and turned it, starting the motor. This is what happened. Everything happened in this way. After hopping onto the cart, my father proceeded just like one of those villagers who drive three-wheeled carts, and with his hand on the throttle, the cart began to move with a warm and quick puttering sound. "Damn it, damn it!" It was unclear whether the voice was excited, upset, or angry. Father cursed repeatedly, and the cart handle shook a few times, and the trunk shook a few times as well. The motorized cart moved down the street—much faster than someone could run, and also faster than a cart drawn by a horse or donkey. There was a chaotic stampede in the streets. The village elders said that it had also been like this when the Japanese troops arrived, and as the townspeople fled and hid from the Japanese, they had similarly been shouting as they carried their things and fled in all directions. On this particular night, this is how things were just as the sun was about to come up—everyone was shouting as people ran in all directions. Some were carrying their sleeping children, while others were carrying their elderly parents. Some were able to keep up easily, and even pulled a handcart loaded with clothes, food, kindling, and rice, as well as young children and elderly relatives. The refugee pulling the handcart had his eyes only half-open, and it was unclear whether he was awake or asleep. The bodies of the sleeping elders and children riding in the cart rocked back and forth, as they kept mumbling to themselves.

"It's not possible that we're dreamwalking.

"It's not possible that we're dreamwalking."

The person I suspected was dreamwalking was half-awake and half-asleep, but even in this indeterminate state, the sound of his footsteps running down the street never stopped, so that he wouldn't lag behind the others. There was noise everywhere. There was movement everywhere. The world was drowned in these sounds, and people were rushing around frantically as if in a nightmare. First it was one family, then ten or more, and eventually it was dozens and even hundreds. It seemed as if the entire town were moving in a nightmare—as if they were all in a liminal state between sleep and wakefulness. My family was awake, and after watching that night's developments, we felt as though we had mastered this night's trajectory. As a result, our awake brains came to function as the entire town's brains—which is to say, the entire town's soul and the entire world's lantern. Riding his motorized cart, Father cut back and forth through the crowd while shouting.

"Don't run away! Don't run away! Wake up everyone who is sleeping, and tell families to guard their houses!

"If you don't guard your houses, you are simply inviting others to come rob you!"

Everyone suddenly came to a stop and stood on the side of the road. People suddenly understood that, in leaving their homes, they were simply inviting others to rob them—to come take their possessions with impunity. By having a lock on the door, they were essentially telling people, "Come on in! No one's home!" Everyone therefore rushed home. Many people ended up returning to their homes. Wherever Father went, he would shout his warnings, urging people to return home and guard their houses for the rest of the night. He urged them to guard their houses for the rest of the night, and not run away. But at this point, dozens or even hundreds of outsiders who were pouring in from the southeast—either because they heard our shouts, or because they had run into some of our relatives—all rushed toward us wielding knives and clubs. When we were a dozen or so paces from one another, they raised their carrying poles, hoes, scythes, and clubs, like a grove of trees swaying in the wind. Instantly, the situation changed completely.

My father turned toward the south, and stood in the street with a frightened look. My mother also turned toward the south, and stood there with a stunned expression. I similarly turned toward the south, and in the lamplight I saw someone running and firecrackers exploding on the ground, and also saw all the raised weapons glinting in the light. The sound of "Kill him, kill him!" drifted across the street. There was an array of bright, dark eyes that did not appear at all sleepy, as if there were people who were completely awake, and who had not dreamwalked. There were several people sprinting, chased by a large crowd who had not dreamwalked. I wasn't sure whether those in front were fellow townspeople or outsiders, nor whether those chasing them were outsiders or townspeople. During this chaos, one person running in front tripped and fell, and without waiting for him to get up, one of the people chasing him slammed a shovel down on his leg, and someone else brought a hoe down on his head and neck. After a shout of "Motherfucker!" he collapsed like a baby swallow falling from its nest. There was a thin, piercing, needle-like cry that was abruptly cut short. Another cluster of clubs and hoes slammed down, and the man on the ground became perfectly still, like a pile of mud. I heard the sound of sticks, clubs, hoes, and shovels slamming down onto his body. One man running in front turned and shouted, "You've killed him! You've killed him!" Before the crowd had a chance to respond, hoes and clubs came raining down on him, so he turned and continued running down the road.

He came sprinting toward us.

The sound of the crowd chasing him resembled thunder or fireworks, and they trampled the man who had fallen as if they were stomping through mud.

My mother stared in alarm. "Quick, run!"

I also stared in alarm. "Quick, get in the cart! Father, quick, get in the cart!"

Father also stared in alarm, and he pushed the cart toward the side of the road to hide. Fortunately, the cart stopped in the opening to an alley that was as dark and quiet as a bottomless well. We dashed inside, whereupon the crowd behind us ran back and forth in confusion.

"They went in here! They went in here!"

Father turned off the cart's headlights, and our entire family slipped into the dark alley as though sinking into watery depths. We became invisible to the people chasing us as if we were mere apparitions in a dream.

The people chasing us came to a halt.

We heard them, as though hearing water lapping on the opposite shore. I don't know how Father was able to see the road in the darkness, or how he managed to turn from one alley into another. It was not only those behind us who were making murderous sounds; people ahead of us were also chasing and killing each other, and there were also sounds of chasing and killing on either side of us. The entire town appeared to have woken up. Just before daybreak, the entire world seemed to have woken up. The sound of chasing and killing descended on the town like a thunderstorm, and the entire world seemed to have descended into a storm of people fleeing and chasing one another. The entire world was engulfed in the sound of screams and murderous beatings. It was as though everyone had suddenly woken up, yet it was also as if the people were all still sleeping. They were dreamwalking, and the people were running around and chasing one another. Sometimes there would be only a handful or a few dozen people being chased, but at other times there would be several dozen, or even a hundred or more. As the numbers grew, the crowds gradually became braver, and sometimes they would stop and wave their sticks and clubs while an avalanche of bricks and stones from who knows where started raining down on the pursuers.

In this way, the pursuers became the pursued.

And those who were fleeing became chasers in their own right.

After a pause, footsteps once again filled the town like a thunderstorm. The noise began. The running began. The explosions began. Clubs were slammed down, raised up, then slammed down again. But Father, seemingly oblivious to it all, rode his cart from the south side of town into the center, and then from the center of town toward the northern end, and finally, via an alley, he reached the outer edge of town. Panting heavily, he hauled us out of town, as though taking us from a state of wakefulness into a dream, and then from a dream back into a crystal-clear state of wakefulness.

3. (5:51–6:00)

Standing at the base of a hill to the west of town, I saw that more than a dozen stars were twinkling in the watery-blue sky. There was fog in that blueness. The town appeared as though it were right below us. It was already so late at night that it seemed as though we could almost glimpse daybreak on the other shore. The sun would soon rise—even on a night like this, full of murderous violence, the sun would still have to rise. There was a cool, brisk breeze, and it surged down the mountain like water coursing down a canal. Our sweat began to pour down, and we began to relax.

I knew that, in making it out of the town, we had managed to escape the murderous violence.

In order to see clearly what had happened there, I got off the cart and, with Father, pushed it halfway up the hill. We parked the cart in a flat area at a turn in the road. We could see the lights in all of the town's streets and alleys, and we could see lights in the classrooms of the town school. The lights rose and fell like water in the reservoir on a clear day. We could still hear the sound of shouting and the pounding of footsteps from the chaotic violence down below. The sound resembled turbulent water in the reservoir on a stormy day, and as the waves crashed into one another, it was impossible to tell when one wave disappeared and when a new one rose in its place. Father stared blankly, as did Mother. My family looked at one another, and then we fixed our gaze on the night town, as though looking at a windswept lake. We were unable to see the houses and trees in the village to the east of town, and we were unable to make out the houses, streets, and trees in the town itself. In the end, the sun had not yet come up, and the world was still engulfed in darkness. The dense stillness in the distance was as terrifying as a volley of black and invisible needles filling the sky. I developed goose bumps, and when I touched my arms, they felt as cold and hard as stone rods. In the nearby field, there was a rustling sound. The leaves of the brambles and wild jujube trees next to the road appeared dark green at night, and there was a rustling sound of something crawling over them. Wild fruits were hanging from the branches like babies extending their fingers. The night was filled with the sound of crickets singing in the wild areas next to the road. There were also grasshoppers singing from some of the jujube trees on the roadside, along the ditch, and at the top of the cliff. At night, the entire world became so still that it appeared as though the world had ended and all that was left was empty air circulating through the darkness. It was as if the world had ended and all that was left was an abandoned grave. Because everything was so still, it was possible to hear sounds and movements that normally you would not be able to hear. A sense of fear and dread permeated the night like blades of moonlight and starlight cutting through the night sky.

Mother and I stood next to the cart. Father stood in front of us, in a spot closer to the world—as though he were standing in the world itself. "How could this be? How could this be?" Mother seemed to be talking to herself, but at the same time she also seemed to be asking Father.

"When I was small, I heard of dreamwalkers, and even encountered some, but who had ever heard of dreamwalkers who simply couldn't be woken?"

"Don't say anything, don't say anything. I told you not to say anything, so why are you still speaking?"

Mother stopped speaking. Instead, she sat down on the ground, as though she were tired.

Father stared at the town as though he were trying to capture some sound, as if he were trying to discern something. With one hand resting on the cart's metal railing and the other touching his still-swollen left cheek and ear, Father stood in the stillness. But, in the end, he was unable to hear, capture, or discern any sound.

Appearing discouraged, Father looked back at us, then gazed out at the mountains surrounding the town.

"What time is it?"

"I don't know."

"This sky seems to be dead. If it doesn't start to brighten soon, that must mean that it really is dead."

He spoke to Mother, but also seemed to be speaking to himself. I remembered that there was a brick-like radio in the cart, which gave the time. I rummaged around the cart, throwing out a couple of empty sacks, until I finally found the radio. When I tuned it, there was a crackling sound, like a shovel being dragged down the road. The crackling sound sent shivers down my spine. I fiddled with the radio, and finally found a channel with music. "Di . . . di . . ." After two notes, there was a crackling sound followed by the sound of a young announcer. "It is currently six o'clock in the morning, on the first day of the seventh month." The voice sounded so pure that it seemed as though it were the seed of a good voice.

"It is six o'clock."

"The sun is about to come up."

Mother and Father said this simultaneously, as though they were thanking time. They were thanking the arrival of six o'clock, as though they were thanking everyone for being about to wake up. In the summer, the sun would appear from behind the eastern mountains at a little after six. On a clear night, the sun would come up at six, after which the sky would brighten and everyone would wake from dreams. At this point, because I shifted my position, the orientation of the radio I was holding also shifted, and the clear sound of a male announcer emerged from the static. It was a long weather announcement.

To our listeners—our vast audience of listener friends:

All the listener friends who are now turning on their radios and tuning them to 127.1 MHz for our weather forecast, please take notice. Please take notice. Last night at around nine-thirty, on account of the hot and dry weather combined with excessive seasonal exhaustion, in some areas of our city there appeared a once-in-a-century mass somnambu-lism. Governmental organizations have already sent a large number of employees to all of the affected counties, townships, and mountain regions, to implement and promote waking-up and self-rescuing measures, and to guard against deleterious behavior resulting from somnambulism. Now, however, the problem to which we must pay very careful attention is that this morning after six o'clock, and for the rest of the day, as a result of topographical and meteorological conditions—and specifically a cold front from the northwest—our city and the surrounding region will find itself in long-term hot, overcast conditions with no sun, rain, or wind. These so-called hot, overcast conditions result from the presence of a thick, dense cloud cover without any rain or wind, producing a long-term state of hot darkness, which will make daytime seem like dusk, and dusk seem like nighttime. Some mountain regions will even find themselves in a state of darkness comparable to a complete occultation of the sun by the earth's shadow, such that daytime will be indistinguishable from the middle of the night. Or, to put this more colloquially, some regions will find themselves in a state of darkness resembling a solar eclipse— which may lead people to oversleep and contribute to an extension of the general somnambulism. Those people who have exhausted themselves while dreamwalking all night will find that, after they fall asleep, their somnambulism has been deepened.

The broadcaster's voice was calm and unhurried, as though he were simply reading an article. His voice was as clear as a bell. But when my father heard this broadcast, he stared in shock, as did my mother. I also stared in shock, as I carefully held the radio. I was afraid that if I jostled it, the announcer's voice might get cut off. At that moment, Father seemed to think of something, and he nudged my hand holding the radio. After adjusting the dial, Father took the radio and headed to the top of the hill to get some thornbush branches. As he walked away, the radio's sound became louder and clearer, even as the sound of the sand and rocks that he dislodged while climbing up the hill also became louder and clearer.

He climbed so high that the noise below faded away.

The announcer repeated the same broadcast, as though replaying a recording. Father stood next to a thornbush above us, holding the radio up to his ear. Every word and every letter the radio announcer uttered smashed down on us like black raindrops and ice pellets.

The broadcast was repeated three times, and the sound smashed down on us three times. With our ears pricked, our family listened to the entire broadcast three times.

The entire world had disappeared, and all that remained was this weather broadcast.

The world had disappeared, and all that remained was the sound of those black ice pellets falling and smashing to the ground.

The radio was turned off. Father stood there in the darkness like a black column, in which should have been the sunrise.

"The sun has died, and the town has expired. The sun has died, and the town has expired. The town has truly expired." Father kept repeating these two phrases over and over, and even as he was coming back down from that higher position on the hill, he continued mumbling these same two phrases. But once he was beside us again, he stopped mumbling and fell silent, as though the sun really had died, or as if the world before him had, in fact, disappeared and died. He stood there silently, gazing in the direction of the town while listening carefully. At this moment, someone else appeared at the foot of the hill, not far from us. Another person was fleeing the mayhem in the town. Three more people. Seven or eight more. They ran and paused in an illuminated spot, then quickly disappeared into the dark night. Needless to say, they were as exhausted as we were, and sat down to rest. It was at this time that the lights above the town once again began to flicker, like the surface of a lake glimmering in the sunlight. In the early morning stillness, all sounds appeared to be amplified, and it seemed as though we could even hear the breathing of ants and other insects. The faint sounds of fighting that drifted up from the town resembled the rumbling of an underground river. The sound of footsteps inching forward were like omens anticipating an earthquake. The town was still alive. It was still breathing. It was still killing. Even after waking up, the town continued beating and killing, as it had when it was dreamwalking. Normally at this hour, at six in the morning, there should have been a fish-belly-like light peeking over the eastern mountains, and a spray of red sunrays should have been spurting through mountain ridges. After a while, that spray of red sunrays would become a shore of light red water, flowing, accumulating, and spreading under the eastern sky. The eastern sky would turn white, then bright red, then purplish-red. The east would turn golden yellow and red. The mountain's trees, rocks, and grass would be dyed crimson. The birds, after sleeping all night, would wake up and begin to sing, and would carry the dawn's red glow from the tree branches into the sky. In this way, a new day would arrive. But on this night, this red dawn didn't arrive. Instead, the eastern mountains remained as dark as a deep gully. The blackness of a dark day followed the previous night's black night, as though the night had never ended, and as though it would never end. It was as if a new day had never arrived. It was as if the previous night had never concluded, and as though the nighttime were an endless ball of black thread.

Father returned and stood next to the cart. He looked at the town as though looking at a bottomless lake. Mother got up from the ground and, holding the cart's railing, stood next to Father, as though she were grabbing the bow of a boat.

Mother asked, "What are we going to do, what are we going to do?"

Father replied, "Let's go back. Why did we have to wake up in the first place? It must have been God who woke us, so that we could warn those who are still sleeping." He then stuffed the radio into my hand and proceeded to turn the cart around.

"We are really going back.

"We have to go back. Our family is in the town, and even if we don't care about the town, we have no choice but to care about our own family."

Finally, Father led Mother away, into the dark night that persisted as dawn was delayed. Step-by-step, they proceeded toward their house in the town at the bottom of the hill.

BOOK TEN

No-*Geng*: There Is Still
One Bird Alive

1. (6:00–6:00)

We didn't follow the original path back into town. The area north of town was very poor, and few houses there had been robbed. On this particular night, poor homes and poor neighborhoods were comparatively safe. We headed to the river north of town, wanting to enter town from the north. On the road we encountered some people who were sleeping on the embankment beside the canal at the base of the hill. There were a couple of lanterns hanging from a small tree below the embankment, and someone was waking up the sleepers so that they could take turns standing guard. It was as if by standing guard, they could prevent the others from dreamwalking. As we passed, voices emerged from the group of sleepers.

"The sun is about to rise."

"If we can just hang in there for a little longer, the sun will come up."

"It's as if the day has died, and we'll never see daylight again. When we fled, we didn't bring our watches or radios, so we have no idea what time it is now."

Father didn't tell them that it was already after six o'clock—past the time when the sun would normally have come up. He didn't tell them that on this day the sun had died, time had died, and the daytime also died. "Go to sleep. Just make sure that one person remains awake to keep the others from dreamwalking. After you go to sleep, the sun will come up, and once it does, everything will be over." Saying this, Father walked away.

We finally arrived at the area north of town.

We were finally going to enter town.

The murky houses were like dark piles of dirt in the mountains. The murky trees were like clumps of grass along the riverbank. The noisy sound of footsteps dissolved into the night's tumultuous din, which would periodically drift over from the town and then die away again. The resulting stillness was as if the town's entire world had died, leaving behind no one and nothing—not even the songs of sparrows and insects. Instead, the only thing left was the occasional calls of night birds. Father parked the cart at the northern entrance to town. It seemed as though there had been no mayhem there, and no dreamwalking. Instead, everyone was sleeping soundly. From that point on, the world was at peace, and the town was also at peace.

Our family quietly returned to town. With the dim beams of our flashlights, we could see the rocks and depressions under our feet. We could see the trees and houses on either side of the road. We could also see many people and things hidden in the darkness. I saw a pair of young women in their thirties standing next to the road, and behind them was a recently built tile-roofed house. The women were standing in front of the entrance like two sisters, and there were lamps hanging from the columns on either side of the entranceway. They lazed about in the light, their eyes half-shut and with a sleepy look on their faces. When they saw that someone was approaching, they smiled. "Who are you? My husband isn't home, so why don't you come in and enjoy yourselves?" Our family quickly walked past, and even after we passed we could still hear them calling after us. "Hey, you, if you don't take advantage of this night to enjoy yourselves, you may not have this opportunity after the sun comes up."

After we proceeded another hundred meters or so down the street, we saw five or six women beneath a lantern, fanning themselves while eating peanuts and walnuts, as they sat in front of a new building, waiting for men. They had bathed and washed their hair, and either were wearing bras or else were simply topless. Some of them had slippers, while others were barefoot. Some of them were holding fans, while others were holding cloths with which to wipe the sweat from their faces. However, all of them had hiked their dresses up to their waists. They were young, and had married and moved to the town from the countryside over the previous two years. Regardless of whether they were attractive or homely, they had caked their faces with blush, like recently painted statues. Sleep hovered like clouds over their eyes. Their husbands had gone off to work. Ordinarily, they would stand around joking and discussing private matters, but tonight after waking up they had gathered under the pagoda tree in the entranceway. Here, they were able to enjoy the coolness while gossiping and waiting for their husbands to return. It appeared they knew nothing about the mayhem that had occurred in the southern and eastern portions of town. It was as though this area to the north of town did not even belong to the Gaotian Town that had degenerated into violence. Standing in front of them, however, was the village chief's wife, who was older than the others. It was unclear how she had ended up coming here, or why she, like the other women, was revealing her eggplant-like breasts, and furthermore was serving these younger women some tea and passing them fans. She even shouted with a voice like fire.

"Hey, who are you? If you are men, then come over here. If you want to sleep with one of these girls, she won't ask you for a cent. And if you are willing to sleep with me, I'll give you one or two hundred yuan. Or even three or four hundred.

"Hey, come here! I am the village chief's wife. The village chief—that pig—left me to go find that woman, Wang Erxiang, leaving me no choice but to find a man of my own.

"Hey, who are you? Come over here! After you come here, I'll do everything you need here in the village. Big things and little things, I'll do them all. Why don't you come?"

We quickly walked past their shouts.

Standing in front of them, Mother released a volley of curses. "How could this be?! How could this be?!" But before Mother had finished, two burly men emerged from an alley to the left and walked over to these women. The men were in their thirties and unmarried. One of them was an idiot—even more so than I—and had a stupid smile on his face. The other one suffered from hysteria, and when he wasn't having an episode, he would always be walking down the street with his head bowed like someone who was lowly and weak. The two men ordinarily didn't see much of each other, and when they did meet they were usually as incompatible as a willow and a pagoda tree. On this night, however, they were walking together, and their faces glowed with excitement—appearing as if they had just eaten honey, drunk wine, or gotten married and were entering their bridal chamber. They were chatting as they emerged from the alley. "I hadn't realized that the Sun family's daughter was so fine. Her body is like water." The idiot suddenly came to a stop and stared at the hysteric's face, as though he couldn't believe what he was hearing.

"Really? But his neighbor's wife was not cooperative, and she wouldn't let me caress her unless I beat her."

The hysteric stopped.

"You didn't do her, did you?"

"Yes, I did her."

"She's as beautiful as a dream."

"A dream is false, but this is real. When people wake up from a dream, they die; but whenever I think of this reality, I quiver with delight."

The hysteric laughed. His laugh was like the morning sun.

"Where are we going now? We should go home and sleep."

"We should take advantage of the fact that the sun has not yet come up, and go find women from another couple of households. Today, and in the future, I will always do as you say, so please take me to find another woman." The hysteric seemed to be pondering something. "Tonight, all the good people are out stealing, killing, and beating people while asleep, and they have left us the women here in the north of town. This street is our personal bridal chamber." The idiot spoke as clearly as though he had glimpsed this night's true essence. As he was speaking, he continued forward, pulling the hysteric with him. In this way, the idiot and the hysteric headed toward us. The flashlights they were holding were as bright as the morning sun, and they shone them on us while shouting,

"Are you sleeping or awake? You don't seem to be stealing, robbing, and plundering."

We stopped. "Do you know what's going on in the town center?"

"Everyone is sick, and people are dreamwalking and beating others to death. Before the sun comes up, the town government plans to expel the outsiders and send them back to their hometowns."

The hysteric said this in a loud voice, sounding completely normal and not ill at all. "Hey, tell me the truth—are there or are there not dreamwalking women standing by the side of the road? Are there or are there not naked women standing in their doorways waiting for me?" Father stared in shock. Mother, who was standing behind Father, also stared in shock. Father shouted, "The fuck there are women waiting in their doorways! If there were, do you think I would have come over here?" Mother shouted, "Why don't you go look in South Street? South Street is bustling with Western-style women." Then she noticed that behind her there was the pounding of footsteps, as though an entire army were running toward her. She heard the screams of women being seized. It sounded as though the women were being beaten, after which they permitted their assailants to do as they wished. My father turned around, as did my mother and I. Behind us we saw a group of men detain those women and take them away—leaving behind only the sound of the women's screams and of the doors slamming shut.

And then . . . and then there was only darkness and stillness, as well as the sound of living footsteps breaking through the deathly solitude.

2. (6:00–6:00)

The town really did die at six o'clock that morning.

The world really did die at six o'clock that morning.

In the darkness, at a time when the sun ordinarily would have been several rod-lengths high in the sky, the town collapsed. The town's deadly battle began. People were as abundant as trees, ants, or grains of sand in the Gobi Desert—as abundant as mountains and oceans, stars and other celestial bodies. The crowds inundated one of the town's streets, then the entire town. They plunged the whole world into a nightmare. There were several hundred people, more than a thousand, and perhaps even two thousand. Most were men, but about a third were women. It seemed as though everyone who had been dreamwalking that night was participating in this town battle.

As for those who were not dreamwalking, they also took the somnambulism as a pretext to participate in this war of looting and pillaging.

This town battle was the climax of the night's events. It was everyone's destination—including both the dreamwalkers and those who were still awake. Initially, the dreamwalkers went to harvest and thresh the wheat, then they went to steal, loot, and kill. The result was like a scene out of some former dynasty. But this town battle that erupted as the dawn was being killed by darkness marked the somnambulism's true source, as well as its true culmination. Our family headed southwest toward the southern part of town, where the population was densest and the buildings were most abundant. We initially wanted to find that bronze gong, and bang it until all of the dreamwalkers woke up. We initially wanted to go home and bring out our pots, bowls, gas, tea leaves, coffee, and realgar ice-crystal medicinal brew, but decided against it. Someone flitted past us, like a dark shadow. Some people flickered into view, like the gleam of a knife. They were wearing white shirts, and were holding knives, clubs, and a variety of weapons. They had cleavers, machetes, bayonets, daggers, and scythes resting on their shoulders. They were holding axes, hoes, and sickles, and someone was even holding a red-tasseled spear that hadn't been seen for years. It was difficult to make out their clothing and dress, much less their faces. Instead, all we could see were their shadows and their weapons, and their muffled footsteps sounded like a river flowing ten or twenty meters underground. Some men, afraid of making noise, had taken off their shoes, and were walking barefoot with their shoes under their arms. Some women running after the men were shouting, "Wait for me! Wait for me! If I'm going to die, I want to die with you. If we're going to die, I want for us to die together." People had tied yellow ribbons around their foreheads, with everyone's ribbon folded two fingers wide. They proceeded hurriedly, without saying a word. They simply looked at one another, and at the yellow ribbons on their foreheads. The ribbons were knotted in the back, making it look as though there were a chrysanthemum blossom growing there. Zhang Mutou, who lived across from my family's house, seemed to be a new man. As he walked past me, he had a steel rod dangling from his waist and was holding a cleaver. He was in the process of tying a yellow ribbon around his forehead, then used the cleaver to cut off the extra fabric. He came to a stop and stood in front of my father, while waving around that two-foot-long steel rod that had been dangling from his waist, and with which he had killed Wang, the kiln worker. "Turn off the light! If you don't want to live, then go ahead and shine the light on your face!"

He spoke very harshly. Indeed, this wasn't the Mutou I had known. I stared in shock, then turned off the light. My father took half a step toward Mutou and said in a low voice,

"Are you awake or asleep? What in the world has happened in town?"

"If you want to live, you need to find a yellow ribbon and tie it around your forehead. If you don't care whether or not you live, however, you can simply continue wandering up and down the town streets." I couldn't see his face, and instead all I could see was him shifting his iron rod and cleaver from one hand to the other, and hanging the cleaver from his waist. He waved the rod until finally someone behind him shone a flashlight covered with a cloth. They both commented on my need for a yellow ribbon, then walked away so quickly it sounded as though they were flying, and their shadows moved so quickly it seemed as though they were being blown along by the wind.

I didn't know what, in fact, had occurred in town. Even Zhang Mutou was no longer his former self. The stillness was broken by the puttering of a cart, as though someone had ignited an entire sheet of fireworks. Everyone who passed us turned to stare at our foreheads. Those who were carrying lanterns and flashlights shone them on our foreheads, and they were initially mute with astonishment, but then continued on. We all knew the people shining the lights, but it was as though none of them could recognize us. Zhang Yuantian. Wang Dayou. Wang Ergou. There was also Boss Gao from the tea shop, who, during the first half of the night, had organized the other shopkeepers and urged them not to sleep, so that they could guard their shops. Some people were standing in a shop that had been left empty after the thieves had carted away all of the electronics. The bystanders looked at the shop's owners, Zhang Ming and his wife, as well as their two burly sons. When we called out their names, they didn't answer, and instead they turned and stared at our heads. They again asked, "Do you not want to live? Do you not want to live?" They kept asking us these questions as we stood, baffled, on the side of the road, and looked out at the crowd like sheep that had gotten separated from their flock. At this point, Uncle Xia walked up to us, then came to a halt. "During the first half of the night, you were awake and rescued my family. During the second half of the night, I was awake and rescued yours. Our families are now even, and neither of us owes the other anything." As he said this, he took out a couple of strips of yellow silk and handed them to my parents. "If you want to live, then fold these and tie them around your forehead. On the other hand, if you want to die, you can simply toss these aside and wait to be decapitated and have your corpse put on public display. Or you can wait for the Heavenly Kingdom to be established, and have your entire family carted off to the Kingdom's new execution grounds."

"Where are you all going?"

271

"We want to go back to the Ming dynasty. To the Taiping Heavenly Kingdom."

"What Ming dynasty? What Taiping Heavenly Kingdom? They both ended several hundred years ago. How are you going to go back to the Ming dynasty? How are you going to go back to the Taiping Heavenly Kingdom?"

"How dare you speak like this? Do you not even want to live? If you don't want to live, then don't bring us down with you, OK?"

"You are dreamwalking. I see that you are definitely dreamwalking."

"You're the one who's dreamwalking! Your entire family is dreamwalking!"

As we were cursing each other, Uncle Xia stalked off. He left as though he were trying to escape us. His footsteps sounded as though he were flying. In the blink of an eye, he dissolved into the dark night. My family picked up the strips of yellow silk that he had dropped, and stood there, stupefied. People around us were muttering under their breath. All around there was the sound of footsteps—a combination of frenzied, quick, and cotton-soft footsteps. The air was full of an evil force, like an invisible wind. Everyone was walking into this wind, and was left dizzy by it. Some were clearly sleeping, but it also seemed as though they were awake. Meanwhile, those who were awake looked as though they were sleeping.

We left the cart on the side of the road.

On the side of the road, we tied the yellow silk around our foreheads. We repeatedly turned to look at the people around us. They were enveloped in sleep, and while asleep they wanted to participate in the bloody town battle. They wanted to live and die while asleep. As Mother was tying the silk ribbon around my forehead, she looked at Father's face. "Why don't you let Niannian go home? He is only a child. Don't make him suffer tonight." After Father finished tying his ribbon, he looked at the ones Mother and I had tied around our own foreheads. "Whoever goes home will have to go through that intersection, and will also have to pass through that group embroiled in the town battle. Let's continue in the same direction. Now that we have tied these strips of silk around our foreheads, that means we have entered the battle. We have become townspeople, and have become just like dreamwalkers. No one will look at us suspiciously anymore. Once people see these yellow ribbons around our heads, they will be reassured and will focus only on hurrying forward through this daytime night." The time should have been that of sunrise. In the past, this would have been the time when the rising sun would be magnificently shining down and staining everything golden yellow— including the town, the river, the forest, and all the houses—and it was the time when the shops below the fields would have opened for business. But in this extended night, people had not yet woken up from their dreams. They had not emerged from their somnambulism. Instead, they continued slipping toward the bloody town battle at the depths of their dreams and their dreamwalking. At an intersection away from the square, the dream stopped and the battle erupted. People crowded around as though attending a meeting, and as they piled on top of one another, the lights flickered on and off and the air was filled with the chattering of their voices. Pieces of news circulated through the crowd, as though red-hot secrets were being passed from hand to hand and from mouth to mouth. Everyone was standing in the street, crowded together like clumps of weeds growing in the wilderness. The lamps were on, and were shining only on the ground and on people's bodies, not on their faces or heads. Many people covered their lamps with their hands, or covered their flashlights with a piece of cloth. "What's going on up ahead?" . . . "The cadres are wearing imperial robes." . . . "What's going on up ahead?" . . . "They say that we're almost at the Taiping

Heavenly Kingdom." . . . "What's going on up ahead?" . . . "The Heavenly Kingdom's great battle is about to begin. They are going to drive out the outsiders who are attacking the town's Heavenly Kingdom, and chop them into mincemeat." This news circulated like the wind or a cloud. The news was like a seed buried in the soil and about to sprout. Although it should have been morning, the sky was still as dark as though it were the middle of the night. The air was jet black, as were the trees, walls, and buildings. Some of the town's streetlamps had originally been lit, but now they were being extinguished. Just as the lamps were being extinguished, we saw the village chief leading away the village widow, Wang Erxiang—that young and radiant woman. Both of them had yellow ribbons tied around their heads, and they were carrying Wang Erxiang's little girl, who was sleeping soundly. They turned and made their way toward an alleyway beyond the crowd. Their complexions appeared clean and pure, and they did not look at all sleepy. Their eyes were as large as walnuts. They ran as fast as monkeys or fish, trying desperately to escape the crowd. They fled into the dark night. They were eloping, so that they could enjoy a heavenly life together. My father called out, "Chief! Chief!" But the village chief acted as though he hadn't heard anything. The village chief and Erxiang left behind the crowd, they left behind the world, which was plunged into darkness. People found themselves sandwiched between the ground and the lamplight. The light was scattered like glowing embers flickering on and off. The air was hot and dry, but it was not yet as hot as a burning stove. A cool morning breeze surged into town and circulated through the crowd and the streets. Many of the silk ribbons people were wearing around their foreheads remained soaked in sweat, which dripped down onto their cheeks and noses. As we were making our way through the crowd, I saw that many people's faces resembled bricks or blocks of wood. They looked as excited as though they were dividing up money at a wedding. Or as agitated as the town's idiot or the town's hysteric. Some people's eyes were only half-open, and there were also many who appeared as though they were not at all sleepy. They looked just like the village chief and Erxiang, except for the fact that their eyes were completely bloodshot—as though they were exhausted but simply couldn't fall asleep. There was a couple whose names I couldn't recall, who were hiding under a roadside electrical pole. Hanging from the pole, about a foot from the ground, there was a lamp with a glass cover and a bean-sprout-like flame. Under the lamp there was a shovel handle and a cleaver, and in the lamplight you could see that their faces, which had already been viciously kicked, were full of nervousness and disquiet. The silk ribbons around their foreheads were so soaked in sweat that it looked as if they had just been washed. "Ma Huzi and Cai Guifen, you two are also here?" My father pulled me away, and my mother followed. Our entire family left the crowd and headed over toward that couple. "We can see that you are awake, so perhaps you can tell us what on earth is happening up ahead?" Ma Huzi stared at my father, my mother, and our entire family, then he lowered his voice until it was barely audible. "I hear that the town mayor has already been killed, as well as some of the townspeople and cadres who were awake and didn't participate in the uprising. You absolutely mustn't say you were rescued by someone who was awake, and you absolutely mustn't reveal that we are awake." Then he looked at the people sleeping and dreamwalking around him. "There is going to be a battle, and all of the town's roads have been blocked off. Even the intersections located farthest from North Street have been barricaded. Impoverished women from North Street have been seized to serve as comfort women for the army, and I hear that these women even include the village chief's wife. It's really extraordinary, that in order to establish a Kingdom of Heaven, the town would be willing to engage outsiders in a deadly battle. An hour ago, those townspeople who were still awake and unwilling to go to battle were tied up and held in the town government building's back courtyard. It's only because we were willing to fight that we are still alive, and were able to come here." Their voices were as soft as a fly, and they spoke as though they had narrowly escaped death. They sounded almost as if they were dreamwalking. "Tianbao, you and your family must leave immediately. Those of us who are still awake must not congregate together. If we do, it would be too easy for those who are half-awake and half-asleep to find us—and if they do, it will be the end." He waved us away, and even gently pushed Father back.

We had no choice but to continue on through the gaps in the crowd and the night. But as we were walking away, Ma Huzi ran over and pulled Father aside. "What time is it? Why hasn't the sun come up yet?" . . . "I don't know what time it is, but I think it must be about time for the sun to come up." As Father said this, he took my hand and, with Mother behind us holding on to our clothing, we made our way through the crowd by following those wearing yellow ribbons around their foreheads. We walked through someone else's dream as though following a small path from one side of the thornbush to the other. I was able to see the color of other people's dreams—they were a mixture of black and white, as though black ink had gotten spilled into some white paint, and then gotten mixed with it. There was a circle of black and a circle of white, together with a swirl of black and white mixed together. Intermixed with the murmurings of people talking in their sleep, there was the smell of sweaty sleep and the pungent odor of morning breath. The sound of their breathing resembled the gasps of someone on the verge of death being oppressed by a nightmare. Awake, we circled the outer margins of the crowd, trying to sneak around under the light of the lamps. Under this lamplight, I could vaguely make out other people, but they didn't look at us, and instead merely focused on tiptoeing toward that square in the center of town, their necks extended like rubber bands.

We arrived at the square.

We arrived at the center of the town battle.

There were masses and masses of people.

On the outer edges of the crowd, there were the people who were half-awake, while inside there were those who were half-asleep, and even farther inside there were those who were sound asleep, as well as the dreamwalkers who could talk and act as though they were awake. After the dreamwalkers began to rebel, they took their knives and their clubs and, staring intently with their sleepy eyes, they gathered below the stage. The stage was constructed from a dozen or so tables that had been pushed together, and on either side there were some wooden poles. Hanging from the poles were oil lamps that were neither particularly bright nor particularly dim. Below the oil lamps there were more than a dozen police from the town police station, together with some of the town youth who had been most fond of fighting. Regardless of whether someone was wearing a police uniform, a white gown, or was simply topless, they would nevertheless have a yellow ribbon tied around their foreheads. The only exception was the man standing at the very center of the stage. This was King Li Chuang—formerly known as Deputy Director Li Chuang from the department of armed forces—who was still wearing the military governor's uniform that he had been wearing during the first half of the night, when the town mayor was wearing his imperial robes. The front and back of his uniform were splattered in blood, as if he had just killed someone. The wooden rings that had been hanging from General Li Chuang's costume were missing, and on the stage in front of him countless beads had fallen and scattered around. The embroidery on his sleeves had come undone, and countless white pearls were hanging from his gown by a thread. Not only was Li Chuang wearing a yellow ribbon around his forehead, like everyone else: he had also tied another ribbon to the front of his uniform. His complexion was the color of coagulated blood, and under the lamplight his hair appeared to be standing on end. He had a handsome face and a complexion that was as resplendent as marble. His eyes were wide open, but nevertheless still retained a look of confusion. His eyes did not appear at all gentle, but rather seemed to project a cold light. It was at this point that someone came and whispered something in his ear, and someone else placed a battery-powered megaphone in his hand. The person whispering into his ear seemed to have mistaken my father for Li Chuang's enemy, Yang Guangzhu—whose father and grandmother had previously passed away, and whose mother had died that same night. After the man finished whispering to Li Chuang and handed him his things, he retreated to stand behind him. Then, dressed in his official robes and holding his megaphone, Li Chuang proceeded to the front of the stage and gazed out at the assembled crowd, and at their eyes glimmering in the lamplight. He cleared his throat, and the crowd standing directly in front of the stage fell silent. He cleared his throat again, and that silence immediately spread through the entire crowd. After waiting for everyone in the square to become silent, he placed his megaphone on a table. "I hereby announce that we will have an uprising. This is our Taiping Heavenly Kingdom. We have already returned to the Taiping Heavenly Kingdom of the era of King Chuang." After a pause, he raised his voice. "Now, the righteous army of the Shun dynasty has been assembled, and we have occupied the town government. Our final battle before the sun comes up will determine the fate of our Heavenly Kingdom. It will determine whether or not we can return to the great Ming dynasty. I know . . ." His voice grew even louder, and even without a megaphone it still sounded as if he were using one. "People from other villages, like Wu Sangui, have already gathered outside town to steal from Gaotian. They want to occupy the houses, roads, and all of the property and livestock of our Heavenly Kingdom's future capital. But they . . ." The deputy director lifted the lower hem of his military gown and laughed a cold laugh. "Those losers with their homemade weapons number only a few dozen, while we have several hundred or even several thousand troops, and if we make a move, we can easily kill them, annihilate them, chop off their hands and feet and hang them from the town's trees and electrical poles. As soon as the sun comes up and they see this, they will retreat, acknowledge defeat, and surrender to us, whereupon we will transition from the Ming dynasty to the Shun dynasty. At that point, our Shun dynasty will finally attain what it deserves, and I, King Li Chuang, decree that anyone who succeeds in killing an outsider will be granted the status of a category seven officer in the Heavenly Kingdom of the Great Shun. Anyone who succeeds in killing two outsiders will be granted the status of a category six officer; anyone who succeeds in killing three or four will be granted the status of a category four or five officer; and anyone who succeeds in killing eight or ten outsiders will be treated like those who have achieved a top score in the Great Shun's military examinations. As for those of you who don't kill anyone, and merely succeed in breaking one of the enemy's arms or legs, or slicing off an enemy's ears or nose, the Great Shun will award you houses, land, and silk based on the number of arms and legs you break, and the number of noses and ears you slice off. The reward for breaking one enemy leg will be one-point-two *mu* of land, and the reward for breaking an enemy arm will be one-point-three *mu*. For those of you who slice off enemy noses or ears, the reward will be ten bolts of silk or five silver ingots for those who offer one nose or ear, and a hundred bolts of silk, eight hundred horses, ten gold bars or five small gold bricks for those who offer ten." When King Chuang reached this point in his speech, his voice became even deeper and even more powerful, as though he were shouting through a crack in a door. "Regardless of whether we return to the Great Shun or remain in the present, this battle will mark a decisive moment . . . Everyone and everything, be they heroes or random weeds, will observe the town's predawn battle . . . Now, everyone listen to me. We must all extinguish our lamps. Everyone must stay silent, and hide in this town's streets and alleys, behind walls and in outhouses, and in funerary shops, restaurants, hair salons, Chinese pharmacies, and in neighboring houses and courtyards. We must make the enemy believe that the entire town is asleep, so that they will boldly enter the town's shops and homes, and steal from them. Then, everyone must continue hiding, and watch for the large gas lamp in the square." King Chuang removed the lamp from the column where it was hanging, and lifted it up. "We will use this light as a signal. When you see that this lamp is illuminated and hanging from the top of the column, you should emerge from your hiding places. And when you see outsiders not wearing yellow ribbons around their heads, you should kill them with impunity. Anyone who kills one outsider will be granted the status of a category seven officer in the Heavenly Kingdom of the Great Shun; and anyone who kills ten outsiders will be recognized for outstanding service . . . Now all should prepare to extinguish their lamps . . . Everyone should help transmit my orders from the front to the back of the crowd . . . Everyone should go and quietly begin looking for somewhere to hide. When you see me extinguish this lamp, you should all extinguish your lanterns, lamps, flashlights, and candles. After the outsiders have entered the town and begun stealing from our houses and our shops, you must be careful not to move . . . But when you see the lamp in the square come on again, and when you hear a deadly commotion in the streets, you should emerge from your hiding places . . . You should kill anyone who is not wearing a yellow band around the head . . . You should kill anyone not from this town . . . You should kill anyone who does not want to return to the Great Ming and help establish the Great Shun . . . Do you hear me? . . . Will you remember what I've said? . . . Have you relayed everything I've said to the people in the back of the crowd?"

Deputy Director Li Chuang shouted while standing at the front of the stage. His voice swirled through the night and through the crowd like a gust of wind. The people in the crowd standing below the stage were buffeted like a clump of grass in that wind, as they turned around to relay to those standing behind them what King Chuang had said. The night looked as though it had been painted black, and the dawn was like a pool of black mud. There was the sound of chirping, as though tens of thousands of feet were jogging over the sandy ground. Then, the lights were extinguished, as though a lake was slowly flowing over the shore in all directions. Our family was standing at an intersection a few dozen paces from the stage. As we watched, we saw the crowd disperse and head toward even darker alleys. "Shunzi, do you want to be a category six or a category seven officer? If you are going to kill someone, why don't you go ahead and kill a high-level provincial official?" . . . "Ma Zhuang, do you want to be county mayor or provincial governor?" . . . "I don't want to be an official. I just want to have a few hundred *mu* of land, and a handful of concubines." . . . "What about you, Wang Yili?" . . . "I don't want to be an official or a landlord. I've spent my entire life as a butcher, slaughtering cattle and pigs, but I don't know what it feels like to kill a person. I want to go back to the Great Ming and the Great Shun, and see what it feels like to kill someone and slice off his nose and ears." The sound of whispering accompanied the rustling sound of footsteps. There was also the sound of people sharpening their blades, as well as the sound of people exchanging their cleavers for larger knives. It sounded like rain. It sounded like feet dashing forward.

There was also the sound of people in the middle of the street relaying the message: "King Chuang wants you to speak more softly. King Chuang orders you to be silent." The sounds were mere whispers, but at the same time their strength was something you would encounter only once in a hundred years. These whispers were like rain falling on a hot pavement, or like midday showers on a field. A mist was swirling over the streets, and there was a heat wave rolling over the entire land. Father initially felt calm and composed, but this heat quickly left him confused. When Mother first saw Father's composure, she herself remained outwardly calm except for the fact that her hands and face became wet with sweat, but after she saw his composure change to confusion, her own face turned pale and her hands began to tremble. "Why doesn't someone go wake up Director Li Chuang? If he doesn't wake up when you tap his shoulder, you can hit him or dump a basin of cold water over his head." Before Father had a chance to say anything, Yang Guangzhu and Zhang Mutou, over in the square, suddenly chopped off someone's head for some reason, and before that person had a chance to finish shouting "Ah!" his head dropped like a melon. "Motherfucker! Those who want to inform, will meet this end. They'll meet this end." Yang Guangzhu and Mutou said this angrily. As they were doing so, they kicked aside the head, which was still spurting blood like a fountain, after which the body collapsed like a wooden stake. Father and Mother both screamed softly, then covered their mouths and eyes with their hands. After this, the world became very quiet. The extinguished lamps shrouded the town in darkness. The streets, meanwhile, were full of movement, disquiet, and the stench of blood. In the disquiet, there was suddenly the scream of someone being killed. "Aiya! . . . Mother!" After this scream, however, the town streets and the entire world became as still as death. All of the lights had been extinguished, and all of the sounds had been silenced. In this deathly still, dark night, there was again the clear sound of Yang Guangzhu mumbling as he dragged something. "Motherfucker! To think that someone would dare inform on us! To think that someone would dare say that our uprising is not an insurrection but merely a mass dreamwalking. Those who dare to say that we are dreamwalking, I'll give them a knife and wake them up." Then, there was only deathly silence. Everything returned to silence, which was broken by the stench of blood and the urgent footsteps of people running and hiding in the night.

My father extinguished his lamp.

My family huddled under a tree at the corner of the street. After we watched Yang Guangzhu, Zhang Mutou, and the rest of the crowd retreat into the distance, Father headed in the direction of the person who was still shouting as he lay dying. Father immediately hurried back, covering his nose and mouth. He didn't say a word, nor did he look around. Instead, he pulled me and Mother by the hand, and we ran for our lives. Even though there was no one behind us, we fled as though we were being pursued by thousands of people wielding knives.

3. (6:00–6:00)

The center of town was only five hundred meters from the bustling area on the eastern side of town. My parents and I covered those five hundred meters as though they were five hundred *li*. We used a tiny amount of time as though it were an entire day, or an entire year. It was as if we were running continuously for an entire day or an entire year. It was as if we were running, sprinting, even flying. Sometimes I would be in front; at other times it would be Father who would be in front. Mother, however, was always following behind us, struggling along like a belly-up fish on the verge of death. The night gave Mother nightmares. The night gave all of us nightmares. I ran to the front, but then went back to support Mother. Father ran to the front, but then also went back to help Mother. In the end, Father and I placed Mother's arms over our shoulders, and continued running. As Father ran, he cursed Mother's leg. "This crippled leg has tormented me my entire life. It has tormented me and Niannian our entire lives!" Mother also cursed her own leg. "It has also tormented me my entire life. If it hadn't been for this leg, there's no way I would have ever married you, Li Tianbao!" Cursing angrily, our entire family ran out of the dream.

We then ran into a new dream.

In the end, no one noticed us and no one pursued us as we escaped into a new dream.

We noticed all of the townspeople hiding in corners, in alleyways, in the shadows, and under trees, as well as in those shops that had been robbed. Everyone was hiding, to the point that the streets were left empty and silent, as though our family were the only ones left. "Who's there?" . . . "It's us, we're wearing yellow ribbons around our heads." . . . "Quick, come hide over here. Do you want to continue on, to martyr yourself as the founding father of the Great Shun and the Heavenly Kingdom?" . . . "If we continue on, we will reach our home. Everything there is familiar to us, and therefore it will be convenient to fight and kill." Just as Father was speaking to the people hiding on the side of the road, someone recognized our family. The darkness was broken by an ear-piercing scream. "Li Tianbao, you ass. Your wife is crippled, yet you still expect her to fight and kill? Is it that you, too, are dreamwalking, and want to return to the Great Shun of King Li Chuang?" Father responded, or perhaps he didn't. He focused only on supporting Mother, as though dragging a sack full of grain. Panting like coarse sand, he attempted to make his way to the house. Mother continued to walk and stop, walk and stop, and she kept wiping the sweat from her face and repeating, "I can't take another step! I can't take another step!" Father continued pushing her, and repeating, "Another few steps and we'll be home. Will it really kill you to take another few steps?" In the end, she walked halfway down East Street, until finally there were no more voices and no more people hiding by the side of the road. It was as if we had left King Chuang's Great Shun on this night on this day of this year.

We once again enjoyed peace and quiet.

There was no longer anyone trying to hunt us down.

The voices of the people hiding by the side of the road gradually faded, but just as we were slowing down to catch our breath, we saw that someone had been killed in the entrance to the Heavenly Fragrance noodle shop. The deceased was an outsider in his thirties or forties, with a square face and jet-black hair. His intestines were leaking out of his abdomen, and his naked torso was perforated with four or five stab wounds. Next to his corpse, there was a cleaver he had been holding, its blade splattered with blood and pieces of flesh. Needless to say, it looked as if he had died fighting someone at close quarters. Farther ahead, in front of the tailor's shop from which even the wardrobes and clothes hangers had been stolen, there was a corpse lying in a drainage ditch. The body was facedown, with the head in the ditch and the feet sticking straight up in the air. Holding his lantern out, Father approached and tried to pull the body out of the ditch, but found he couldn't budge it. "He's dead," Father told us, as though describing a withered branch that had broken off from a tree. "The corpse doesn't even have a trace of breath. It appears there was a battle here, and this resembles a cleaned-up battlefield. It doesn't look like the site of a robbery, but rather the site of a town battle." Shocked into silence, we proceeded eastward. In the deathly quiet, our footsteps resonated hollowly. Every few steps, Father would mutter to himself. Mother didn't say anything, but began walking faster than us. It suddenly appeared that she was not as crippled as before, and was now able to walk like a normal person. Eventually, the entrance to our family's New World funerary shop appeared before us. When Mother saw the shop entrance, she increased her pace even more, as though she were finally returning home after having been away for countless days, or even years. But when she was about to reach the entranceway to our home, Mother came to an abrupt halt in the middle of the street, as though she had just noticed that she had taken a wrong turn and was standing in front of the wrong house. The entrance to our shop was wide open. One of the doors had fallen to the ground, with half lying inside the shop and the other half lying outside. The shop's wreaths had been torn apart and were scattered over the floor and in the entranceway. Even in this pitch-black night that should have been daytime, I could tell that those paper blossoms and leaves were splattered in blood, as though countless white leaves had fallen into a pool and gotten stained by the foul water. The red blood on the white blossoms appeared alluring, thick, and purplish-black. The blood on the green leaves appeared dark, black, and purplish-blue. The sharp stench of blood lingered on the ground and in the entrance to our house. There had been a violent struggle here, a battle. Mixed with the blood and the paper, there was a cooking knife and an ax. There was also a wooden club that had been used as a weapon, and had been left in a pool of blood like a long leg bone. Everything was very still. It seemed as though hidden in the stillness, in the night, in the still night, there was a faint sound. Father shone his light in front of him, deciding he might as well stop covering the light. In front of him, he saw a hoe, some clothing, and several shoes that had been left there. The batteries of his flashlight were about to run out, and the light was as weak as a thin layer of yellow cloth. He could hear a noisy ruckus two hundred meters away, near the town's east entrance, as if the sound of a mountain being moved was being transmitted from the other side of the world. "The sun is about to come up?" This question was from Mother, who was standing in the doorway to her house, staring in shock. "The sun won't come up." This response was from Father, who was staring at the bloody mess in the entranceway. Then, everything became quiet again. In the stillness, it almost seemed as if you could hear the corpses breathing. This tiny, frigid sound resonated through my brain and through my joints. My entire family stood in front of that pool of blood and in front of those paper blossoms. We saw that in the doorway to our shop there were bloodstained paper blossoms, a bloodstained shirt, and a new pair of those "liberation shoes" worn by PLA soldiers. We didn't shout in surprise, and instead merely stared impassively at the scene before us.

Along this stretch of street, there had been a battle and a deadly beating.

"You should go back. Now that we are awake, I have no choice but to go to East Street to have a look."

Father's voice seemed to have little relation to the scene before me. He handed Mother the flashlight he was holding, and looked at her as though looking at something he had long wanted to throw away but had never been able to. "You should go back. Did you hear me? You should go back. If you don't want to live, then don't go back. Otherwise, you should go back, and don't come out even under threat of death. You must close and lock your door, and even if you hear a sound as loud as heaven, you mustn't come out." Mother didn't accept the flashlight, acting as if it wasn't worth it.

"You have to go. Even under threat of death, you still have to go and take a look, and then you can return."

This was said in a very loud voice. Mother said this in a very loud voice, but it also sounded as though she were simply telling Father goodbye on an ordinary day as he went down to hoe the fields. No one thought of me. No one mentioned what I should do. A feeling of loss descended over the night, and over my heart. It was as if I were superfluous to the night, and superfluous to my own family. I watched as Father headed toward the town's eastern entrance. I watched as Mother made her way home through the paper blossoms and the bloodstains, but when she reached the door, she turned around and said something very intimate and recriminatory.

"Niannian, why aren't you coming with me and your father? Why are you just standing there?"

When I caught up with Father, Father also said something very recriminatory.

"Niannian, why are you following me, and not staying home to look after your mother?"

But Father still pulled my hand. I followed him as though following an eagle capable of lifting its legs and flying away. The road was filled with objects left behind after deadly fights, including sickles, axes, hoes, shovels, and carrying poles. There were also red flags and scythes, as well as cloth shoes, sneakers, leather shoes, and cheap plastic sandals. Originally, there had been only a few lamps in the town's eastern entrance, but by the time we arrived there were many. An entire world of lamps was illuminated, and the town's entrance was so brightly lit that it seemed as though it were daytime. Meanwhile, the people scurrying beneath these lamps each had a white cloth tied around the left arm. A large truck was parked at the entrance to the village, and was loaded with bundle after bundle of red flags and red silk fabric. An oil lamp was hanging from each of the truck's banner rods, and there were two banners as large as bedsheets on either side of the truck's hood. They both had writing on them, but neither Father nor I could read it. All we could see was that in the truck there were a couple of young people who not only had white cloths tied around their left arms but also had white bloodstained bandages wrapped around their heads. One of them was wearing glasses, and the other was wearing a short-sleeved shirt. They were taking turns holding up the loudspeaker and shouting.

"Fellow elders." . . . "Brothers and sisters, the predawn general offensive has begun." . . . "We must cross over the dark night and enter tomorrow, to seize Gaotian Town." . . . "From this point on, we will no longer be villagers. From this point on, we will no longer be left-behind peasants. Instead, we will become future masters and modern urbanites. We will begin enjoying luxurious lives, in which we can have whatever our hearts desire. We will be able to go to the market and get whatever we need, without having to get up in the middle of the night to come into town. We will send the townspeople to the countryside and into the mountains, where they will have to live the kind of bitter lives we ourselves have lived, growing crops and raising livestock, and when they want to go to the market, it will be they who will need to wake up in the middle of the night to come into town." . . . "To come to our city." . . . "Fellow countrymen." . . . "Fellow comrades." . . . "For the sake of tomorrow, and for the sake of the future, we must charge!" . . . "Fellow countrymen." . . . "Uncles and aunts and brothers and sisters." . . . "For the sake of tomorrow and for the sake of the future, we must kill!" . . . "Whoever succeeds in seizing a restaurant will get to keep it." . . . "Whoever succeeds in seizing a store will get to keep it." . . . "Whoever attacks anyone who is attempting to resist us, or attacks anyone who doesn't have a white cloth around the left arm, tomorrow you will be rewarded with a house in town. And if you attack resisters with a hammer, then in the future, when the town becomes a city, you will be rewarded with a building in a busy intersection. Anyone who is attacked to the point of being covered in blood or dead, you will be viewed not as criminals but rather as heroes, and tomorrow this town will be our town, these streets will be our streets, and everything under heaven will be ours. These streets, and all of these houses, stores, train stations, post offices, banks, markets, and so forth and so on, they will all belong to us. At that point, all will get what they deserve, and will take what they need, and if they want prosperity, they can have prosperity, and if they want liveliness, they can have liveliness." . . . "We must attack for the sake of tomorrow!" . . . "We must bleed for the sake of our grandchildren!" . . . "Fellow countrymen." . . . "Brothers." . . . "Charge!" . . . "Charge!" . . . "For the sake of tomorrow, for the sake of the future, and for the sake of our grandchildren, take down Gaotian, kill Gaotian, and charge!"

Those two youths hopped down from the truck and charged forward while holding up the oil lamp and the red flag. The crowd similarly grabbed red flags, swords and spears, lamps and clubs, and followed them toward town. There were maybe several hundred people, or even over a thousand, or perhaps even over ten thousand. They all surged down the streets, waving their clubs and farming tools in the air. "Our family wants that grocery store." . . . "Our family wants that hardware store on the side the road." . . . "For years, our family has long had its eye on that butcher shop." Shouting and pillaging, they all ran toward town. They sprinted through the shops on either side of the street. It was unclear whether they were awake or asleep, or whether they were dreaming or dreamwalking. In the lamplight, the white cloths they were wearing around their arms resembled white flowers blooming in the dark night—white flowers that were surging through the air. The sound of everyone running resembled countless war hammers pounding on countless leather war drums. It sounded as though a hailstorm were pounding down on the drums. "Here are some people who don't have white cloths around their arms . . . Here are some people who don't have white cloths around their arms . . ." The shouts rang out as though the crowd had just found a bank vault, or as though they were standing in front of a locked door and had just found the key. Father grabbed my hand and pulled me into an outhouse on the side of the road. I didn't know whether this was for men or women, but the open-air portion of the outhouse was only half the size of a typical room. I had never been inside this particular outhouse, which had been constructed by one of the town's old men, who would come by every evening to collect the night soil left behind each day by people on their way to the market. But now, the outhouse became a fortress that would save our lives. The walls of the structure were made of stone and mud, the wall was lumpy and uneven like the town's swollen and bruised face. Father pulled me against the wall, then ripped the yellow bands from our heads and tossed them into the latrine. "Niannian, don't be afraid. If someone comes, say that we are outsiders. You mustn't say that we are from this town." Seeing that I was trembling from head to toe, Father hugged me close, as though hugging a bunny. I grasped his arms with both hands, fingernails digging into his skin. As I grabbed him, I also calmed down and began to listen to what was happening outside. The footsteps of people running past the outhouse sounded like an army or cavalry. Like a thousand-man army or a ten-thousand-man cavalry. Wave after wave of horses and people ran by, kicking up a cloud of dust that smelled even stronger than the inside of the outhouse. The smell of the dust covered the stench of the outhouse, and also covered the dark scent of the predawn sky. "If only we had white cloths tied around our arms right now, we would be fine. We would be safe, and nothing would happen." Father was talking to himself, and also seemed to be thinking about something. He reflexively patted his pockets, and as he did so, he turned on the light in the outhouse. The light came on explosively, making it appear as though a sun were suspended over West Street. On West Street there was a loud rumble, after which there was the sound of a shout and a counterattack. "For the sake of the Great Shun, everyone must kill!" . . . "For the sake of the Great Shun, everyone must attack and kill!" Meanwhile, there were also shouts coming from East Street. "For the sake of tomorrow, for the sake of the future, for the sake of our sons and grandsons, let's go kill!" . . . "To ensure that tomorrow's Gaotian is still our Gaotian, let's go kill!" The odd thing was that no one was speaking about the present. No one wanted the present. This was a war over the past and the future. More specifically, this future was the future that was written about in books, and the past was that of the town battle. This great war had erupted over the future and the past. As for the present of this night of this month of this year, it either had been completely forgotten, or had been transformed into a nightmare. There was no present. The present had disappeared. It was as Yan Lianke had written in one of his novels: *What arrived was the time and history of the future and the past.* And now we were going to die in this nightmare. The lamps in the sky were flickering and swaying, like a sword dancing in midair. The footsteps in the street were running, as the sound piled up until it was over our heads and extended into the air. The sound became a mountain. It became an ocean. It became a mountain range, an ocean, and an entire world. Someone was cursing, "Grandma, grandma, fuck your grandma!" Someone else was screaming at the top of his lungs. "Ma . . . Ma . . . My head is bleeding! . . . My head is bleeding!" It was as though all of the townspeople and the peasants had gathered outside the outhouse to fight. It was as though they had gathered to have a deadly fight. A knife fell from the sky and landed next to our feet. A shoe also fell from the sky and landed on my head. Father hugged me close, the way one might embrace a lamb. I grasped him tightly, digging my fingers into his waist. This way, even as people outside were fighting and yelling, we were hiding inside the outhouse, trembling and holding our breath. The outhouse walls swayed precariously, as though they were about to collapse. Similarly, the street and ground also swayed and cracked as though they were about to collapse. The flashlight's batteries finally ran out and its light was extinguished. As the outside descended into darkness, it came to resemble a pool of ink, while the outhouse, which remained illuminated, resembled a pool of light. The light in the outhouse was so bright that you could make out the latrine pit down below, as well as the thousands of maggots that were thriving in the heat of this night of the sixth lunar month. White larvae crawled up the latrine walls, heading toward Gaotian. As they crawled along, the vibrations from the deadly fight that was raging outside knocked them back down, back down into the latrine. This is how things went. In this way, it seemed as if the sound of the deadly fight moved west. It appeared that the outsiders had fallen into a trap set by the townspeople. The lights from both sides shone onto the square, and the sound of fighting shifted west, even as the sound of footsteps and shouting also shifted east. It appeared as though the outsiders were being driven out by the townspeople, who were chasing, killing, and expelling them. But after a while—after a short while—the outsiders once again surged into town until they reached the square. The townspeople and the outsiders then proceeded to attack and retreat, attack and retreat—repeatedly moving back and forth outside the outhouse, like a handsaw. Shouts and screams rained down like hail onto the outhouse and the entire town. In my father's embrace, I began to breathe quickly as I struggled to move. I felt there was something on the ground sticking to my feet and shoes, making it feel as though I were trying to walk through a vat of rubber. Blood was flowing into the outhouse along the cracks between the floor stones, as though it were rainwater. First there were several streams, and then there was a large pool. A pool of blood half the size of a standard tatami mat, or as large as a door. Blackish-reddish-purple, the blood flowed into the outhouse, and in the process it had picked up and carried away dirt and weeds that had been lying on the ground. The smell of blood overpowered the stench of the outhouse. Black, thick, sticky blood flowed in toward the latrine pit.

At this point, Father also noticed the blood flowing into the outhouse. He saw that a stream of blood had curved around his foot. He stared at the bloody floor in astonishment, then picked me up out of the way of the blood, carrying me to an empty area in the center of the outhouse.

"What time is it? Is the sun really not going to come? Has the sun really died?"

I remembered the radio dangling from my waist, and quickly brought it around to the front. After pressing the "on" button, I held the radio up to my ear, then I brought it down again and hit it a couple of times. Finally, it began producing sound. The announcer's voice sounded slightly frantic as he methodically read the broadcast, as though a tape were being played over and over again. *The problem that we now must attend to is* . . . Father grabbed the radio and turned the volume almost all the way down, such that only the two of us could hear it.

Because of the terrain and airflow, as well as the cold front that has moved in from the northwest, several regions in our city will find themselves in long-term hot, overcast conditions with no sun, no rain, and no wind. This means that there will be dense cloud cover but no rain or wind. The result will be long-term hot and overcast conditions, such that at midday it will be as dark as dusk. Furthermore, some regions may witness midday darkness like that of a solar eclipse, making the day look as though it were the middle of the night.

When the broadcast reached this point, Father turned off the radio.

Upon turning off the radio, he wanted to say two completely extraneous phrases. Two dreamtalking phrases.

"Where can I go to find a sun that can make me wake up?"

"As soon as the sun comes up, the night will end and everyone will wake up."

And then, and then he straightened his back, and very urgently—yet at the same time very woodenly—stood there and listened to the sound of people running around and fighting outside. He walked away from me, then stood stealthily in the entrance to the outhouse, as though standing in the doorway to his dream. With one step, he would be able to enter his dream, and with another he would be able to emerge from his dream and wake up. Father stood in the entrance to the outhouse, with his neck extended until it was as long as a rope, stealthily watching the fighting that was going on outside in the night. After waiting for the commotion to calm down, he dragged me from the outhouse. Sneaking along beneath the roadside wall, we fled east, to the area outside town.

It was as if we were running into a dreamwalking state.

It was as if we were running out of a dreamwalking state into a state of wakefulness.

BOOK ELEVEN

Rise: The Final Bird
Flies Away

1. (6:00–6:00)

Once again, we ran out of town.

The town streets were full of people who were wounded and bleeding. In the light and in the shadows, they were shouting, "Help me! Help me! For better or for worse, we are all fellow country-folk. Help me! Help me!" The wounded were bleeding. They were awake, and had expressions of remorse. "I think I'm dreamwalking. I think I'm dreamwalking. I had already fallen asleep when I heard someone whispering in my ear, saying that I should go into town to steal, and that tonight many people were going into town to steal, and I don't know what happened, but the next thing I knew I was following this person to go and steal and kill." A thin, middle-aged man's face was covered in blood, and he was holding his head in his hands. "I saw people stealing televisions, quilts, and sewing machines, but I didn't steal anything myself. Instead, I got my face slashed." Holding his wounded face, he removed the cloth from his arm and handed it to Father. "Use this to wrap my head. Use this to wrap my head." Father took the cloth and proceeded to rip up his own shirt, and then wrapped the man's head. But as Father was doing this, he kept muttering to himself, "I'm so sleepy, yet you demand that I wrap your head! I'm virtually dreamwalking myself, yet you demand that I wrap your head!" Father wrapped the man's head using strips of cloth from his own shirt. Then Father and I supported him as though escorting a wounded soldier back from the battlefield.

The peasants were wounded and bleeding. They had all emerged and congregated beneath a large truck, where they were talking and hugging one another. They all woke up and ran away in every direction, toward their respective homes. "This is extraordinary dreamwalking! This is extraordinary dreamwalking!" Those who were dead and no longer bleeding weren't able to wake up, but those who were awake were heading home, while those who were still dreamwalking continued surging into town. Those who were awake but pretending to be dreaming, meanwhile, also mixed in with the dreamwalkers and proceeded into town with them. It seemed that some had finished shopping at the market and were heading home, while others were still heading to the market. Those who were heading to the market were walking confidently down the middle of the road, while those who were awake and returning home after having stolen things were walking along the road's outer edge. When members of these two groups encountered one another, they either didn't say anything or else simply exchanged a few pleasantries.

"Aiya, how did the town end up like this?"

"Go quickly! If you are too slow, then there won't be any stores left. There won't be any goods left."

Empty-handed, the awake people returned home, while encouraging the dreamwalkers to rush into town. The people in the street carrying empty shoulder poles, pulling empty carts, or driving empty cars were proceeding into town draped in red flags and carrying all sorts of lanterns. They resembled a cavalry, and their lights illuminated the entire street. The town was going to meet its end because, no matter what, the townspeople would have no way of fighting off this wave upon wave of countryfolk. Father and I had both tied white cloths around our forearms. The thin, middle-aged man with the bloody head, whom we had left to the east of town, was now running out of town. He was running along the outer edge of the road as he headed toward the southern part of town, running against the tide of people who were surging into town. The entire way, Father grasped my hand, and I heard him mumbling.

"Niannian, it seems that Father is dreamwalking. He is going to do something extraordinary!

"Niannian, Father is dreamwalking. Don't wake him up. Father is going to do something extraordinary!"

I realized that Father really was dreamwalking. I realized that he had been tired and had fallen asleep, at which point he must have been infected by the hysterical dreamwalking that had affected the entire town. Because I was stupid, I knew that Father had fallen asleep and was dreaming, but I didn't attempt to release him from his dream. Instead, I merely followed after him, following him as he dreamwalked out of town. From the east side of town, we proceeded south until we arrived at an intersection and waited there. Group after group of countryfolk heading into town passed in front of us, and in town we could hear the screams of people beating others, and of people being beaten. This dry, cracked sound hovered over our heads. The air was full of the smell of blood, as though it had been burned or boiled. There was also the woody smell of that old pagoda tree behind us—the burnt smell of battle. This had previously been an ice cream and popsicle stand. My father and I were here, our bodies covered in the smell of sweat and confusion. The empty spaces in town were either illuminated or full of murderous screams. All of those sounds that emerged from the light either flew overhead or dropped down to earth. The boundary between light and darkness resembled diluted ink that was permeating everything around it. You could see layer upon layer of leaves in the trees, leaves so thick that they came to resemble splotches of ink in their own right, and the sky resembled an enormous black sail erected overhead.

The night had already ended.

The night coolness had also already ended.

Based on the heat, it was clear that it was already the time of day when the sun would ordinarily be several rod-lengths high in the sky. It was the time of day when the sun would ordinarily be prepared to blanket the earth with its heat. In summer, this time of day was between eight and nine o'clock, when people would be eating breakfast. But time died at six o'clock. It died inside the deathly blackness just before the sun should have come up. The weather was as the announcer had described—hot and overcast. As the announcer had said, the sky resembled a total solar eclipse. Even in the middle of the day, all you could see were the objects and shadows directly in front of you, and if you were three to five meters away, you wouldn't be able to see anything clearly, as it would all be a dark blur. In this darkness, in this murderous fighting, in the chaos in which the daytime had died, we watched and listened, as Father sat on the ground and leaned against the pagoda tree. As he was resting, I took advantage of a ray of light that was passing overhead, and could once again see the whites of his eyes.

His eyes resembled a dirty white rag. The white part of his left eye was as large as his right, his right eye was as large as his left, and his blackish-yellow pupils resembled two drops of sewage that had fallen onto the rag. It looked as though Father had fallen asleep. He must have been so exhausted that he fell asleep. But even as he slept, he continued dreamtalking as though he were awake. "We must find the sun. If we can find the sun, we'll be able to save the people of this village, this town, and this entire region. If we can bring out the sun, we'll be able to save the people of this village, this town, and this entire region." There was a murmuring sound in my ears, and there was a murmuring sound hidden in the world. As Father was speaking, he turned to look at the area above the town. "The fact that the lights above the town are still swinging back and forth indicates that the people are still fighting." After he said this, he again turned his head in that direction. "We must try to go and find the sun. We must go and find the sun. I always feel that the sun is hidden somewhere on my body, but I can't remember where I left it—the same way that you might want to speak to someone, but you open your mouth and realize you can't remember the person's name." As Father was saying this, he stood up from where he was sitting under the tree. I was very surprised that Father would stand up while asleep, as though he were awake. But then my surprise gradually faded, as I remembered that during this night of somnambulism, everyone was dreamwalking, and if you didn't dreamwalk, that was considered to be very odd. Father stood there and seemed to be searching for something on the ground, while also feeling around in his pockets. He circled halfway around that pagoda tree, and then he came to a halt. He knocked twice on the tree, then beat his own head, as though the sun were hiding inside his skull. It was as though, by pounding his own head, he could squeeze out the sun that was hidden inside.

"I know how to bring out the sun!
"I know how to transform the dark night into daylight!"

2. (6:00–6:00)

This is what happened.

This is really what happened. If only I weren't stupid—if only I weren't stupid, I could have found a way to release Father from his dream. If only I weren't stupid, I would have been able to release Father from the madness of his dreams. However, I was, in fact, stupid. I really was a bit stupid. When Father asked me to go with him, I went with him, and when he didn't ask me to wake him up, I left him to his dreams. As we were walking, Father kept telling me over and over that he knew how to bring out the sun, that he knew how to make the sun rise. Then, we headed south, in the direction of the embankment where the crematorium was located. After proceeding a few steps, Father looked back to see whether or not I was following him, then he shouted into this daytime darkness,

"Niannian, come with me.

"Don't you want this town to be saved? Don't you want the entire world to be saved?"

I followed in Father's footsteps. It seemed as though I was following him not so that he might save this town, but rather in order to see *how* he was going to save it. "I have to roll all of the barrels of corpse oil out of the cave. I have to roll them up to the eastern end of the embankment. In the past, that is where the sun would always appear at dawn, and when people at the base of the hill see the sun emerging from the eastern side of the embankment, they will all wake up from their dreams." Father kept talking to himself on this day that looked as though dusk had just transitioned to night. I listened to Father talk to himself, as we both proceeded toward the embankment. I wanted to see how deeply Father was sleeping, but the darkness obscured his face. It completely obscured his face. Several times, I walked ahead and then turned to look back at him—as though looking up at a bird's nest hidden in a tree, but unable to see the nest or even the branches around it. All I could see was a dark shadow that appeared to hover in midair as he proceeded forward. Sweat dripped down from Father's face onto mine. It was bitter and salty, and had a slight stench. It was on account of this sweat that I stopped turning around to look at him. It was the strength in his hand as he was leading me forward that convinced me that he was capable of going through with his plan. I therefore didn't doubt him, nor did I attempt to stop him. Given that he was my father, how could I stop him? Given that he was my father, how could I doubt that he could be capable of bringing out the sun and transforming the dark night into day? Our footsteps were as fast as windblown raindrops. For every two steps that he took, I had to take three. When he took long strides, I had to jog just to keep up. This daytime night was already as dark as a lake of black ink, and as we walked along we kicked the darkness as though wading through a river of ink.

This was the third time that night that we had walked along this stretch of road. When we reached the point where we would ordinarily turn to go to Uncle's villa in the scenic compound, Father came to a stop.

A miracle quietly occurred there.

It was at that moment that I became convinced that Father was capable of bringing out the sun. I completely believed that he could make daytime return. Someone arrived at the intersection. He was pulling a handcart with an oil lamp hanging from the handle. When the man approached, Father called out to him, and the man came to a stop. "You must be heading into town to steal things?" The man squinted at Father. "Everything in town has already been stolen by others!" Father looked at him. "Let's go up to the embankment and move some barrels of oil from the west to the east side of the embankment. For every barrel you move, I'll give you ten yuan."

The man stood there, looking shocked.

"Twenty yuan."

The man stood there in shock.

"For every barrel you move, I'll give you fifty yuan. If you don't want to do this, then you can proceed into town and see what you can manage to loot. But beware the townspeople wearing yellow ribbons around their heads, as they may try to beat you to death."

The man lowered his head and followed us. "If you don't give me the fifty yuan, there'll be hell to pay." We saw a few more dreamwalkers, some of whom had come outside to wander around, while others wanted to take advantage of the somnambulism to make money. Father said some things along the same lines. He said some even more startling things. "For each barrel that you move from the west side of the embankment to the east side, I'll give you a part of a house . . . If you push two barrels, I'll give you the majority of a house. If you push three barrels, I'll give you a house facing the street. If you push ten barrels, I'll give you the entire New World funerary shop." Upon hearing this, the other people followed him. It turned out that dreamwalkers are like homeless wanderers, or a flock of sheep without a bellwether. As long as they had a leader and somewhere to eat and sleep and make money, they would definitely follow along. In the blink of an eye, we were soon being followed by five or six people, and then by five or six more. Some were empty-handed and some were pulling carts, but they all followed behind us. A large gaggle. A large contingent. A large mass. A large crowd. All gathered chaotically. The way that chickens, ducks, pigs, and dogs all follow behind their master. This is how things were, and this is how the world was. My father was a dreamwalker. But he was no mere dreamwalker, he was a dream master—a dream emperor. In the amount of time it takes to drink a bowl of water, he managed to assemble several dozen dreamwalkers. Whenever anyone approached, Father would shout out to offer a reward. "If you want money, I'll give you money. If you want a house, I'll give you a house. If you want a woman, then after you've finished moving the oil barrels, I'll tell you where you can find the woman of your dreams." Some ignored him, then headed straight into town. Others, however, heard him summoning them, and followed us to the cave in the embankment where the oil was stored.

They formed a large procession, a large crowd, and everyone proceeded halfway up the embankment. They went to the intersection that led to the cave. Father was sleeping, but he ran to the embankment like someone who was awake. He led those dreamwalkers to the cave. "I know how to get people to move these barrels! The more people there are and the quicker they are, the better. The sooner we can bring out the sun, the sooner the town will be saved, and the sooner the people will be saved." Hearing these shouts, I continued toward the embankment. There were always some people wandering around there, and always some people walking up and down the road. "Do you want money? For each barrel you move from the western side of the embankment to the eastern side, I'll give you fifty yuan when the sun comes up . . . Are you asleep, or awake? If you want the sun to appear, then you must help move the barrels. On the other hand, if you want the sky to remain dark forever, then simply keep dreamwalking in the darkness and don't worry about doing anything." I stood on the side of the road on the western side of the embankment. The muddy road looked as though there was a gray cloth spread out under our feet. Beneath the embankment, the villages, towns, and trees were shrouded in darkness. All that was visible was a bare light in the town, which swayed and flickered as though there were a fire burning. The sound of pounding drifted down from above, like the sound of horses' hooves. People's shouts pierced the darkness like arrows shot from a considerable distance. The lake water that was flowing down the embankment was calm and clear, and produced an inky-green glow—a glow that dissolved into the dark night. The night was heroic, and the sky was also heroic, and the people were like a solitary tree or a bush growing between the heroic sky and the heroic earth. Everything was swallowed up by this heroic sky, but the sky was supported by this tree and this bush. There was an array of shimmering lights all around, as though the night were full of ghosts and specters, and whenever I saw a light approach, I would stand at the top of the embankment and shout, "Are you awake or are you asleep? . . . If you are awake, do you want a house and land, and to have the sun come out? . . . If you are asleep, then do you want to earn some money, or do you want to go into town and try to steal things, and possibly get beaten to death? . . . We fled from that town, and even though many of the people who were pouring in did not steal anything, they were nevertheless still beaten black-and-blue by the townspeople, who left them with bruised noses, swollen faces, broken arms and legs, and the streets looking like rivers of blood . . . Outside town, there are piles upon piles of injured or maimed bodies, and there isn't a single one of them who doesn't feel regret, and there is not a single one who will not wake up and cry and shout and, bleeding profusely, attempt to return home."

Some people came.

Some people left.

Someone who was awake passed by and asked me if I was dreamwalking, to which I replied that if I were awake, why would I be shouting like this? "What a joke! If you were awake, would you be claiming that you could make the sun come up? Would you be claiming that you could bring back the daylight?" The joker walked away, and as he swaggered off, I shouted at his departing shadow, "I'm not going to argue with you . . . Just wait and see . . . Just wait and see!" People who were dreaming were standing around me. There were ten or more, or even several dozen, and they all stood in a group—a heroic group. They were going to accompany me to the cave, to help move the oil barrels. They were going to help us bring out the sun, and to transform the night into day.

There were several, a dozen, or several dozen of these dreamwalkers. I led them to the entrance of the cave in the middle of the hill.

3. (6:00–6:00)

As I was summoning one group of dreamwalkers after another, the neighbors arrived. Uncle Yan, the author, arrived. He had been summoned by all of the shouts up on the embankment. Such an extraordinary person, he was like a lamb that can't find its pen, or a chicken, cat, pig, or dog that can't find its home. Standing one-point-seven meters tall, in the deadly black night he resembled a wounded carp in a storehouse. He was wearing leather sandals, oversize underwear, and a wrinkled T-shirt. His face was pressed flat from having been slept on, looking as though it had been hit with a hammer. His face and his body were flat. Even his heart had been flattened.

I took a path back from the western side of the embankment. The light from my flashlight resembled dead fish eyes watching the world. "What's wrong with you? . . . What have you been shouting about for the past half night?" The neighbors walked over and shone their lights in my face, and over my body. They shone their lights onto my words, as though shining them onto an unbelievable pearl. I stared at Uncle Yan's light, and at his face . . . "Uncle Yan, are you awake or are you dreamwalking? Do you want to make the sun come up, or do you intend to spend your entire day here in the dark? The whole town is in tumult. Everyone has gone crazy. Countless houses and stores have been robbed, yet you are here and don't know about it? Both sides of the main street are drenched in blood and full of screams, and the ground is covered in flesh and blood, yet you are here and haven't seen it?"

Then, he came over. He stood there, gazing down at the town—gazing at a point in the distant sky that was beginning to heat up.

"What time is it now?

"The town is truly in tumult.

"Can you really find the sun, and replace the dark night with daylight?"

I looked up at the sky, then down at the ground. Finally, I looked at Gaotian Village, sitting at the base of the embankment. I didn't know how Father, while dreaming, had managed to organize all those dreamwalkers to move the barrels in the cave. How was he able to arrange for the dreamwalkers to roll them out of the cave? The first group of dreamwalkers had already emerged from the cave pushing the barrels of corpse oil, and they were followed by one group after another. They followed Father, who was holding a lantern to lead the way. The rumbling of the barrels cut through the dark night and gathered the darkness that blanketed the earth and sky of that summer day. It was as though the wind were blowing the dark night hot and cold. As the dreamwalkers pushed those barrels uphill, their labored breathing was as coarse and heavy as a rope, but once they reached the flat road along the top of the embankment, they no longer had to work as hard. Their breathing became more regular, and as the barrels rolled along the muddy road, the thudding sound they had been making was replaced with a soft jingling. Meanwhile, the oil inside the barrels was initially thick and viscous, but after the barrels had rolled for a while the oil became thinner and could be heard sloshing around inside. There was a long procession, with several dozen barrels and several dozen dreamwalkers pushing them. "Come with me, come with me." Father stood in front of the dreamwalkers and shouted, as though someone were driving a lead car, or as though a general were leading his troops on a nighttime expedition. All the dreamwalkers and all the barrels were rumbling along evenly and heroically, like carriages following a lead car. They rolled downhill, around a corner, then arrived right in front of us. "As long as we can get this oil to the east side of the embankment, I'll issue everyone's money . . . Together, we'll roll out this year's, this month's, and this day's daylight, and everyone who has helped roll the oil will be received as a hero . . . As soon as daylight arrives, everyone will thank us and toast us . . . Quick . . . quick . . . The sooner we can roll out the sun, the fewer townspeople will be killed, and the less blood will be spilled . . . Hey, you . . . quick! . . . If you slow down, it slows down everyone behind you . . . If you slow down, it may very well mean that yet another head may be chopped off and end up lying in the streets of Gaotian . . . and there will be yet another person with a bloody hole in place of a head."

Father was up in front yelling at the sky and at the dream-walkers. The dreamwalkers passed noisily in front of us, rolling the barrels of oil. Without looking at anyone, they followed Father's lead and rolled barrel after barrel of corpse oil from the west side of the embankment over to the east side. It was as though a string of railway cars hauling oil went rumbling past. This midday night was pitch-black, and the water was clear and murky. The air was muggy but there was also a breeze. The oil from the barrels had a greasy, foul odor that mixed with the scent of warm summer, as though some grease had been heated on a stove. No one said a word, and no one paused to rest. Instead, there were just those dreamwalkers bent over oil barrels, and countless pairs of eyes that appeared to be staring off into space. Rumbling along, the dreamwalkers walked past us. Like Zhuge Liang's legendary fleet of handcarts, known as the Wooden Oxen and Gliding Horses, these figures walked past us transporting vast amounts of oil. The sound they were making gradually faded away, the same way that the seasons progress from summer to winter, or from spring to fall.

"What kind of oil is this?" I heard Uncle Yan say this in his sleep.

"It's not any kind of oil."

"Really, what kind of oil is it?"

"It is machine oil, gasoline, and oil that we use to cook our food, all of which is prepared year in and year out here on this embankment."

"Ah . . . ah . . . ah."

This was the last time Uncle Yan ever said "Ah" to me. As he was sighing, he saw that in the procession of dreamwalkers, there was a man in his sixties who was rolling a barrel as though attempting to roll the entire mountain. Uncle Yan placed his flashlight in his pocket and went to help the old man, and in this way he, too, joined the procession of dreamwalkers who were attempting to make the sun rise and to bring about daytime. It was as if he wanted to reach out and see whether the dream was hard or soft, hot or cold. It was as if he wanted to personally confirm whether the story was true or fictional.

The sky was black and murky.

The world was silent, but also contained some hidden sound.

The embankment and the village and the forest located between one hill and another resembled murky black masses. The light that flickered up from the town at the base of the embankment was chaotic and scintillating. The shouts people made as they beat one another continued to pierce the gap between the atmosphere and people's ears. Meanwhile, the barrels were being moved from the west side of the embankment to the east side, and after everyone walked away, the sound became as faint as that of someone grinding his teeth in his sleep.

4. (9:01–9:30)

In this way, the dreamwalkers transferred all of the barrels of corpse oil from the western side of the embankment to the eastern side. They made seven or eight trips back and forth—I can't remember exactly how many. Perhaps it was eight or nine. At any rate, they took all of the barrels to a peak on the northeast end of the embankment. After placing the barrels there, they faced in the direction of Gaotian and looked, and listened. They saw those lights flickering on and off, and it seemed as though they could also see the slaughter. They could see people with broken arms and legs, and the streets were completely splattered with human blood and tissue. They could hear screams of "Attack!" and "Kill!" It seemed as though they could also hear people moaning as they bled out and died. The dreamwalkers' faces were pale—as pale as the white blossoms that New World would sell to grieving families. Their eyes increasingly revealed a sense of disquiet. In fact, as they dreamwalked, the muscles in their faces would twitch and convulse. Their faces were covered in sweat, and had a terrified expression. As they stared straight ahead, their eyes revealed a feeling of confusion and bewilderment. They followed my father and imitated him, while at the same time muttering to themselves,

"Is the sun about to come up? Is the sun about to come up?

"Quick, make the sun come up!

"Quick, make the sun come up!"

They frantically followed my father to the west side of the embankment, where they rolled and pushed the barrels of corpse oil.

They were endeavoring to summon the sun and the daylight. They made one trip after another, carrying one load after another. One trip and a load, followed by another load and another trip. Eventually, it was no longer necessary for my father to tell them what to do, and instead they rushed around of their own accord, rolling the barrels from the west side of the embankment to the east. They were like a machine or a procession of cars. They were like a flock of geese, and if the one in front flew into a sunlit mountain, the others would inevitably follow. It was as though they were sentient draft animals running back and forth along the mountain, and if the one in front jumped off a cliff, the ones behind would surely follow.

On the northeast corner of the embankment, there was an earthen ridge. There, the yellow earth was so deep that it would be possible to bury villagers for years to come. Originally, this ridge had a basin with a small pool. The basin was one *mu* in size, but over time it gradually filled up and became home to an assortment of trees and weeds, feral cats and stray dogs. It became the home of hares and birds. People normally wouldn't go there, visiting only after their family's pig or child happened to die. But these days, pigs rarely died of illness, and there were few dead infants. The pit, accordingly, had been abandoned. Father, however, knew that the pit was there, though I had no idea how he knew. In the past, when you watched the sunrise from Gaotian, it would appear as though the sun were rising out of that pit. Daybreak would start from that pit. The only variation was that in winter, it would appear as though the sun was emerging from one side of the pit, while in summer it would appear to be emerging out of the other side. They rolled the oil barrels around that pit. As the dreamwalkers pushed over more barrels, Father pried open the lids with a pair of pliers, such that all of the black corpse oil flowed directly into the pit. He did this for one barrel, then another, then for a hundred or more. The contents of one barrel after another were poured into the pit. Initially, the liquid appeared black and dirty, as though it were a pit of black mud, but as more oil was added, the black, dirty liquid acquired a brown glow, and under the lamplight the pit came to resemble a greenish-blue lake. The barrels that had been brought over surrounded the pit, and some of them even fell in, producing a gurgling sound as though the pit contained hundreds of fountains spouting water. The empty barrels were tossed to the side, like countless tree trunks. It was as though there were a field of enormous mushrooms growing on the mountain. So, it turned out that a dream could produce an extraordinary event. It turned out that while dreaming, people could accomplish countless things.

All of the oil was transferred from the western side of the embankment to the eastern side.

All of the oil was poured into the sinkhole.

The path leading from the western side of the embankment up to the top of the hill was several dozen meters long, and the vegetation on either side of the path had been crushed flat by the endless procession of barrels that had rolled over it. The grass had been stained dark by the oil, making it look like a long stretch of asphalt. Under the lamplight, this path of grass and asphalt stretched out toward the embankment's northern peak, like hair that is combed back. The ground was covered in the smell of broken grass and the stench of corpse oil. The entire world was filled with the smell of oil and sweat, and the dry odor of darkness. The irritability and turmoil of this daytime darkness brought everyone back to a boiling point. The lampshades of the dozen or so lanterns that were hanging from the trees around the pit were covered in burn marks and water stains. The lamplight became progressively dimmer, as though this daytime night was becoming progressively deeper. Next to the oil pit, there were several chinaberry and pagoda trees. There were also two mulberry trees with trunks as large as rice bowls. The trees' leaves, having been baked black by the lanterns, were drooping down. The insects on the leaves crawled out of their cocoons, and then stared intently at the people.

The lamplight projected the trees' shadows far into the distance. It also projected the people's shadows into the distance.

In the pit that resembled a wheat-threshing ground, the oil was as deep as a man's thigh, and the flat surface produced a dark glow and an astringent odor. When you leaned over to look in, you could see countless fish-scale-like lights. The process of relocating the oil barrels took two or three hours. After rolling the barrels, everyone lay down next to the pit and fell asleep. One person, after rolling his final barrel, collapsed next to it and immediately fell asleep. Another person was rolling a barrel but stopped on his way to the pit and fell asleep in the middle of the road, and the sound of his snoring was just like the sound of the barrels rolling down the road. Another, after he finished, chatted for a while, then used some grass to wipe the oil from his hand. At the same time, he didn't forget he had been doing this for money. "Where is my fifty yuan for each barrel?! . . . Where is the house I was promised?! . . ." These questions about where he should go to get his money and his house hung from his lips like leaves from a tree, or weeds covering the ground. But even as he was asking, he fell sound asleep. His voice grew soft, and soon there was no sound at all. He slipped into a deep sleep. Next to the oil pit, Father was busy rushing around telling everyone about the compensation. "I'll give you your money right away . . . As soon as the sun comes up, I'll give you your money." After he answered several people, no one else dared ask about the money and the houses that had been promised. Instead, one after another, they all lay down and fell asleep. From a state of dreamwalking, they returned to an ordinary dream state. Father, however, continued dreamwalking, while remaining fast asleep. He was dreaming and dreamwalking as he continued running back and forth through this crowd, taking the empty barrels and rolling them away. He no longer needed to attend to those people who had been pushing the barrels, nor did he need to reinstate his promise that he would give fifty yuan for every barrel that anyone rolled. He didn't return to his promise that if someone pushed three barrels, Father would give him a house; and if someone pushed ten barrels, he would give him a street-side store. Instead, now all he did was push the empty barrels out of the way while running around and talking to himself. His pitch-black excitement was like something out of an insane opera.

"We can light a fire, and the sun will come up!

"We can light a fire, and the sun will come up!"

By this point, I realized that Father had fallen into a deep dream state. He had been awake all night running and shouting, so he must have been so exhausted that he would fall asleep as soon as he had somewhere to rest his head. Even though he was sleeping, his head remained erect, and he continued running around incessantly. I assumed that as soon as he ignited the oil in the pit, everything would be finished and he would lie down and fall asleep—and even if the flames were licking his body and burning him to death, he might not wake up.

In order to prevent Father from getting burned alive, I ran after him.

I was concerned that after Father ignited the oil, he might fall into the fire.

But at this moment, there was a new development that startled both the dreamers and the dreamwalkers. Just as Father finished moving the final empty barrel from the edge of the pit and was wiping his hands with some dry grass, he turned to everyone and shouted, "The sun is about to rise! . . . The sun is about to rise!" Just as Father was about to take an oil lamp down from a tree and use it to ignite the oil, Yan emerged from somewhere in the crowd and stood in front of Father, his entire body and his face covered in corpse oil. I didn't know whether he had gotten dirty while the dreamwalkers were pushing the oil barrels, or if it had happened while he was following Father down to the pool of oil. In any event, Yan stood in front of Father, and it was as if a dark cloud had appeared and blocked the sun as it was about to come up. Yan stood a step away from Father, and made a few ordinary remarks—actually, some truly earthshaking remarks.

"If you ignite this now, it will only produce a flat surface.

"If you want this fire to resemble the rising sun, you will need to transform this flat surface into a giant fireball.

"I've given this a lot of thought, and the only solution would be to install a pole in the middle of the pond, and then place a pile of oil-soaked hay on top of it, such that after you ignite the oil you also ignite the pole with the oil-soaked hay, which will then burn in midair, and from a distance it will look like a fireball, and will look like the rising sun."

Father stood next to the oil pit. The others were either squatting next to the pit or else lying in the grass. They were lying around like bales of hay or overturned barrels. Under the lamplight, everything was dark and murky—the tree shadows were dark and murky, and the entire world was also dark and murky. I stood on a mound next to Uncle Yan and examined his expression. Then I turned my attention to his shoulder, and saw that his shoulder bone resembled a withered yellow rib. I saw that his face resembled the lamp's yellow light, and was fluttering like a silk sheet and shimmering like a red flame, such that it appeared as though his face was hiding a sun beneath it. I stared at Yan. I thought about what he had said. His eyeballs moved, as though there were a pair of fireballs burning and spinning inside his face. Father began looking for something in the crowd of sleeping people. From under the tree and next to the pit, he removed a couple of straws from one of the bales of hay, then stood in front of Yan. Suddenly, he noticed that those sleeping, dreaming people had removed their oil-soaked clothing and left it scattered. Father began to grin happily, like someone who returns home and finds his keys, or like a baby that manages to find something someone else has lost. Or like the time I found a wallet someone had dropped on the way to the market and, after a brief hesitation, I picked it up and hid it.

Father was silent. He was silent for a long while. He was silent for an entire lifetime. Finally, he shifted his gaze from Yan's body back to the oil pit. The oil's surface was perfectly calm and flat, like an enormous sheet of black silk fabric shimmering in the light. Shadows of trees and human figures were projected onto the oil's surface. Initially, the foul odor of the corpse oil was oppressive, but after a time you no longer noticed it. No one knew that the oil came from humans, that it was corpse oil generated by the crematorium over a period of more than ten years. I was the only one who knew. Only Father and I. But I can't remember whether at that moment I was awake, asleep, or dreamwalking like Father. I really can't remember. I now believe that I must have been awake—but if I was awake, how could I have let my father do such an imbecilic thing? Even cats, dogs, pigs, chickens, and other domesticated fowl know you shouldn't do what he did. In the end, I was a stupid child. I really was a stupid child. I was awake, yet I let Father proceed with his plan. I let him do the thing that he most needed to do, yet which was also what he shouldn't have done. In Gaotian, at the base of the hill, the lights were still blinking haphazardly. The sound transmitted from there was urgent, chaotic, and murky. On one side there was the reservoir, while on the other side there was the village at the base of the mountain ridge. Behind us there was the scenic compound with Uncle's house, which was brightly lit but had no sound. What on earth was going on in Uncle's house? Who had time to worry about what was going on over there? Who knew what was going on in that scenic compound? Who even had the energy to think about it?

The pit had been filled with oil, and was about to be ignited.

The sun would emerge from this pit.

Daylight would drive away the darkness.

I stared at Father's face, and at Yan's riblike shoulder. He had originally been wearing a T-shirt, but I didn't know where the shirt had gone. At any rate, he was now shirtless and covered in oil, and one would never have guessed from his appearance that he was a prominent author.

He, too, was a dreamwalker.

His dreamwalking was no different from anyone else's. His hair was white, his eyes were half-closed, and he breathed through his mouth, not his nose. What time was it? I didn't know where I had left my radio. If this had been an ordinary day, then it should have already been the morning, and the sun would be approaching its zenith. But the world was completely confused, the same way that at night you are unable to see the ocean. Time had died. The sun had died. But now, the sun would come back to life, and time itself would come back to life. Father and Yan stood there and looked at each other, but it seemed as though they couldn't really see each other. They were both dreaming, they were both dreamwalking, and they were engrossed in their respective dreams and thinking about their own concerns. They were surrounded by the sound of people breathing and yawning. In front and in back of them, there was the sound of snoring and of people talking to themselves. Apart from these sounds, the world was extremely still, and everything under heaven was extremely still. Several dozen meters from the oil pit, there was a field, in which there was a hissing sound. It was as though a snake had crawled out of the weeds. Perhaps it was a wild hare that came running out. The sound fell into the darkness like a blade of grass falling into the oil pit, or a stone falling into the oil pit. The sound of snoring and people talking in their sleep slipped into the dark night and slipped into that oil pit that was one *mu* large. The oil pit was extremely still. The mountains, fields, and villages surrounding the pit were so calm that it seemed as though the sun and time itself had died. Next to this deathly still pit, Father's nasal breathing sounded like a dragonfly fluttering around. Meanwhile, Yan was breathing through his mouth, which resembled the uncovered top of a soy sauce bottle, or an uncovered well on the side of the road. They silently watched each other for an entire day, an entire night, an entire season, an entire year—but it also seemed like an infinitesimally short flash of silence. At this moment, Father's face suddenly became rigid and red. And beneath this rigid redness, a vein was pulsing.

"Brother Lianke, you can use tonight's events as the basis for a novel."

Yan gazed at my father and seemed as though about to say something.

"I don't doubt you'll write this into a novel. This is the sort of story you find only once every hundred or thousand years."

Upon seeing Yan, Father didn't say anything else. Instead, he went over to the tree and lifted several of the lanterns hanging there, as though trying to determine how heavy each of them was. He selected a heavy one and brought it down. Like a child, he kicked his shoes into the oil pit, one after the other, and when they landed, they didn't produce the sort of plopping sound and white splash that you would expect after throwing a stone into a pool of water, and instead they were engulfed by the thick, viscous oil as though they were being swallowed by a large tarp. Then, Father rolled up some wormwood grass he had picked, and also grabbed a large bundle of tree branches. He also took the clothes of some of the dreamwalkers and hugged them to his chest. In this way, as though he were moving to a new home, he carried, pushed, and dragged all this and the lantern and went over to the edge of the pit.

For some reason, either because I was stupid or because I happened to fall asleep at that precise moment, I saw Father as though I were watching a dreamwalker from within a dream. This dream, however, gave me nightmares, and the dreamwalker brought me such terror that I became convinced I would die. It was as though I were dreaming and didn't realize I was actually sleeping in my own bed, with my fists resting on my own chest. I wanted to move my fists, but even if I used all my strength, I still couldn't budge them. I wanted to warn my father not to enter that oil pit, but even if I used all my strength, I wasn't able to open my mouth or make a sound. Father was going to accomplish a great thing. The dream was able to realize a great thing. Dreamwalkers were able to realize and accomplish the greatest possible thing under heaven. So Father, carrying the kindling, made his way toward the center of the oil-filled pit. He proceeded step-by-step, and although sometimes the corpse oil didn't reach his knees, at other times it buried his thighs. The wormwood branches paddled through the surface of the oil, releasing an oily stench that spread over the ridge, over the mountain, and over the entire world. I didn't know what Father wanted to do. Yan, who was in a dreamy stupor, didn't know what Father was going to do either. In fact, no one—including those who were sleeping, awake, and dreaming—knew what Father was going to do. The sky was gray, black, and murky. The land was black, dead, and murky. The people were black, gray, dead, and murky.

"Father, what are you going to do?"

I shouted as though I had spent the entire day running home, but was now standing in the entranceway to my house and wasn't seeing my parents.

Father turned to look at me and said something that no one in the world could have understood.

"Niannian, at this time our Li family has repaid its debts, and even after you grow up, you won't owe anything on my behalf." His voice was hoarse and happy, like a sheet of white paper over a grave, happily fluttering in the wind.

Yan stared at Father as he walked into the distance.

"What are you doing? Can you carry all that?"

There was no answer.

The world was so still, it was as if it didn't even exist. Father waded through the waist-deep oil to the center of the pit. He stood in the middle of the pit for a while, then took the grass, branches, and clothing he was carrying, and dipped them into the oil. Finally, as though he were taking a bath, he bent over and splashed the oil all over his body. Then he proceeded to an area where the oil reached his thighs, squatted down until the oil reached his neck, and stood up again. He walked back and forth through the oil until he had transformed himself into a veritable oil man. He seemed to be look- ing for something, trying to find something beneath the oil with his feet. Finally, he succeeded in finding it—perhaps a stone or a pile of dirt—beneath the oil, and slowly climbed onto it, so that now the oil reached only his feet. He placed the oil-soaked grass and sticks all around him, then stood up straight and looked in our direction.

He gazed at us for a while. He watched us for an entire lifetime. Then he opened the cover of the oil lamp.

"Brother Lianke, when you write your novel, you must remem- ber to render me as a good character!"

This is what Father shouted. It was like something an awake person might have said. After shouting this, Father proceeded to pour the oil from the lamp onto the oil-soaked branches and grass in front of him. Then, he placed the lamp itself—with the cover removed—on top of those oil-soaked branches and grass. He didn't hear the popping sound of the lamp oil burning. But as soon as the oil on the surface of that viscous oil pool was ignited, it immediately produced a conflagration—a sheet of fire as though it was a sheet of red silk suddenly blown into the air. I didn't know what Father was trying to do, but Yan did. He exclaimed, "Ah! . . ." and his body tensed up and leaped forward, as though he were suddenly waking up from a dream.

"Brother Tianbao, you've gone crazy . . . Are you dreamwalking, or are you awake?"

Yan took a flying leap into the oil pit.

But after he had advanced only a few steps, he saw, in the center of the pit, the fiery conflagration reaching for the sky. Yan came to a stop and stared in shock. He saw my father—whose body was covered in kindling, grass, branches, and clothing, as though he were a living fireball—standing in the center of the pit and swaying back and forth. Yan moved back toward the edge of the pit, as though he were trying to get as far away from this fireball as possible, and heard Father screaming in agony.

"I'm awake! . . . I'm awake! . . ."

Following these shouts, the conflagration that had been my father simply took a couple of steps, then came to a stop. The conflagration paused for a moment, but it also seemed as though it had been stopped for Father's entire life. Then the conflagration proceeded to the center of the pit, so that it could yield the largest fireball possible. Once the conflagration reached this point, it stopped again.

Father didn't cry or shout, and instead he stood there and let the burning oil envelop the kindling, branches, and clothing he was holding. The conflagration also continued to envelop his own body. He let the flames climb the pile of kindling, grass, and branches, and soon an enormous fireball emerged out of the fiery conflagration. The oil pit's burning surface was initially only as large as a tatami mat, but eventually it became larger than a house. In the blink of an eye, the fire enveloped the grass and kindling, and climbed up Father's fiery column. The fire reached upward and spread outward in all directions, quickly engulfing everything around it. There were red and blue flames, and when the fire reached the point where the oil touched the grass and kindling, it became a golden yellow fireball. I saw Father standing in the fire like a fireball on the spire of a fiery tower. That spire was swaying precariously back and forth, but didn't topple over.

"The sun has come out! Write me into your novel as a good person!"

I believe that these were the last words Father uttered, but I couldn't tell whether he was awake or was talking in his sleep. His shouts were like a blade cutting through the night, jolting me from my stupor, but just as I was about to jump down into the pit, the fire's heat pushed Yan away from the edge.

As Yan emerged from the pit, he pushed me away from the edge. By this point, he was completely awake. He was staring in confusion, as though he had no idea what had happened. He grabbed his head with one hand, then grabbed his face with both hands. As he was doing so, he started shouting to the people who had gathered around the pit. "Heavens! . . . Heavens! . . ." Then, he looked at the fire that was leaping out of the pit and, like my father before him, began screaming frantically at the crowd.

"Everyone run to the embankment!

"Everyone run to the embankment!"

By this point, those who had been sleeping and dreaming along the edge of the pit had woken up. They had all gotten to their feet and were staring at the flames. Most of the oil pit had already formed a fireball, and a wave of searing heat surged out like a tsunami.

"Everyone run up to the embankment! . . . Everyone run up to the embankment!"

Everyone ran after Yan. The footsteps mixed with his shouts, like raindrops pounding on a grassy hillside. A pungent yellow burning smell filled the air like a sandstorm pounding my face and pounding everyone's nose. The explosive sound of cold oil burning, together with people's screams as they woke up, resonated to the top of the mountain. I could see the fire's red glow in the air, and I could see the flames reflecting off the surface of the reservoir, like the reflection of the sun at dawn. Ash from the burnt oil flew around us like sparrow or phoenix feathers, and rained down on everyone's head, hair, and face. People were running away and heading toward the embankment—running so fast that it seemed as if they were fleeing their own execution. They didn't stop until they arrived at the rear of the hill, where the fire had not yet reached. When they looked back, they saw that behind them there was no conflagration, but rather a sun hovering over the eastern side of the embankment, looking as though it were about to rise. The sun's flames reached as high as a tree, as high as a house, as high as a multistory building. A semispherical orb appeared to be hovering over the mountaintop, as though it were attempting to leap into the air but kept getting pulled back.

It was like the instant when the winter sun is about to rise in the east.

It was like the instant when the summer sun is about to set in the west.

The mountain range was glowing red.

The land was glowing red.

The entire world was burning bright red.

Beneath the red glow, the trees, rivers, villages, houses, and livestock were brightly illuminated, like a landscape or an entire world fashioned from agate. Led by Yan, we ran to the front of the embankment, whereupon I suddenly found myself extremely thirsty. My body felt so parched, I wanted to leap into the reservoir from the top of the two-hundred-meter-tall embankment—to drink some water and drown. I stared down at the reservoir, which was illuminated by the firelight. It occurred to me that Father would surely leap out of the water, like a fish. As everyone was staring intently at that fiery sun, I was staring instead into this boundless reservoir. My lips were cracked, my throat was cracked, and my heart was cracked, to the point that I wanted to leap into the reservoir and drink myself to death.

At this point, I heard shouts coming from somewhere.

These were ear-piercingly loud cries.

"The sun has come up!"

"The sun has come up!"

"Daylight has arrived! The sun has come up in the east!"

This sound was coming from the western side of the embankment. Everyone turned to look, and saw that the fiery sun was illuminating the embankment as brightly as if it were daytime. The sky was illuminated, and everything under heaven was illuminated—including the villages, rivers, mountains, the trees and crops and flowers by the roadside, as well as both the harvested and the unharvested wheat and beans. They were all illuminated and clearly visible. In a village to the west of the embankment, there were countless people standing in the entrance staring up at the fiery lake on the east side of the embankment. "The sun has come up!" . . . "It is light outside!" . . . "The sun has come up!" . . . "It is light outside!" . . . They shouted, jumped up and down, and clapped their hands, as though the entire village and the entire world were full of children celebrating the New Year. The residents of the villages below the embankment all walked out of their homes. They all ran out of their homes. They stood in the village entrance, which was bathed in daylight, where they were banging their gongs, beating their drums, and shouting at the oil-fire sun on the eastern mountain. "The sun has come out!" . . . "It is light outside!" . . . "The sun has come out!" . . . "It is light outside!" . . . These shouts came in waves, like the endless waves of grain that fill the fields at this time of year, or like people celebrating the arrival of rain to break a summer drought. The entire land was illuminated by the red glow of this sun rising over the eastern mountains. The entire land was illuminated by the clear, bright light of the sun rising over the eastern mountains.

Following these shouts, the cocks in one of the villages finally began to crow, after which all of the villages were soon filled with the sound of crowing cocks.

From somewhere, there was the lowing of recently awakened cows, and soon all of the villages were full of the sound of lowing cows.

At this point, the sun came back to life. Time also came back to life. The lively sound of cocks crowing and cows lowing was transmitted to Gaotian Town. People were banging their gongs, beating their drums, and shouting. "The sun has come out!" . . . "It is light outside!" . . . "The sun has come out!" . . . "It is light outside!" . . . Suddenly, the lamplight and fighting disappeared from the town. The sunlight hovering over the eastern mountain shone down on the town, illuminating everything that had lain in darkness during the Gaotian night, which had reduced every sound to deathly silence. Everything now seemed to come back to life. For a long period, Gaotian had been trapped in a state resembling death—a predawn stillness before the sounds that typically signal dawn. This was an atypical stillness, resembling the sort of stillness that lingers, just before dusk, after the daytime noises have disappeared. This was an atypical stillness, resembling the sort of deathly silence that one finds at the instant when daytime and nighttime exchange places. Following this deathly silence, another sound came rumbling through, as the world came back to life, and time itself came back to life. After that extraordinary silence, I heard a coarse and heavy buzzing, after which people began pouring out of Gaotian and the surrounding villages, shouting crazily at the eastern sky and the eastern hill.

"Quick, come look! It appears as though the eastern hill is on fire!"

"Quick, come look! It appears as though the eastern hill is on fire!"

Some people emerged from their homes, while others stood in the town's streets. From our position up on the embankment, we could see that the town's streets were full of people. The open areas outside town were also full of people. There was the sound of gongs and firecrackers, together with jubilant shouts and raucous applause. It was as if in the crowd that had gathered at the entrance to town, my mother was also shouting and jumping around. She, however, was jumping more slowly than everyone else, and every time she landed her body would bend awkwardly, as though she were about to topple over. In the end, she always managed to remain upright, and each time she bent over she would leap up again and resume shouting.

"Daylight has arrived! . . . The sun is alive and has risen! . . .

"Daylight has arrived! . . . The sun is alive and has risen! . . ."

The outsiders began surging out of town, heading back to their respective villages. Some were driving carts, while others were chasing after them. One group after another, like soldiers fleeing a devastating defeat. Most of the carts were empty, and everyone was empty-handed. If the carts were carrying anything, it would invariably be fellow villagers who had been wounded or the bodies of those killed while dreamwalking. The outsiders pulled their empty carts and their wounded companions, and watched the sun rise in the east. From a distance, we could see that they were depressed and demoralized, and we could also see that the townspeople were chasing after them and attacking them with stones and carrying poles. The outsiders did not fight back, as though they felt they deserved to be beaten. Instead, shielding their heads and faces with their arms, they fled, rushing back to their respective villages and homes.

They all returned to their respective villages and homes.

They returned to the new day.

Postface:
Nothing Else to Say

1.

What else is there to say? This is simply what happened.

This is what happened in that year, in that month, and on that day.

Bodhisattvas . . . heavens . . . gods and masters . . . as well as Chinese Zen Buddhism . . . temples . . . lofty realms . . . epiphanies . . . Laozi . . . Zhuangzi . . . Confucius and assorted celestials and deities from other sects. I don't know how many people died while dreamwalking that night, or how many people died in the entire world. All I know is that in the town of Gaotian, 539 people died that night. I saw the complete list, from which I can recall the following:

Yan Lianke

1) Shen Quande, male, thirty-six years old. While dreamwalking, went to a field and began threshing grain, but touched an electrical line and was electrocuted.
2) Wang Ergou, male, forty-one years old. While dreamwalking, joined the town battle and was killed.
3) Hu Bingquan, male, eighty years old. While dreamwalking, jumped into a river and drowned himself.
4) Yu Rongjuan, female, sixty-seven years old. While dreamwalking, jumped into a river and died.
5) Zhang Mutou, male, thirty-seven years old. While dreamwalking, became a martyr for the Great Shun, and died.
6) Hu Dequan, male, sixty-eight years old. While dreamwalking, became thirsty and fell into his home's water tank and drowned.
7) Ma Huzi, male, twenty-seven years old. While dreamwalking, joined the town battle and was killed.
8) Yang Guangzhu, male, thirty-five years old. While dreamwalking, became a martyr for the Great Shun, and died.
9) Niu Dafeng, male, thirty years old. While dreamwalking, tried to steal something and was killed.
10) Niu Xiuxiu, female, twenty-six years old. While dreamwalking, tried to steal something and was killed.
11) Yu Xiaoshen, female, sixty-five years old. While dreamwalking, hanged herself for some reason and died.
12) Ma Mingming, male, eighteen years old. While dreamwalking, raped a woman and was killed.
13) Zhang Cai, male, forty-one years old. While dreamwalking, had a fight with his wife, then hanged himself.
14) Gu Lingling, female, twenty-three years old. While dreamwalking, committed sodomy with someone, then drowned herself in a well out of a sense of shame.

15) Yu Guoshi, male, thirty-eight years old. While dreamwalking, participated in the town battle and was killed.

16) Yang Dashan, male, twenty-six years old. While dreamwalking, participated in the town battle and was killed.

17) Yang Xiaojuan, Yang Dashan's sister, sixteen years old. While dreamwalking, a man tried to rape her, in response to which she took her own life.

18) Liu Datang, male, thirty-five years old. While dreamwalking, participated in the town battle and was killed.

19) Li Tianbao, my father, forty years old. While dreamwalking, immolated himself while making the sun rise.

37) Ma Ping, female, thirty years old. After her husband died while dreamwalking, she jumped into a well and drowned.

47) Qian Fen, female, thirty years old. After her three-year-old son fell into a ditch and drowned, she jumped into a river and drowned.

77) Li Dahua, female, thirty-six years old. Normally kind and diligent, was beaten to death after trying to steal things while dreamwalking.

78) Sun Laohan, male, ninety-one years old. While trying to wake up other dreamwalkers, was pushed down by a dreamwalker and died.

79) Zhou Wangzhi, male, forty-nine years old. Teacher. Suddenly began weeping inconsolably while asleep and died.

99) Tian Zhengqin, male, fifty-two years old. Town mayor. While dreamwalking, was killed during the popular uprising organized by Li Chuang.

100) Guo Dagang, forty-eight years old. Deputy town mayor. While dreamwalking, was killed during the popular uprising organized by Li Chuang.

101) Li Xiaohua, female, four years old. Because her father carried

her into the town battle and then dropped her, she was trampled to death.

202) Sima Lingxiao, forty-eight years old. Deputy town mayor. While dreamwalking, was killed during the popular uprising organized by Li Chuang.

303) Li Chuang, male, thirty-one years old. Originally served as the deputy director of the town's department of armed forces. A descendent of the rebel Li Zicheng, he led a popular uprising while dreamwalking and established the Shun dynasty, after which he was hanged.

404) Hao Jun, twenty-seven years old. Manager of a grocery store. Was killed trying to prevent dreamwalkers from robbing his store.

505) Hao Junwen, sixty-seven years old. Committed suicide after watching his son die.

506) Gao Zhangzi, male, forty-seven years old. Manager of a farm tools store, died while dreamwalking owing to unknown causes.

507) Little girl, about three months old, nameless. Her mother carried her when going out to harvest wheat and then put her down beside a field, whereupon the girl died of unknown causes.

508) Mao Xiaotiao, twelve years old. While dreamwalking, was trampled to death by troops fighting in the town battle.

538) Zheng Xiuju, eighty years old. Was scared to death by the actions of the dreamwalkers.

539) Zheng Junjun. Committed suicide after the rest of his family was killed.

Buddhas . . . bodhisattvas . . . divinities, landlords, and Jade Emperors—these are some of the 539 people from our town who died during the great somnambulism. I don't know how many others died, or how people died in neighboring towns. All I know is that this government-compiled list of the deceased from Gaotian Town was ninety-five pages long. It was as long as a book—almost as long as one of Yan Lianke's novels. It seemed as though virtually every family lost someone, and virtually every household had someone who had been injured, and corpses were strewn throughout the streets like autumn leaves or fallen grain. Several days later, graves began sprouting up like mushrooms in the abandoned fields outside town. A few days after that, the town established a new government and, in order to help guard against the infectious diseases that the decaying corpses might bring, the new town government brought in twenty carts with a total of 420 barrels of antiseptic—approximately as much antiseptic as the amount of corpse oil my father burned that night. In the scenic compound where my uncle lived, an additional ninety-nine people died that night. My uncle and aunt also died, having been beaten to death while trying to take the dreamwalkers some food. After my uncle and aunt died, all of their belongings were stolen, including their tables and chairs, their bowls and chopsticks, and their curtains and light bulbs. Even the flowers and saplings in their courtyard had been dug up and taken away. Every town had dozens and dozens of dreamwalkers, and it was reported that in the county seat and in the provincial capital they were even more terrifying. In all, the night lasted more than thirty-six hours, and at least a thousand people were killed in the ensuing uprisings and riots. By the time the sun finally came up and brought an end to this once-in-a-century stretch of darkness, the television and radio stations in the county, city, and provincial seat began simultaneously broadcasting the same announcement, stating that in Henan Province there had been only a small number of locations where dreamwalkers had managed to create a disturbance. Meanwhile, the afternoon editions of the city papers—in the "local oddities" column positioned in the lower left-hand corner of the front page—also carried an identical announcement:

IN OUR CITY'S MOUNTAIN REGION, THERE APPEARED SOME
SMALL-SCALE CASES OF SOMNAMBULISM

Recently, it has been hot and people have been busy harvesting wheat, and a set of peculiar meteorological and geographic conditions generated a phenomenon of seasonal darkness. As a result, in some of our city's mountainous regions—including a number of roads and villages bordering Shuihuang Township in western Chuanbei County—people began to dreamwalk as they transitioned from a state of exhaustion to a state of brisk activity. Some went out to harvest and thresh wheat while dreamwalking, while others stayed awake and tried to rouse the dreamwalkers, in the interest of social order and interpersonal relations. In Zhaonan County's Gaotian Town, there were false rumors about large swaths of dreamwalking-related deaths and social disturbances, and in order to put a stop to these rumors and promote a stable social order, the government sent in a large number of national cadres and public security officers to conduct an investigation and also help the masses to regain a good and productive social order.

2.

Bodhisattvas . . . gods . . . there is one more thing that I need to tell you. In our town, 539 people died, more than 490 were seriously injured, and there is no telling how much property damage there had been. Every household suffered either a fatality or a serious injury, and was also subject to looting or vandalism. Every household either had people who were dreamwalking, or had people who were taking advantage of the general somnambulism to wreak havoc. After this devastation, however, few households appeared to be particularly distraught, and few families were weeping. I was initially bewildered by this. Normally, after someone died, everyone would react as though the sky itself had collapsed, and half the town would be in tears. Some people even died from heartbreak after their relatives were killed—while weeping, they would take one breath and choke on the next. Sometimes two people died on the same day, or five people might die over a three-day span, and the townspeople could never rest easy. The weeping drowned the town for two weeks or a full month. However, on this particular day three months ago—on the day that the nighttime was extended interminably—539 townspeople died, to the point that virtually every household felt an impact, but most residents were rather subdued, and simply waited until dawn the next day. When the sun finally appeared, the surviving townspeople quietly came out of their homes and began collecting the corpses.

There wasn't a single drop of crying.

At that point, in the western sky there appeared a corpse-fire cloud like the one that had risen over the eastern embankment. The ensuing sunlight gathered in the western sky, where it drove away the clouds and the darkness. In this way, the nighttime ended, as though having been blown away by the wind, leaving behind a community full of shattered doors and windows, and discarded clothes and shoes, as well as assorted hand fans and cart wheels. There were also jet-black bloodstains, cut hair, and severed limbs, and the hoes, sickles, and axes that had been used as weapons—and even after all of this had been cleaned up by the relatives of the deceased, the streets nevertheless remained as still as death.

The nighttime had finally ended.

The sun really did rise in the west.

But after the nighttime concluded and the daytime arrived, there wasn't a trace of the happiness that daylight had returned. The town government sent someone to put desks in the most crowded areas around town, where cadres proceeded to calculate the number of deceased and the amount of property damage each household had suffered, but most families were reluctant to make a report.

"Will every family that has had a relative pass away receive compensation from the government?"

"Not necessarily."

"If not, then what's the point of registering?"

"Isn't it just so that they can have some data?"

After that, there were no more questions, and no more responses, and after reporting their families' deaths, injuries, and damages, the residents slowly trudged home in the sunlight. One of the cadres recording the data remembered something, and shouted, "Given that the weather is so hot, you should take this opportunity to bury your dead. The government no longer cares whether the dead are buried or cremated, so you should take this opportunity to go ahead and bury them."

Some of the people walking away didn't look back, while others turned around and said, "If we weren't going to bury them, why would we be letting the corpses lie in our homes?"

Actually, it wasn't that the government no longer cared whether the dead were buried or cremated, but rather that the crematorium had been destroyed and reduced to a pile of debris. I don't know whether the crematorium was dismantled by dreamwalkers or by people who were awake but were taking advantage of the general somnambulism to destroy it. The crematorium's furnace had been pushed over and rolled into the reservoir, and the furnace room had been detonated with explosives, such that there was now a small hill of shattered bricks and tiles in the courtyard. Everything else had been carted away—including not only things of value, but also worthless items. All that was left were two empty houses and courtyards on either side, with some trees and plants, plants and flowers, flowers and wild birds, as well as an assortment of wild sparrows, wild hares, wild badgers, and weasels. It was a field of ruins—a field of ruins and wilderness. I didn't know where Juanzi had gone. Perhaps she had returned home to her own village? I didn't know where the crematorium workers had gone either. Perhaps they, too, had returned home to their own villages?

The crematorium was very still.

The embankment, ridge, and mountain range were very still.

The entire world was very still. Our Gaotian Town was very, very still.

Half a month later—just half a month—the town gradually began to recover its former vibrancy. Everything that had to be bought was bought, and everything that had to be sold was sold. It was as if nothing had happened. The sun rose when it was supposed to, and set when it was supposed to. It rose from where it was supposed to, and set where it was supposed to. In the fields outside town, after the wheat was harvested there was an extended period of rainy weather—and after the skies had cleared, the fields of green grass were so thick that they appeared black. The thousands of freshly dug graves were covered by a layer of new grass, but apart from the fact that this grass was lighter, thinner, and more tender than the surrounding grass, these new graves were scarcely different from the older ones. In the threshing grounds, the area of the field that had been flattened didn't have a single grain left, but the new wheat sprouts were growing so vibrantly that it was as though someone had deliberately planted them there.

This is how things were.

This is how the world was.

In the clothing store, the owner cleaned up the shattered doors and windows, and reopened for business.

The electronics store suffered enormous losses, but the owner took out a loan and reopened, and business turned out to be even better than before. In fact, it was much better, as there was a steady stream of people from town and from the countryside who wanted to buy electronics.

There were shops selling beef and mutton, stores selling packaged food and groceries, and street-side stalls selling fruits and vegetables. There were also the people who came in from the countryside to go to the market. Everything was as lively as before, and as noisy and bustling as before. The only exception was the farm tools store next to our house. The owner had died that night, and I don't know where his wife had gone. Perhaps she had returned to her parents' home. At any rate, she was originally not from this town, and after she left, the store's front door remained closed and the sign in front—which read PROSPEROUS TOOL STORE—quickly became covered in cobwebs.

On that night, Mother had followed Father's instructions and barricaded the front door from within, to keep out the battle being waged outside. Although countless people from the town and surrounding villages died that night, blanketing the ground like fallen fruit following an infestation or toppled crops following a windstorm, business at our New World funerary shop actually did not improve. In fact, it didn't improve in the slightest. This is because my mother stopped making burial shrouds and papercuts for wreaths and funerary objects. I'm not sure why she stopped making papercuts, but over the next several days—as local families were conducting funerals for their deceased—my own family went up to the embankment's east hill and collected a handful of charred soil from what had been the oil pit. Then, using this soil to stand for Li Tianbao, we symbolically buried him. As we were collecting the soil from the pit, we saw something very odd. At that moment, the pit—from which the flaming corpse oil had risen up as a new sun—resembled an overturned brick kiln, and the soil was charred and burnt. The entire pit—in fact, the entire world—was filled with the smell of burnt soil and sulfur from making bricks. However, in the fissures that had formed in the dry, burnt soil, someone had planted countless wildflowers, including red ones, yellow ones, and green ones. There were wild camellias and chrysanthemums, with long strings of purple and red blossoms, and also coxcomb blossoms and small orchids. In order to permit the plants' roots to reach the soft earth beneath the top charred layer, whoever had planted these flowers had lifted up chunks of charred soil, as though removing the lid from a pot, and had then dug small holes in the soil, such that only the tops of the plants peeked out through the charred soil. It looked as though the flowers had been planted only three days earlier, and they hadn't yet begun to thrive and instead were simply draped over the charred soil. We proceeded to this flower garden in the middle of the pit and collected several handfuls of soil to serve as Father's ashes. We then placed Father's soil and ashes in a room in our shop, assuming that in the future, whenever townspeople saw us and saw Father's ashes, they would feel grateful and indebted, and would greet us with a smile. This, however, turned out not to be the case. Although during the first few days after the calamity, whenever the townspeople saw Mother and me, most of them would express their gratitude, later they stopped responding in this way, and instead would pull Mother aside and say, "You claim that that night your family wasn't sleepy? . . . That night, your husband also dreamwalked. If he wasn't dreamwalking, then how could he have thought of using that method to make the sun come up? If he wasn't dreamwalking, how could he have brought himself to jump into that pit of burning oil?"

Within another half a month, they stopped saying even this sort of thing.

Afterward, there was another minor incident that I should probably recount. One day, Mother was straightening up the dust-covered debris that was still scattered on the table, when someone walked in. He had gray hair and was of average height, and he was pulling a suitcase and carrying several bundles. Upon entering the house, he left his suitcase in the doorway and handed Mother some eggs, milk, and pastries. When people from around here pay someone a visit, they always offer these sorts of goods as a gift. After giving my mother the gifts, he gazed at my father's funeral portrait without saying a word. He was silent for a long time—for what seemed like an entire day, an entire month, an entire year, and even an entire lifetime. Eventually, he began to remove several books from his suitcase, until he formed a pile—an enormous pile of books. The books had titles like *Kissing Lenin's Years* and like *Water, Ballad, Hymn, and Sun; Ding of Dream Village;* and *The Dead Books.* There was also *The Days, Months, Years* and *My Gaotian and Father's Generation.* The visitor placed the books in front of Father's funeral portrait, then lit them on fire. As he was doing so, he didn't kneel down, nor did he light any incense sticks. Rather, he merely stood there watching the fire, and looking at my father's black-and-white portrait. After the fire began to die down, the man gave Mother a final look, then caressed my face and patted my head.

"If I don't succeed in writing the book your father asked me to write—a book that would function as a warm stove in winter and a cool electric fan in summer—then I won't ever return to this town."

He said this in a quiet voice—a cold and listless voice. Then he left. Pulling his wheeled suitcase, he left our house. My mother and I escorted him out to the entranceway. We assumed he was heading to the train station in order to return to his home in Beijing, but it turned out that his family in Beijing thought that he was still writing his novel in his old home in Gaotian. So, no one knew where he was, and it was as if he had vanished from the face of the earth. He disappeared without a trace, like the books he burned in front of my father's funeral portrait. We never heard from him again, but before he disappeared, the last thing he said to me was, "Go to that charred-soil pit, and look for Juanzi. She goes there every day to wait for you."

I didn't go.

I simply couldn't believe that Juanzi would go there every day to wait for me. Why would she be waiting for me? How could I be worth waiting for? In the end, however, I couldn't resist going to take a look. I wanted to see whether or not she was, in fact, waiting in that charred-earth pit. And, if so, what was she doing there? I went on a market day. On market days, the sun is like a winter fire. The sun was as bright as the sun, and there wasn't a trace of dust or pollutants. The streets were thronged with people, and the sunlight was abundant. The autumn sun shone down on the houses, walls, and streets, making them look as though they were glowing. The trees looked as though they were glowing. The shops, doors, windows, and goods all looked as though they were glowing. The street sellers hawking vegetables, clothing, brooms, and plows—everything looked as though it was glowing. The heads and shoulders of the people walking on their way to the market were as bright and transparent as jade, to the point that you could see right through their clothing and flesh, and see their hearts and veins. Feeling completely listless, I wandered up and down the street. Listlessly, I remembered the final thing Yan Lianke had said before he left. Listlessly, I remembered that Juanzi's family lived in one of the villages near the former oil pit. The memory of Little Juanzi suddenly stabbed my body like a hot needle. It stabbed my heart. I decided to go to that charred-soil pit to look for her. I walked and then ran out of town, as if I were fleeing, and headed straight to that charred-soil pit. When I got there, however, I stared in shock. Along the path where Father and the dreamwalkers had rolled the oil barrels that night, the grass was now knee-high, and there were layers upon layers of small yellow flowers reaching for the sky. Autumn bees were busily buzzing around the flowers, and hundreds upon hundreds of floral fragrances shimmered yellow and red in front of me, like a sheet of silk. I waded through the floral fragrance until I was standing in front of the pit, and although I didn't find Little Juanzi, it did seem as though the black pit full of charred earth suddenly penetrated my heart. It turned out that those flowers growing out of the fissures in the charred soil were alive! Where previously *the flowers had been growing sparsely, now they were tightly packed together. The charred, black earth in the pit was covered by the flowers, such that not a speck of soil remained visible. Red and yellow chrysanthemums were blooming in the area around the pit, and the floral fragrance was so strong that it seemed as if the wind would not be able to blow it away. The autumn bees and butterflies were flying around those flowers as though it were spring. The shadows of the bees and butterflies—together with the fainter shadows of the sparrows and other birds flying overhead—passed over the flowers, like a boat drifting through a lake. The sunlight was extremely bright, such that you could even see the puffs of breath that the flowers and the birds exhaled, the sound of which was as soft as sunrays and specks of dust doing battle in midair. At the same time, it was as clear as the stars sparkling in the sky above.* This, I think, was taken from the end of Yan Lianke's novella *The Days, Months, Years* . . . or perhaps it wasn't! As I was hesitating over whether the text was or wasn't taken from this work, Juanzi suddenly appeared on the other side of the pit, using a carrying pole to bring buckets of water to irrigate the flowers. "Ay, ay, ay!" Her braids and the carrying pole shimmered in the sunlight, like the wings of butterflies and dragonflies.